A Love of Adventure

Also by Joan Druett

JOAN DRUETT

A Love of Adventure

A LOVE OF ADVENTURE

AN OLD SALT PRESS BOOK, published by Old Salt Press, a Limited Liability Company registered in New Jersey, U.S.A.

For more information about our titles go to
www.oldsaltpress.com
Text © 2012 Joan Druett
Cover Art © 2012 Ron Druett
Interior art © 2012 Ron Druett
ISBN: 978-0-9941246-1-6

Publisher's Note: This is a work of historical fiction. Certain characters and their actions may have been inspired by historical individuals and events. The characters in the novel, however, represent the work of the author's imagination. Any resemblance to actual persons, living or dead, is entirely coincidental.

Prologue

The black ship would not have been sighted for perhaps another hour if a Portuguese seaman called Viera had not been so conscientious. It was hot, and eight bells—change of watch—but Viera stayed at masthead lookout, for no one had come to relieve him.

Viera was worried, because the *Pandora* was sailing in dangerous waters. At latitude 15 the bright heave of the ocean was lonely and the tropical islands that smudged the far horizon were a weight at the back of his mind. It made no difference to him that the captain was actually steering for one of those islands, to pick up a store of coconut oil. White riffraff castaways lived on those atolls, leading gangs of savages in a violent existence, preying on unwary ships that ventured into these parts—or so he had heard. The easy canvas billowed lazily in a descending series of wings below him. Viera shaded his eyes, scanning the sea. Then, as the *Pandora* rolled slowly and lifted her prow to crest a swell, he saw the black ship.

For a moment his mouth was too dry to shout. The ship was full-rigged, with all her canvas out, and as she tacked to run down to them she was like a menacing moth. Six months previously a ship had been taken by pirates in these waters. The pirates had cut up the body of the ship's captain and fed it to the captain's own ship pigs. Or so Viera had been told.

Finally finding his voice, he hollered urgently to the mate.

Captain Sherman's wife, Frances, was half asleep in her rocking chair on the deck, under a light awning her husband had rigged to shade her. A startlingly beautiful young woman, she was in the last week of her pregnancy, yet in every pose she was graceful. Her hair was a rich copper-red; her small face was square, and she had wide sea-colored eyes, rimmed by thick black lashes.

When she heard the note in Viera's voice, she stood up very slowly and carefully, and went to the rail to see the ship the Portuguese had raised. The black ship was coming down so quickly that Frances saw the sails at once. She stood very still, one hand on the rail and the other propped in the ache at the back of her waist. A sense of dread slid inside her. Then she heard Nathaniel join her, and turned to look up at him.

Her husband, Nathaniel, was a sturdy, middle-sized man, fair and ruddy in coloring, with a broad, alert face. He was seventeen years older than Frances, and to her he looked huge and reliable. She watched him uneasily as he frowned at the ship, running a professional eye over the canvas. The *Pandora* had only about two thirds as much sail as the ship that came on so relentlessly. The sun was hot and blinding, and the sparkle on the water made Frances feel ill. Nevertheless she stopped at the rail. The wood of the rail was warm and dry under her hands, absorbing the sweat in her palms. She leaned the weight of her abdomen on the rail and silently waited as the black ship neared.

The wind was capricious. It came in hard, small gusts, so that the sails slatted every now and then, despite the helmsman's care. Water swished and spars creaked. All seven of the *Pandora* crew were on deck, even those who were not on duty. Frances could hear them muttering. The ship neared ... two miles, one. There was no ensign flying. Frances could fancy she saw menacing faces in the rigging ...

and then a flag flew up at the spanker gaff, and the wind gusted.

She sniffed. She couldn't believe it. The other vessel smelled like a manure heap! Frances heard her husband shout with laughter. He cried, "A guano ship! A confounded guano carrier!" Men were guffawing all about the deck. The wind gusted again and the odor of bird droppings was unmistakable. The guano ship luffed in an invitation to speak, and Nathaniel, grinning, ordered the ship put aback.

The men ran with a will to the braces, and canvas slapped smartly as the yards were brought around. The *Pandora* slowed to a near stop. Frances held on to the rail and stared at the black ship. It was almost still, sitting like a magpie on its own blurred reflection, and then, jerkily, it lowered a boat. Six men scrambled into it, and Frances watched them pull across the half mile between the two ships, clopping their oars in and out of the water.

The man in the head of the approaching boat was ... singing. Frances shifted uneasily. Broad for his height, he had stiff reddish hair that stood out all around his head. The sun bounced away from his shiny pink face and his mouth was wide open as he bellowed a chantey.

"Now bend tae ye oars, me boys," he exhorted as the boat came near. He was keeping time with a bottle. "Ho, me boys, 'way ho!" he sang, and urged in his lusty voice that they "make the boat fly, skip o'er the briny, 'way ho!" Then, as the oarsmen obediently agreed in a wavering gruff chorus that the boat must "fly, 'way ho, fly," Frances turned and slowly made her way to the little sitting room in the after cabin. It was no longer right that she should be on deck: a ship was a man's world. She heard the visitor's boat rattle against the *Pandora*'s side, and she could hear the stamp and clatter as the men began to climb on deck. The visitor seemed harmless, she thought, but foreboding shifted inside her. She washed her hands carefully and tidied her hair, and then she sat down on the sofa to wait.

The visitor was a half-head taller than Nathaniel, half again as broad, and about the same age, in his mid-forties. He strode up to him with a grin that sent apple-red cheeks in different directions and with his hand held out most jovially. "An island trader, eh?" he cried. "And a bonny sight indeed, I say!" He was as Scotch as a thistle, and looked like one, too, with his stiff head of hair and shiny round face."McGhie's the name, Broderick McGhie," he said. "They call me Broddy and me vessel is ship *Glens ae Scotland."*

Then he shook Nathaniel's hand again. He was not as drunk as he pretended to be, though in his other fist he held a brandy bottle, quite full. "Ye'll sell me a wee bit oil for me lamps?" Nathaniel, grinning, nodded and introduced himself, and found the bottle thrust at his chest. "A wee dram a-fore we talk trade!" McGhie boomed.

Frances stood up slowly as the two men clattered into the cabin. One hand held the chart table for support, but she managed a dutiful smile as the visitor stopped short. Round blue eyes like marbles bulged and McGhie cried, "A lady?" He seemed vastly amazed. "A lady!" he cried.

Frances smiled and then sat down again, carefully, easing her weight. Nathaniel was busy filling two glasses with brandy. Then she saw his eyes resting on her face.

His jovial grin faded. He frowned. It had not occurred to him that Frances might not like it if he brought the visitor down to the cabin. She was usually a most sociable hostess. She was white, he thought, and nervous—he could feel it. When she had shifted in her chair a little gasp had escaped her, more like a sigh than a groan. Something was troubling her. Nathaniel sat down but kept shooting little glances at his wife while he listened to his guest's loud rambling.

The Scotchman did not seem to sense that anything was amiss. "New Zealand?" he demanded. "Ye sail tae New Zealand, after picking up your oil?" He was seated with his knees wide apart, his brandy glass circled with a capacious

4

fist, his expression vastly approving. "New Zealand is the place tae make a wee bit o' fortune, for certain, Captain Sherman."

Then he looked about and lowered his voice. "I ha'e the offer of a wee small island in Cook Strait. Te Rauparaha hisself offered me the place for a station, at a price. 'Twould be jest the thing for a fine shore whaling station, oh, aye, indeed, if I could find a man wi' the money and the urge tae invest. What d'ye think of that, eh? A shore whaling station, tae fill your barrels wi' the guid black oil."

Nathaniel was at once intrigued. An island—where a shore whaling station could be established? There was certainly money to be made in New Zealand oil ... so long as the English kept their fists off the land. And such land, he thought. He could afford to buy a large number of New Zealand acres with the profit from his coconut oil, the boxes of trade tobacco in his holds, and the monies owed to him in Sydney for the China goods he had brought into town. If he bought land now and held it for a future profit, he could certainly amass a fortune. If he had the land and a shore whaling station, and kept the brig *Pandora* to trade between Sydney and the islands, he could collect money from many directions...

McGhie finally left the brig *Pandora* at six, carrying the can of lamp oil that Nathaniel had pressed on him, refusing to accept payment. Nathaniel accompanied the Scotsman to the rail, but Frances stopped below—and it was that which made him wonder about his wife again. Frances was usually so courteous—and she had not even offered McGhie any supper. When Nathaniel had made the offer in her place, he had thought that he saw her lift a hand in mute protest.

Broddy, however, had refused. "In Nae Zealand!" he said now with a wink, then scrambled down the side to his boat. It bounced up and down as the boat's crew settled in their places, and pulled for the guano ship, with its captain singing and waving.

Nathaniel stood and watched the boat's jerky progress. McGhie was more than a little drunk, and Nathaniel felt a little benign and shiny himself, intoxicated with dreams and schemes as well as good brandy. The brief tropical twilight was upon them. Within a moment, the sun was gone and the sparse southern stars flicked into the velvet tropical night.

McGhie's lusty, tipsy voice, blurred with geniality, bobbed away into the darkness and towards the dim, oil-starved lamps of his odoriferous ship. *"Has a love of adventure, a promise of gold,"* came the distant boom, *"e'er tempted ye o'er the old briny world?"*

Then the chantey was lost to the night. Nathaniel stayed by the rail, staring into darkness, absorbed with the pictures in his mind. Land in New Zealand, he thought, and a partnership in a fine shore whaling station, a partnership with this invigorating Scotchman, based on Nathaniel's money and McGhie's expertise, on an island that was most profitably sited...

It had been an amazing day, one to quicken the blood and fire the spirit. It was as if fate had taken a hand in his affairs and nudged him in the right direction. After a long, long while he roused himself and slowly, musing, made his way below to the cabins.

Frances was not in the cabin where they had entertained McGhie. Puzzled, Nathaniel went into the captain's stateroom.

Frances was stripping the big swinging bed. Her movements were jerky. She, who was normally so graceful and agile, looked cumbersome and awkward. She was crying — tears smeared her cheeks as she looked tremulously up at her husband. She was ashamed of betraying her pain and fear, but she couldn't help it.

Why was she so frightened? It was ridiculous, she thought, that she should be so afraid. After all, she knew better than most what the next hours held. Nevertheless her hands were trembling as she laid out towels and spread the rubber sheet. There were tears on her lashes and she had to swallow before she could speak. Her throat hurt and all she could say was, "Oh, Nathaniel." She laughed a little then, through the tears, and said faintly, "Oh, Nathaniel, I did think Captain McGhie would never go away. He was a very pleasant man, but I really did fear that he would never get up and leave."

Her husband frowned at her. Then she saw the horrified comprehension fill him. "Oh, God," he said hollowly. "Oh God, oh Frances." He began to help her, clumsily. His hands, too, were trembling.

The confinement took four hours — four hours of clumsy frightened labor. The big callused hands that could grip barrels and shift them and heave at tons of wet flapping canvas were awkwardly gentle. My God, Nathaniel kept on thinking, what a woman. What an incredible, wonderful woman. He felt helpless adoration, amazed more than ever that his beautiful Frances had married him and come to share his strange existence at sea. She was a perfect, wonderful lady who had sat in the transom cabin in the throes of childbirth, terrified but too embarrassed to make excuses to a male stranger. It was impossible to understand how she must have felt all that long afternoon — but easy to imagine her mortification, and how endless the drinking and jovial masculine conversation must have seemed.

The baby was another lady. They laughed, Frances cried, he cried, and their daughter hollered fit to deafen the ship. They both trembled as Nathaniel held the infant in his big rough hands, awed by this gift, hardly daring to believe they owned her, that the sweat and struggle and indignity of confinement could end in something so precious.

"She's beautiful?" said Frances.

"She's beautiful," Nathaniel confirmed. He gazed lovingly at the bright red, crumpled, furious little face, convinced of her loveliness. The girl was going to be blessed with her mother's glorious copper hair, and Nathaniel was certain that those tight-shut eyes would prove to be a luminous sea color. Love for both his women filled him to bursting.

"11th April," he wrote with immense pride in his log. "Begins with a moderate breeze from SSE with flying clouds, steering SE. Spoke guano freighter Glens of Scotland, McGhie, he boarded us after some oil for his lamps. At 9:08 moments PM sea time My Wife Brought Forth a Daughter all well thank God and I call her Pandora Sherman."

"You certainly do not, Captain Sherman," Frances said in her crispest tones next day. "Her name," she said, "is Abigail."

One

Abigail Pandora Sherman reined in her horse and sat upright in the old saddle, surveying the tiny settlement of Mangonui and the bay beyond as a monarch might survey her domain.

The hill swept downwards before her, bare in patches, grassy in parts, gullied by the rains of past winters, falling in rounded swerves to the beach. The weather was brilliantly sunny. The harbor was almost landlocked, so that it lay as still as a millpond, in colors of deep blue, turquoise, and silver. Far to Abigail's left a ribbon of thick dark green bush hid the winding course of the river, and on the little headland below, late-blooming pohutukawa trees blushed an emphatic orange-red.

Seventeen whaleships were anchored down in the bay. Seventeen! Abigail couldn't remember when she had last seen so many in this place. In Auckland and Port Nicholson there was a constant bustle of little sloops and big trading vessels, and in Sydney and Hobart Town the shipping lined the wharves, but there in this almost deserted spot the ships came only in fours or fives.

Those seventeen whaleships bobbed at their cables, bowing to their reflections and each other. Some had their sails furled, others had their sails drying. Abigail clicked her tongue and rattled the bridle, and the mare sighed gustily and began to clop a zigzag path down the hill, along the edge of a gully, heading for the trees by the river.

As Abigail descended, her home bobbed out of sight behind her; the plain front door and front verandah went first, then the silver-weathered wooden cladding of the upper story, and finally the iron roof and the two brick chimneys. Abigail began to hum as she neared the trees; then she broke into merry song, ducking her head to avoid the branches.

"Has a love of adventure, a promise of gold," she caroled, "ever tempted you over the watery world?" She knew exactly where she was going; her fishing gear was stowed in the burlap bag that hung from her saddle. Cool shadows surrounded her. The kahikatea and totara trees that grew along the river course were enormous, a century old perhaps, with thick, clotted foliage that blotted out the sun. Ferns brushed at her feet and at the horse's hooves.

Her voice seemed to ring flat in the damper air, but she sang jubilantly, "Have you listened to the lookout cry, There she blows?" The horse's ears flicked back and forth, and the bush was silent, unmoving save for the rustle of Abigail's busy progress. It was as if the whole vegetable world was listening to her cheerful chantey.

"Our waist boat splashed down," she called as the mare forged steadily along the track. "And sure got the start." Ahead coins of sunlight fell onto the ferns, and the ferns gave way to grass; she was near the bank of the river. Then she could see the water reflecting the overhanging branches. Exposed rocks gleamed in the middle. It was a private place, her very own fishing spot, a fine deep backwater where fish slowed for a rest and giant eels lurked.

"Lay me on, Cap'n Brown," sang Abigail. "Bow oar pull me on—for 'tis *hell* that I am with a dart!" Then, with a jolt, she stopped short and scowled. Her private fishing place had people in it.

A graceful whaleboat bobbed in the backwater, held in place with the skilful dipping of a couple of oars. The boy in the head of the boat was standing at a steering oar, and five other boys were sitting—and all six of them were gazing silent and open-mouthed in Abigail's direction.

Abigail watched in a silence of her own that was as intimidating as she could make it. Boats' crews did not scare her; she had known sailors all of her life. Sailors were fellows who were kind and indulged her; she had shelves of handiwork presents to prove it. These sailors, moreover, were very young, very unseasoned indeed, she thought. So she smiled with perfect confidence and said, "This is *my* fishing place."

The sailor boys all gaped as if they had never seen a red-haired girl in a blue drilling dress in their lives before. They were dressed most dashingly themselves, in liberty pants with wide bottoms and shirts in a variety of colors. Their leader, the callow young gentleman who stood at the steering oar, was wearing white pants and a bright blue shirt and had an exuberant red sash tied round his middle.

He said loftily, "We got here first."

"But I live here!"

"You do? And who is *you*, anyways?"

"My father," Abby said, "is the American vice-consul." Then she slid off the horse, landed firmly on her feet, unhooked her burlap bag, and started to take out her fishing gear. If she acted as if the boys were not there, she reasoned, they would take the hint and leave.

Then, to her chagrin, she saw that the young sailor's superior grin was still firmly in place. "Vice-consuls' daughters," he said scornfully, "do not sing sea chanteys, and they particularly do not sing sea chanteys like the one what our disbelievin' ears perceived when you came out of them trees."

Abigail could think of nothing to say; she felt most

irritatingly bested. Seizing their advantage, the boys paddled their boat close to the bank. They tied it to a tree and all jumped up onto the grass, and Abigail resignedly began to pack up her gear, ready to give in and move out.

Then the boat-header said in the most sugary of tones, "Don't go."

Abigail ignored him. She was not even supposed to be fishing alone—though her father was usually lenient about it, she could imagine all too easily his reaction if he found out somehow that she had led the whaler boys to expect her company.

Then the young man said, "We'll give you half if you stay."

Abigail stopped winding the line. Her father was out for the day; he had taken someone unknown but important out riding—and she was sorely tempted. There was no reason her father should find out what she had done in the long sunny unchaperoned hours.

She said cautiously, "I get half the catch?"

"Yep," said the officer. "Half. If we catch twenty, you get ten; if we get a hundred, you get fifty."

"And if we get eels you won't keep the big ones and give me the little ones?"

While the young man thought about it, Abigail unraveled her line again. The five other boys produced lines too, sat down in a row, and began to cast, giving her sheepish friendly grins as they did so. They looked more like farm boys than sailors, she thought, and she said to the one nearest her, "Do you have a name?"

He blushed. He had jug ears and knobbly hands that seemed too big for his wrists. "Michael," he mumbled. He came, he said, from Wethersfield, Connecticut.

They all fished. Abby felt relaxed and confident, for after all, she had chattered with sailors all of her life, on the brig *Pandora* and on other ships she had visited. The crewmen of the brig had been unfailingly wonderful to her; they took her along to visit their families when the *Pandora* was in their home port, and to shops in foreign places, and bought her all the lemon syrup she could drink. Sailors had made up her large childhood family, treating her as a daughter or a sister: they had read her their letters, told her their yarns, and filled her head with romantic stories.

The sun was warm. It was very peaceful sitting in a row in the sun. Abby turned to the officer and said very kindly, "And what are you called?"

To her amusement he dropped his line, leapt to his feet, flourished his hat, bowed very deeply, and then said in his acute American accent, "Consider West, third mate, *Erasmus* larboard boat, at your service, *ma'am!*" Then he sat down, put on his hat, and went back to fishing as if he'd never stopped.

"*You*, a third mate?" Whaleship crews were notoriously young, but she doubted that this fellow was more than eighteen.

He said derisively, "*You*, a vice-consul's daughter?" Then he said, mimicking, "And do you have a name?"

"Of course I do! And, what's more," she added, "my name is not a riddle." He looked so flummoxed that her spirits rose and she recited, "The wind was west, and west steered we, the wind blew right aft, so how could that be?"

She had to tell him. Because Third Mate West was at the helm, of course! Everyone laughed except Mr. West. He said grumpily, "And where did you learn that doggerel? I warrant it weren't at a school, not in this outlandish place."

Broddy had taught her the riddle: nevertheless she retorted, stung, "Of course I went to school."

When Abby was six, her mother had taken a strong stand. She herself had taught Abigail how to read, and print some, and draw pictures and tinkle the keys of a piano. And a kind mate had taught her some arithmetic.

Abby and her father had both been convinced that this was enough. However her mother had said that shipboard

13

life was not sufficient education for a shipmaster's daughter. So she had made inquiries.

"I went to a school in Auckland," Abby declared now.

It was one of the first schools in colony, housed in two rooms in a wooden building in Shortland Street. Mrs. Sherman had found a boarding place nearby, and she and Abby stopped in Auckland while Captain Sherman went off on the brig *Pandora* on his own. Only in the summers did Abby and her mother join him on the vessel.

"It was run," said Abby, "by Miss Ellie Clark." Miss Ellie Clark was a large middle-aged lady who had travelled from England to New Zealand to make her fortune, or perhaps—who knew?—to find a husband. For all Abby knew, she had discovered neither.

Abby remembered her vividly. She giggled and said, "She had such a lot of black hair, a mass of it." Miss Ellie Clark arranged her dusty hair in a sort of tower, with a little lace cap jammed on the very crown of the edifice, and how uncomfortable it looked—"I couldn't take my eyes away from it," Abby confessed. "It looked so heavy."

Then, as Miss Ellie Clark had questioned her new pupil to find out how much Abigail had learned already, Abby found that Miss Clark had a most fascinating habit. "As she talked she scratched her head with a pen," she said. "She talked and talked and the pen slid in and out of her hair ... and every time the pen slid in, the hair rose up, just a little, and every time the pen slid out, the hair would drop with a little plop."

As the pen had slid in, she had thought she glimpsed a tantalizing flash of pallid baldness. "I must have seemed exceedingly stupid," she confided to the row of rapt boys, "for I was very vague about the answers to Mss Ellie Clark's questions."On and on the pen handle had scratched, in and out, in and out, and then, yes!

Before Abby had thought to clap her hands on top of her impulsive mouth the exclamation had come bursting out.

14

"It's a wig!" she had cried, and guffawed. Two of the boys at the back of the class had giggled too, and Miss Ellie Clark caned the three of them.

Caned? Michael's eyes were very round; there was no caning, he declared, in American schools. "Well," said Abby, "New Zealand schools are different."

There were two methods of caning, Abby had found, one for girls and one for boys. The girls got "palmies" and the boys got "stretched bums." Naughty boys were gripped by the scruff of the collar and laid squirming and mortified face-downwards on Miss Clark's voluminous lap, and the cane, with whistling strokes, briskly stretched their breeches.

Abby, being a girl, was shrilly commanded to put her hands out palm upwards and keep start-still. She couldn't believe that Miss Clark was going to hit her, not really, not until the cane came zipping down. Nine years later the memory still made her flinch. At the time her hands jerked back of their own accord, and she received the vicious stroke on the tender tips of her fingers. She had screamed and had been informed that she was an arrant little coward, and then, frozen with shock, she had stood like stone to receive the rest of her punishment.

The second room of the school, where the children learned to cipher, was called the counting house. The teacher in this room was Miss Ellie Clark's employee, a younger lady who also taught the piano. As Abby was patently unable to demonstrate her musical ability that day, the teacher had sweetly suggested that Abigail Sherman might favor the class with a recitation of her favorite poem.

Abby was delighted to oblige. Her offended spirit bloomed with warm gratitude for the kindness, and she knew, of course, any number of jaunty ditties. She stood four-square in front of the rows of desks, smiled brightly and took a big breath.

"If to your starboard red appear," she chanted, and waved an injured hand to her right—

It is your duty to keep clear.
But when upon your port is seen
A vessel's starboard light of green,
There's nothing much for you to do,
For green to port steers wide of you.

Then, as Broddy had taught, she stamped her feet and shouted, "*Roll and go!*" The teacher had not been amused; Abby had been kept in when school was over for the day. "Miss Ellie Clark said," Abby told the whaler boys, "that obedience, decorum and respect must form the first lesson, for both children and Maoris—just as if little Maoris are not children!"

Maori children did go to the school, so that as well as writing and arithmetic and the need for decorum, Abby learned how to speak the Maori language. The Maori mothers paid the fees with money they made selling fish and the clams they called "pipis," and kumara and fruit in season, all spread out on mats at the foot of Shortland Street where the harbor waters lapped. When Abby first started school, her mother would buy a basket of peaches from one of the women, paying sixpence for it, or perhaps an old shirt instead, and the Maori woman would give Abby three juicy peaches for her school dinner.

"Surely you didn't go to school every day!" one of the boys said.

"Oh yes, I did," Abby answered. "Every single day except Sunday."

The Maori lady had a grandson called Tamati, the Maori version of the English name Thomas. Tamati was only four years older than Abby, but did not go to school. Indeed, he had never learned to read or write. Abby envied him greatly. He carried the baskets for Mrs. Sherman, and he and her mother escorted her all the way to the door of the school, to make certain she did not escape. The whaler boys greeted this revelation with horror: in America, they assured her, boys and girls went to school only if the planting or the

16

harvesting or such other important occasions did not get in the road of it. Children wandered in and out of classrooms as if they were their own casual kitchens. Abby envied them, too: they were almost as fortunate as Tamati had been.

When Abby's father had moved to Mangonui to be the American vice-consul, the Maori woman who gave Abby the peaches gave Tamati himself to Mrs. Sherman. She called at the boardinghouse where Mrs. Sherman stopped to deliver the boy; Mangonui was wild enough, she said, and Mrs. Sherman needed a boy, for a daughter was not sufficient. Tamati had not seemed upset in the slightest at the notion of being given away like a handful of peaches: he became Sherman very rapidly, and everything Sherman was "ours." For a year he helped Mrs. Sherman in the garden and the scullery, and then he had gone to do crew work on the brig and had become a talented seaman.

Today, however, Tamati was not on the brig: he was out riding as groom with Captain Sherman and his anonymous visitor. The *Pandora* was somewhere on the Tasman Sea on the way to Melbourne with a hired captain, carrying a load of 40 tons of Mangonui potatoes, 21,537 feet sawn timber, 200 bushels of barley, four knocked-down houses, 60 barrels of black oil from the shore whaling station in Cook Strait, and six doubtlessly seasick passengers. Broddy McGhie was at the shore whaling station, and Captain Sherman and Tamati were riding with the guest.

Who could it be? It must be one of the captains of the seventeen ships in the bay—but who? And why? Captain Sherman had never done such a thing before. He never even had guests to dinner, except for Broddy, of course, and Broddy didn't count, for he was part of the family. When Broddy was in Mangonui, he and her father never went riding: they inhabited the billiard room and the dining room exclusively. The house resounded all day and most of the night with the loud echoes of chanteys, the softer sounds of billiard balls clicking on felt, the clink of bottles, and the hearty noises of full-bodied Scotch laughter—and that was the extent of the hospitable activity.

It occurred to Abby that it would be a wonderful coincidence if the mysterious guest was none other than these boys' master. She said, "Who is your captain?"

"Cambridge," supplied Michael.

The name meant nothing. Abby smiled and said, "Is he kind?"

"Our old man?" Consider West threw an arm in the air. "*Kind?*" And the boys all had a good laugh.

"Perish the thought," said one.

"A poor matelote boy gets a-seized up in the riggin' if he so much as breathes to wind'ard," said another.

"Oh," said Abby. She knew they were teasing, but still pulled a face. Her father did not believe in flogging.

"However," said Consider West magnanimously, "we forgive 'im —for ain't he the luckiest master in the whole broad Pacific? And the governor of New Zealand himself has expressed a wish to see the ship *Erasmus!*"

Abby stared. "*Who?*"

"Aye," said Mr. West. "Mr. George Grey himself. He said it in the Bay of Islands, but he didn't have time to look."

Abby wondered whether to believe him. Then she forgot it. Her line gave a mighty tug and she surged to her feet, shrieking like a whistle, whipping the line out of the water with a triumphant cry. A huge eel came flapping up the bank, slapping at the grass in furious s-bends. Abby yelled again and got out of the way very fast.

The eel was as round as a man's arm and twice as long, and it had a huge mouth chock full of sharp vicious teeth, which it snapped with great ferocity. The boys all hollered at once and leapt up and assailed it with lumps of wood, but for quite some moments the eel gave as good as it got. Each time they thought they had it conquered, it lunged around and laid its teeth into a handy boot, while Abby bobbed about on the outskirts, shouting unheeded advice.

18

Finally, with a last ferocious lunge, the eel subsided. "Good Godfrey and bless me," said Consider West, with most unaccustomed awe. "That sure be the most ugliest fish I ever did see. Do they all grow that huge in New Zealand?"

Abigail had never seen an eel that large, but was certain that eels, like peaches, grew larger in New Zealand than anywhere else. "Of course," she said.

"Well, ma'am," said Mr. West, and fetched another bow, "he's yours. We," he declared, "will keep the little eels."

Abigail and the boys had an excellent morning's fishing. The whaleboat crew had carried a bag of hard bread for dinner, and they cooked some fish by wrapping them in leaves and mud and baking them in a fire. Then Abby scrambled onto her horse and led the way through the bush to a wild peach tree on the fringe of the forest. It had plenty of ripe bursting fruit, dripping juice and sweetness, and the boys stripped the branches with a great deal of horseplay. Then, to Abby's consternation, she found she had no horse; Rosie, the mare, had sighted the uphill path to home and oats and wandered off, leaving her mistress stranded.

Abigail and the boys went back to the river and retrieved their lines. Then they shared out the catch. Abigail, ruefully aware that she would be hauling the burlap bag home on her back, gave the boys the biggest eels.

"We could row you," said Michael.

"What?"

"Yes," said Mr. West. "You could come with us as far as the beach. In fact," he added as if inspired, "you could come on board the ship *Erasmus* and view how beautiful she is."

The offer was remarkably tempting. Like Sir George Grey, Abby would dearly love to see the *Erasmus* – but the idea was quite impossible. She shook her head.

"Why not?"

She shrugged.

"You're gallied," Consider West jeered. "You're scared."

"That is not true!"

"Then why don't you come? 'Tis proper," he hastened to add. "There's a lady on board. Cap'n Cambridge carries his wife."

Abigail could remember only one other time that a whaleship had carried a woman into Mangonui. That particular vessel had arrived under most imprudent sail, considering the squally conditions, and Abby's mother had been summoned on board the instant the anchor was dropped. Abigail had gone too, to assist—which meant she had been given the job of warming towels by the cabin stove. Two weeks later the whaling master had sailed away, properly grateful and carrying his wife and a dear baby boy.

Abby's own mother had been a pioneer female voyager. She had told Abigail many stories about how scandalized her friends had been when they learned she was determined to sail—and not even on a whaleship! Everyone had disapproved of a woman's going with her husband on an East Indies trader to the barbaric Orient and south Pacific— women were meant to stop at home and look after the money and the children.

It was no wonder, Abby considered, that her mother had never returned to New Bedford. What unimaginative folks people must be, to think so old-fashioned! Abigail had no relations in New Bedford that she knew of, except her father's cousin, Mrs. Jezekiel Mitchell. When her mother had died, Captain Sherman had almost concluded to send Abby to New Bedford to learn manners from this lady, but of course Abby hadn't gone. She refused to contemplate the notion. What would her father do without her?

Anyway, she belonged to New Zealand, not New Bedford. Her father was a landowner here: he was wealthy. He owned hundreds of acres of New Zealand soil, as well as the brig *Pandora* and half the shore whaling station. Abby was an heiress.

She smiled kindly at the boys and said, "Do you enjoy

having a lady on board of your ship?"

The boys all pulled faces. Whaling, they declared, was a man's business. "But don't she make gingerbread for all hands?" said one dissenter.

They all contemplated this and slowly nodded. "Mince pies, at Christmas," said one. "Doughnut mixture, to cook in the trypots, for each thousandth barrel," said another, and they all nodded again, absentmindedly licking peach juice from their fingers.

Abigail watched them with amusement. Each thousandth barrel, she thought, just as if the thousandth came up every few days. Other whalemen were pleased enough if they carried home one thousand barrels plus a few hundred, but Abigail had already been informed that the *Erasmus* report was astounding. It was traditional for the crew to be treated to doughnuts at such times, but even so, Mrs. Cambridge sounded a warm, friendly person. No doubt, Abby thought, she kept the log, as her mother had, and wrote up the books and worked the navigation when her husband was busy catching all those whales and then cutting them in. The thought of paying a call on Mrs. Cambridge was becoming very tempting.

However, she said, "Only to the beach."

"The mate is a capital fellow," Mr. West said, and smiled just as complacently as if Abigail had agreed to visit the ship. Then the boys launched the whaleboat.

Abigail thoroughly enjoyed her sail. The whaleboat had rather a lot of water sloshing about in the bottom and was consequently rather low in the water, but the craft was so graceful and slender at both pointed ends that she thrust lightly and eagerly through the silky brown flow. The river chuckled softly in time to the creaking of the cedar planking. Shadows of thick dark trees flowed over them, and at the fringe of the bush, a vanguard of graceful tree-ferns dabbled their gritty drooping fronds in the secret brown ripples.

No one said a word. The boys seemed sleepy, content

21

with their fishing expedition. Abigail's burlap bag in the bow thumped a bit as the bilge water reached it and one of the eels came to life. The boy at bow oar set a boot on it, and the eel quietened. Then, slowly, the whaleboat eased round the final river bend, and the full expanse of the bay was revealed.

The current at the mouth of the river made the boat dance. The light was blinding, sparkling scintillations off the surface of the sea in a dazzle of blue, green, brown, and gold. The bare green hills reared up towards the tiny puffs of cloud in a blue sky that was edged with a distant mauve haze. Abigail could just make out the glint of a window in her father's house, but the other three European homesteads were hidden by the pohutukawa trees on the headland. Whaleboats were drawn up on the beach.

The whaling vessels seemed huge as the boat moved among them. The nearest vessel was the *Chandler Price*. Abigail read the name on her stern. She had her sails drying in the little breeze, the canvas almost luminous in the brilliant air. Abigail could see the buntlines hanging like rattails in rows, and men working on the yards. All the whaleships were busy with port-time activities. A whaleboat towing a raft of heavy water casks pulled out from the beach very slowly. Another whaleboat with two men in the amidship thwarts was on the way to visit one of the ships, but which one Abby could not see, for the boat pulled out of sight between two of the anchored vessels. Another great stern loomed overhead, massive and black. The copper sheeting beneath the great bulge of the hull gleamed in the darkness of the water. Abigail craned her neck to see the huge gold carved eagle on the stern, above the four round holes of the sternlights. *Erasmus* of New Bedford, she read on the sternboard, and then the boys pulled so the whaleboat slid around the starboard quarter.

Both the starboard quarter and starboard bow boats were hung in their cranes on the outside of the ship. Abigail knew that the starboard quarter boat was traditionally the captain's boat—so the captain was at home. She felt abruptly nervous, and was glad when the boys rowed on.

The men on board were painting ship. They hung from bowlines with brushes in their hands and shouted out gleefully when they recognized Consider West and saw that he had a girl on board. The cutting stage, lowered outwards when the officers were cutting the blubber from a whale, was lashed up and men were painting it black. The tryworks bricking, which surrounded the great cauldrons in which the oil was boiled out of the blubber, was being neatly whitewashed. The ship *Erasmus* looked as spick-and-span as any housewife's kitchen, and it was easy to believe that a lady lived on board. The hurricane house, built on the after deck on either side of the wheel, had a roof to shelter the helmsman and little deck cabins within it; it was painted a pretty green.

Abby was relieved when the boys did not stop but kept pulling. The whaleboat slid gracefully on, past the huge anchor chain with its rust and encrustations, and past the blunt prow and thrusting jibboom, and then on through the bay. The boys, it seemed, were giving her a tour of the harbor. They passed other ships—*Marengo, Minerva*—whose great hulls rose up and up to shadow the sun when the whaleboat pulled beneath their sterns. Soon they were circling the furthermost ship of the fleet.

She was called *Pierrot*, and was small and somehow shabby, whereas the others had been grand. Her black coat of paint seemed dusty rather than somber. Instead of an eagle on her stern she had a ribbon and a mannequin in motley. There was something hanging in her mainmast rigging...

It was a man. He looked grotesque and larger than life, seized up in an obscene spread-eagle shape, as if to make up for the lack of an eagle on the sternboard. Abigail saw the strips of bloody bruising that crisscrossed the pallid back.

Then they moved closer, and the bulwarks hid the dreadful thing. She heard the high-pitched wail of the man's wild cursing, however, and felt sick.

Her father considered it barbaric. The first time Abby had seen a flogging on his brig was when the *Pandora* was docked in Hobart Town. As soon as they had made port, Mrs. Sherman had been called away to assist in a birthing, so that Abigail was left alone. Captain Sherman was busy with the mate on business on shore, so the stern second mate put Abby into the care of the seventeen-year-old steerage boy, Jim.

Jim was conscientious to a fault. The second mate gave him very strict instructions not to take the captain's daughter near any grogshops, so when the two dollars that Captain Sherman had given Abby had been spent on lemon syrup and fruit, Jim took her along to view a hanging instead.

In the marketplace four men had been hanged, convicts who had killed a man when they made a bid to escape. Jim declared afterwards that it was "an 'orrible waste of four good men," and Abby thought it was a waste of more than that, for they had both been thoroughly sick in the dirt. Then, when she and Jim returned to the brig earlier than said because of their inner conditions, they found a dreadful scene on deck: the second mate was flogging one of the men.

Abby couldn't remember the second mate's name, but she knew the seaman he was flogging very well indeed. He was Ichabod Jones, a quiet young fellow who was one of her favorites in the brig. He read her stories out of a book written by a man called Dickens, and he had taught her how to knot macramé edges to the covers she made for sea chests. It had nearly broken her heart to see him treated so, to see him with his thumbs tied up in the shrouds so that only the tips of his boots hit the deck. Each time the rope's end had curled over his back, he had grunted and flinched, and she had remembered Miss Ellie's caning, and how it had felt.

Abigail wondered if she had acted the way she had because of Mss Ellie's caning—or was it because of the hangings she had seen? She had flown onto the brig, thrown herself at the mate, and grabbed the lash away from him. She had had no right, for when her father and the first mate were away, the second mate was in charge of the ship. No doubt he had thought he had good reason to flog poor Ichabod Jones; young Jones had a dry way of speech, and the mate said he had come on board saucy.

"Your daughter flew at me, a right little vixen, she," he reported furiously to her father that evening. "And, what's more," he said in the most righteous of tones, "she used the most unhandsome language."

Abigail wondered what had happened to Ichabod Jones after that voyage. As soon as Captain Sherman had returned to the brig, both Jones and the second mate had asked for their discharge. Her father had been very angry, and Abby's punishment had been banishment from the brig. Her father had negotiated with Miss Ellie Clark as soon as they got back to Auckland, and Abby had been condemned to live at the school while both her father and mother sailed away on the *Pandora*. That, too, had nearly broken her heart.

Her mother had not come back. Abby thrust the memory away—and all at once, while she was lost in her musings, they had arrived back at the ship *Erasmus*.

Abby said, "Look, I don't think..." The boys ignored her. They were on the larboard side, out of sight of most of the harbor, and abruptly, before Abby could say anything more, five of the boys quit the boat.

It rocked wildly and the water sloshed in the bottom, wetting Abby's skirts. She watched them shin up the side of the ship like a passel of monkeys and bit her lip. She was not dressed for visiting, she thought apprehensively, and, what's more, she had not received a proper invitation.

But she had often visited other vessels, she argued to herself, both at sea and in port. The captains and crews had always been polite and correct and extremely hospitable, and the women she had seen, on English merchant vessels, had been delighted to entertain Captain Sherman's daughter.

Consider West steadied the boat with a hand on a rope. Then he pushed on the thick solid side of the ship, moving the whaleboat along until it lay beneath the larboard quarter davits. The davit falls dangled, and then were hooked on; suddenly the other boys appeared on the roof of the hurricane house, and with a shouted *Heave!* they began to haul the boat up.

The whaleboat rocked and jerked and banged on the side of the ship. It must sound deafening from inside the cabins, Abigail thought with trepidation. She wondered again about her welcome, and all at once was very conscious of her state of dress and the sailors gawping about in the rigging. When the boat reached the level of the top of the house, Consider West put out a hand to help her. Abigail ignored him. She grabbed her burlap bag, picked up her skirts in the other hand, and stepped neat as a fly onto the ship.

A couple of sailors whistled. Abigail stood awkwardly, wishing she had stopped at home. Then, as she watched the boys secure the boat in the cranes and let the water out of the bottom, slowly she became aware that a second boat had arrived at the ship, on the other — starboard — side.

Abigail could not see who was in the other boat; the passengers were hidden by the side of the ship. She watched great silvery coins of water fall out of the whaleboat to flop down on the sea, and she gnawed her lip, listening to the voices below. But surely Mrs. Cambridge would be glad to see her, particularly as she was bringing with her a fine mess of fresh fish... Of course she would be pleased! Abby, with decision, walked over to the ladder that led from the roof of the house to the deck, picked up her skirts, and began to descend.

Her father's voice thundered, "Abigail!"

Her foot slipped. Strong hands caught her about the waist, and set her down. She stumbled, clumsy with consternation, and the hands caught her again, holding her wrists.

They were cool sailor's hands, their bones stretched and hardened with years of grappling with stiff canvas. Abigail gazed upwards into the face of a stranger. Arched questioning eyebrows looked down at her.

She released herself hastily and looked wildly around. Captain Sherman was only two paces away, and never had she seen him so red-faced, astounded, or thunderous. She took a deep breath, bracing herself for the tirade. Mr. West and his boat's crew, she saw to her disgust, had made themselves scarce. She was alone with her father and his companion and all the fascinated seamen who were hanging about in the rigging.

Then she saw to her chagrin that her father's companion was thoroughly diverted. He had his arms folded. Those black eyebrows were infuriatingly high. Who was he? A sea captain, by his clothing—though his broadcloth coat was dusty—and a whaling master, by his bearing. He had all the broad-shouldered dignity of the species, despite his youth, and despite the rakish way he wore his peaked hat. It was thrust to the back of a tousle of curls, and his face was so tanned and those curls so black that she thought for a moment he was Portuguese. Then, with an odd little jerk inside her, she met his eyes. They were narrowed with silent laughter—and they were the most brilliant of blues.

Abby gave him a challenging look and then braced herself to face her father. He was dusty, too, and she could smell the sulfur on both the men, and knew then where they had been riding that morning. They had gone to the pumice valley, where Te Wharenui's people took healing baths in hot mud puddles. There were other pools—of warm water, set in among trees and ferns, where the young people bathed before they made love. It made the women languorous and the men very strong.

Or so Abigail had been told. She flushed and said to her father, "Don't be ... be cross. I only came to pay a call on Mrs. Cambridge."

"Mrs. Cambridge sent an invitation?"

Abby bit her lip and said, "No."

"So you just took it into your head to burden her with your company?"

Abigail winced, made more uncomfortable by the man with her father, who still watched her, his demeanor lazy and amused. He leaned one shoulder on the corner of the hurricane house as if he was very content to stand there and view her discomfiture for as long as her father kept on scolding. She cast him a sideways resentful glance — and anger lent her inspiration. She whirled round to her father, held up the burlap bag, smiled radiantly, and declared, "I thought I'd bring Mrs. Cambridge a present."

The bag immediately bounced; apparently an eel had flopped into life with the motion. Abby's father glared and shouted, "And what the devil is it, miss? A confounded litter of kittens?"

The black-haired captain cleared his throat rather abruptly, with a strange muffled sound. Who was he, anyway? Why didn't he have the decency to straighten up and set off on his own business? She had thought him rather grim at first, but laughing at her like that, he seemed very young to be a ship's master, even by whaling standards. He was perhaps only twenty-four. Abby's flying thoughts came to an apprehensive halt: firm proprietorial bootsteps were coming up the after stairs. Captain Cambridge, it seemed, had become inquisitive about the shouting on his after decks.

Abby had never met the master of the *Erasmus* before, but Captain Cambridge's bearing and appearance gave him away at once: he was so bluff, so red-faced and hearty that his identity was unmistakable. A big, burly man, with stiff, fair square-cut whiskers, he had a most self-satisfied look about him.

Sighting Abby's father, he boomed, "Captain Sherman, glad to see you!" Then he saw Abby and stopped short, pulling at his whiskers. Then, finally, he saw the black-haired captain, and his smile widened even further. "Good Godfrey!" he cried. "Seth, by thunder, 'tis good to see you!" He pounded this Seth on the shoulder and turned to Captain Sherman and exclaimed, "You've met my cousin? Captain Seth Morgan? Master of ship *Pierrot?*"

Oddly, Abby thought, this Captain Seth Morgan did not seem as gratified to meet his cousin as Captain Cambridge was to see him. He straightened, and his mouth and eyebrows straightened, too. However Captain Cambridge didn't seem to notice. "I sent a message th'instant I heard *Pierrot* was in the harbor," he cried. "Was afraid you'd miss it. You'll stop for tea, of course!"

Then, all at once, the name of Captain Seth Morgan's ship registered in Abby's mind. She frowned, and her mouth set in a line of disdain. She thought of the *Pierrot* and the man dangling in the mainmast rigging, the man who had dangled like a chill echo of Ichabod Jones. When Captain Morgan suddenly met her stare she lifted her chin and did not drop her eyes.

One black eyebrow arched high, in puzzlement. Then he shrugged and looked away. His cousin Captain Cambridge had him by the hand and was pumping it up and down with hearty delight. "How long, Seth?" he demanded. "How long since we last saw each other? Three years? Four? Oh, this whaling business!" He shook his head ruefully, grinning all the time. "I remember the place it was," he informed Captain Sherman, and chuckled. "The Okhotsk Sea, in a fog. When was it, Seth? The forty-four season? Or the forty-five? He was mate of the *Omega*." And he shook with hearty laughter and waved a genial arm at the clear blue sky and the summer hills surrounding the bay. "Quite a change of circumstance, eh? Seth has his own ship now," he declared, and demanded in jocular fashion, "What sort of report have you, Cousin Morgan? How well are you doing?"

A muscle jumped in Captain Morgan's jaw. He said quietly, "I hear your report is extremely gratifying, Obed." His voice was even, deep, and husky, the voice of a man who had spent a lot of his boyhood singing out in the rigging.

Obed Cambridge waited. They watched him until he opened his mouth and said with slow, creamy satisfaction, "Six thousand, six hundred."

There was dead silence. Captain Sherman was astounded. Seth Morgan was stunned. It would make New Bedford history, that amazing report. Six thousand, six hundred barrels of sperm oil. A voyage worth, at the most conservative estimate, two hundred thousand dollars. It was too much money to imagine all at once.

"I've had a deal of good fortune," Obed said, clasping his hands lightly behind his back, like an admiral. "When I was homeward bound from my last voyage, I was in Lahaina when the *Wilmingon and Liverpool Packet* was condemned. I bought one thousand barrels of her oil—for fifty cents a barrel—and stored it in the hulk against my return."

Fifty cents a barrel. There were thirty-one and one-half gallons in each barrel—and sperm oil sold at ninety-nine cents a gallon. It was a profit of thirty thousand dollars, just from that one transaction. "I shipped the oil to Manila," Obed said, "and sold it for the London market."

So he had not even paid taxes: he had sold it as British-caught oil to avoid the duties. Devious, but perfectly legal. Captain Sherman's expression held a wealth of respect, and that muscle jumped again in Seth Morgan's jaw.

"From Manila we cruised the Sea of Japan," Captain Cambridge recited relentlessly, "and boiled two thousand, eight hundred barrels there—in fifty-seven days. Went back to Manila and shipped all but a thousand back to London. Then we came to the New Zealand ground and cruised from the north to the Line. Now we are bound to Cape Horn and home—full."

The last word lingered in the air. Then Obed boomed, "Well, Cousin Seth, how have you been faring, eh? What is your report? Give us your tally, Cousin!"

Seth flicked a narrow glance at Sherman and his daughter and said shortly, "Seventy-five barrels."

The silence was as stunned as that which had greeted Obed's report, but the quality was altogether different. Obed almost whistled. Seth saw his cousin's lips purse up, but Obed stopped himself just before committing the tactless blunder. He cleared his throat with an awkward noise and said heavily, "You've been out how long? A year?"

"Fourteen months." There was a bitter taste in Seth's throat. Fourteen months, he brooded: fourteen months of bent harpoons and parted lines and whales that gallied to windward, an eternity of incompetent officers and cowardly boatsteerers and mutinous crews, and—by far the worst—fourteen months of an endlessly empty sea. Hunting the whale was the same as hunting any fortune. The world was desperate for oil, and would pay highly for it, but only the astoundingly lucky succeeded—lucky men like Obed.

With a ponderous attempt to soothe the air, Obed said, "There have been worse voyages..." Seth didn't bother to answer. He moved his shoulders irritably, shoved his fists into his jacket pockets, and stared unseeingly at the bay. The hills were darkening as the sunlight lengthened from behind them to the west, the long shadows rippling on the grass and the water. A little coastal steamer was nosing around a headland from the direction of the open sea, just coming into sight. It was flying the British ensign.

Obed said to Captain Sherman, "You'll stop to tea, of course!" Sherman glanced at his daughter, who blushed, and

31

Obed boomed, "Most welcome, most welcome! Mrs. Cambridge will be first-rate gratified to receive a visit from a female. She loves a woman-gam, and this is almost as good—a girl-gam, eh?" He roared with laughter at his own feeble joke and firmly ushered his guests below.

Captain Sherman was a bulky man, and both the cousins were big men. As they crowded the narrow, dark stairway, they had to move with care. Obed went first, Seth following him as he opened the door to the transom cabin. The light was dim; Seth paused in the doorway, conscious of the scent of roses and furniture polish, and an unexpected sense of coming home. Seth's mother had died when he was eleven and he had never had a home since then. His father had immediately sold the family home and moved into a New Bedford boardinghouse. Seth could have gone to live with Obed's parents, but he had chosen to go to sea instead.

Now, he was afflicted with intense nostalgia. He had almost forgotten what it was like to hear the soft swish of petticoats as a woman stood up to greet him, and how it felt to step into a warm aura of domesticity. He had never met Obed's wife before; as his eyes adjusted to the dimmer light he became aware of soft curves and utter femininity.

"Victoria, my wife," said Obed, as complacent as when he gave his report. "Victoria—Seth Morgan, my cousin."

Seth took the little hand, holding it very carefully. Victoria Cambridge was demure and rounded. Her gown was cut high in the waist, emphasizing her abundant curves. Her shoulders sloped just a little from the pure white ruching of her collar, and she had a pink-and-white complexion, matt as ivory. Her dark hair, gleaming as smooth as two wings of oil, was parted in the middle and caught in a flawless chignon in the nape of her tender neck.

She was perfect. Envy twisted cruelly inside Seth again: first, Seth thought hungrily, that incredible report, and now this most enchanting lady. Would Obed's good fortune never falter? Seth grimly pictured his dank cabin and his cranky old vessel and his appalling first officer, and his slovenly crew who talked of mutiny behind his back. This cabin, in stark contrast, was a home, a perfect, respectable parlor. It was incredible that the presence of a woman should make such a difference. The sofa had a knitted cover and there were crocheted lamp mats on the lockers.

Where had Obed found this jewel? Obed's mother — Seth's aunt Fanny Morgan Cambridge — was a dreadful old besom, in Seth's opinion, full of shrill and unseemly ideas. His Aunt Fanny had been the major reason Seth had gone to sea. Anything was preferable to living at the Cambridge house with that old blue-stocking. The contrast between Obed's mother and Obed's bride was as emphatic as the difference between Obed's ship, and Seth's.

The little hand in his felt delicate. Seth stood looking down at the smooth hair and curved cheek. A swelling bosom trembled above the high waist of her gown. Obed had all the domestic comforts: the reassurance of dutiful companionship in the daytime, and warm company in the captain's bed at night. The door behind Mrs. Cambridge was ajar, and Seth could glimpse the corner of a crocheted bedcover; he looked down at the hand he had been holding too long, lifted it, and touched the back of it, very gallantly, with his lips.

Victoria gasped. The fingers trembled, and the dark lashes flew upwards, and round hazel eyes stared shocked into his. Then Victoria looked quickly at her husband.

Obed had a distinctly gratified twinkle in his eye: he obviously considered it a compliment to his ineffable good judgment that his handsome young cousin should so openly admire his wife.

Victoria said breathlessly, "Captain Seth Morgan? Our ... cousin?" She blushed, and said, "Even ... even if at first acquaintance, it is a privilege to meet with a relation — and especially so in such a lonely far-flung spot." When Captain Sherman and his daughter came in, she turned to them with manifest relief.

Abigail looked absurdly young—and untidy, terribly untidy—beside Mrs. Cambridge's neat dark-gowned figure. The copper hair was tumbled and far too vivid and her wide, black-lashed, gray-green eyes were too candid.

When she smiled an awkward, unhappy smile, there was a tiny triangular chip out of the corner of one of the even white teeth. Her face was as square as a kitten's. One cheek held an uncertain dimple. Victoria Cambridge made Sherman's daughter look—gauche. It was apparent that she felt it: the copper ringlets stuck in tendrils to her flushed cheeks. She smelled most distressingly of fish, and she hung on to the cord of her burlap bag as if she felt it was a lifeline.

"Sit down, child," said Mrs. Cambridge. She smiled kindly but Abigail blushed again as she sat diffidently on a straight-backed chair to one side of the little chart table, while Mrs. Cambridge perched neatly on another. The cabin was narrow and over furnished, and the men were seated like poultry in a row on the sofa. There was an obvious attempt to make the cabin look like a New Bedford parlor, with daguerreotypes and framed prints on the walls, all a little askew because of the vessel's slight motion.

Obed Cambridge poured out three glasses of brandy, and then, just as the atmosphere relaxed and became a trifle convivial, the burlap bag gave a loud little hop.

Abigail went red. Her father gulped brandy and said to Mrs. Cambridge, "My daughter has brought you a puppy or some such."

Mrs. Cambridge said blankly, "A dog?"

Abigail swallowed and said, "Fish. I was ... was fishing, and ... and the catch was good. I hope you like eels."

"Eels?" Mrs. Cambridge seemed more startled than ever.

Nathaniel Sherman barked, "Fishing? What's this? You went fishing alone? When I specifically told you not to?"

Abigail winced and muttered, "I was not alone."

34

"With the Butler girls?"

Abigail was silent. Sometimes, she thought, her father was so preoccupied with his lands and this mysterious new scheme that was going to make him as rich as Croesus that he had little idea of what went on in the real world about him. Captain Butler was the other important settler in Mangonui, an Englishman who had arrived with his family a year or so ago, and lived on the point, up a pretty creek. He had a chandlery and a house where visiting captains stayed, and styled himself the "harbor master." Like Abby's father, he procured provisions and men for the whaling vessels in season, on commission. Captain Butler and his wife certainly did have daughters, but those girls were in England learning parlor manners, and they had been away for quite some months.

It was, however, very tempting to leave her father with this delusion. If he believed—at least until they got home—that Abigail had had female company, then his wrath would lose its potential to embarrass.

So, she said nothing. Then, to her horror, she heard Mrs. Cambridge say, "Mrs. Butler paid me a call this morning. Such an admirable woman. Oh, what trials she has endured, and how she admires you, Captain Sherman, in your resourcefulness during your troubles. She led me to believe that her daughters were in England at this moment to further their education before returning to the family bosom. Are there other girls in the family?"

Abigail's cheeks were fiery. Not only had Mrs. Butler gossiped, but Abby's diplomatic silence now looked like a downright lie. Her father roared, "Abigail!"—and then she was saved by a tap on the door.

A Polynesian steward came in. He was wearing dungarees and an apron. Mrs. Cambridge pointed to the burlap bag, murmuring, and the man bent and hefted it. When he looked inside, he grinned and said something. Abigail did not hear what it was, for Obed was saying importantly, "We expect an illustrious guest on the steamer, the governor himself. When we met in the Bay of Islands, he indicated a desire to look over an American whaling vessel, so of course he received an invitation to pay a social visit when he arrives this afternoon in Mangonui. There was no time," he explained, "while we were anchored off Russell."

"Is that so, by thunder?" Captain Sherman said politely, and Seth Morgan seemed equally unimpressed.

Obed's lady, however, looked quite animated. As the steward left the cabin, carrying the bag, she said brightly, "We seem to be well-off for eels today. The steward informs me that our larboard boat's crew went a-fishing up the river, and that they caught a fine mess of eels as well. One of the eels, he tells me," she said demurely, "is enormous."

Captain Sherman shouted, "Abigail, you were fishing with that boat's crew!"

Abigail muttered, "They're only boys."

Mrs. Cambridge had her hands folded in her lap and her lips were pursed in a rosebud shape as she regarded Abigail. She said, "Our third mate, Mr. West, is quite respectable, but impulsive, I fear. Young people are so..."

Abigail said hotly, "Mr. West and his boys were perfect Yankee gentlemen!"

"Abigail, you're a disgrace!"

"They shared the catch, Father!"

Captain Sherman pushed his hand through his hair in despair, and said, "Oh daughter, daughter, don't you ever think? Abigail, has it ever occurred to you that you shame me?"

Abigail bit her lip, fighting back tears. She could think of no reply.

"Fifteen years old," her father despaired. "Nearly sixteen, sixteen come April. And too damn—" He broke off abruptly, to say to Mrs. Cambridge in heavy tones, "I do beg your pardon, ma'am. And I do apologize for my daughter. Obviously her presence on this ship is one of her block-headed escapades. I have failed in my paternal duty," he sighed, and swallowed brandy as if he needed it.

Abruptly Abigail's conscience pricked her. Her father's angry look had turned to a gray, weary pallor. If they had been at home now she would have hugged him penitently and promised to be better in the future. She looked down at her hands in her lap and heard him say dully, "When my dear wife died..."

"Mrs. Butler," said Mrs. Cambridge, "told me that your daughter is motherless. And that your lady was, oh! ... such a woman. She was much in demand, I heard, for her gift of midwifery."

Abigail's throat felt tight. She begged silently that her father would say nothing, that he wouldn't tell this woman about her mother. Instead, she heard him say with difficulty, "My dear wife, Frances, expired nearly four years ago." Abigail's fingernails dug into her palms. Stop, oh, please stop, she silently implored. But he told it all, how her mother had nursed him and three of the crew on the brig *Pandora* and then had succumbed and expired within one feverish day. Abigail had not been there, on that fatal voyage: Abigail had been banished to school.

She remembered when her father had come to the school, alone, to collect her, and she listened now with wild resentment to him telling these people about that awful moment. His voice said unevenly, "It was a blessing that Abigail was not on board to be taken with cholera, too." He sighed and added, "When I took her away from the school, I should have set her on the next ship for New Bedford."

Mrs. Cambridge's soft voice murmured, "Truly, in the midst of life we are afflicted with pain. No one knows when he will be called by his maker." There was a pause, and then she said, "You have a female relative in New Bedford who would take your daughter and the responsibility of her education?"

Abby froze. Her father said, "My cousin, Mrs. Mitchell,

in New Bedford, is the only female relative I have."

"Mrs. Mitchell? Not Mrs. Jezekiel Mitchell of Boat Train Road?" Mrs. Cambridge's voice held surprise. "Merciful heavens," she said, "but I know her quite well. Her older son, Jireh, is master of the whaling vessel *Lizzie Ann*, and her younger son, William, is mate of ... Merciful heavens," she said again, and stared at Seth Morgan. He met her gaze expressionlessly. She cried, "Obed, isn't William Mitchell Captain Morgan's first officer?"

Captain Morgan said briefly, "He is." Then his mouth snapped shut.

There was an awkward little silence, then Abigail's father said, "That is why I was going to the *Pierrot*, to meet my cousin's son. I had hoped to take him riding today, to view—" He broke off and coughed. Then he muttered, "He couldn't come, so Captain Morgan kindly kept me company instead."

So, Abigail realized with apprehension, she had a cousin on the *Pierrot*. Her wide eyes shifted to Captain Morgan, who was staring broodingly at his brandy glass. A sick feeling turned coldly inside her. It was traditional for the first officer to stop on board of his ship when in port, for the first mate was in charge while the captain did business on shore. But why had William Mitchell not paid at least a short token visit to the vice-consular house?

"Yes, we were on the way to the *Pierrot*," her father said. "Captain Morgan having kindly given me the invitation— when I was treated to the sight of my daughter gallivanting about on your ship. That is why I am here. And I should send my girl to New Bedford. You're right, my dear lady," he said. "A motherless girl requires female guidance. My daughter is an impulsive hoyden, and 'tis my fault entirely. I have failed in the exercise of my paternal duty."

Abigail wanted to cry, *No!* He had been absent-minded lately, with his enigmatic scheme in his head, and often as cross as a bear with his worries, but he had never been

38

unkind or ungenerous. She had never felt without love. They argued—of course they argued. How could they not? For they were so very alike. She might resemble her mother amazingly, but her nature was her father's: impulsive, romantic, single-minded, and obstinate. She stared at him and wanted to cry, Don't forget the *Pandora!* — for when they were at sea, all differences were forgotten and they were both sublimely content. How could he manage without her? Who would supervise the Maori girls in the kitchen, and who would nurse him if he fell sick? She had pulled off his boots for him often enough, and undressed him as well, when he was a little the worse for his liquor.

Mrs. Cambridge said sedately, "Fifteen is young. It may not be too late."

Obed Cambridge cleared his throat and looked at his wife proudly. "Captain Sherman," he said, "listen to me wife's advice. 'Tis unfailingly good."

"We will help you, and be glad to do it," Mrs. Cambridge declared. "We are homeward bound," she said, and smiled. "Full. We will make a fast passage, we hope. And I, of course, as a sympathetic friend who knows the trials of your situation, would be most willing to improve your lot. And, I must admit it," she said with a sweet little laugh, "I should be most grateful for the opportunity of female companionship. We would be perfectly willing to stop an extra day or so while your daughter packs her things. Then we'll take her passenger with us and deliver her safely—God willing—into the responsible care of your cousin, Mrs. Mitchell."

Abigail was frozen with horror, watching her world fall apart but unable to do a thing about it. Then Captain Seth Morgan got to his feet. His tanned face was expressionless as he nodded politely to his cousin's wife.

"If you would excuse me, Mrs. Cambridge."

Captain Sherman stood up, too. He cleared his throat and said, "Captain Morgan, if you would be so kind as to take us to your ship..."

Abigail pushed herself to her feet, her wide eyes focused apprehensively on Seth Morgan. There was a taut white line about the straight shape of his mouth. Then he looked at her, and said abruptly, "Not your daughter."

Abby saw her father's puzzled frown. He said, "But..."

Seth Morgan shook his head. "No," was all he said. There was another dead silence. Abby's mouth had gone dry. Her father didn't know about the flogged man, she thought. Then she heard Mrs. Cambridge say, "But of course it would not be right for Miss Sherman to call on board of the ship. It would be most improper, I do assure you. Obed," she said, turning her sweet smile on her husband, "I'm certain we could lower a boat and deliver Miss Sherman to her home while her father goes a-calling."

Captain Sherman said, "But we cannot presume on your kindness ..."

"It's no trouble at all," Mrs. Cambridge replied. She smiled again, and the subject was closed. Abby found herself ushered up onto deck and into a boat, and a crew was assembled to take her on shore, and then it was lowered.

A whaleboat flying the English flag pulled up to the side of the *Erasmus* as they were leaving. Abby recognized the man in the stern: the elegant willowy figure of Sir George Grey was unmistakable. The broader figure of his secretary, Gould, was seated further forward. She saw the two of them stand up and begin to climb up the side. Mr. West stood behind her with the steering oar under his arm and his crew grinned sheepishly at her as they hauled at their oars, but when Consider West tried to speak to her, Abby ignored him.

Tamati was waiting on the beach. How had he known that she needed an escort? Her father was strict about that at night, not because of the sailors or natives, but because of the packs of half-wild dogs. Tamati was sitting barebacked on his favorite horse and had Abby's mare, Rosie, on the rein.

When Abigail heard the boat's crew mutter and laugh about him, she haughtily tossed her head. Tamati was a strange sight, true, for he liked to wear an assortment of rags such as would be scorned by the most miserable wretches in the shantytown village. Wearing rags was Tamati's eccentricity.

When he went a-courting—and he was in love with the daughter of a chief—he dressed up in a splendid blue suit with a hat and cravat, but the rest of the time he wore shreds. It made Abby's father furious. "What kind of scarecrow will folk think I keep?" he demanded, and the other Maori boys teased Tamati about it, saying, "Who is that young taurekareka who belongs with Captain Sherman?" But Tamati cared not a hoot.

Now he ignored the Yankee derision with superb contempt, clicked his tongue, and led the way up the hill to home. He didn't bother to speak to Abby, either; his entire loyalty was to her father, and—apart from the daughter of the chief—girls counted for naught.

It was growing dark. The long shadows on the hills were merging with the twilight, and the ripples on the placid bay were distant and mysterious. Abigail reined in on the crest of the hill and turned to look down at the huddle of ships. Dark was gathering fast; a scatter of dim lights specked the darkness where the ships were collected.

The ship *Pierrot* was distinctive because she was anchored apart from the rest. She had two dim lights, but there was no sound from her direction. Abigail wondered with trepidation if her father was on board, and whether he was discussing her with his cousin's son William Mitchell. Or was he still on the *Erasmus?* He *couldn't* send her away; she wouldn't go, she thought fiercely. It was not possible or right that he should send her to live with the Mitchells.

The Mitchells. The sun was quite gone, and the stars glimmered out. Her mother had barely mentioned the

41

Mitchells; Abby thought with an abrupt little shock that her mother had not liked them—and yet the Mitchells were the only relations Captain Sherman had. Mrs. Mitchell, Captain Sherman's cousin, was married to a merchant, and most seamen hated and feared most merchants. He owned the whaling ship *Lizzie Ann*, which his older son, Jireh Mitchell, commanded. He owned...

Abigail had to stop and think; her mind darted from one vague memory to another. Her father had talked about the Mitchells after her mother had died, in that dreadful time when he was wondering whether to send her to New Bedford. Mrs. Mitchell was married to the owner-merchant Jezekiel Mitchell, and she had three children. There was the son Jireh, Abby dimly remembered, and ... a daughter, Charity. Charity was a nice name, she thought, but she did not want to meet its owner. Then there was the second son, William—William Mitchell, first mate of Captain Morgan's ship. First mates were good men, she desperately thought. They did not get that sort of promotion otherwise. Unless...

Then she remembered. The second ship that Jezekiel Mitchell owned was the ship *Pierrot*.

Captain Sherman was very late returning home but Abigail was awake. When she heard his step in the porch, she grabbed a shawl, threw it over her nightdress, and ran down the stairs.

Her father's face was bleak in the lamplight. She could smell the brandy on his breath, and his thinning hair was damp with sea mist. She thought with a horrid shock that he was old, for he looked it, and then she said hurriedly, "Please, Father, please can we talk?"

His eyes were haggard. He said curtly, "Sir George Grey and his secretary will be here at noon for dinner; please make certain the meal is fit for such illustrious visitors."

The words were so utterly unexpected that for a moment she did not understand him. Her mouth fell open as he said brusquely, "And dress up and look nice for the occasion; Sir George has expressed a wish to meet you, so you will preside at the table. It is your chance," he added dryly, "to prove you own the table-and-parlor manners you declare you possess."

Then he turned on his heel, went into his study, and firmly shut the door.

Two

It was her chance. Abigail was up at dawn.

She flew around, harassing their Maori maid and housekeeper, Wikitoria, into a frenzy of dusting, polishing, taking up the carpet covers, wiping the glasses, and shining the silver. The flock of silly clucking hens was herded briskly into the horse paddock, safely away from the scullery, much to the annoyance of both Tamati and the rooster. Tamati was sent off to the beach to get fish, and the rooster perched on the paddock gate, crowing loudly to voice his displeasure.

Abby had forgotten to feed the yeast two days before and Mrs. Butler had none to spare, so Abby and Wikitoria had to make saleratus bread instead, with lemon water and sieved flour. To Abby's relief it rose, and was only a little burned on the crust. The butter, thank the Lord, had not gone rancid and was easily freshened with some cold well water. Abby washed her hair as well, shivering and gasping as she rinsed it under the pump. Then, when the table was finally finished, she dashed upstairs to her comb and her wardrobe.

One hour later every garment she possessed was piled on the bed, and both her bed and her hair were in wild disorder. Abby was still in her shift, hovering about in an agitation of uncertainty. Her father loved to buy her pretty things, and had a standing order with the seamstresses in Auckland and Sydney and bought silks and muslins from the captains of incoming ships, so that Abby was never more than a year behind the London modes — but nothing seemed right for the governor of New Zealand. Sir George Grey was handsome. All the matrons of Auckland sighed over him and he was renowned as a walking model of elegance. Abby knew with despairing certainty that he possessed an infallible eye and exquisite taste. Time was fleeting fast. She could hear 'Toria doing heaven-knew-what in the dining room. With a gasp Abby grabbed her most formal gown and jerked it over her head. It was an elaborate flounced taffeta, in a tartan pattern. With anxious fingers she did up all the buttons, then twirled her hair into long glossy ringlets and arranged them in formal bunches over her ears. She could hear the sounds of horses ridden up to the porch as she grabbed a flowered silk Chinese shawl and ran helter-skelter down the stairs.

The instant she saw Sir George Grey she knew she had made a dreadful mistake. He was not dressed in the slightest as she had expected him to be. He did not have epaulettes, or a uniform; he did not have a hat with nodding ostrich plumes, or a sword. Instead he wore checked trousers and a dusty shooting jacket and he looked just like any colonist, or even like his own secretary, Gould, for that matter. Abby knew with a sinking heart that she was hopelessly overdressed. She didn't even know whether to curtsey or not, so she made an awkward bob instead. Her too-elaborate dress made a deafening rustling commotion when she did it, and Sir George seemed gently and mortifyingly amused.

Frank Gould, a short stolid man, took Abby's hand, shook it briefly, and then dropped it, all without a word. Abigail did not dare look at her father's expression: instead she turned with a muttered apology and led the way into the dining room.

That, at least, looked decent. She and Toria had polished the heavy thick rimu table until it glowed with an unaccustomed shine. The glassware was clean and the plates were unchipped. Abigail sat apprehensively at the foot opposite her father, and the governor and Frank Gould took their places on either side.

Wikitoria served them in a most uncharacteristic silence, and Abby slowly relaxed. The men were chatting and had apparently forgotten her, and the food was certainly fine. That freshened butter had been cut into neat little twirls, specked with glinting drops of fresh water, and the saleratus bread was only a little bit tough. There were cold sliced meats and pickles, and even cold roast rabbit. Sir George complimented her on that, saying gravely that he had not tasted rabbit since he had left New South Wales, and how he wished that more rabbits would grow here, for he was certainly fond of the dish. Abby sat straighter, helplessly charmed, and then she stood, pushing back her seat, as Toria brought in the one hot course.

It was a huge tureen of chowder. Abigail had agitated endlessly over what dish to serve, and the chowder had been an inspiration. Green vegetables were very short in Mangonui, but there was an endless supply of potatoes and onions, and salt pork and fish. She had good milk, and—after all—it was a Yankee dish. It smelled marvelous. When Abby picked up the ladle, the three men watched her expectantly. Even her father was smiling.

Lumps of potato and fish bobbed about on the steaming surface. Sir George Grey turned to her father and said affably, "It was an amazing sight." Abby listened with only half an ear as she dipped the ladle and moved it gently to stir the thick soup. Sir George went on, "I was thunderstruck to see such a fleet of whalers in such a far-flung place"—but Abby did not hear her father's answer. She was staring, horror-struck, at what had bobbed to the surface.

It was an insect. Her nerveless fingers let go of the ladle and the soup stilled. The insect floated sluggishly on top. It was a cricket, a huge cricket from one of the hordes that devastated the fields at this time of year. With the clearing of the primeval forest and the destruction of the native birds, insects had become a plague in New Zealand—but Abby could not conceive how this specimen had got into her chowder.

"Seventeen vessels, such a fleet," Sir George Grey was saying. Abigail paid no heed, frozen in a trance of horror. The insect was huge, at least two inches long, and it was most unmistakably dead. It had cooked to a bland gray color, and its lusterless eyes were baleful. She dimly heard Sir George Grey say, "So it is, that a few American whalers enter some secluded bay and, lo, in a twinkling, a settlement springs up. But," he said reproachfully, "the captains never stop to sell their oil. Instead they try to cheat the duties by selling in the Manila market."

Where in heaven's name had the confounded insect come from? Abigail had washed the vegetables herself, and Tamati had gutted and scaled the fish, and the milk had been clean. It must have fallen off the wall, she thought wildly, while the cauldron was steaming on the stove. Otherwise her mind was blank. Then she heard Toria arrive behind her. The Maori girl was perfectly capable of seeing the insect and letting out an entertained shriek: as if of their own volition Abby's fingers grabbed the ladle and poked the insect back under the mess of potatoes and fish.

Wikitoria went away. Abby took a big breath and very slowly, very carefully, she filled the governor's bowl and passed it over to him. For many years, she was certain, she would have nightmares of serving the governor of New Zealand an insect, but he merely smiled, and nodded his thanks. With equal care, she filled bowls for his secretary and for her father. Then, with her own bowl in front of her, she stared down into the tureen again, and heard the governor sneeze.

Then he said in startled tones, "Hulloa, what is this?" She gasped, and jerked round to stare at him, fully expecting to see him poking a spoon at his soup. Her heart seemingly stopped forever inside her—but he was merely regarding his handkerchief.

Handkerchief? It was a small American flag. Abby looked at her father, and saw that his florid cheeks had turned ashen. The haggard look was back in his eyes. The silence dragged on while she numbly served the insect to herself. Sitting down, she promptly dropped a piece of bread into her plate, hiding the nasty corpse, but her fingers insisted on trembling—and not because of the insect or the fright that the governor had given her. Her father, she knew, gave those little flags to dissident chiefs, and she sensed he was in danger.

Sir George Grey's smile was bland but definitely menacing. "Now," he mused aloud in deceptively gentle tones, "I wonder where I found this? H'm?" Captain Sherman's face sagged as Sir George Grey continued, "Ah! I remember. Te Rauparaha gave it to me. He declared that you gave it to him, Captain Sherman, to fly at the head of his canoe. He told me most interestingly how you preached the way of the American Revolution, and how you gave the flag to favored chiefs ... But surely you do not preach dissension to the natives?"

To Abby's horror, the governor seemed to be thoroughly enjoying himself. "Surely," he murmured, "you did not contemplate the incitement of rebellion against the English government? No natives are treated more kindly than the natives of New Zealand! They have prospered greatly from intercourse with the peoples of England."

Nathaniel Sherman blustered, "The Maoris prospered greatly from trade with American whalemen. Since the British claimed New Zealand, that prosperity has ceased. Surely they are entitled to have second thoughts? Before your countrymen brought taxes and duties and punitive laws, the American brought trade worth many thousands of dollars a year—trade that is now going to Honolulu, in the Sandwich Islands. Now that America is a presence in the Pacific, sir, it is logical that New Zealand have links with America, not England."

"Ah," said Sir George. The sound was light, almost amused, but his eyes were chipped with ice, and his cheeks had gone red with anger. "I believe you are still the owner, Captain Sherman, of several thousand acres of New Zealand land?"

Still the owner? Abigail was bewildered. Of course her father owned land—he was rich. But instead of replying he went whiter than ever.

Sir George said smoothly, "There is no need for an answer, for Frank, I believe, has the list entire."

Frank Gould put down his spoon, and recited the list of her father's holdings, without notes. He knew the holdings, it seemed, as if they were written in his head. He had a wooden voice and the list seemed to go on forever. Abigail would never have believed that her father owned so much.

At last the pedantic voice stopped. Nathaniel Sherman sat perfectly still. Sir George cleared his throat and said, "Is Frank's list correct?"

Abigail's father seemed quite unaware that she was listening. He didn't look at her or at Sir George: he seemed to be looking at some bitter picture in the air. Then, the thought occurred to her that the secretary had not mentioned her father's arrangement with the old chief Te Wharenui, concerning the pumice valley, which he reckoned held some mysterious fortune. Nathaniel Sherman, however, did not correct him. Instead, he nodded, his big fists clenched on the table.

"None have been missed?"

The secretary had not listed the shore whaling station share, either. Was it registered in Broddy's name? Abigail

49

waited, bewildered, but her father merely said, "None."

There was another silence. Then Gould said tonelessly, "I must by law inform you that possession of New Zealand land by foreign national is now illegal. You must sell out: Americans are not allowed to own property."

Sell out? Her father sell out? Abigail couldn't believe it; her father was a New Zealander, just as she was. She had been born and raised here.

She had not. She had been born at sea. She heard her father say, "Well, I'm sixty. I guess it's time to retire. I'll sell out."

"That," said Sir George, "is required by law, regardless of your age."He paused, and then added, "Frank has your vouchers."

Vouchers? Then Abby remembered. When the English claimed New Zealand, all landowners had had to register vouchers, certifying how they had obtained their land and what they had paid for it. When she had learned about the system in Miss Ellie Clark's school, it had seemed quite fair, for then other men could not come and claim her father's land, and fight him for it, since it was all written down and legal.

Now she wondered if it was really fair, for her father seemed stricken. Confused, she heard Gould begin to speak again. He cleared his wooden voice and said, "According to law, Captain Sherman, the land you bought now belongs to the Queen of England. You must sell it all, to an English national — at the exact same price you paid."

Nathaniel Sherman shouted, "*What!*" It was a roar of outrage. Abigail jumped nervously and her spoon clattered into her dish. Soup spattered on the table and the bloated insect bobbed into view but she didn't at that moment care, for her father's veins were standing out on his forehead. She was terrified that he would throw a fit or have an apoplexy. He whispered, "My God, I've slaved and schemed for fifteen years, and you English bastards want to take it all."

His fists were clenched so tight on the table that his knuckles were white rocks, and he said in that terrible trembling whisper, "You bastards know what I paid for the land — blankets and tobacco and cloth and fishhooks — and now because of you English I'm ruined. And, my God," he said, his voice rising into a shout of pain and fury, "you didn't even claim this country for a proper reason! Don't you go canting bout the natives and prosperity. No — for the American whalemen did that. No," he said thickly, "you English were perfectly uninterested in New Zealand. You didn't want the place until you conceived the notion that the French might claim it first."

Abigail could hear his heavy, uneven breathing. She tried to swallow, but her mouth was too dry. Sir George paused in thought, and then said, "And guns, sir — I'm fully persuaded that you trade in guns."

That was untrue: all her life Abby's father had declared that any man who armed a native race was a fool, and before she could stop herself she shouted, "That is not so, sir!"

All three faces jerked round to her. Sir George Grey's eyebrows were lifted inquiringly; his secretary, Gould, had a drop of grease on his chin. Her father snapped, "Get out."

Abby's whole body jerked with bewildered humiliation. She stuttered, "Wh-what?"

He roared, "Go!" — and she lurched to her feet. Her chair fell over with a crash, and to her fury hot tears were spilling down her cheeks. Her father shouted, "Go to your room!" Abigail made a wild snatch, mumbled inarticulately, and backed clumsily out of the room. Her last glimpse, as she turned and fled, was of Frank Gould getting up to help himself to more of the soup.

Abby did not go to her bedroom, but instead ran outside — because of what she had snatched up as she had so precipitately flown. The corpse of the cricket was bloated and obscene in the palm of her hand, so disgustingly greasy

51

that she thought she'd be sick. Instead she stopped on the path to the horse paddock and threw it away with all of her might. The rooster squawked, flapped heavily down from the gate, and nipped up the prize in his greedy beak, and Abby ran, head down, round the corner of the hayshed — right into the solid chest of a man who was rapidly striding towards her.

The man grunted with shock and said, "Goddammit."

Abigail, after one appalled glimpse of startled black eyebrows, flinched away, tripped on the overabundant flounce of the hated gown, and crashed full-length to the path. Seth Morgan said, "What the devil?" and Abby found her hands gripped as he hauled her to her feet. When she angrily tore free of him, Seth frowned down at his palm and wiped it on the side of his trousers. Then he asked, "Are you hurt?"

She snapped, "No!" Then she saw Tamati come up the path from the hill. The Maori was wearing his usual choice selection of rags, and she focused on him rather than look at Seth Morgan. Her knee was smarting where she had knocked it on a stone, but she ignored that, too.

A hand came out and tipped her chin and hauled it around. She scowled up at him, and Captain Morgan let her go. He demanded, "If you're not hurt, then why are you crying?"

Because she had been thrown out of the dining room; because her father had been humiliated and had turned on her in his grief; because she had tried so hard to prove she was a lady, and she had worn the wrong clothes and served the governor of New Zealand insect soup. "I am not crying!"

"You're not?" Seth Morgan surveyed the gown and her hair, looking at her slowly up and then down. There was a familiar twitch of amusement in his face, and she hated him more than ever. Then Tamati wandered over. Seth Morgan nodded to him and said to Abigail, "Is your father busy?"

Abby snapped, "Yes!" and Tamati frowned at her and

tut-tutted.

"How much longer will he be?"

She shrugged, and Seth Morgan sighed and said, "I need to see him soon. I have two deserters to report, and I'm determined to sail tomorrow."When she said nothing, he said sharply, "Tomorrow is Thursday."

She already knew that—and knew, moreover, why the day was important. If Captain Morgan did not get away the next day he would be delayed a further forty-eight hours, for no whaling master worth his salt would depart from a port on a Friday. It was very bad luck to do so, and whaling depended so much on good fortune.

Seth said, "I want your father to post a reward and see the local chief about getting back my men."

That was usual practice, too. The vice-consul passed on the captain's message to the natives, and the Maori boys went out a-hunting. It was fun for them and profitable, too. The captured men were slung from shoulder poles by their lashed hands and feet and were delivered like hogs. Abigail felt sorry for them, so kept obstinately silent.

However Tamati grinned, and said, "I'll take you to Te Wharenui, Cap'n."Abigail whirled and glared at him, but he paid no attention, saying, "Come along o' me, sir, and we fix all up. We get them little buggers pronto, you wait and see. How about you horse?"

Seth Morgan was given a horse. Abby, seething and miserable, watched them trot away over the crest of the hill, going inland, heading for the village where Te Wharenui and his people lived. She moodily kicked at a stone. Then, when Tamati and Captain Morgan were out of sight, she limped into the hayshed to inspect her smarting knee.

The shed was dim and dusty, with motes dancing in the light from the half-open door. She propped her foot on a sawhorse and pulled up her skirt with a loud rustle of taffeta. Her knee was oozing blood, and her white stocking was torn. She inspected it disconsolately, and then shrieked with shock and fright as a hand descended over her mouth.

The rustle of her dress had hid all other sounds, so there had been no noise of movement to warn her. The scream was muffled, and Abby wildly jerked her head from side to side, trying to shake loose to shout louder. She kicked and squirmed desperately, and a man whispered urgently in her ear, "Please don't holler, miss. Edmund won't hurt yer."

She stilled. Her blood was thumping with panic in her ears. The man whispered again, "Please, miss. I don't mean no 'arm."

The hoarse voice was scared and persuasive. Then, cautiously, by degrees, the man moved his palm from over her mouth. The grip on her arm eased too, so that Abby was able to turn around. The man stepped back, into the shadows at the rear of the shed. He seemed very frightened. He had his hands held up, pleadingly. He smiled coaxingly, and said, "Please, miss."

He was middle-sized and stood with a curiously hunched posture that made his arms look unnaturally long. In the dim light it was impossible to tell how old he was. Where had he been hiding? There was straw sticking out of his clothing. How long had he been in the shed? If Tamati had seen him, he would certainly have raised the alarm, so this man — Edmund? — must have been here quite a long time. Abigail opened her mouth to scream.

Edmund said wheedlingly, "Please, miss, you look to 'ave a kind 'eart. Don't report me, don't 'and me over. Don't send me back to that hell-ship."

He was a deserter. Abby whispered, "From ship *Pierrot?*"

"Aye. I heared ye talkin' ter Cap'n Morgan, rot his..." The last two words were a mad hiss, quickly quenched. The man said, "Excuse me, miss. 'Tis a long time since I talked ter a respectable lady."

Lady? The word warmed Abby's heart. She whispered, "When did you escape?"

"Me an' my mate, the steerage boy, Jack Rawlings, we

stole a boat last night." He added quickly, "We 'ad ter get away. Don't report us, miss—not till the *Pierrot* 'as sailed. Give us a chance ter git clear."

"Wh-where is this Jack? R-Rawlings?" She looked around, expecting to see another furtive figure in the shadows. The musty air was warm and still. She could hear the horses in the paddock and the croaking cluck of the hens.

Edmund was watching her closely. His hands hung loosely by his sides, the fingers curled. He said hoarsely, "Jack's down at the river, a-watching the boat. If we 'ad some food, we could sail upstream."

"But ... but the river will be the first place Te Wharenui's people will look," she protested. "You'll never get away. Deserters never do, here. You're best to ask my father for help."

"Your father?" He took a step closer.

"He's the American vice-consul. He's a fair man. I'll intercede for you."

Edmund put up his hands and rubbed his face with his palms, dragging down his cheeks and shaking his head in dejection. "Never," he muttered. "You're too innocent an' sweet, miss. You don't know the harsh truth of life. A poor Jack sailor never wins—never—and poor Jack Rawlings is but a boy, and so mistreated it would break your tender 'eart. It's starvin', he is—we all are—an' worse'n that, on that hell-ship. You've no notion what torture is practiced on that floatin' hell of misery, never in yer young life."

Abigail hesitated. Then, with a movement that was so abrupt that she nearly shrieked, Edmund twisted around and presented his back to her. She watched, bewildered, as he scrabbled at his shirt, dragging it up to display...

With sick pity, Abby realized that this was the man who had been seized up in the rigging, and that the flogging had been by no means the first. Old black bruising and scarring marked the fish-white expanse, underscored terribly by long open cuts in the skin. The new wounds oozed pus and watery blood. Abby imagined she could see the vertebrae, luminous in the exposed strips of gristle, like stepping-stones in the swollen white flesh. She looked away, fighting sickness. For a moment the vision of the hanged men in Hobart Town was as vivid as yesterday. When she looked at Edmund again, he was facing her and eyeing her closely.

His hunched posture now made terrible sense. She whispered, "Did Captain Morgan do that to you?"

"Cap'n Morgan?" The hoarse voice was derisive. "It's the bucko..." Then, oddly, he broke off, as if he'd registered the tone of her voice, and muttered, "They're all as bad as one t'other, on that hell-ship."

"But why? Why mistreat you so?"

"I could tell you stories, but what's the use? All we want, poor Jack and me, is food, and yer silence, and the chance to get away. Jes' bring us some food ter put in the boat, and you'll never hear more of poor Edmund again."

Abigail hesitated. Then, taking a breath, she nodded. Edmund's voice hissed with triumph. "Down at the boat, miss, if you could bring us food a-fore dark..."

"Just food?"

"Meat," he said. His tone was avid. "Bread, hard bread, if yer've got it." The boat was hidden at the fishing spot. Abby nodded, turned, and ran, as quietly as she could, to the back door and the scullery.

Toria was in the kitchen. Abigail mumbled something incoherent and kept on going, along the hall and up the stairs to her bedroom. She could hear Sir George Grey's voice in the dining room. Shutting the door, she tugged off the taffeta gown and threw it in a corner. Toria could have it, for she would never wear it again. She took off her four lace-edged petticoats too, until she stood in her shift. Then she pulled on a dark-colored work dress and ran back down to the kitchen.

Toria, to her fervent relief, was gone, perhaps to take

coffee in to the men. Abigail's hands were clumsy with haste as she filled a burlap bag. There were plenty of scraps because of the dinner, and even some saleratus bread. She filled the bag up to the mouth, and pulled the string to close it, and all the time was imagining Edmund running furtively down the long grass of the gullies and through the bush to the boat and the river. Her ears were stretched for shouts of discovery, but she heard nothing. She grabbed up the bag and ran.

Rosie, the mare, was with the hens in the paddock. Abigail fetched a bridle and saddle blanket, and five minutes later set off down the hill. The heavy burlap bag knocked by her knee as Rosie zigzagged along the descending track at a reluctant trot. Where the grass was trampled by the wild peach tree, Abigail ducked her head to avoid branches. Then she was in the forest. There was no sign or sound of Edmund. The worn path wound in and out, and ferns scraped against the horse's hooves. The canopy thinned and they were beside the river. The backwater was empty, the clearing deserted.

Abigail slid uncertainly to the ground, the string of the bag tight in her hands. She said, "Edmund?" Her voice sounded shrill, louder than she had intended. As she opened her mouth again, Edmund touched her shoulder.

Abby nearly screamed. She whirled around and saw Edmund clearly for the first time. He was filthy. His eyelids were scabbed, and his head was bald in grotesque patches. She stepped back, repelled.

Edmund did not seem to notice. He snatched the bag with a grunt and yanked the string open. Then he shoveled food into his mouth. He ate openmouthed, drooling saliva like a dog. Abigail stepped further away, looking around for her horse.

Rosie had moved up the path, whickering a little, her ears twitching back and forth. Abby moved stealthily towards her—and Edmund's face jerked up.

Abigail stopped short. She said, "Wh-where is Jack Rawlings?" The mare moved again, brushing backwards into the ferns, keeping out of reach.

Edmund had stopped chewing. Food dribbled onto his chin. He said, "Upstream."

Abby realized she was very frightened. She took another step towards her horse. Edmund reached out, and grabbed her arm.

"Please let me go. I—I've done what you asked."

His fingers dug in like claws. She could smell his vile breath and see the slime in the stubble of his beard. Then, to her horror, he smiled, a voracious grin, like that of some predatory dog. In a dreadful caressing tone, he said, "Oh no, you don't, my pretty. Edmund ain't finished with yer yet."

She gasped, "No!" and jerked away.

She didn't see the blow coming. It landed solidly on her cheek and ear, and her whole head rang and hurt. She screamed as he punched her again, and she fell. Then, dimly, she heard a shout.

Hooves pounded. The newcomer yelled again, and all at once she knew who it was. She screamed and heard Edmund scream too, like a maddened horse. "You touch me, an' I'll kill yer, Cap'n Morgan, Edmund will, he'll kill yer, fer what yer done ter poor Jack 'n me, you an' yer bloody bucko—" Then the voice broke off as a fist sapped into flesh.

Abby scrambled to her feet. Seth Morgan had Edmund in the grip of one big fist, pounding him with the other, slamming into the deserter's face as if he was intent on murder. Abby stumbled in the direction of a ... horse ... not Rosie, Rosie had run away. It was Captain Morgan's horse— and then she was brought up short by a triumphant demented yell.

Seth Morgan was sprawled on the grass, struggling dazedly to get back on his feet, and Edmund—Edmund had a knife that he'd snatched out of his boot. She watched in horror as he dragged it open and raised it. With a desperate effort Abigail grabbed the lump of wood that Consider West had used to batter the monster eel, and screaming like a devil possessed, she whirled the timber around her head.

She hit Edmund with all the fear and fury that the dreadful day had given her. She shrieked and laid into him with all her might, and he squealed like a stuck hog. The knife went spinning up into the air and landed on the riverbank. Abigail dropped the timber and threw herself after it.

She grabbed it just as Edmund hit her between the shoulders. She collapsed to the grass. The knife flipped, blade over handle, and hit the water with a tiny plop. Abigail struggled wildly, sensed Edmund raise himself to slam her with his fist—and felt the riverbank beneath her crumble. Edmund swung, the dirt sagged, Abigail twisted—and the bank collapsed. She and her assailant fell together, head over heels in a clumsy struggling commotion, and then she felt the water close over her head.

The cold liquid slap took away what breath she had left. Struggling, she sank to the bottom. Weeds curled around her arms. Abruptly Edmund's horrid weight washed away from her, but her dress was holding her down; she was drowning. She grabbed her skirt with frantic fingers and ripped. The stitching tore, and Abby kicked her way out of the gown. Then, with bursting lungs, she bobbed to the top.

The first three breaths hurt like fire. She couldn't see Seth Morgan. The current had taken her away from the clearing, around the next bend in the river. She struggled to the bank but it was too steep to climb. Abby swam, slowly and with difficulty, upstream. When she arrived at the place where the bank had crumbled, Seth Morgan reached down a long arm and hauled her up onto the grass.

There was a graze on his cheek and his clothes were dirt-stained and rumpled. Abigail sank to the ground and sat hunched over, her chest heaving as she struggled to slow the urgent pounding of her heart. Her throat felt raw. The sodden shift that was all she wore clung in a chilly embrace. Finally, she was able to stand. She turned and looked up at Seth Morgan.

He had his arms folded. He looked her up and down and said, "What did you do with your dress?"

She flushed. The shift reached only halfway down her thighs and the wet fine cambric clung to her breasts. She snapped, "I had to take it off to swim."

"Did Edmund rape you?"

"He did not rape me!" She was as angry as he. "And I'll thank you to stop staring!"

He lifted on sardonic eyebrow, and for a shocked second she saw that he thought she was lying. She lifted her chin and glared at him, and a reluctant trace of respect twitched his lips. Then, with belated gallantry, he took off his jacket and gave it to her. She took it without a word and struggled into its warm capacious folds with chilled clumsy movements, resentfully aware that he didn't bother to look away. It was as if any modesty that Abigail Sherman might happen to possess was of little importance.

Seth was wearing a white French shirt, cut full in the sleeves and the gathers of the yoke, surprisingly modish for an American whaleman. When he folded his arms again, the loose collar pulled away from his strong brown throat. He observed, "I would have thought you learned your lesson yesterday."

"I don't know what you mean."

"If you insist on wandering to the river alone ... unfortunate encounters are inevitable."

She retorted, "It's lucky for you I was *wandering*, as you put it, or you would be dead and done this minute."

"What?" He laughed. "That was a lucky blow that Edmund got in. And if you had not been here, pretty Miss Sherman, I would not have been fighting in the first place."

"No?" she snapped. "You were riding, were you not? And you were hunting for Edmund? Oh, you most certainly would have been in a fight, Captain Morgan, and if I had not been here, there would have been no one to save you when he produced that knife!"

"What knife?"

"His knife—a jackknife. He had it in his boot."

"So where is it now?"

"In the river! I hit him and I grabbed it and it fell into the river when he knocked it out of my hand."

"A likely story." Then, to her alarm, he strode over the the burlap bag and hefted it. She opened her mouth quickly, but no words came. Numbly, she watched him open the bag to look inside.

He said softly, terrifyingly, "You incredibly stupid little bitch."

She flinched. "Captain Morgan..."

"You bloody little idiot." He bit out the words, moving forward. She stepped hastily backwards until the edge of the bank stopped her. He kept coming and gripped her shoulders and shouted in her face, "You were hiding one of the goddamned deserters!"

"No!" To her fury, her eyes were stinging with tears.

"And what about Jack Rawlings? Is he somewhere here too?"

She shouted, "I've never met this Jack Rawlings! And I hope to hell he gets away! I saw the way you flogged that Edmund, Captain Morgan and ... and I despise you, and I don't regret doing what I did!"

For a moment she thought he was going to shove her away from him in disgust. Instead, he hauled her over to where his horse was nervously waiting. She cried, "Let me go!" He ignored her, and sobbing with fright and rage, she found herself tossed up onto the horse like so much lumber. Then, with an angry thump, Seth Morgan arrived in the saddle behind her.

She cried, "I can get home by myself!"

"That is impossible, for two good reasons, empty-brained Miss Sherman." The horse jolted into a painful canter, and his voice snapped in her ear, "For one, you're in no fit state to wander further—and for the other, I want a long and serious discussion with your father. It's time he knew exactly how irresponsible you are!"

Four days later Abigail sailed for New England. It was a brilliant morning, New Zealand at her most lovely. The rounded gullied slopes of the hills were drenched with early sun, and the water danced and sparkled, tossed up by a brisk fair breeze. The whaleship *Erasmus* pitched a little on the end of the cable, eager despite her heavy cargo of oil.

"All hands!" the mate, Mr. Allen, sang out. "Prepare ship to get under way for h-o-o-ome!"

The patter of footsteps on deck was hurried and excited. "Man the windlass!" Twelve brawny pairs of shoulders were set to the brakes before the first mate could suck another breath.

"Man the windlass for home!"

"Ohh—don't ye hear th'Old Man say—" cried the second mate in a nasal chantey.

"Goodbye, fare ye well, goodbye, fare ye well," came a deep gruff chorus. Feet stamped and the brakes were shoved to waist level with a great cry of, "Heave!"

Ohh—don't ye hear th'Old Man say—
Hooray, me boys, we're homeward bound!

"Heave away!" cried the mate, and the ship inched up to the anchor.

Home. Abigail felt sick. Her hands were icy cold and her fingers were clumsy, like frozen toes. She had her own tiny stateroom, a wedge-shaped cubbyhole at the end of the short passage that led from the starboard end of the transom cabin to Captain Cambridge's stateroom. Her narrow berth was reached by two steps, and there was no door. That was all the space there was: the two steps and her berth, and that was it. A single sidelight provided dim illumination. The wooden bunk was coffin-shaped, narrower at the stern end than it was at the bow end. Her bags were stowed tightly underneath, and the bunk had a wooden lip to stop her mattress from falling out.

Despite all her efforts at rigid control, Abby could feel her lips trembling. She concentrated on making the bed. She had brought her own bedding, of course, but the sight of the embroidered sheets and the quilted cover her mother had made did not help. She automatically put her soft pillow at the wider, bow end of the bunk: the bed ran fore and aft, and when the vessel pitched, she would be shoved sternwards with the motion. This way, her feet would hit the bulkhead, and not her head. When she was small, her father and mother had often found her curled in a ball at the end of her bed under all the covers, sent there by the motion of the brig and yet still deeply asleep.

She swallowed, very aware of her father watching her. He stood brace-legged at the bottom of the two steps, in the doorway of the transom cabin. His lower lip stuck out, and he had his arms folded over his chest.

"Don't you shame me," he barked. "None of your exploits, miss."

"I won't," Abigail muttered. She didn't dare look at him. Never had he seemed more beloved. "You know I won't. You know I can behave."

"Aye?" he queried grimly. "I know you can behave yourself, Abigail—you can certainly do that—when it suits you to be good."

She turned and smoothed the quilt, her hands trembling over the bright patches of color. The ship pitched smoothly under her feet as the anchor cable tautened, the windlass shortening the chain link by link as the men heaved and grunted on deck. It all felt unreal, like a dream. She had dreamed last night that she was sailing away from her father and Mangonui, and for an instant, when she awoke, she had been filled with wild joy that it had been only a nightmare. Then she had remembered.

Nathaniel said sternly, "I have to send you, and you know it." His cheeks wobbled as he said, "You'll be content, if you have the sense to learn some discipline. Bridle yourself, and you will find New Bedford acceptable."

Abigail knew, achingly, without any shred of doubt, that the wind always blew nor'nor'east in New Bedford, and that the roofs of the houses were hunched with cold. New England was a place where feet and hearts were always frozen, and in New Bedford laughter was indecent and passion an embarrassment. Two drops ran down her cheeks and sparkled briefly on the bedcover before she angrily scrubbed them into little dark blotches.

"And 'tis not forever," Nathaniel said. His voice was awkward and his eyes tried hard to be reassuring. "You'll come back, as soon as, as soon as..." He broke off and pulled out a handkerchief and loudly blew his nose. "Things is hard for Americans at present and — well, you heard it, Abby — I may have to sell out. The English..."

His voice broke again. She heard him take a deep breath, and he said, "Any American who trades here has to pay a discriminatory tax, an imposition of five hundred percent. And times could get dangerous. If the Maori Sons of Liberty rise up against the English tyrants there could be war."

"Then come with me, Father. Sell out and then we can sail together, in the brig."

He shouted, "I can't!" She could see him trembling. "I'm not walking away, Abby, and leaving the English with the profits that are mine by right!" Then, with an obvious effort to calm himself, he blew his nose again and said gruffly, "I'll come through, never mind. It takes a better man than an Englishman to hold old Captain Sherman down, and when old Te Wharenui and I have beat out the way we'll make our fortune..."

Abigail cried desperately, "What fortune? You've talked

about it but all I hear is some romantic dream. Father, I don't believe it exists, and if I have to wait for some pot of gold at the end of a rainbow, then I know I'll be away forever, Father, and I can't bear it."

The uncontrollable tears were pouring down her face. Her father's blurred face twisted. He reached out. She felt his big trembling hands grab her so that she came off her feet. He swung her down and hugged her, while she clung and angrily sobbed, "We should be together, Father, together on the brig. Forget the fortune, forget the English — sell up and sail away."

He said incoherently, "I can't." Then he let her go and blew his nose again. His sagging cheeks were damp. He said, "I'll beat the English never fear. And the brig..." He broke off and coughed. Then, to her confusion, he reached into his pocket and fetched out a bundle of papers.

His hands were shaking as he handed them to her. He said awkwardly, "I can't tell you about the scheme, not yet, but when the time comes and I think of a way to tell you the secret, you'll be an heiress, never fear."

Abigail stared numbly down at the copperplate writing on the documents. She heard her father say, "'Tis best this way, Abby, for if the English should seize all I own, or summat happen to me..."

The words, very slowly, made sense. The topmost document was a Bill of Sale: "Contract of Nathaniel Sherman and Abigail Pandora Sherman relating to Sale of Brig *Pandora* ... Whereas Nathaniel Sherman has this day sold to Abigail Pandora Sherman of Mangonui, New Zealand, and wherever she may be, Brig *Pandora* and outfits as she now sails from the Port of Auckland, New Zealand, in consideration of One Dollar..."

Her father had sold her the brig. The rest were the brig's shipping papers. He had sold her the brig for the sum of one dollar. She heard him say, "And I'll be writing, Abigail, and will let you know about the fortune as fast as I am able" —

and she knew with a sudden tragic certainty that her father did not believe they would ever see each other again. She begged, "Oh please, please, don't make me go."

From the deck came the cry, "Avast the heaving!" It was time for Nathaniel to be on deck, in his capacity of pilot. He would stop on the quarterdeck until the open sea was in reach, and then a boat would take him back to shore. "Lay aloft and loose sail!" came the cry. Footsteps rattled the deck planks, and then rope thrummed as men sprang aloft in the yards.

"Come on," Nathaniel said. His hand gripped her elbow. Abigail hugged her shawl convulsively about her as they climbed the after companionway to deck. The wind clutched at her hair, frisking tendrils into her eyes and sticking them to her damp cheeks. The men aloft were shipping off gaskets, working on earrings and buntlines, grappling with reef-tackles and clewlines as the sheets hauled home.

Home! "We're homeward bound to the gals of the town," cried the chantey singer in his nasal voice.

"Goodbye, fare ye well, goodbye, fare ye well," and, "Heave!" from the men on deck at halyards. Yards creaked and squealed as they rose.

"Then heave away, me hearties, we're all homeward bound."

"Hooray, me lads, we're homeward bound!"

Obed Cambridge stood four-square on the quarterdeck by the skylight with his fists in his pockets. His whiskers jutted skywards as he watched the canvas jerk out and billow and bell tight. Nathaniel left Abigail to take his station by the captain. Abby stood awkwardly, knowing she should keep out of the way but reluctant to leave her father. On the brig *Pandora* she would have been at the helm, or at lookout in the bow. She felt abandoned already, and miserably lonely. Mrs. Cambridge sat sedately in the little deck cabin she had in the hurricane house; Abby could see the groomed head at the window, but instead of joining her hostess, she turned her back on the ship, staring blindly over the taffrail at the hills and the bays of Mangonui.

The other vessels in the bay were flying their flags in salute, and men crammed the rails. The *Erasmus* had all her colors flying: she was bound home, gloriously full. Nathaniel Sherman said briskly, "Haul in port mainbraces and star' forebraces." The ship had to bear left as she quit the bay. The mate and then Mr. West in the waist deck repeated the order. All the sails except jibs were set: the ship shuddered with impatience, held back only by the short, taut anchor chain.

"Man the windlass!"

Strong backs bent and straightened at the handles. The entire anchor chain vibrated, creaking with small sharp noises as barnacles and rust popped free. The links squealed against each other, clanking as they were dragged one by one up the hawse pipe. Then, as the ship began to move, the huge anchor sucked loose and came up dripping.

"Hoist away the jib!" The wind plucked at the curls by Abigail's left ear, and she could feel helpless tears streaking a miserable path on her face. The orders as the anchor was secured to the cathead sounded very distant, almost in a foreign language. The lovely ship seemed poised for a frozen second, on the lip of an ebbing wave, and then, in the space of a heartbeat, the *Erasmus* dug in her prow, lifted again, and left New Zealand, bound home.

Three

The Maori boys delivered Jack Rawlings the same morning that the *Pierrot* sailed. The seaman was trussed hand and foot to a carrying pole, like a hog. There was no sign of Edmund—surely he must have drowned. Very few seamen could swim. It didn't make any difference that no one had seen him. The current would have carried the body past the moored vessels and out of the bay to sea.

The *Pierrot* sailed one man short, steering east-nor'east, and for five days Jack was given a hammer and set to chipping rust off the anchor chains, on the foredeck. At night he was put down in the forehold, along with his straw mattress and blanket and as much hard bread and water as he needed.

On the sixth morning Seth gave instructions that Jack was to be returned to normal duty, to sleep in the foc'sle and have his regular watches below. Instead, Mr. Leonard, the second mate, came to the skylight and called down to Seth. He said, "Jack refuses to come up on deck."

Seth swallowed a mouthful of scorched, half-raw beans and said, "What?"

"Jack refuses duty."

The second mate's head was just visible, bobbing above

the small square panes in the skylight that was set into the deck to illuminate the after cabins. Seth frowned, feeling puzzled. Rebellion was totally out of character for Jack Rawlings, who had the guts of an earthworm.

The boy had been a confounded nuisance since the moment they'd weighed anchor off New Bedford, and not just because he was gallied. He had burst into tears the first time he was ordered aloft; he was girlish, no doubt shipped off by his family in the hope that sea life would turn him into a man. For a while the first officer, William Mitchell, had made a pet of the boy; then abruptly, for no apparent reason, Mitchell had turned vicious, making Jack Rawlings the butt of his spiteful temper. Then Edmund Davis had taken him over: Edmund had been flogged because he stood up for the boy when William Mitchell had struck out at Jack in one of his nasty moods.

Seth said impatiently to Mr. Leonard, "Haul him aft, and I'll deal with him."

There was a pause. Then the second mate's voice was strained. "Cap'n," he said, "Mr. Mitchell is at the forehatch a-dealing right now, and I think you should come."

Seth's belly clenched. When he arrived on deck, at first glance everything was peaceful. It was unusually pleasant weather for that latitude, and all sail was set. The sea was empty, a limitless dark blue heaving of water. But Mr. Leonard had been knocking around Cape Horn for many years now, and Seth trusted his instincts—and almost the entire crew was gathered around the forehatch.

The helmsman was staring at the huddle instead of paying attention to the sails, and the ship was about to fall off the wind. Seth snapped, "Look lively," before setting off for the foredeck with Mr. Leonard hurrying anxiously alongside him. The men all looked over their shoulders as they arrived. William Mitchell was by the side of the hatch, in throes of one of his ranting fits, and Seth could feel the sullen hatred in the air.

He paused deliberately to choose a cigar from his top jacket pocket, put it between his teeth, and light it as he looked around, summing up the situation. There were seven men in the rigging. Four were in the crosstrees and should have been looking for whales, but were watching the first mate's antics. The other three were in the maintop: the third mate, Charlie Lisbon, and two men were overhauling some reeving. One of the faces was tattooed: Seth's boatsteerer, the Maori Tom Kanaka.

Seth interrupted Mitchell, snapping, "What's the problem?"

"The boy Jack Rawlings has gotten ideas above his station, Captain. He has the arrogance to refuse his duty."

Mitchell spoke in a kind of spiteful womanish whine that Seth disliked intensely. The first officer's face was skull-shaped, with cavernous cheeks, framed by long dark hair that straggled about his tiny ears and leaked from under his round black hat. His thin lips writhed as he went on, "He requires informing of who he is, Captain, and I intend to inform him with a rope's end, Captain, inform him with the cat o' nine tails that he happens to be the lowliest deck-walloper in this whole blessed ship."

Mitchell's flat, black eyes watched Seth avidly. Seth took out his cigar and studied the end with distaste. Then he said, "We'll see about that. Send a man down to fetch the boy up, and bring him aft. Then I'll decide what to do."

Mitchell didn't like that: the eyes flashed hatred. The first mate was in charge of the discipline of the ship, and Mitchell cherished his prerogative. He shouted, "José Manuel, you there! Get down there and clinch Jack Rawlings, take him aft and seize him up in the mizzen rigging—seize him up, I say! Make a spread-eagle of the mutineer, and we'll flog him for desertion."

Seth's diaphragm clenched. It was open insolence for Mitchell to misinterpret his instructions so blatantly. He shouted, "Belay that!" and then realized his mistake.

The voyage had been wretched and the men were rebellious. The crew had been kept in line only because they were all terrified of William Mitchell's hysterical ragings.

José hadn't moved. Mitchell shrieked. "Haul Jack on deck and seize him up, I say!"

There was sudden movement in the rigging. Tom Kanaka slid down a backstay and dropped like a cat on the planks next to Seth. His tattooed face grimaced. "Take care, Cap'n. Them buggers has had enough."

"And with the blessed cat o' nine tails, I'll peel off his hide," Mitchell was bawling. Spittle flew from his lips. He jerked his head from side to side, holding the sullen men still with the force of his hysterical temper, while José stared at Seth, apparently paralyzed while he waited for his captain to confirm or countermand the order.

A crazy line from an old poem jumped like a flea in the back of Seth's mind: "*They haze thee, and flog thee, 'til thee ain't worth a damn.*" He muttered, "With me, Tom," and shoved through the crowd to the forehatch. The necessity was obvious: he had to go down and get Jack himself.

The short strong ladder led down into utter blackness. Seth climbed down two rungs and then paused and swung around to peer downwards, waiting for his sight to adjust. All he could see was the shape of the mattress near the bottom. The smoke from his cigar stung his eyes, and he stubbed it out on the rim of the hatch. Tiny sparks drifted down into the hold and something rustled in the darkness.

Seth's skin crawled. The sound did not come from the direction of the mattress. Over to his right the fresh-water tank bulked huge and square. Elsewhere, massive oil casks were stacked in tiers, full of gaps and hiding places.

He descended two more rungs, moving carefully. Jack Rawlings's mattress was empty. The handcuffs lay open on the blanket, and his tin pot was overturned. *Someone had released the boy.*

The hairs on Seth's nape were crawling. Jack sobbed

with terror – over behind the water tank. The rustle had come from over by the casks. Mitchell was ranting overhead, quoting hellfire and rage from the Bible. Seth could smell old oil, and sweat, and rats. The deckhead was braced with heavy beams, which acted as enormous rafters in this dark low space. If the man down there with Jack was armed...

Seth backed up to the deck. The light was blinding after the almost impenetrable darkness below. The men all stared at Seth, but Mitchell, lost in the thrall of his rage, did not seem to notice. "Shall smite thee in the knees, and the legs," he bawled, "with a sore botch that cannot be healed, from the sole of the foot unto the top of..." He sounded utterly insane. Seth jerked his head at Tom, then turned and ran to the afterdeck.

Leaving the Maori by the skylight, he hurried below to his stateroom where, clumsy with haste, he fumbled with the lock of a cupboard. Crazily, the back of his mind was quoting doggerel again. It was as if the crisis had freed a part of his brain to pointless recitation:

> *They seized me up by my two thumbs*
> *And they flogged me till the bloody gore run.*
> *They cut a net across me back 'n bum*
> *Until we rebelled, on the good ship Pierrot.*

Had the poem really run like that? No, of course it had not. Seth had a Jennings repeating rifle and a pair of pistols. The rifle would not be much good in the low confines of the forehold, but nonetheless he loaded all three. When he came back on deck he gave one of the pistols to Tom Kanaka.

The scene was apparently unchanged: the men still stood in an angry irresolute huddle about the forehatch. But Mitchell's raving had stopped. Something had happened. Seth began to run, with Tom close behind.

Mr. Leonard broke away from the group to meet him by the mainmast, wearing a look of utter consternation – and a blood-curdling scream echoed from the forehold below. The crowd of men around the forehatch exploded apart, scrambling onto the foredeck and behind the windlass. *Something* was coming up.

Seth said, "My God, what has happened?"

Mr. Leonard gasped, "Mr. Mitchell forced José Manuel to go below, and when he didn't come up ... Mitchell ... went below himself." The round eyes in his dark face were white around the rims. Seth thrust the butt of his rifle into his hand. As he ran up to the hatch, Mr. Mitchell ... came ... crawling ... out. His mouth was open in a soundless howl. One arm was clutched in front of him. He was cradling something bulky in his shirt. He gaped, tried to gasp, and then fell, sprawling, to the planks. Blood showered as he fell.

Behind him out of the forehatch exploded ... a howling creature that whirled the enormous blade of a long-handled boarding knife around his screeching head. The weapon whirled and whistled like a scythe, and thumped down on Mitchell's writhing form. The madman was Edmund. When the razor-sharp blade flashed up again it was dripping red.

Seth fired wildly, and knew at once that he had missed. Edmund plunged down the forehatch again. Seth heard the thump as he hit the floor, and then the rattle of the huge knife. Then came another wild shriek, and a scurry of footsteps.

Seth's hands were shaking as he reloaded the pistol. Something lay bleeding beside the fallen first mate—a severed arm. Edmund must have cut it off with that savage swing. William Mitchell—surely—was dead. But as Seth watched, horrified, the first officer tried to get up. Intestines fell out of Mitchell's shirt, into a slimy pile on the deck. Then Mitchell collapsed on top of the gruesome mess. Seth did not want to touch him. When he did, Mitchell was dead.

Seth straightened, sick with disgust and fear. He jerked his head at Tom and moved to the forehatch, saying to Mr. Leonard, "Hold the men back. Shoot, if you have to." With every fiber of his body stretched taut, he set his boot on the first rung and ducked his head.

The deckhead of the forehold was so low and the beams so heavy that after he jumped away from the bottom of the ladder, he had to walk doubled over. The floor was black and slippery. Tom's shape behind him blocked out the light from the hatch. Then the Maori was down in the hold. Seth took a cautious step, and Tom followed.

There was a ghastly huddle of bloodstained rags at the foot of the water tank. The mouth was open wide, frozen in a scream of terror. It was the seaman José Manuel. Seth stepped round the pathetic bundle, further into the darkness.

No sound, no movement. He could sense Edmund watching, waiting, biding his time, relishing the suspense, changing his grip on that dreadful scythe. The blade of the boarding knife was honed to cut through whalebone and gristle. It could easily remove a man's head with one swing, but the long handle would be a disadvantage in this cramped space.

Seth took another long sideways step, to give Tom room. He felt horribly constricted by the low weight of the beams, and the light was behind him, making him a vulnerable silhouette. An icy trickle of sweat ran into his collar. The shadows between the casks were thick. When he heard Jack Rawlings gasp from behind the water tank to his right, Seth nearly cried out. He took a step in that direction — and there was a blur of vicious movement from his left.

Seth spun around, his heart thumping — and from the corner of his eye glimpsed Jack come out from behind the tank. When Seth whirled again, the boy was holding a knife. Seth lifted his pistol — and with a demented shriek Edmund burst out from between two casks, scything with that dreadful blade. Seth's pistol clicked, misfired, jammed. He backed off rapidly and felt Tom thrust the other pistol into his left hand. He dropped the faulty one and fumbled to get the good pistol to his right.

Edmund shrieked. The bloodstained blade sliced from Seth's left to Seth's right. He jumped back, and collided with Tom. Seth heard Tom Kanaka curse, and shouting from up on deck. Sweat ran into his eyes, and he banged his ear on one of the cursed rafters when he shook his head to clear it. The boarding knife swished again, and he felt its passage like a sliver of ice on his belly. Backing rapidly, he skidded in blood, getting tangled in Manuel's body. Seth could feel blood running into his belt, and for an instant he was terrified that he was cut like Mitchell. Jack rushed forward with his knife raised—and with an ululating war cry, Tom grasped the boy and threw him backwards, just as Edmund's blade descended.

The boy screamed and jerked and fell to the floor. There was blood gushing everywhere. Edmund shrieked in an appalling sound of loss and fury and swung the blade up out of Jack's twitching corpse and at Seth. Seth dodged wildly. The blade jerked up, and banged into a beam, and jammed. For an instant Edmund's face was totally in focus, filling Seth's entire vision. And then, as Edmund cursed and struggled to free his weapon, Seth's pistol fired.

He had no recollection of pulling the trigger. The ball entered Edmund's left temple. Seth saw the burst of blood and a flying splinter of bone. The body arced and fell to the planks, and the knife, freed with the jerk, crashed with an echoing clang to the floor. Then, as if in slow motion, a chip of wood fell from the rafter and stung Seth's cheek.

The echoes of the shot seemed to ring in Seth's head forever. Then, numbly, he heard the cries from the foredeck. Tom said urgently, "C'mon, Cap'n, them buggers is 'ysterical, on account of they think us is dead."

Pulling himself out of his stupor, Seth sprang for the ladder and up onto deck. The men who had gathered about the hatch again stumbled backwards, crying out, then froze, seeing it was not the maniac.

Seth grinned stiffly, feeling blood on his cheek. He opened his mouth with no real idea of what words were in his mind.

"Cap'n Morgan!" cried Charlie Lisbon from the maintop. Seth's neck cracked as he turned his head to look. The young third mate was pointing towards the heaving sea on the larboard bow.

"There blows, sir!" he cried. "Blows, blows, blows! And sperm, at that, sir!"

Seth felt instantly galvanized, his trivial wounds forgotten. He bellowed, "Where away?" —and the lookout at the fore masthead cried, pointing, "Three points on the lee bow, sir!"

"How far? Tell me how far." Seth's pulse was thudding. How close? Would the ship overrun the school and gally the fish?

"Three miles, sir! There she blo-o-ows! A big school, sir, a big gam, sir. By God, sir, there she blows!"

Seth spun around, snapping, "Hard down on the wheel—get the craft in the boats—line tubs." Then, with a jerk, he remembered he did not have a first mate to pass on his orders, and cried, "Mr. Leonard, take charge!"

The Brava man's stubbled face gaped briefly; then Leonard ran to obey. Seth said, "Tom, you'll have to head Mr. Mitchell's boat. And get that corpse stowed on the carpenter's bench, with a tarpaulin over it. Lash it tight."

The sooner the reminder of the ghastly affair was hidden, the better. The mess in the forehold would have to be cleaned up later.

Then he forgot it. Men were excitedly running about. It was the best tonic in the whole salty world, this sight of a gam of whales! Boats' crews ran to their slung boats, piling in their gear. Cooper climbed the mainmast to take over the lookout, while the men who had been aloft skidded down to the deck.

Seth strode to the companionway to grab his spyglass from the wall just inside the door, and ran to the foremast rigging.

The deck there was stained, but Mitchell's corpse was gone. Seth scrambled up the shrouds and over the top. "Sing out, Cooper, sing out!"

"They've gone down, sir."

So they had. Which way would they run? Seth's heart was thundering. The ship must not overtake them. When would they breech? A minute lumbered by, then ten, then twenty, and the cooper shrieked, "There she blows! Two mile off, four points on the lee bow, and closing!"

Seth had seen them. A mile and a half was more like it. A pod of whales—he had seen at least ten spouts and an equal number of gigantic black backs. He cried, "Clear away larboard and bow!" Swinging onto the weather stay, he wrapped his fists and ankles about it and skidded down to deck with barely an instant's hesitation as he jumped the spreader. No sooner had his boots hit the deck than he was striding aft. Mr. Leonard was there. Seth snapped, "I'll have steward in my boat, and Jim Savage for 'steerer." Then he turned away and roared, "Lower larboard and bow boats!"

Men dashed to the boat falls. Down went the boats with a rattle, and the crews scrambled after them. A few yards, and their masts were stepped, and sails jerked up and seized the wind. Whales to leeward! They were in hot pursuit. Seth started for the foremast again.

"There blows, sir! Another school, sir!" Cooper's gravelly voice shouted. "She blows, two points to weather quarter!"

The ship was in the midst of whales—whales to both sides of her! Seth cried, "How far?"

"Two miles and a half, sir!"

Seth roared, "Main yard aback—heave her to! Ready the star' and waist boats—prepare to lower! Cooper, keep those signals running." Even as he hollered, he was striding to the ladder, and scrambling up to the hurricane house roof. His oarsmen waiting there, jiggling with excitement. Seth sprang into the slung starboard boat, followed by Jimmy Savage, and with a rattle the boat splashed jerkily down to the water as the boat falls were released. Seth steadied it with the huge steering oar, and Jim took his place in the bow. A series of thumps as the four oarsmen joined them. Steward was looking scared—this was his very first chase.

These whales were to windward, blowing and breaching. "Pull ahead," Seth ordered. He saw flukes—the whales were beginning to sound. Seth looked up, at the signals the cooper was running. Which way would they go?" Pull like hell," he said to the steward, who was gaping up at him from the thwart in front. He grabbed the end of the oar, pushing, giving the man the rhythm. "One—two. That's it, follow the others." And don't jump overboard, he prayed silently; don't get so gallied when the whales rise that the sea looks a great deal safer than the boat.

The men all pulled at their oars, four of them grinning. The steward sweated. Jimmy Savage, at the bow oar, was singing exultantly in some Pacific tongue ... and the whales began to rise.

They breached in rapid succession—a gam of cows and square-nosed bulls, so close! Where was the other school? Seth turned to stare at the ship. "Signal!" cried Jim Savage. "Red flags at fore and main."

"Whales right ahead!" Seth cried. His whales—the whales that rose and rose ahead of him now. "Ten minutes more, and they're ours! Pull! Pile it on!"

The boat danced through the water. Spray flicked up. There was a commotion in the water dead ahead. An unbelievable stretch of ocean heaved, and water rushed and gurgled as thousands of barrels were displaced. A new island rose to the surface of the sea and shining water ran down monumental flanks. Then the bull settled in the water.

"Easy, boys, easy."

The muscles of Seth's braced thighs trembled as he stood at the steering oar. He was barely conscious of five faces looking intently up at him, trying to read the size of the whale in his expression. With a stinking belch the bull whale spouted, so close that Seth was sprayed.

Seth said softly to the steward, "If I say pull ahead, pull, and if I say stern all, then push astern. Quiet now, quiet, don't gally the fish."

The school of cows was playing, breaching, blowing and fishtailing, as the bull lay logily in the water, blowing. Then, with a gurgle, the old bull arched his back, ready to sound. The whaleboat slid over the lethal flukes. "Stand, Jim," Seth whispered. If the bull rose under the boat... The taste in his throat was coppery with excitement and fear. With a stealthy rattle Jimmy Savage stood and wedged his thigh in the notch that had been cut to brace the harpooner. They were directly in line with the hump.

The boat slid forward like silk. "Stern two," Seth whispered. The two starboard oarsmen dug their oars in the water. Seth leaned all his strength on the steering sweep, the boat bobbed sideways—and the whale spouted.

"Let him have it, Jim!" Jimmy Savage raised his harpoon—and with a wild howl, he drove the iron deep, just behind the fin.

"Fast!" Seth bellowed. "And man the oars for your life! Stern all, stern all!"

The boat quivered, wobbled, shot back like retracting rubber. The harpoon line sang, and Seth reached down and snubbed the line to the loggerhead. "Stern three!" he cried, watching the whale. The boat spun crazily and bounced as great flukes lashed the sea in the very spot where they'd been an instant before. Then with a tremendous lurch the whaleboat straightened and surged ahead, tugged along like a toy as the whale ran. With round eyes and gaping mouth the steward stared wildly about at the sea that was rushing past them. He held his oar high in the air.

Seth bared his teeth in a grin of exultation, and he and Jimmy Savage, treading carefully to avoid the smoking line that sang out after the whale, changed ends in the boat so that Seth was at the bow, ready to lance the bull when they pulled up to him.

"Well placed, Jim," he said as he settled. "Up to the hitches and for'ard of the hump." The boat was running at railroad speed, in a gigantic rushing circle. The huge whale towed them up near the waist boat, and Seth saw young Charlie Lisbon through a mist of spray; the third mate's sweaty face was red with excitement. He glanced back at the ship, in the distance astern, and his heart jerked. Flags to fore and mizzen! Another boat fast! They had fastened a whale in the leeward school! And Seth's bull was rising, tired of running at last.

An upheaval in the ocean just barely sensed, a slowing of the rush of the boat, and—"Haul in the slack," Seth sang out. Steward was taking the manila hand over hand, and someone was showing him how to coil it in the bottom of the boat. Seth faced forward.

His thigh was braced in the notch. The wood bit into muscle. The ash handles of the lances were to hand in a crotch by his knee. The whale was rising, rising. Then, with a rush, the great square head was clear, and the huge beast spouted.

Bow oarsman reached forward and groped for the rope in the water. Up came a bight of it in his big callused hands. With a grunt he put his shoulders into the bone-cracking task of hauling the boat up parallel with the side of the bull. The boat jerked sideways and bobbed, bow oar grunted and creaked with exertion, and then with another jerk they were up to the gigantic hump.

The ash was solid in Seth's fist. He swung and struck with all his strength. The lance bit into blubber and reached for the great chambers of the heart. Then, as the great bull shuddered, "Stern all!" he cried.

80

Oar blades hit the water in a single panic-stricken thrust. Line sang out again; then the boat whipped backwards in the agitated waters. The whale lifted its great head to the sky, crashed it down with wide-gaping jaws, plunged, and gnashed. Great peglike teeth in the narrow lower jaw seized an oar and snapped it to splinters.

"Stern three!" roared Seth. The whale had seen the boat. It rushed at them with its long jaw open wide. The boat spun sideways and danced out of reach. The bull snapped and tossed its great head in pain and fury. Steward was baling with his hat, yelling like a banshee; Jimmy Savage was chanting—and the whale spouted blood.

He sounded with a crash, swam shallowly, and almost at once came up again—but not alone. "Hold on," cried Seth. Three huge bodies had joined the dying bull, fat sleek cows from his harem, come in response to his agony. The entire sea convulsed.

"Mr. Lisbon!" hollered Seth, as if the third mate could hear him. He held back his lance from the killing thrust: as soon as the bull was dead the cows would leave him. "Mr. Lisbon!" Seth roared in desperation, for there would never be a better chance to take another whale than this—and then, like magic, the waist boat was there, and Charlie Lisbon was yelling at his harpooner.

The bull was shivering. He began to circle on the surface of the ruptured water. The cows darted about in anxious little rushes. The boatsteerer in Mr. Lisbon's boat lifted his arm—and thrust a harpoon in the sleek gray flank of one fat cow. Another thrust—two irons fast! Then Mr. Lisbon's half-heard shriek, "Stern all!" and the other boat was off.

Seth's bull rolled, and went into his flurry. He gnashed his jaws at the sky and rushed in a savage circle. The fastened cow pursued him, tossing from side to side to rid herself of harpoons. The boats were dancing crazily in the tumult.

Seth set his jaw as his thigh jolted in the notch and he bit down the pain. The cow went by—and he darted. The lance shot in and whipped out smoothly. He grabbed it by the warp, positioned himself, and lanced again.

The cow rushed on—and then the message reached her vitals. She threw her fifty-ton body clear into the air, turning over and over, tangling up line. Crash!—the huge mass thudded down, and a wash of water half filled the boats. Mr. Lisbon's crew were hauling in line and pulling forward, set for the final thrust. One more lance to finish her, and...

Seth's bull died. The huge body swept wearily from side to side. The head splashed forward and back in a last protest at the sun, and the great whale tipped slowly over onto his side, one flipper projecting pitifully at the lambent blue of the sky. And then the cow died, flinching just twice before she finned out; she, too, died with her head to the sun.

She had fought hard and died fast—and she was enormous. The blubber on her would be a half yard thick. The bull, too, would make a hundred barrels. Seth raised a jubilant arm at the sky. At last he had grease! Three whales—and two at least were buster ones. And the men were cheering—cheering! Grease had made them a crew again.

"I was born," declared Abigail, "in latitude fifteen, longitude one hundred and fifty, under double-reefed forecourse and main topmast stays'l, sharp on the wind, heading sou'east."

There was a moment's stunned silence. Captain Cambridge, in his armchair at the head of the cabin table, seemed almost embarrassed. Mrs. Cambridge, on his right, went rather pink.

The table was built around the foot of the mizzenmast. Captain Cambridge's chair was at the end opposite the mast, and everyone else sat on the benches that had been built in on either side. Abby was on Captain Cambridge's left, opposite Mrs. Cambridge. Mr. West, the third mate, sat by Abby, and Mr. Taber, the second mate, by Mrs. Cambridge:

it was their watch below. The first mate, Mr. Allen, was on watch on deck; he would have his dinner later. The ship *Erasmus* creaked powerfully as she creamed up the sea on the ninth day of her homeward passage.

Mrs. Cambridge murmured, "So you are not a New Zealand national?"

Abigail shook her head. She was not sure what nationality she had, if any.

"But your parents were both New England folks: your mother was the daughter of a Fairhaven physician."

Abigail said, "Yes." She didn't want to talk about her mother; it was painfully obvious, she thought resentfully, that Mrs. Butler and Mrs. Cambridge had enjoyed a capital gossip about the Sherman affairs while the *Erasmus* was in Mangonui.

The dinner was excellent—ham, Mangonui potatoes, beer, coffee, and bread and *butter*—but instead of eating she thought about Mrs. Cambridge, and the way she had interfered in her life, and how she relished her food. It was no wonder, she brooded, that Mrs. Cambridge was plump and growing plumper.

"And no doubt," Mrs. Cambridge pursued, "your mother employed the nursing skills she learned from her father on board of your father's ship?"

"And in the ports," Abby agreed reluctantly. She thought of all the times when the *Pandora* had dropped anchor to find an urgent messenger pulling out from shore, and how her mother had packed up her grandfather's old medical bag and gone off on the instant. Tears stung her eyes; never had she missed her mother more. Mangonui was hundreds of miles away. She swallowed and said, "My mother was famous for her medical lore." And Mrs. Cambridge silenced, looking pleased, while Captain Cambridge cleared his throat, for no apparent reason at all.

After the meal, as always, Abigail and Mrs. Cambridge went to the room that was Mrs. Cambridge's private place on deck in the hurricane house. It was perfectly splendid, Abby thought: quite six feet by eight, because the *Erasmus* was such a fine large vessel, and furnished with a divan and a chair and a table, with a cabin stove in the corner for little items of cooking and heating the irons.

But Abby felt trapped. She might as well, she thought drearily, have been in prison. The door was ajar, and she could see the man at the helm, his face tipped back to watch the sails through the special gap in the roof. The man was steering full-and-bye, and Abby felt certain she could have done better, for every now and then a little water splashed over the taffrail as the wind got too far abeam.

Mrs. Cambridge said pensively, "Was it difficult for your mother, I wonder, to raise an infant on board of a ship? And then later, when you were a growing girl..."

Abby said indignantly, "I had lessons." Her tone was righteous, despite the fact that she had been expert at playing truant on board the *Pandora*. There were too many places on a brig where a small girl could hide. Her mother had scolded and sighed, and on one voyage, the first mate had tut-tutted and tried to improve the situation himself by teaching Abby to figure.

Abby remembered that he had got very impatient with her grasshopper mind when she refused to believe that one dozen peaches was the same as twelve apples. Everyone knew that apples kept better on board ship! Her mother used to fill a small barrel with apples, and then pour molasses over them until the cask was brimming. The apples were still delicious six months later, but peaches that had been preserved that way were fit only for the hogs.

She said, "My mother taught me to read and write." The first mate had let her help him keep the log, and in return for his kindness she had helped him write long sentimental letters to his sweetheart. They had mused for hours over flowery words, all the time munching the cake that his sweetheart had packed in his sea chest.

"The duties of a mother," Mrs. Cambridge murmured then, "are grave and serious, and surely the care of the precious gem that God has delivered into a woman's care is even more of a challenge when that child grows up on board of a ship, in the company of rough-and-ready men."

Her tone was still thoughtful, and her cheek was flushed pink as she bent her sleek head over her sewing, but Abby was too angry to pay much heed. "Sailors were kind to me!" she said. Sailors, she silently fumed, were her friends. Mates had carried her about as a baby, and comforted her when she took her first tumbles on the pitching deck; sailors had taught her to sing and swear and make fancy rope work, and introduced her to all the wonderful ways of a ship.

"They paid you much attention?"

Abby muttered, "Yes." But she got a lot more attention on this ship, she thought rebelliously. Whenever she ventured out on the open deck the men all stared. She did the washing for Mrs. Cambridge as well as herself, as Captain Cambridge had asked her, and of course she could not refuse, and the washing, when she hung it out, got an uncommon lot of attention as well.

The men talked about her, she knew it, and Consider West strutted about like a cock-a-doodle-doo, just because he was the one who had first brought her to the *Erasmus*. He tried to engage her attention a-constant at the dining table, but Abigail ignored him; she, too, remembered that he had brought her to this ship.

"But," said Mrs. Cambridge in that same pensive tone, "I am convinced that your father had rules. The men, no doubt, were instructed to recognize the special gentleness and respectful consideration due to a girl."

Abby said shortly, "They were always polite, if that is what you mean."

"And," said Mrs. Cambridge, "I am equally sure that your mother supplemented your education with more creative employments. For instance," she said, and smiled kindly, "your mother taught you to sew."

Of course her mother had taught Abby her stitchery! But, Abby thought mutinously, she had not indulged in this sewing, sewing, *sewing* that Mrs. Cambridge thought so wonderful. Abigail loathed the activity. Her own husband, no matter how important a shipmaster—and a captain he would be, Abby was certain of that—would have to survive with his slippers and his nightshirt unembroidered.

"And," said Mrs. Cambridge, "she communicated her skills in the art of nursing?"

Abby hesitated, surprised at the tone of Mrs. Cambridge's voice. She sounded most unusually awkward, as if she'd had to brace herself to ask the question. Abby had certainly helped with the nursing: she had carried her mother's bag, and had hung out bandages after they had been carefully washed and then soaked in strong vinegar, but that was as far as the assisting had gone. During the actual emergency times Abby had been sent to play outside with the patient's children.

Abigail said slowly, "I have her medical books." The two well-thumbed books and her bed linen were all she had to remind her of her mother, now that she was so far from home. She looked sideways at her hostess, thinking about it. The averted cheek was flushed, and Mrs. Cambridge was bent over her sewing much further than needed.

Then Abby completely forgot it—for the man at masthead called out that he'd raised a sail.

"'Tis the ship *Pierrot*, by thunder," said Obed Cambridge ten minutes later. "I'd recognize that old single tops'l box if the archangel Gabriel himself were a-trumpeting—and, by thunder, she's a-cutting in whale!"

He was on the roof of the house, but not alone in his amazement: Abby was standing uncertainly beside him. Her feet had carried her out of Mrs. Cambridge's room and across the deck and up the ladder as if of their own accord. It was the first vessel raised in more than eight days.

"I'll speak him," he said. "And find out where he found that whale—and show you how we whalemen do it."

They would speak the *Pierrot?* Abigail was not at all sure how she felt about that. Seth Morgan was on board of that ship, and a cousin Abby did not want to meet. Her mind was full of unpleasant things—of the confrontation by the riverbank, and Edmund, and the dreadful flogging, and the future that lay ahead of her in New Bedford. However, her feet insisted that she stay where she was: speaking a ship—any ship—was far too exciting to be missed.

The ship *Pierrot* was a full six miles off, her staysails, jibs, and mainsail all furled. The main and mizzen topsails were braced full on the starboard tack and the foresail was hauled up tight, so that the old ship puddled about like a duck, with the sun on her sails from the west. "Good Godfrey!" Obed expostulated, peering through the glass. Abby hopped from one foot to the other with suspense, his tone was so confounded. "I do believe that Seth has more than one whale!" The distant ensign jerked up the *Pierrot* mizzen. "Aha," said Obed, "he's seen us. Aha," he said with evident glee, "we'll sail around him, and show him what sailing is like."

"Sit there," he said to Abby, pointing at the larboard boat where it sat braced in the cranes, level with the roof of the house—"You'll have a capital view." She obediently scampered over, clambered in, and sat on a thwart. As he had promised, the view was tremendous.

Time went by in a swish of water and a racket of readying the ship. All hands were on deck, bright-eyed and grinning, and most had grabbed a chance to spruce up their looks. The sight of a fellow whaler, no matter how grubby, was a welcome diversion after all that empty water. Obed stood on the quarterdeck by the lee mizzen shrouds where Abby could look down on him. Consider West was beside him, resplendent in blue shirt and white bandanna and buckskin trousers tied with leather thongs at the knee.

The *Erasmus* swayed majestically, close-hauled on the wind, her wake foaming a bubbling light green. No order had been given to reduce sail, even when the *Pierrot* was less than a half mile away, and Abby hoped that Captain Seth Morgan had nerves of steel.

"Wear ship!" hollered Obed, and in a flurry of orders and hauling of ropes, the *Erasmus* wore round her stern so her bowsprit pointed right smack-dab at the *Pierrot* weather waist. Abby, her fingers clutching the sides of the boat, could see the cutting stage lowered so it spanned the great bobbing carcass of a whale. There were men on the plank, holding long implements with bright sharp blades. Their heads were turned as they stared at the ship that was bearing so remorselessly down on them. A huge strip of blubber hung suspended over the *Pierrot* starboard rail, glistening in the sun as the *Erasmus* approached.

Then, at the ultimate teeth-clenching second, the *Erasmus* tacked. Obed boomed the orders out, red-faced and laughing. Round the other ship's bow the *Erasmus* sailed, so close it almost seemed that she would snag the jibboom. Around the larboard side of the *Pierrot* she creamed, past one—no, two!—huge logy bodies secured on lines. Then, with a singing out and a heave at the braces and a pull at clewlines, the great arcing wake of the *Erasmus* darkened and slowed, and the ship braced round, very slowly, and sheered past the other ship's stern.

Captain Seth Morgan was standing brace-legged on the roof of the *Pierrot* hurricane house. He was wearing dungarees and rawhide boots and he had his arms folded. The *Erasmus* was so tightly sailed, was gliding by so slowly and close, that Abigail could see his grim expression. She ducked, involuntarily. Then she heard Obed clamber onto the roof nearby.

Obed said, with a bluff chuckle in his voice, "Ship ahoy."

She could have sworn she heard Seth Morgan sigh. Then

he acknowledged the playful formality. "*Pierrot*, of New Bedford."

"*Erasmus*. You've had some luck."

"I have."

"And you want to gam?"

"I'm too busy—and dirty—for that, but I'd be obliged if you'd come on board for an hour."

"It would be more logical for you to come here," Obed objected, "your ship being in such a state."His voice held a tinge of envy. "How many whales? Three?"

"And three last week."

"What!"

"My luck has improved." Seth's tone was dry.

"It has, by thunder!" Then Obed said, "You'd be glad of a good supper."

The gap between the two ships was widening, as the *Erasmus* gradually lost way. Seth Morgan raised his voice, and shouted, "Is the Sherman girl on board of you?"

Abby ducked further down in her boat. She heard Obed say in puzzled tones, "Aye, Seth, she is."

"Then you must come here. I have bad news, and I don't want to break it myself."

The *Erasmus* moved on, slowly, slowly; it was too late for further conversation. Then the *Erasmus* stilled, a half mile from the other vessel, her main yard aback.

Four

Obed said in tones of the utmost consternation, "I won't tell the girl that—not me, Seth, no sir."

Seth surveyed his cousin with weary impatience. His eyes were sore and rimmed with grit. How long was it since he'd slept? It didn't matter, he thought: he had oil. Six whales in six days!

He also had a blubber room between-decks full of strips of fat, and chopped horse-pieces of blubber piled deep all over his decks. He snapped, "Obed, you have to tell the girl, and you know it. It's your place to do it—as long as she's on your ship, you're her guardian. It's impossible for her to come here and I'm a deal too busy to dress up and be social."

Obed said plaintively, "How can I upset the pretty little thing? Anyway," he said, catching Seth's infuriated look, "she will no doubt have questions that only you can answer."

Seth knew why Obed was so against upsetting females; anyone who had a mother like that old besom Mrs. Fanny would learn fast to read warily in dealings with the sex. Nevertheless he felt extremely impatient. "For God's sake, Obed, how can I possibly tell the girl the grisly details?"

Obed stared unhappily into his brandy glass. Then he muttered, "Bad business, by thunder."

Seth didn't bother to answer. Instead, he shut his sore eyes. The two men were in the transom cabin; a tarpaulin cover had been thrown on the sofa, and the two cousins sat on that. Seth was sprawled, his stockinged feet propped up on a chair, and he held his brandy glass on his stomach. He could hear Mr. Leonard and Charlie Lisbon entertaining Obed's third mate and his boat's crew on deck. Seth's men were being treated to a glass of rum as well; they had worked hard enough to deserve it, and they seemed amenable enough—for the moment. Seth thought grimly that two weeks without whale would see them rebellious again. Because William Mitchell had intimidated them, they had no idea of the strength or weakness of their captain. At the first opportunity they would try him out, to see if they could bully him.

Obed observed, "You've been lucky."

"I suppose so." Seth still had nightmares about that confrontation in the forehold. In his dreams he was trapped down there with Edmund and that giant knife, and the pistol failed to fire...

"Apart from those murders, I meant." Obed went on enviously, "Three whale—and buster ones, in the bargain."

Seth relished the moment. Obed was dressed respectably in a broadcloth suit, while Seth had not bothered to change out of his dungarees, but for once Seth felt the equal of his cousin in this highly competitive whaling business. For six backbreaking days he and his men had been chasing whales, and killing them, towing the ponderous dead weight of carcasses to the ship, or cutting the huge strips of blubber free, or baling the clear spermaceti from the monstrous foreheads, or boiling out the good yellow oil.

As captain, Seth had had to drive himself twice as hard as he had driven his men, and now he was functioning on the dull edge of exhaustion. But it was worth every ache. He said, "One of the cows we took last week made a hundred and fifteen barrels."

Obed whistled. A sperm whale that made a hundred barrels or more was a rarity; in the oil-hungry market the oil boiled out from just that one whale would fetch three thousand dollars. Then he added slyly, "You'll have to report the murders, as well, to the father."

Seth's eyes snapped open. "To Captain Sherman?"

"No, no. To Jezekiel Mitchell."

Who was the owner of the ship, as well as the father of the murdered first officer. "Oh, God." Seth shut his eyes again. He loathed the business of making reports, even the most mundane ones, and this would be an exceedingly grim one to write. Then he said, "You're homeward bound—can't you break the news to him?"

"Good Godfrey, no!" Obed's expression was horrified. "The weather's fair. I'll wait while you have the letter written, and then, as a neighborly gesture, I'll make sure that Mitchell gets it." Then he paused and said thoughtfully, "I can send over some men to help with all that cutting in, if you wish."

Seth grinned. If Obed helped cut in, he would be entitled to half the oil. He said, "I think we can manage alone, thank you."

Obed did not look disappointed: he had expected no less. But it was second nature for an alert Yankee businessman to try his chances; he would not have been Obed if he hadn't.

Seth changed the subject, saying, "Obed, what's my legal situation? Do I have to report the murder to anyone else?"

"I don't know, confound me if I do." Obed's brow was furrowed. "I've never come acrost the situation afore."

Neither had Seth. "Perhaps I should ask an American consul," he said, thinking aloud. He could call in at the

Chilean port of Talcahuano, where he was acquainted with the American consul, Mr. Crosby. Talcahuano was a notorious port for desertion, as so many whalers recruited there that runaways could always find another berth. He might lose half his crew—but would that be a loss? A lucky captain had little trouble shipping replacement men. And at long last Seth was lucky; he shut his eyes again.

Obed said suddenly, "Your log."

"What?"

"When I first shipped as mate, the captain gave me a list of must-dos and mustn't-dos for keeping the log. It was your mention of a consul that brought it to mind. There was a ruling about shipping a man in a place without a consul. The captain has to put his name in the log the day he is shipped, and have his mate witness the entry. Then the captain ships him again when he finds a consul, and it's all shipshape and legal."

"And what the devil has that to do with my problem?"

"It proves it," Obed said earnestly. "It proves that your log is a legal document. All you need to do is be certain that the murders are written up in the log, and get a consul to sign the entry when you find one."

It sounded too easy, Seth thought. Then Obed checked, "You do keep a log?"

"Of course I keep a log. At least," Seth amended, "my mate keeps one." He unhitched his feet and stood up to pour more brandy. He could hear the din of conversation on deck, as his men relayed their ghoulish yarns to their undoubtedly riveted visitors. The gruesome affair would be the talk of the Pacific within weeks.

When Obed took his glass, his brow was furrowed again. "But," he said, "if William Mitchell kept the log, who wrote up the murders?"

"Charlie Lisbon," Seth said. Mr. Leonard was now first mate, but Mr. Leonard couldn't read or write. Seth stretched up an arm, unhooked the big blue book from the shelf over the chart table, then slumped back down by Obed and cocked his feet up on the chair again.

He turned the pages. Obed, with blatant curiosity, craned his neck to read. For a while there was silence.

Most of the log was kept in the crabbed thin writing that was so like the man that William Mitchell had been. "Friday 26th January," Seth read. "Begins with dead calm the 3 Kings off our beam about 15 miles off Latter part New Zealand in sight steering for Mangonui, at 3 AM Edmund Davis seaman and Jack Rawlings steerage boy were put in the foremast rigging and flogged for insolence I seize them up and striped their hides with three dozen to learn them their places So Ends."

"At three in the morning?" Obed demanded. His face was round with consternation. "He flogged two men at three in the morning — without bringing them aft?"

Seth said tiredly, "He did." He remembered his impotent fury when he had found what had happened. But what could he do? The master and first officers had to present a united face to the crew; or rebellion would follow, as sure as night followed day.

"At anchor in Mangonui," came four entries later. "At 11 AM Edmund Davis made assault on Mr. Mitchell the first officer and threatened my life, he not having learned his lesson He was put in the rigging and I stripped his shirt over his shoulder and made a net of his skin so that those which remain shall hear and fear and shall henceforth commit no more any such evil Deuteronomy chapter nineteen So Ends."

"Good Godfrey!" Obed's tone was appalled. "Mind you," he said, lowering his voice, "there were stories back home about William Mitchell. His father was overfond of the whip, the way I heard it, and Mrs. Mitchell protected the other one, Jireh, so that William got most of the whipping. There was talk," he heavily mused. "I remember a yarn about a boy strung up in a tree when William Mitchell was just a schoolboy, and a fire lit under him. Jireh Mitchell heard of it and came and got the fire out before the boy was dead and done. Afterward the boy swore it was William that done it," he said. "At the time folk reckoned William was twisted. And it does, from this, seem pitifully likely that your first officer wasn't in his right mind."

Mitchell had not been the only one to go insane, Seth brooded. He turned to the entry for the day of the murders, and found it easily, for the writing was very different, being large and ingenuous.

"Begins with fine weather," Charlie Lisbon had carefully penned. "Moderate winds from NNW, middle part shortened sail for the night, at brekkfast time a stowaway was discovered, and he murdered William Mitchell first mate and Joe Manuel seaman before being overpowered and Jack Rawlings steerage boy died of his wounds Captain Morgan shot Edmund Davis and killed him at 7:15 AM raised a school of sperm whales, raised by Charles T. Lisbon Third Mate (MySelf) at 7:30 AM raised another, Captain Morgan struck a large Bull and Bow Boat (My Boat) struck a large Cow killed and saved them both, ends pleasant wether ship working up to the dead whales, another whale taken by Mr. Leonard in the Leward school."

Obed was silent, frowning. Seth read the entry again, his own eyebrows lowered. "Do you think that covers it?" he asked at length. He felt very doubtful, but didn't dare make additions or alterations.

"It's not witnessed," Obed said. "And where is the burial? You have to note the burial."

Seth turned the page. "There it is." It was in the next entry.

"At Sunset we buried William Mitchell first mate and Joe Manuel seaman and Jack Rawlings steerage boy and Edmund Davis seaman with the usual burial service Captain Morgan read some verses from the bible and it was a very solem occasion after 3 greusom murders on board As Mr. Mitchell is dead I now keep the log, so Ends, cutting in three buster whales."

Obed pulled at his whiskers. Then he shrugged and said, "I'll tell you what. I'll make an entry in my log certifying to what you told me."

"That," said Seth, with a sense of profound relief, "would be most neighborly."

"And," said Obed, watching him slyly, "I'll wait about until you've written that letter to Jezekiel Mitchell."

Seth said dryly, "Thank you." If his astounding run of luck continued, then any whales raised while his ship and Obed's were in company would belong to both ships, half the oil each.

"And," added Obed, saluting Seth with his glass, "you can be the one to break the dismal tidings to Abigail Sherman."

"I'm damned if I will," said Seth.

When Consider West's boat brought Captain Cambridge back from the gam, Abigail was hovering in a state of dreadful suspense. The boat clunked on the ship's side and the oarsmen scrambled out. As soon as the boat was at the level of the roof of the house Abigail ran up to him, but he merely gave her a brooding look before going to the ladder and then clumping below. As he passed her she could smell the brandy he had drunk. She looked about rather wildly and then grabbed Mr. West's arm.

She said, "Did you hear what Captain Morgan had to say? Had he spoken a merchantman out of Mangonui? Oh, please, was it about my father?"

Consider West had the momentous look of a man who was bulging with gossip. Scathingly he said, "Of course it wasn't. How could it be? Cap'n Morgan sailed a-fore us, and there ain't no ship what sails faster than the *Erasmus*."

His boat's crew grinned, just as superior as he, and then they left the house in a rush, apparently in a race to get to the foc'sle first.

They, too, it seemed, had sensational gossip to relate. Abby transferred her gaze back to Mr. West. Giving him a coaxing smile, she said, "What did he have to say, then?"

Consider West sniffed, smarting, it seemed, from all those snubs at the dining table. He said haughtily, "If I told you, you'd faint."

"What?" She laughed with relief that the news was not about her father. "Me? That's impossible. I've never fainted in my life." Stepping to the larboard boat, she clambered into it, and sat down on a thwart. Then she patted the thwart in front of her, and said, "Do please tell, Mr. West, kind sir. And if I faint you won't have to catch me."

He sat down grudgingly. Then he said in grumpy tones, "Charlie Lisbon told me all about it. William Mitchell was foully murdered, six days out from Mangonui."

"What!" She stared, aghast. For a moment the world went out of kilter. The notion that she would arrive in New Bedford at the exact same time that the Mitchells learned that they had lost a son—by murder—was peculiarly distressing.

As if from a distance she heard Mr. West say in tones of disgust and alarm, "Hey Miz Abby, you've gone all white when you said you would not. And I ain't even told you the gory bits, yet."

Abigail spent a sleepless night. The *Erasmus* lay uneasily, alive with unfamiliar noises. Sails slatted as the ship lay to— but it was not that that kept Abby awake. She lay staring at the darkness, listening to Obed's snoring, and grappling with her conscience.

When dawn grayed the sky beyond the sidelight she crept out of her berth, dressed in a blue gingham dress, and went in search of Mr. West. He was on duty and should have been on deck, but he took some finding. Eventually she discovered him stretched out full-length in the bottom of his boat with his hat over his eyes, snoozing.

She woke him with a well-placed toe and said without any preamble, "I want to take me to the ship *Pierrot*. I have to talk with Captain Morgan."

He gawped.

"And don't argue. You owe me a favor, and this is it."

"You're jestin'!"

"I jest not. You got me in this mess, Mr. West, and you owe me. If it were not for you I'd still be in Mangonui instead of on this ship and packed off to New Bedford."

"That's ridiculous. Anyways," he said very firmly, "if I did it, Cap'n Cambridge would have me for stealing a boat, and send me for'ard. And what d'you want to see Cap'n Morgan about, anyways?"

"Captain Cambridge demote you? Never! You're far too valuable for that, and you know it."

"In my eye, I do," he said flatly. "He'd wear me intestines for a bandanna."

"Really? Oh dear, is he so strict? I wonder what he will say, then, when he finds out that you were sleeping on duty."

"You wouldn't!"

"I would. And," she added virtuously, "if you are caught for stealing, then I will take the blame—unlike certain young gentlemen I know."

Ten minutes later Mr. West and his crew stealthily lowered the boat with Abigail in it, and pulled away. "I jes' don't know," he moaned at the steering oar. "And I don't know what Cap'n Morgan is going to say, neither."

"Oh, do be quiet," said Abigail.

Seth, unaware that visitors were on the way, was sitting at the breakfast table and was in the worst of moods for company. His eyes were as foggy and gritty as ever, despite the sleep. The first whale had been cut in after Obed had gone, and the great skull had been baled of the clear spermaceti oil within it. When the huge stripped carcass had been let go to sink, the men had brought round the second whale and secured it, ready for cutting in next morning. Then they had all headed off to their berths, except for a lookout. The sleep had been desperately needed.

Cutting in and trying out was pure hell, with only the prospect of casks full of oil to keep a man laboring at the ghastly task. Seth's mouth felt sour and his head felt full of gun-cotton wadding. How did his crew feel? Equally bad-tempered? Seth hoped not: there were two whales to be cut in today, and there was a mountain of blubber to be boiled in the pots.

Mr. Leonard came to the skylight while Seth was still contemplating his breakfast. It was like a chilling echo of the morning of the murders. He said, "Cap'n, better come up. The men for'ard are after trouble."

Already? The confrontation had come much sooner than Seth expected. Nowadays the Jennings rifle and the pistols were always loaded, always handy. Seth picked up the rifle and went up on deck. He glanced around quickly, taking in the scene, his mind clearing into a kind of exhausted brilliancy.

The *Pierrot* was as she had been for two days, snugly held back with the helm tied hard down. A boat was pulling out from the *Erasmus* towards him. Obed? Seth put it out of his mind. The entire foremast crew was gathered on the amidships deck. The seamen's feet were braced aggressively amongst the heaps of waiting blubber; the deck of the *Pierrot* was a slippery, dangerous place.

Seth said, "What's the problem?"

The ringleader seemed to be one Jim Pott, a quarrelsome Irishman shipped five months before in Talcahuano. He stalked two paces forward, and said, "It's the grub. It ain't fit for a goat. You 'spect us ter cut in and work the windlass with this rubbish in our bellies?"

Seth considered. The food was always second-rate on the *Pierrot*, because Jezekiel Mitchell had provisioned her so cheaply, but admittedly the food this morning was worse than awful.

He said mildly, "Send for the grub and show me."

The men all muttered, and shifted closer. The mildness had emboldened them. Seth stood quietly, the gun held loosely in his hand. Mr. Leonard said nervously, "You think this be a good idea, Cap'n?"

Seth did not reply. He watched the wooden kid that held the foremast men's rations as a boy brought it up onto deck. Then it was passed from hand to hand until Jim Pott held it. Jim lunged forward, shoved it under Seth's face, and shouted, "Take a sniff'er that, Cap'n. Take a sniff'er that! It ain't fit fer a pig!"

"You're right," Seth admitted. He turned and said gently, "Mr. Leonard, I should be grateful if you would send down for my plate. It's on the table, still untouched—and these boys might like to look at it."

The plate was tin. Mr. Leonard brought it up himself, in a worried silence. Seth looked at the greasy chunks of sour salt meat and rusty beans and weevil-ridden biscuit, and then, with his left hand, he took it and gave it to Jim Pott.

"Well?" he inquired. "Is my grub very different from yours?" At the edge of his vision he could see the *Erasmus* boat pulling nearer. The heads of the oarsmen were turned to gape at him, and their oars stirred the water to slow the boat. There seemed to be an argument going on inside it, but he ignored this, turning to stare at Jim Pott instead.

"It's the same," Jim Pott said grudgingly. All the men shifted and growled, unimpressed.

"You don't think much of my breakfast?" Seth still spoke mildly—but then he shouted at the top of his lungs, "I don't think much of it, either, Jim, and you can damn well throw it overboard!"

Jim gaped. Then, with an aggressive smirk, he threw the plate over the rail.

It sailed over the sea high and wide, spilling grease and beans. Seth swung the rifle and fired. The tin plate sang and jerked sideways. He tipped the rifle, heard the second round roll down the tubular barrel, and fired again. The plate rang loudly, and jerked again, before it dropped with a splash.

Seth roared, "And now, by God! I'll go hungry—and you'll either eat your mess or go hungry too!"

The men said nothing. They were skidding in grease and falling all over each other into heaps of blubber in their rush to get forward.

Seth nodded grimly and then looked over the rail. "And what the devil do you want?" he demanded.

Consider West and his oarsmen had all thrown themselves flat in the bottom of the boat. Abigail was sitting bolt upright on her thwart, her eyes wide. Then, she put up her hands.

"Please don't shoot me, Captain Morgan," she begged. "Couldn't we parley, instead?"

If Seth was amused, he managed very successfully to hide it. He ordered that the boat be hoisted, while Consider West and his boat's crew scrambled up the side and vanished forward. Abby was left alone, facing Seth Morgan on the roof of his hurricane house, feeling nervous hiccups bubble inside her as she met his aggressive scowl.

He snapped, "I suppose this is Obed's idea."

Abby blinked. "Does it make any difference if it is?" She couldn't imagine how Captain Morgan had conceived such an unlikely notion, but she was prepared to go along with anything, if it would only improve his temper.

He shouted, "Yes, goddammit, it does!" She winced, and he muttered something mysterious about yellow-bellied cowards. Then, to her amazement, he shut his eyes, took an audible bracing breath, and said, "I regret I must inform you of the untimely death of your cousin William Mitchell."

She said, "Oh."

"You're not surprised?"

"No. I already knew it."

He said incredulously, "Obed informed you that Mitchell is dead?"

She wished she could say yes, but her conscience did not allow it. Captain Cambridge had said not a word on the subject; perhaps, she thought, he did not want to upset his wife. She mutely shook her head.

"Then how the devil did you hear about it?"

Abigail flushed, and muttered, "Someone told me."

To her alarm, Seth went red too. "My God!" he roared. "You've been gossiping with the *Erasmus* crew!" Abby flinched and retreated: he strode forward, and she stepped hastily into the larboard boat. It rattled on the davits.

She gasped, "I had a right. William Mitchell was my cousin. Second cousin. Or was it third?" she mused aloud. "But I had an undeniable right to know that he had been murdered."

Seth was towering over her. He shouted, "Sit down!" She sat on a thwart with a thump. "My God," he said with angry disdain, glowering down at her from the deck, "you've been gossiping — no doubt with the same silly young man who carried you onto the *Erasmus* — and no doubt this *excursion* is your own idea: you came here to gather a little more of this sensational gossip!"

"That is not true!"

"You want me to believe it was Obed's idea?"

"No, it wasn't, but I have a very good reason for coming."

"Yes? And what may that be, Miss Scatterbrain Sherman? Did you hope to learn more about the man you helped when he deserted? Or did you think you'd learn more gory details of the murders?"

Abigail was white. She said quietly, "I already know much more than is comfortable, thank you. I already know that William Mitchell was a brute and the author of his own fate."

For a moment, Seth Morgan seemed bereft of words.

Then he said blankly, "I beg your pardon?"

She said with dignity, "As you say, I listened to gossip. I didn't think of it that way. All I knew was that the news you carried concerned me, yet Captain Cambridge had concluded to keep it a distressing secret."

"He had?" Seth Morgan's voice was much lower, more thoughtful, as he studied her earnest expression. He rubbed his bristly chin with one broad palm. Then one eyebrow arched and he said, "Well? Are you going to put me out of my suspense? Come, tell me why you came here. What scamp-headed notion sent you in my unfortunate direction?"

"There's no mystery about it," she snapped. "I only came to apologize and set matters right."

"You ... *what?*"

"Apologize," she said. She was deeply regretting having bothered; plans made in the throes of a wakeful night, she realized, were often not very sensible. She took a breath and said, "I called you a brute, and other things I don't like to remember. And I know now it wasn't you. It was my cousin who was bucko."

Seth Morgan was very still and very silent. Then, to her great alarm, he came over and stepped into the boat, setting it to rattling again. He sat down, facing her, and he leaned so close she could see the white line of fury around his mouth. "Are you insinuating," he asked icily, "that I am not responsible for the discipline of my ship?"

Consternation filled her, and all at once she was very glad she was sitting down. She said rapidly in a low voice, "I also want to apologize for taking food to Edmund. It was very foolish of me and I feel very bad about it."

"And rightly so!"

"And..." She gulped, and wanted to shut her eyes, but couldn't. "And I should be so very grateful if you would not mention my transgressions in the letter to Mr. Jezekiel Mitchell."

Dead silence. Then Seth Morgan said flatly, "So that's it."

Abby said cautiously, fearing the worst, "What is?"

"Obed had to give some reason for laying aback, so he said he was waiting for a letter, right? And once you heard the gossip about Mitchell's death, you realized that the letter was for Mitchell's father — right?"

Abby said shakily, "Yes." She could smell him, a blend of cigar smoke and sweat and oil, and she wished she was a thousand miles away.

"And," said Seth with merciless logic, "you began to worry that the letter might give news of Abigail Sherman as well, h'm? In fact, you began to feel mightily concerned that it might tell rather a lot about your exploits."

He had outlined the progress of her nighttime thoughts very accurately indeed. Abby said desperately, "But I really do apologize, Captain Morgan. I feel dreadful that Edmund might have killed you, especially when I realized that you had not flogged him at all. He was horrid. He had me fooled when I first discovered him in the hayshed, because I couldn't really see him. And I do hold strong views — very strong views! — on flogging, Captain Morgan. I really did believe at the time that you had done that awful thing..."

She paused, looking at him with wide, candid eyes. "I must be a hypocrite," she confided, "because after I found out what Edmund was like I must admit I *enjoyed* whacking him with that lump of wood."

But Seth Morgan wasn't listening. He was clambering out of the boat. "Wait there," he instructed, and strode off across the roof of the house to the ladder without another word.

He came back a surprisingly short time later, a folded paper in his hand, Consider West and his crew sheepishly following him. Seth was looking grimly pleased with himself.

He handed the letter to Abigail, who took it hesitantly,

turning it over in her hands. It was folded twice one way and three times the other in the usual fashion, so it made a small tight shape that did not need an envelope. The last fold had been sealed with a red blob of sealing wax. On the other side it was addressed to Jezekiel Mitchell Esq., Boat Train Road, Dartmouth, New Bedford.

"You will oblige me," said Seth Morgan, "by giving that to Cousin Cambridge with my thanks for the offer to deliver same, and also please bid him goodbye for me, with good wishes for a swift and pleasant passage home, and also my congratulations on the happy event when it happens."

His grin was wolfish. "For," he said, "there is no need for him to hang about here any longer." He turned with the evident intention of striding off, but on an afterthought he turned again, saying casually, "You can tell Obed if you like that you came to see me at my request, so I could break the sad news in a proper manner."

Abby said not a word. The boys lowered the boat in a sheepish silence, but she scarcely noticed Consider's open relief. They pulled away from the side of the ship, and all the time she frowned at Seth Morgan, who had run out onto the cutting platform and was back at work without even a farewell wave.

Happy event? What happy event? Surely Captain Morgan didn't mean...?

At breakfast Mrs. Cambridge resumed a twenty-four-hour-long campaign of oblique questioning and veiled complaint. Her husband had failed to provide an explanation for the very odd events during the speaking of the ship *Pierrot*, and evidently his officers were under instructions to keep quiet too, for Mr. West shuffled uncomfortably about on his bench during meals, and the first mate, Mr. Allen, was as glumly silent as ever.

Mrs. Cambridge finished her tea, put down the cup, set her hands on her swelling abdomen, and said, "Obed, I must

105

confess a certain amazement that you should have allowed Miss Sherman to go a-gamming on our cousin's ship alone."

Abby tensed. Mr. West shifted uncomfortably. Obed looked at neither of them. He said gruffly, "It was necessary."

"But the impropriety..."

Abigail said quickly, "I do assure you I did not go below on Captain Morgan's ship. We simply had a brief conversation on the roof of his hurricane house."

"But I am certain from what I have heard of your mother that she would not have allowed you to call on a ship that did not have a lady on board."

Obed barked, "There was a compelling reason."

He was red in the face and obviously building up a head of angry steam. Consider West made a muttered excuse and disappeared up to deck. The second mate came down, cast one look at the gathering around the table, and went into his stateroom. Abigail looked down at her plate.

Then she heard Mrs. Cambridge's reproachful voice say, "But I am utterly unable, Obed, to conceive of any reason for such blatant impropriety. I am responsible for Miss Sherman, and I feel I should have been consulted. After all, Seth Morgan is our cousin, and if the circumstances were so very urgent, I should have been most happy to chaperone Miss Sherman on board of his ship."

Abby quelled the twitch of her lips. So that was it, she thought: Mrs. Cambridge was piqued that they had sailed away without her seeing Captain Morgan. Seth had kissed her hand ... and he was young and handsome...

Obed, looking horrified, spluttered, "But Seth was in no fit state for gamming. He was cutting in!"

Mrs. Cambridge smiled, and said, "Exactly." Then, with neat movements of her hands, she began to peel a peach. Obed glared at her, then tugged at his whiskers, and mumbled, "Abigail went on a family matter."

His wife stared at him, her hazel eyes more round than

ever, and then looked at Abigail. Abby warily said nothing. It was beyond her to decide why both captains were so set on protecting her reputation, but she was thankful enough all the same. Obed hauled at his beard again, avoiding both feminine pairs of eyes, and muttered, "It was news that only Seth was competent to give her."

"Family news? How interesting. But it could not have been news of Captain Sherman, for we sailed quite four days after the *Pierrot*. So ... it must have been news of Miss Sherman's cousin, William Mitchell."

Obed shifted about in his chair, disconcerted to find such perception in the ladylike person of his wife. He mumbled, "There was an accident."

"To William Mitchell? Oh dear," Mrs. Cambridge said. "Was he injured during whaling?"

"No," said Obed glumly. "He was murdered."

Abigail found her appetite had gone, and pushed aside her plate. Mrs. Cambridge cried, "Murdered?"

"Aye."

"In manhood's prime?"

"Yes, Victoria."

"He was murdered by a mutineer?"

"The murderer is dead. There were ... several deaths."

"Oh, dear heaven!"

Abby kept silent, and Obed was silent, too, obviously determined not to reveal any more. She heard Mrs. Cambridge murmur, "In the midst of life we are truly in death," and then her voice rose as she said, "And we carry a letter from Captain Morgan to the poor bereaved?"

"Aye, Victoria."

"How doubly unfortunate, then, that we are the ones to carry such dismal tidings. Hard on the heels of the loss of a cherished son," Mrs. Cambridge dolefully pronounced, "they will receive a young female cousin in his place."

That night, when the *Erasmus* was creaming up the star-tipped sea on the next leg of her brisk homeward passage, as Obed's snores were punctuating the serene warm darkness, Abby crept out of bed, pulled on shirt and dungaree pants, ran barefoot on deck, and climbed the mizzenmast.

It was exhilarating, it was marvelous, it was absolutely terrifying. Abby had run the rigging of the brig *Pandora* since she was old enough to reach from ratline to ratline and climb the ladderlike shrouds; just as children on shore learned the branches of their backyard trees, Abby had learned the *Pandora* hamper. But the rigging of the mighty *Erasmus* was a very different proposition.

Abigail had also never climbed in the dark. Her father and Broddy, who otherwise thought her running the rigging a very big joke, and useful at times in the bargain, had sternly forbid her two things—to climb out on the dolphin-striker, and to lay aloft at night. But oh—the magnificent height of the truck of the *Erasmus*! Abby hung on to a lanyard, spinning slowly, fighting not to shriek as the distant decks rose and fell. The phosphorescent wake of the ship was a hundred feet below her, and at times she felt convinced that she was one with the nighttime clouds. The *Erasmus* carried all canvas because she was on passage, and with the sails braced full the ship was a heavenly mountain, a downward-falling pyramid of moonlighted canvas. The ship was so beautiful her breath tugged sharp in her throat.

As the nights went by Abigail explored the ship from spanker gaff to fore-topgallant crosstrees, and she slid down every stay and brace in the dark. Her exploits became more and more daring: one night when she climbed the mizzenmast she stopped at the topmast staysail stay and stretched full-length upon it. The sail was set and braced full, a taut thrumming canvas hammock tight with hard breeze. Abby was a full eighty feet above the deck. She rolled into the tight furrow in the top of the triangular sail by the stay that held it up, and then she let go with both hands. She slid—zip, slam—all the way to the maintop. If her father had been there she would not have been allowed on deck for a week. If the wind had left the sail at that single split second she would have thudded to the deck. It didn't. Abby grabbed her balance and scrambled all the way to the main topgallant crosstrees.

It was her favorite perch. The ship was like a little bottle, suspended miraculously beneath a luminous splendor of canvas. Only on passage was a whaleship as lovely as a merchantman, for it was only then that a whaleship set all her sail. Now the *Erasmus,* scudding through a moon-sparked sea towards Cape Horn, was utterly wonderful, and from this perch life held promise, too. Here in the crosstrees Abby's troubles were molehills instead of mountains, and she knew that one day she would be sailing home...

The rigging vibrated. Someone was climbing the topmast. *There was someone else in the main topmast rigging.*

Abby froze. Then she turned, ducked, and wriggled frantically down to the nearest stay.

Just before she could hurl herself into dark anonymity, however, a horridly familiar voice gloated, "Well, well, what d'ye know? 'Tis Abby, ho, ho." Consider West cackled and then continued, "I didn't credit me ears, I did not, not when Michael told me a female were in the riggin'. No, no, sez I, thee's moonstruck. There he was, at the helm, and in the riggin', he persisted, up there a lady, and in dungaree pants, no less."

Jug-eared Michael, Abby thought furiously, must have the sight of an owl. She said coldly, "I will thank you to call me Miss Sherman."

"As befits a lady? And what will Cap'n Cambridge think, I wonder, when he hears tell there's a female sailor in the ship—not to mention what his wife will say?"

Abby winced. The thought of Cambridge thunder and scandalized reproof was very nasty indeed.

She said stiffly, "I would be grateful, Mr. West, if you

would keep your counsel and conclude not to rat."

"But," he cried, "what would I say — and how would I feel, if one mornin' your lifeless frame were discovered prone on the deck?"

Consider West, Abby thought with fury, was having the time of his life. "That won't happen," she said scathingly. "I never fall. I learned to climb when I was very small, and I've done it all my life on my brig *Pandora*."

"Fibs," scoffed Mr. West. "Fabrications."

"I'm telling the truth — I've been climbing the rigging for years."

"But you do not own a brig."

"I do! The *Pandora* is mine!"

The papers for the brig were under her bunk, in the little folding writing desk that her father had once made for her. "The brig *Pandora* is mine, my father sold her to me," she said proudly — for her father had told her to inform everyone in New Bedford that he was rich and that she herself was an owner.

Then she said in more anxious tones, "You can tell Captain Cambridge that and welcome, but I would be most obliged if you would kindly refrain from informing him that I climbed the rigging on his ship."

From the noise he made, it seemed Consider West was laughing until the tears ran down his face. Abby listened grimly and wished that she dared reach out and push him over.

"And what will happen to me," he inquired at last, "if Cap'n Cambridge somehow learns I kept quiet about our female sailor?"

"Nothing," she said roundly. "Just as nothing happened when you carried me to Captain Morgan's ship."

He lapsed into a thoughtful silence; then, as bright as a terrier and twice as irritating, he asked, "But how can I forebear to tell when female sailors make such entertainin' telling?"

110

Abby could have wept with frustration. She snapped, "Oh, do stop going on about female sailors. I don't believe there is any such thing."

"But of course there are female sailors," he cried, and to her alarm, he reached up for a backstay, ready to slide down to deck. "We spoke a ship what had a female greenhand only this year. She shipped as a foremast hand, and she lived with the men in the foc'sle all unsuspected, ate from the common kid, went to work aloft like all the rest, and pulled an oar in a boat."

"That's nonsense," said Abigail, certain that life in the foc'sle was far too public for a female to hide her female frailties.

"'Tis true," Consider West said loftily. "They found her out," he added with ghoulish relish, "when the mate stripped her for a flogging, after she got into a fight with the big black cook."

Abby stared, aghast, almost moved to blushing. "She shipped to be along with her sweetheart," Mr. West said sentimentally, "but, silly gal, she picked the wrong ship."

With that he slid down the backstay he was holding. When she heard the thump as his feet hit the deck, Abby followed him. She caught up with him in the shadow of the house and grabbed his arm. Then, with a lurch of utter horror, she saw the helmsman's grinning face.

"That's not Michael!" she hissed.

"Naw," said Mr. West, and guffawed. "But 'twas Michael what spied you first—oh, quite two weeks ago, it must've been. He and my watch have been a-watching you for quite a while."

He detached his arm from her grip and took himself below with yet another chuckle, while Abby watched his retreating back, riven with furious suspense.

"I was a-talking to Miz Sherman," Mr. West announced smugly at breakfast next morning.

"I was astounded," he declared.

Obed Cambridge scarcely bothered to lift an eyebrow. He was buttering bread and piling baked beans onto it. Mrs. Cambridge sedately poured coffee for them all. Mr. West, undeterred, said, "I must admit, sir, that I found it unbelievable."

Mrs. Cambridge said, "Coffee, Mr. West?"

"Thank you, ma'am." He took the cup, saying, "Never, in all my life, have I come acrost the like."

Abby was on the verge of screaming. Wild possibilities rushed through her mind — of throwing a cup, or a fit. She prayed for a squall, for a freak wave to sweep the decks and come down the skylight onto Consider West's impenitent head.

"I never did know it was possible," declared the young man, "for a young girl to..."

"Yes, Mr. West?"

"... own a brig," he said, and smirked at Abby.

Abigail produced the brig's papers. She felt odd about it, for her father's instruction to tell all of New Bedford that he had sold her the brig seemed so strange. Obed Cambridge, however, seemed to see nothing unusual about it. In fact, he seemed struck with admiration.

"That's shrewd, by thunder," he said, pulling his whiskers and nodding his head. His face, Abby saw with amazement, held respect. Would all of New Bedford be similarly admiring? Did all of New England esteem those who owned ships? "Aye," said Obed to Mr. West, and chuckled. "'Tis certainly possible for her to own a brig, and she does, by thunder, she does — and all for the sum of one dollar!"

"How very remarkable," said Mrs. Cambridge, looking from the papers to Abby and back. Her expression, too, held an unusual approval: the ownership of a valuable vessel, it seemed, had made Abby herself more valuable. Was this why her father had done it, so the Mitchells would respect her?

The Mitchells. Later that day Abigail escaped from the sewing and hunted for Mr. West. After all, she thought, he might have teased her unmercifully, but he hadn't ratted. She even felt a little friendly towards him, as if by his silence he had made them comrades of sorts. She found him at work on his boat, and said, "Tell me, do you think that William Mitchell was as bad as the gossip made him out to be?"

"Worse," he said, as objectionable as ever. "Crazy as a bedbug, and no doubt about it."

Abby bit her lip. "Are they all like that, the Mitchells?"

Consider West hesitated. They were on the main deck, and above Abby's head the main course creaked. The ship plunged and rose evenly, eating up the miles in perfect whole-sail weather.

Then he mumbled, "I can't really claim to know 'em. Jireh Mitchell..."

He broke off, as if the topic of William Mitchell's brother made him uncomfortable, and bent to hammer a nail into a warped cedar plank.

If Abby had been on the *Pandora* she would have helped by holding the turning iron to bend the nail as it came through the wood. Instead, with foreboding, she said in a low voice, "Is Jireh Mitchell bucko, too?"

Mr. West stood up and pursed his lips, looking reflectively up at the rigging. The watch was busy aloft, unbending light sails on the foremast and bending on the heavy ones, readying the ship for Cape Horn and its ice and its gales. Abby's nights in the rigging were numbered, as the *Erasmus* forged swiftly sou'sou'east.

"Oh, Jireh Mitchell is a handsome, jovial fellow," Mr. West declared. "A dear boy for the gals." And he smirked at having fooled her.

Exasperated, Abby walked to the taffrail and looked moodily at the foaming wake. The bubbling green trail led all the way to New Zealand, far over the horizon. Jireh

Mitchell handsome? A dear boy for the girls? It was impossible to believe it.

Involuntarily, however, she imagined him, this cousin she had never met. Black-haired, she thought, blue-eyed and broad-shouldered, a tall, romantic, swashbuckling figure who amazed the world with his flamboyant ways. Then, with a lurch, she remembered the murder. Jireh Mitchell did not know that his brother was dead. He might not hear for months, or years. Letters often went astray in their progress from ship to ship in the wide Pacific.

Seth Morgan did not like writing letters, and Obed hated being the bearer of bad news. Jireh Mitchell might not hear the terrible story until the day he arrived back in New Bedford — to find Abigail staying at his parents' house.

Five

In early March, in longitude 125, in the Tropic of Capricorn, Seth made a landfall at Capricorn Island. From the sea it looked very beautiful. The slopes of the mountainous interior were covered thickly with trees, and the coral-sand shores were rimmed with graceful palms. The placid lagoon looked enticing, but when the *Pierrot* was still a mile off Seth ordered the ship luffed by the wind and studied the shore through his spyglass.

There was only one gap in the broad reef that circled the island, and that gap was very narrow, perhaps only one hundred feet—one ship's length—wide. The surf was high, thrown up into great fifty-foot sprays as the weight of the Pacific hit the coral wall. Beyond the reef three whalers were anchored in the calm lagoon, but Seth still hesitated. With a strong on-shore wind any ships there could be helplessly windbound, trapped for weeks or even months while they waited for a change. All Seth's professional instincts warned him that that could very easily happen. Furthermore, the reef was so broad and the gap so narrow that a wind shift while the ship was maneuvering out of the lagoon could send the ship crashing onto the reef. It happened all the time, in the savage Pacific, so often that the loss of a vessel on a reef because of bad piloting or a wind change merited less than a column in the dry reporting of the New Bedford whalemen's shipping paper.

The gap was deep, however; the sea had no chance to form a comber. Those three whalers, obviously, had made the passage safely. Seth could see the distant thin lace of a tumbling waterfall on the slopes of the island, and the *Pierrot* was desperately short of fresh water. Ordering the after yards squared, he strode forward to join the lookout in the bow.

As he stood between the knightheads, Seth could hear orders given behind him to ready the anchor for dropping. The jibboom pointed directly at the passage. Then, as the ship's momentum impelled her onwards, the jagged clumps of coral loomed on either side. The top of the reef was as broad and flat as a highway, a gleaming, pitted gray expanse glimpsed through the dashing spray. The smooth water of the lagoon beckoned.

Seth shouted, "Haul up the fores'l."

"Aye, sir!"

"Jibs!"

"Aye, sir!"

The ship slid forward, slowing as the weight of canvas left the wind. One of the anchored vessels was almost dead ahead. Then there was an inviting space, and then a headland. As the *Pierrot* entered the bay beyond, the other two vessels were hidden behind the outcrop of land. Canoes gathered around the *Pierrot*, paddled by muscular warriors.

"Starboard the wheel."

"Starboard the helm, sir!"

The air was full of the scent of vegetation and warm fertile dirt. The men in the canoes broke into a chant that Seth hoped was a song of welcome.

"Brace up tops'ls!"

"Tops'ls, sir!"

Seth waited. Then, "Hard to starboard the wheel." He heard the echo from the man at the helm.

"Clew up tops'ls."

"Aye, sir. Stand by the anchor, there!"

The flukes, reddened with rust, plunged down, wetted for the first time since leaving the mud of New Zealand. The lagoon rippled and then stilled, as glassy as a millpond, so clear that Seth could see coral sand four fathoms below.

A canoe paddled up to the martingale chains and powerful hands hoisted a wizened old man up to the jib-boom. The old fellow scrambled the rest of the way to the foredeck by himself. He was almost toothless and very bowlegged, and his skin was scaly. He wore a loincloth and many strings of sharks' teeth.

"Cap'n," he said to Seth, and then explained in rapid confident broken English that he was chief minister to the local chief. No, he regretted that there was no American consul here, or any white men at all, apart from the visiting sailors. Then he stated his business. Seth had to establish his credentials by buying a bushel of yams from the king. For ten dollars, the old man said, grinning.

He meant the big silver Chilean dollars. Amazed that coins were the currency here, Seth paid over without comment, and the money disappeared like magic in the folds of the loincloth. Seth guessed he would never see a sign of the yams; the natives, he mused, had learned about the white man's duties and taxes.

"Now," declared the old man, "you trade with the people, plenty. And tomorrow you come see the chief."

Seth agreed that he would pay the king a call, and then, with shrewdness that would have done a New Bedford crimp credit, the old man began to dicker for tobacco and guns. Seth admitted that he had tobacco, but he had no intention of making future visits to Capricorn hazardous by dealing in arms. The old man did not seem disappointed. "We have wood to trade, plenty nice water," he said.

"Native men carry, you pay tobacco, not much, just a little. Sea slugs, pearl shell. Bananas, yes, very good coconuts, pigs — mats, hats."

The other captains were very happy with their trade, he communicated. Then he told Seth the names of the other ships and their captains. One of them was the *Lizzie Ann*, commanded by Captain Jireh Mitchell, who had been very happy with what was offered.

Seth said, "Goddammit!" Jireh Mitchell certainly did not know that his brother was dead: he was fated, Seth brooded, to be the bearer of bad news.

Looking alarmed, the old man queried, "Missionary man on ship?"

Seth shook his head, wondering why the fellow asked.

"Wife, perhaps? Lady down in cabin?"

Seth shook his head again, puzzled, and the old man, looking highly relieved, offered him a girl.

"Goddammit, no," said Seth, and sent the fellow packing. Then, scowling, he ordered the starboard boat lowered.

The *Lizzie Ann* was one of the two ships on the other side of the headland. She was the *Pierrot*'s sister ship, so Seth studied her curiously as his boat pulled towards her. My God, he thought, the *Lizzie Ann* was only one year older than the *Pierrot*, but she looked more than ten years worse. He would not have thought it possible. Her black varnish had worn in patches to a leprous gray; her chains were rusty and her yards were unpainted. She made the *Pierrot* look almost decent.

There seemed to be no one at all on board. Seth reached out, grabbed a dangling boat fall, and shouted, "Ship ahoy," but there was no reply.

Water chuckled about the boxlike hull. The breeze from the shore was humid and scented with flowers, and tiny bright fish nibbled at the blade of Seth's oar. The noon sun was very hot, and he was sweating under the prickly weight of his broadcloth gamming suit.

Then, just as Seth was about to give the order to return to the *Pierrot*, a man materialized on the roof of the hurricane house. He was a tall slim sailor, so deeply tanned that his fair hair seemed yellow and his moustache quite white. His face was stubbled with short silvery whiskers. Bare feet and ankles stuck out of the bottoms of baggy black pants; his long shirt glittered with gold-thread and bright silk, and was caught at the hips with a thin gold sash. Seth stared, dumbfounded. He had never seen Jireh Mitchell before, but this exotic figure bore no resemblance whatsoever to either Jezekiel or William.

"Captain Mitchell?" he said cautiously.

The other fetched a deep bow. "And your name, sir?"

"Morgan."

"My God," cried Jireh Mitchell. He clapped one hand to his chest. "A pirate! A Morgan buccaneer!"

Seth winced, thinking that passing on bad news to this clown was going to be an even greater challenge than feared. "Seth Morgan," he elaborated, adding, "ship *Pierrot*."

"*Pierrot?*" Mitchell visibly started, and then came forward to study Seth with lively interest. "Jehovah," he said, with every appearance of sympathy, "we're brother mariners and fellow sufferers, and I take off my hat to you, sir."

He had no hat to take off. Seth paused, and then said, "I have a message for you."

"From the pen o' my father?"

"Ah ... no."

"Then thank God for that. Come aboard, Captain Morgan!"

Jireh Mitchell's transom cabin was as unconventional as he was. The sofa was draped with a huge American flag and bales of Chinese brocade served as footstools. Jireh Mitchell waved a hospitable hand at the chair by the chart desk, saying in hopeful tones, "The message is good?"

"Unfortunately, no."

"I was afraid o' that." He paused, but when Seth opened his mouth, Jireh said hastily, "Not yet, please, Captain Morgan! A drink, first — to prepare the way, so to speak."

Seth watched as Mitchell poured a fine French brandy into dusty cut-crystal glasses. This was William Mitchell's brother? Jezekiel Mitchell's son? It didn't seem possible. Jireh smiled all the time, as if he had been smiling coaxingly and winningly since the moment he'd been born. Seth abruptly remembered what Obed had said about Jezekiel Mitchell's whippings. Was this how Jireh had avoided the floggings, with this constant charming and apologetic smile?

Jireh perched on the sofa, one bare foot propped on a bale of brocade, the other tucked beneath him. He looked like an Oriental nabob.

Mitchell said, "I presume your report is excellent?"

"Just over fifteen hundred barrels. Sperm."

Fifteen hundred. The words rolled off Seth's tongue. His greasy luck had held. Ten more months the same as the last and he'd be back in New Bedford.

"Excellent!" Jireh said warmly. "The heartiest congratulations. My father will be most gratified. The *Lizzie Ann*," he said, and his brown eyes took on a light of laughter, "is clean."

Clean? No oil taken? What a misnomer, Seth thought, glancing around: the cabin, like the rest of the ship, was grubby. The old *Lizzie Ann* radiated flamboyant squalor.

Jireh Mitchell twinkled, reading his thoughts. He said, "We have no steward."

"No?"

"The first one, a Portuguese, deserted at Canton. Then the Chinese replacement I shipped in Manila couldn't be found, not anywhere at all. We thought he'd gone overboard."

Canton? So that, thought Seth, accounted for the silk brocade cloth. He eyed the bale that served Mitchell for a footstool, remembering the old native man's mention of pearl shell and sea slugs. What other trade was Mitchell doing? Tea? Chinese porcelain? Holds filled with such exotic cargoes meant no room for mincing up blubber and storing casks of oil. All Mitchell's men were on shore, it seemed: were they smoking bêche-de-mer—sea slugs, sold at high prices as a Chinese tonic for virility in the Manila market? What the devil kind of whaling voyage was this?

"Then behold," quoth Jireh, "we found him."

"Who? The Chinese steward?"

"Aye. He was down in the run." Mitchell's long finger indicated the small afterhold beneath the cabin floor. "I had a small cargo stowed down there, on my own account, you understand—boxes of cigars, chocolate, raisins, indigo, preserved ginger, delicacies in jars. The rapscallion steward had shut himself in with them," he said, and a note of outrage tinged his tone, "and was living the life o' a sultan. There were a few some barrels o' brandy and Madeira, too, and he'd equipped himself with a straw. Now, I have no steward, for I discharged the rascal here. He's probably setting up a village chophouse."

Seth couldn't help it: a bark of laughter escaped him. Mitchell was a rascal himself. How the devil was he going to tell him that his brother had been foully murdered?

He asked, "Do you do much of this Oriental trading?"

"I often think, Captain Morgan, that I was born into the wrong generation."

Seth sipped pensively. Jireh was right, he thought: he would have fitted better in the flamboyant hordes of traders who set out from Salem late last century, shaking in their seaboots but somehow surviving the hostile Orient, coming home with fabulous cargoes, like treasures in an Arabian legend.

"I vastly prefer it to whaling," Jireh candidly admitted. "It takes uncommon courage to chase and kill the greatest fish in the sea, Captain Morgan, and a strong stomach to face the filthy hard work afterwards—just so my father and merchants like him can reap huge profits and make their fortunes. A bloody business, don't you agree?"

Seth stared. He had been whaling since he was eleven years old; he had never thought about it. Abruptly, he felt uncomfortable, almost as if he were a gullible fool, and he drained his glass to hide his face.

Jireh was watching him as closely as ever. "More brandy?"

Seth shook his head, mentally bracing himself. Clearing his throat, he said, "Captain Mitchell, I regret that I must inform you—"

The door to the captain's stateroom opened, and a doe-eyed girl came gliding in. She was about fifteen, brown and beautiful, with a great deal of bouncy black hair. Her smile was wide and friendly as she gazed admiringly at Seth. She was wrapped in a length of brightly patterned calico.

"This," said Jireh with a wink, "is the replacement for that Chinese rascal—my substitute steward. I've named her Mary, after a certain old biddy who lived in Boat Train Road. A neighbor, you understand. I used to steal her apples, and when she caught me she smacked me acrost the bum. It gives a certain spice to certain activities."

Seth was acutely embarrassed. The girl stood by Jireh, leaning on him and smiling cheerfully at Seth as her master caressed her round bottom. It was impossible to know if she understood.

Jireh said, "When you ship kanaka, how do you call them?"

Seth was silent, though he knew what Mitchell meant. When islanders were shipped on whalers, captains found it impossible to spell their native names, so gave them nicknames instead. Most were called something convenient, like Seth's own Tom Kanaka and Jim Savage, but some men, with a more robust and irreverent sense of humor, inflicted innocent islanders with names like Ruddi Scoundrel or Spun

Yarn.

"I call mine after the merchants of New Bedford," Jireh said. "It can make teaching them their seamanship an uncommon' amusing exercise, and swearing enjoyable." He chuckled, and stroked the girl's flank. "Have you completed your mite o' business with the king's minister?"

"If you mean have I paid my ten dollars, then the answer is yes."

"Ah. Did he offer you a girl?"

Seth flicked an eyebrow. "He seemed worried that I might have a wife on board."

"You don't, I trust?"

"I'm not married."

"And you would not have the lamentable lack o' judgment to carry one, if you had one."

It was obvious, Seth thought, that Jireh Mitchell would find a wife an encumbrance. He said, "I saw my cousin Obed Cambridge not long ago. He carries his wife and doesn't seem inconvenienced by her."

"And his report?"

"Excellent."

"Ah, then no wonder he's an advocate o' the strange custom. Undoubtedly he believes his wife brings him luck."

Could that be so? Seth was startled.

"And Obed Cambridge, if I know him — and I know him well — was never one for dallying with the dusky beauties." Jireh chuckled as his hand stroked the native girl's thigh, now fully exposed.

Seth looked away, and snapped, "Obed has a well-kept ship and an excellent report. His wife behaves admirably."

"Oh, I'm sure, I'm sure," said Jireh soothingly. His smile was apologetic. "No doubt," he murmured, "she keeps out o' his way when she's seasick."

"As far as I know, that has never been a problem."

"Lucky man! Or should I say, lucky woman. And no doubt he enjoys squiring her about on tourist viewing, and to proper portside functions. And," Jireh went on with a malicious glint, "he'll enjoy it even more when she concludes to litter, and in a dead calm, a hundred miles from a midwife."

Seth blinked. How had Jireh guessed? "That is a possibility," he admitted.

"What? His lady is with child?" Seth nodded, and Jireh guffawed. "How one would love to be a viewer o' the panic and commotion. Poor Obed! I spoke a merchantman once— she had a complement o' twenty-five passengers the day before we spoke, and twenty-six that morning. The captain was extreme grateful o' a glass o' good brandy. The lady who performed the miracle was the only female in the ship."

"Obed won't have that problem."

"Oh?"

"No. They carry a female passenger."

My God, Seth thought, was that why the Cambridges had made that apparently disinterested offer to carry Abigail Sherman? Mrs. Sherman had been known for her midwifery, he remembered.

He said slowly, "The passenger is your cousin."

"My—what?"

"Nathaniel Sherman's daughter. Abigail. Her father is sending her to live with your mother."

Silence. Mitchell's eyes were narrowed. "Sherman," he mused at last. "My mother's cousin. A bluff, noisy sort o' man, with a truly beautiful wife."

"She's dead. Sherman is a widower."

"So I heard." Mitchell's expression was regretful. "Red-haired," he said, "and vivacious. Spirited, as well as beautiful, with a radiant smile. I was fourteen when they sailed from New Bedford, and looking back, I do believe I was in love with her, in a calf-brained kind o' way, for I've had a weakness for redheads ever since. Is she pretty?"

"What?"

"Abigail."

Seth frowned. Unsettlingly, he remembered that Abigail had very pretty breasts. She had shown spirit, shouting at him there on the riverbank, wearing only a sodden shift.

Minx, he thought angrily. He had found her diverting when he'd first seen her. Like this rascal of a cousin, she was vivid. He fancied he saw a family resemblance.

He snapped, "She's redheaded, if that pleases you."

Jireh's eyebrows shot up. "Oh, it does, it does," he said in his apologetic way. "Though I doubt my father will relish having a pretty redheaded girl in his house, particularly if she is as spirited as her mother." Then he asked slyly, "Is that the message you have been trying so hard to deliver to me?"

"No, it is not! I've been trying to inform you as tactfully as possible that your brother is dead!"

The moment the words were out, Seth regretted them. Jireh's face had gone perfectly blank. Then he smacked the girl lightly on her hip, letting her wrap fall down again, and said, "Mary, go away."

When Seth arrived back at the *Pierrot* there were native men in the martingale chains and a babel of noise and movement on the deck. Native girls were swimming naked about the ship, and being hauled on board by their men.

Seth roared, "What the devil?" Then he sprang onto the deck himself, and ran forward, barging his furious way through a crowd that was plying a trade in women. The whole ship stank of lust. A grinning Jim Pott was giving a girl a small plug of tobacco with one hand, and shoving her toward the foc'sle with the other.

When Seth yelled, the woman dived overboard, shrieking, and Jim disappeared rapidly down the ladder. Within seconds three native men had been thrown over the bulwarks, and two dozen others had taken flight. Then Seth strode below to confront Mr. Leonard, who had been left in charge of the ship.

He was shuddering with rage. Jim Pott and two others had a venereal disease, and would not have been allowed on shore to infect the native women. My God, he thought incoherently, this was a problem that Cousin Cambridge was never forced to face. No wonder the old native had been so concerned that Seth might have a wife on board!

He arrived in the after quarters in a clatter of angry bootsteps, but Mr. Leonard did not hear him. His back was turned to Seth and he was busily and obliviously doing a native woman. As Seth arrived his stringy buttocks hammered a last time between her thighs, and he grunted in a high-pitched tone, and fell forward on the woman, panting. The woman stared at Seth over Leonard's shoulder. She jerked her hips to unseat the mate, beckoned to Seth, and said, "Tobak."

Seth's roar of fury rattled the deck planks. Ten minutes later there was not a native soul near the *Pierrot,* and the men were sullenly slushing masts and scraping yards. Other skippers allowed prostitution on board of their ships because they knew that if the men went onshore to find women they were more likely to run away — but Seth didn't care about that.

Goddammit, he didn't care if his men all ran away, as long as he got to Talcahuano first. My God, he thought, and stared at the island without seeing it, seeing in his mind instead the sedate afterquarters of the *Erasmus.* He would never, he thought with grim passion, see his ship a floating brothel again.

Before he left New Bedford again, he would take a wife — and take her to sea.

The *Erasmus* made the icy seas off Cape Horn thirty-five days after leaving the *Pierrot.* It was a month and four days of overhauling rigging and sails, of checking guys and back ropes, of reeving new braces and making new clewlines. By the time the *Erasmus* reached longitude ninety the crew had prepared themselves as well, with heavy clothes mended, and tarpaulin hats and rawhide boots generously coated with tar.

Four days off Tierra del Fuego the ship was laboring in a heavy sea, and the decks were constantly wet. The *Erasmus* dug in her prow because of her heavy cargo. The men slept in damp bedding and woke up to choose the least wet of their clothes to wear on deck. Nevertheless every manjack of the crew was content. They were all—except Abby—going home.

"Home, sweet home," said Mrs. Cambridge, contemplatively stitching tiny gowns. She and Abigail had long since been driven out of the room in the deckhouse into the transom cabin. "I can hardly realize," she said, sedately adjusting her now considerable weight as the *Erasmus* pitched, "that three years have passed on our little wooden home. Verily, time waits for no man. As one ages," she declared from her pinnacle of twenty-five years, "one finds that years pass as rapidly as months did in one's childhood. Before we know it, we will all be safely home, delivered to that cherished spot that lingers in our hearts."

Abby was silent, her head bent over the red square of flannel she was hemming. Home seemed impossibly far away, and she was struggling with claustrophobia. She had never spent so much time below decks before, and the sound of the sea and the pitching of the vessel gave her a headache and made her nervous. Whenever she could find an excuse, she wrapped herself up in her seal-lined cloak and went on deck, where the tumult of sea and wind and orders was comprehensible and reassuring. Here she knew that everything was under control. The rigging was stiff with frost, and the wind was icy, but nevertheless she stopped up on deck as long as she could.

Off Cape Horn the sky and sea were the color of steel. The bow dug deeply, and the *Erasmus* seemed reluctant to rise and shed the tons of water on her decks. Obed looked alert, standing holding on to the mizzen shrouds, his whiskers jutting as he probed the weather. The wind was hauling aft, and water splashed over the taffrail. Two men were sweating with their shoulders to the wheel, and the waves had pools of foaming white on their flanks. There was no sun, just the ominous metallic under-shine to the racing clouds. Obed ordered the mizzen topsail furled and the fore and main topsails double-reefed. An hour later the main topsail was close-reefed and the foresail furled. The gale was in the increase. Abigail was sent back to the after cabin.

It was very dark below. The lamps dashed back and forth on their hooks. Every dish and spoon was on the move. Supper was a hurried affair of holding on with one hand and eating cold food with the other. It was too noisy to talk. Bootsteps hurried back and forth above on deck, and the rigging whistled with the rising wind. The officers ate hurriedly, with one eye on the barometer; Obed did not come down at all.

The barometer stood at 29.25 and was falling. It was cold but too rugged to light a fire in the cabin stove. By eleven that night the mercury had fallen to 28.10. All the sidelights were shut and battened down, and Abby was struggling with claustrophobia again. Mrs. Cambridge had gone to bed, the big swinging bed in the captain's stateroom — the best place, in her condition.

At midnight the *Erasmus* shipped a sea that swept away the bow boat. Abby heard the crash, incoherent shouting and the urgent thud of running boots. She couldn't help it — she scrambled up the companion stairs, much of the way on hands and knees, and staggered through the door at the top.

The *Erasmus* was lying to, under a fore topmast staysail and main spencer, her head to the wind. The gale was tremendous. The ship was pitching her head down and then settling her stern with a crash. The whole of the vessel shuddered with each concussion, and blocks squealed. The waves rolled in from an endless night, spume at their tops beaten by the wind to a horizontal steam. The men were struggling to lash down the waist boat, bottom-up on the tryworks. Their heads were down as they struggled against the wind and the pitch of the decks. A wave reared up out of the night and smashed over the foredeck as the bow dug in.

Abby dodged backwards and slammed the door in the face of the wave—but too late. She half fell, half stumbled down the stairs, and a foaming waterfall came with her. When she helped the steward mop up they lurched into a bulkhead or a locker with every pitch of the ship.

Surely Mrs. Cambridge must be terrified, listening uncomprehending to the commotion? It was bad enough for Abigail, who knew something about what was being done to save the ship and their lives. When the steward went back to his steerage quarters, Abby retired to her berth. It was hard work to stay in her bed. She could only do it by lying on her stomach and digging in her feet and right hand between the mattress and the bulkheads. Tremendous seas crashed only inches from her head and the walls streamed with water. Then, in a tiny lull, Abby heard a groan.

It came from the captain's stateroom. Abigail unhooked her feet and arm and fell out of her bunk and down the two steps. She grabbed a shawl, dragged it on over her nightgown, thrust her feet into wet boots, and snatched a lamp from the transom cabin. When she stumbled into the captain's stateroom Mrs. Cambridge's white, strained face looked up at her.

With a lurch of horrified comprehension, Abby realized that Mrs. Cambridge's time had come. It had been obvious for weeks that she was in a delicate condition, but the pregnancy had never been mentioned. It had been impossible to ask what Captain Cambridge's plans were— though surely he must have taken advice? But now Captain Cambridge was on deck, and it was impossible to summon him. His responsibility was the ship.

Abby whispered, "Oh, dear merciful heavens."

Trembling, she hung the lamp on a hook. Mrs. Cambridge shut her eyes convulsively, and her breathing became fast and ragged. She shuddered for a long moment while the bed swung, and then that awful little mewing groan of pain escaped her again. Mrs. Cambridge was cold and sweating and in labor, and Abby had not a notion what she should do for her.

She thought of all the times her mother had taken her along for a birthing. Her job had been to carry towels and squares of sheeting for receiving the baby. Inspired, she pulled open drawers and lockers, stumbling as the ship pitched and the bed swung back and forth. She couldn't ask Mrs. Cambridge where things were stowed, because it was impossible to hear a word over the din of sea and tortured rigging. The sounds of the ship and the storm overwhelmed everything except those little moans of distress as each pain reached its peak.

Then she realized that the pains were coming about every four minutes. That was what Abby's mother had always asked when she had arrived at the patient's house: how far apart were the pains? Four minutes, Abby thought apprehensively, probably meant that the matter was becoming urgent. Articles of clothing fell out of the lockers as the ship rolled; she grabbed towels and flannel squares, thrust the rest back and slammed the doors, timing her movements to the lurching of the ship.

The bed swung so violently now that its side hit the deck with every starboard lurch. Abby, with her armload of linen, clambered onto it. Mrs. Cambridge winced, but the bed, with extra weight, settled. The rhythmic slamming stopped. Mrs. Cambridge shut her eyes with another contraction, and Abby, with dim memories of her mother, shuffled about on hands and knees and rubbed the small of Mrs. Cambridge's back. It helped, her mother had said; she had often said wryly that a woman's wage was an aching back, and it was up to other women to soothe it.

To Abigail's amazement, it worked. Mrs. Cambridge sighed and relaxed and murmured thanks. It became a kind of routine, a pattern of a pain beginning, Mrs. Cambridge whimpering, and an energetic rubbing of the poor tortured back, going on forever, through a terrifying night.

Obed—she heard Obed. With a gasp of relief she heard his bootsteps coming down the stairs. His gruff voice hollered out, "Hey, how's she doing?"

What could she say? *Oh, please, your wife, she's in pain, and I'm scared to death because I've never been trapped below before during a storm, and I've never been present at a birth.* Then, while her frantic mind was framing words, the mate's voice called back, "She ain't moved a hair."

They were talking about the barometer. Abby could have wept. She heard Obed turn and go back up the stairs.

Mrs. Cambridge rolled over onto her back, braced her bent knees, and groaned on a different note. Oh, God, what was happening? Mrs. Cambridge seemed to be off in a hardworking heedless world of her own, deaf to anxious questions.

At seven in the morning a sea broke over the *Erasmus* forward, and carried off bowsprit, topgallant mast, and all the rigging that went with it. The crash was deafening. The bed swung and the ship lurched and Abby, trembling violently, found a squalling infant in her outstretched hands.

Abby shrieked and the baby shrieked back. Then, gathering her wits, she grabbed a flannel napkin. The infant was most terrifyingly slippery. It was ... a girl.

Victoria had her head back, sweat on her face, and to Abby's distress she bore down again. The afterbirth gushed out and for a dreadful moment Abby thought she was going to be sick. Victoria was sighing with relief. Then she opened her eyes and lifted her head and looked at her baby—and smiled.

One hour later Abby went up on deck to tell Obed that he was a father. Victoria and baby were both asleep, tidily arranged in a tidy clean bed. The medical books had told Abby how to tie the cord, and how to clean up. Now she felt drained and weak, with a deep exhausted conviction that she would never be the same girl again. Obed, by contrast, was jubilant. He thought he and his wife were amazingly clever, and that Abigail Sherman had done quite well, too.

"We'll call her Abigail," he boomed. The deck was a grim sight, littered with rigging and damaged spars, but the storm was over. The watch was aloft, taking down the main topgallant mast. The sea was still rugged, but a watery light suffused the world.

"I don't think so," Victoria said firmly later.

Abigail said hopefully, "Pandora?"

"Emily, after my poor deceased mother, who would have celebrated this day."

"Emily Erasmus Cambridge," said Obed smugly.

At that moment, Abby felt reluctant admiration. Obed looked battle-worn, and the waves still marched like jackknives over the horizon, but he had brought the ship through. And Victoria—Victoria had groaned, but she had never once complained. Now that Abby had had a chance to read the midwifery sections of her two medical books, she was horrified by all the things that could have gone wrong. In Victoria's situation, in a storm, giving birth, Abby would have been scared out of her wits. It had been bad enough being a helpless spectator.

"Weren't you frightened?" she said later.

Victoria was nursing, looking down proudly as the baby tugged at one plump breast. "Frightened?" she said. She didn't even stop to think. "Of course I wasn't frightened — how could I be scared? I knew at every moment that our little wooden home was in the very best of hands."

Mrs. Cambridge may have thought that with the production of little Emily a fine job was well and truly done, but Abby found that her work had only just started.

The medical books declared that hemorrhage and puerperal fever and other appalling things were very likely to occur if the new mother did not lie flat for at least three days, and remain in bed a full two weeks after that. The books did not say who was supposed to do all the washing and changing and settling of baby in a little swinging cot between nursing times, but obviously that person had to be Abigail herself.

So, while the decks of the *Erasmus*, like the weather, cleared, Abby smoothed pillows, brought soothing foods, and did endless, endless washing. Men on deck cleaned ship, set up new ratlines, painted yards and the hull outside, and slushed and tarred and scrubbed and whitewashed, but all Abby saw of it was what she could glimpse when she hung all that washing out. She crossed the Equator for the very first time in her life, and no one even noticed.

By the time Victoria could take a daily walk on deck, they were far enough from the Line for the weather to be pleasant. The horizon was dotted with vessels, trudging south or flying homewards. Abigail carried the baby and said apprehensively, "What is New Bedford like?"

"Large," said Victoria. She smiled; her expression held understanding, as if she knew full well that the thought of a large city would intimidate a girl from the tiny settlement of Mangonui. "Quite twenty thousand people, and the most prosperous city of its size in the whole of the world."

Prosperous — on the whale oil and bone that the ships brought in from the broad Pacific. Right whales caught off New Zealand had financed mansions in County Street. And schools, said Victoria — only they were called *lyceums* — and libraries, which were called *athenaeums.* The names were supposed to be impressive, and Abby, unwillingly, was impressed. The Cambridge family, Victoria told her with demure satisfaction, lived in County Street; the Cambridge family was wealthy. Obed's father had a partnership in a bank, and he and Obed had the entire ownership of the whaleship *Erasmus* and her buster cargo of oil. Now they would be richer than ever.

Obed was an only child, the heir to all this. When he had married, just weeks before he and Victoria had sailed, the entire second floor of the mansion had been made over to them. It was like a whole house, with a front parlor and a balcony, two large bedrooms, and facilities. Obed's mother, the redoubtable Mrs. Fanny, lived in her own apartments on the floor below. Mrs. Fanny wrote for the papers and believed in Women's Rights. Her views, said Victoria, were inspired by a young woman who lived next door, one Martha Cady. Martha Cady lived with her widower father, who, unfortunately, found it amusing that his daughter was a *blue-stocking*.

A what? Abby had never heard the word before, and Victoria had to explain. But, as Victoria confided as the days wore on, Mrs. Fanny had always been formidable. In her prime she had been a supporter of President Andrew Jackson: Mrs. Fanny believed, said Victoria, that President Jackson's ideas concerning the great worth of the common American working man applied to women, too. Abby found it almost impossible to believe that Obed and Victoria had someone so disreputable in their background. Was that why Victoria had agreed to sail?

All at once they were in the Gulf Stream. At nine in the morning the temperature of the water was over seventy degrees and half an hour later it was only sixty; but Abby was the only one to find that remarkable. For all the others it was just a sign that they were mere days away from New Bedford. Gulfweed bumped against the sides of the ship, and the men scooped it up and exclaimed merrily over the signs of home they saw there: crabs, and shrimp, and tiny drab fish.

In latitude 35°25′ north, the ship was as bright and clean as the day she'd left home, and the men carried out a very strange ritual. All hands set to tearing down the bricks of the tryworks furnace. The big iron pots were scoured and scrubbed, turned upside down, and lashed to the deck. Then the men waited, poised.

All heads were turned to Captain Cambridge. He was standing by the mizzenmast, his expression benign. Then— "Throw them over, boys," he sang out, and a race commenced to be the first to throw a brick overboard. It was always done, as Consider West informed Abby while all the men relished the celebratory issue of grog—except perhaps on some of the scruffier Atlantic whalers. The bricks were discarded at this spot, and a new furnace was built before the next voyage. Abby imagined a pile at the bottom of the Atlantic Ocean, growing a little more with every homebound vessel. Would the pile ever reach the surface and make a tryworks atoll? Obed Cambridge guffawed at this and put up a bounty of a bottle of wine for the first man to raise Block Island.

The landmark was raised at eight next morning, on Abigail's sixteenth birthday.

Six

The ship was oddly silent as the crew lined the rails. Abby wondered what they were thinking. Three years would have brought change that perhaps some were scared to contemplate: many of the men might not have heard from home at all. Children might be dead, or born, brothers run off to sea, sweethearts snapped up by other men. Some of the crew lived outside New Bedford and had to catch the cars or the stage to find what news was in store for them. Others were transient citizens and would have a short exultant holiday before shipping quickly again. But none of them, she thought, could be half as scared as she was.

The big sand heap of Block Island was on the port bow, six or seven miles away, its hillocks dabbed with green. Buzzards Bay was dead ahead; and Cuttyhunk, Newport with its jetties and mansions; and the great bluffs of Gay Head. Then Sakonnet, Nasha Wona, Hen and Chickens, Acushnet: Obed pointed them all out and told her the names, and it was like a poem to his home.

A small boat ran out to them, and Obed ordered the ship luffed to, so they could take on the pilot. Abby's bags were packed. It was a sunny spring day — spring, in April! — but she hugged her cloak about her. Her cheeks felt numb.

The pilot clambered aboard and then the ship kept on her course, thrusting through the choppy glitter of the water with her braces taut and her canvas creaking. "The gals of New Bedford are pulling us home," said Obed, and the pilot laughed as if he had not heard the saying a thousand times before. Then the two went briefly below. When they came back they smelled of brandy.

Abigail listened silently to the pilot's three years' worth of gossip as he told it to Obed. In January a carpenter by the name of James Wilson Marshall had found a great lode of gold at Sutter's Mill in California, and for the last three weeks the papers had been full of it, gold was on everyone's lips; the captain of the ship *Christopher Mitchell* had discovered a female sailor on board; and there was a cholera epidemic in south America. Abby hardly heard a word of it. She was staring at the rush of traffic on Buzzards Bay and the Acushnet River; at the multitude of craft tacking busily back and forth. Palmer's Island, Clark's Point light, Fairhaven, New Bedford, smoke in the blue spring sky, and whaleships, at anchor, moored to wharves, hove down in the disarray of repair, or loading or discharging, or, in the distance, a-building. It was too much to comprehend.

The pilot and Obed had broken off their gam to holler instructions, and the men were leaping about on deck and in the yards, bunting up and furling:

Oh, down the starboard side of Union Street
Lives a gal so young and fair...

Union Street and Centre Street lay before Abby in a welter of buildings and flags and smoking chimneys. Carryalls and carriages rattled in the streets, and sirens hooted. There were mansions in the distance, with cupolas on their roofs that glittered like diamonds.

The men on the yards scrabbled up canvas for the very

last time.

> *Oh, pray we, may we never never be*
> *Leave her, Johnny, leave her*
> *She's a winsome witch, oh, the likes of she*
> *But it's time for us to leave her!*

They were singing about the ship. The *Erasmus* slowed and slowed ... curtseyed to the town that had given her birth, and then waited, majestically, to be hauled into the end of Merrill's Wharf.

There was a great brick building at the head of the wharf. The air was full of the commotion and smoke of prosperity. The very wind smelled of wealth — of oil and salt and smoke. Oil casks lay in complacent rows on the great squared timbers of the jetty.

Suddenly the ship was invaded by a ferrety crowd of furtive men in caps. They shoved everywhere, on deck and below, hunting down sailors, each shouting coercions louder than the others, offering lodging, grog, whores, blandishments, their fingers snagging the shirts of poor confused boys who'd been accustomed to a quiet sea and a silent horizon.

"They call them crimps, or runners," said Obed. "The boardinghouse-keepers and the agents send them out on commission, but their true name is land shark, and they're a deal worse than the sea variety." Abigail believed him. The crew had to shove the crimps aside so they could furl the last sails. The sharks even invaded the pantry, as if salt beef that had doubled Cape Horn more than once was a delicate dish, to be stolen and prized.

Then, all at once, the ship was empty. All the men had gone, and the land sharks with them. The alleyways around Union Street and Centre Street had gulped them up. Only the Cambridge family was left on board. Abby was given the baby to hold, and she cuddled the little girl apprehensively.

Where would she sleep tonight? Her bedding was

packed in a bundle. And, how would she know Jezekiel Mitchell, when—if—he came to fetch her?

A carriage rattled onto the wharf through the thinning crowd. Abby's heart bumped. A short fleshy man clambered out and strode quickly over, leaving an elderly coachman to take care of the horses. Was this Mr. Mitchell? He had a tall hat, a gray suit, and bushy white whiskers. When he walked onto the deck and looked about, she knew he was, for the resemblance was unmistakable: this was Obed Cambridge's banker-merchant father.

The two men shook hands and slapped each other many times on the back, exchanging loud, bluff congratulations on the success of the voyage. Victoria received a benevolent kiss on the cheek. For Abigail there was nothing but an eyebrow-wagging look, when Mr. Cambridge came over to inspect the baby.

Obed assisted Victoria down the gangway and across the wharf to the carriage. Abigail followed them, simply because she was holding the baby. She didn't know what she was expected to do, and half thought she'd be sharply told to wait on the ship.

Then, when she handed her up to Victoria, the baby woke up and began to scream. Victoria frowned and said to Abby, "Come on, get in." She gave Emily back before Abby was even really settled, saying, "Why does she cry so?"

The baby howled piteously, her little arms threshing about, real tears streaming down her little crumpled face. When the carriage rocked as Obed and his father got in, the crying hesitated but then redoubled. Then the carriage lurched and set off, and little Emily silenced again. Timbers thundered under the wheels, and cobblestones jolted the carriage. When they turned into Union Street the *Erasmus* was abruptly out of sight, and Abby felt like crying, herself.

On either side were awning-fronted shops, a commotion of silversmiths, hatters, tailors, saddle-makers, and the sidewalks were crowded with swells strolling past all the bow-fronted windows, tapping canes and shouting over the thunder of traffic, escorting bell-skirted ladies. Victoria, her face pressed to the carriage curtains, exclaimed about changes in fashion.

Abby hardly heard her. She was straining to listen to Obed's father, who was clicking his tongue and shaking his head, and saying, "Dear lord, what a business." They were talking about the murder, she was certain.

Obed shook his head, too. "Aye, indeed."

"This is the first I have heard of it. Mitchell undoubtedly believes his son still alive."

Obed sighed and added, "And does not know the girl is coming."

"You carry a letter?"

"Two. One from Nathaniel Sherman—about the girl, begging their indulgence. And the other from our cousin Seth Morgan, with the news of the murder."

There was a long pause, and then Mr. Cambridge cleared his throat. "It ... ah ... appears to be your responsibility to break the news."

Obed said glumly, "Yes."

"At the same time that you deliver the girl."

The street was running uphill. Mansions were all about them, all with rows of sixteen-paned windows, and pillared porticos in front. The houses were set in grounds of thick spring grass, with fences made of pickets, or of iron railings shaped like harpoons. The was no smell of oil here, just the evidence of the wealth it brought.

The carriage hesitated, and then turned into the entrance of one of the grandest houses. The portico had four sets of triple columns and a broad flight of steps.

Obed said to his father, "I'll send the letters by a man," just as the carriage lurched to a stop. The baby abruptly started screaming again. Otherwise, it was silent. A squat woman in a black gown and lace cap was waiting at the top of the steps.

The coachman dismounted and opened the carriage door. Victoria said, "Thank you, Thomas," and descended on her husband's arm. The woman in black came down the steps to meet her, walking slowly and heavily with the aid of a cane.

This, it seemed, was the notorious Mrs. Fanny, Obed's mother, because she and Victoria kissed each other on the cheek. Abby, carefully holding the baby, mortifyingly close to tears, descended the carriage and looked up, to meet a pair of small, sharp, very shrewd eyes, that looked her up and down. But instead of saying anything, the woman led the way inside.

It took a whole ten minutes before Mrs. Fanny addressed her first words to her. Then she bellowed, "I was acquainted with your mother—another Fanny!"

They were in Mrs. Fanny's private parlor downstairs, and Abby was still holding the yelling baby. Victoria had neglected to tell Abby that her mother-in-law was deaf; she had had to deduce it for herself. Mrs. Fanny shouted all the time—perhaps, thought Abigail, in a hint to her listeners that they were to shout right back.

She took a big breath, braced herself, and yelled, "My mother's name was Frances!"

Victoria winced. Mrs. Fanny took her trumpet out of her ear, looked at it, shook it, and then rapped her own head with a sharp slap of her knuckles. "There's no need to scream, girl!" Abby bit her lip, and Mrs. Fanny shouted, "Frances, Fanny, what's the difference? A modish name in its time, it was—Fanny Kemble, Fanny Wright. Then Fanny Trollope spoiled the game!"

Abby blinked. Was Mrs. Fanny mad, as well as deaf? She said, "Fanny ... who?"

"Fanny Trollope is an English girl, and she has no warmth in her heart for President Jackson, bless his name. She wrote about the manners of common Americans, trying to change us with her fastidious carping. For who supported the president's stand? The common salt of America, you mark what I say — cursing, sweating pioneer folk, not fine-mannered men and pernickety women! Now, if men curse or spit on the floor, other folk cry, *A Trollope! A Trollope!* And it serves the interfering woman right!"

Abigail stared, completely at a loss for a reply. Victoria was sitting very straight in her chair, her lips pressed together, and the baby cried and cried.

"Your mother was Fanny, and I remember the talk when she sailed off," Mrs. Fanny roared on. "A pretty red-haired lass like you, and people swore she went about in trousers."

Abby flinched. For a horrid moment she thought that Mrs. Fanny had somehow deduced that she had spent most of her childhood in dungaree pants — which had been only practical, on board ship.

She shouted, "My mother wore skirts!" Angry tears stung her eyes; she was at the end of her tether, on the verge of wailing like the baby. "Even in the tropics she wore a dress," she cried. "And I don't care a pin what people here said, for they're wrong! She held no nonsense about four flannel petticoats in a hundred degrees on the Equator, just because it was winter in New England — but my mother wore a gown!"

Mrs. Sherman had not worn petticoats at all — she had worn dungaree or calico pants under her skirt instead, because, she said, it was more modest and more convenient. But Abby didn't mention that: she merely stared challengingly at Mrs. Fanny. Victoria had her hand over her eyes.

Mrs. Fanny seemed most confounded. She shook her ear trumpet, and muttered, "One day all females will be habited in trousers — President Jackson would have ruled upon it, if he'd thought of it."

Abby blinked at her, lost for words again, and the old woman barked, "Oh, do go upstairs with the infant, she's giving me a headache," and Abigail followed Victoria upstairs with a profound sense of relief.

Victoria's apartment on the second floor was perfectly palatial. Abigail, juggling the screaming baby as she looked about, felt intimidated. The parlor was larger than the billiard room in her father's house, and would look even bigger when the clutter of bags and baskets and trunks and bundles had all been unpacked and tidied away. The bedroom was huge too, with a bed so large the posts were of the dimensions of marble columns.

There was a dressing room with washstand and *piping* and another bedroom that Abby surveyed with positive longing, with a dainty bed with muslin curtains and a window with a tree just outside. The windows of the apartment were almost as amazing as the water-piping, for they had white wooden shutters that slid magically into a gap in the wall on either side. The walls themselves were paneled and hung with paper from China, and there were prints and daguerreotypes in rows, and curiosities in cabinets and on shelves. There was no sign of Abby's bags, and she dared not ask where they were.

Then, while the baby cried and Abby did her best to help Victoria tidy the parlor, Obed arrived up the stairs. He was red in the face and refused to meet Abby's apprehensive gaze. She thought sickly that he had come to say that the carriage was ready to take her to the Mitchells — but then she saw that he had one of her bags over his shoulder.

He looked about, cleared his throat uncomfortably, and put the bag in the second bedroom. Then he went down for the other things. Thomas, the coachman, helped him. No one said a word. Abby hid her face in the baby's neck, light-headed with relief. Even twenty-four hours was a blessed respite from the dreaded Mitchells. Tomorrow she might feel braver.

When Mrs. Fanny woke up in the morning she felt old and stiff and frowzy. She had her son at home at last, and a granddaughter, which was surely cause for celebration — but did she have to celebrate the fact that the child had howled all night? The unaccustomed noises in the normally silent upper floor had gone on and on, and kept her awake.

Once, she had heard Victoria exhaustedly weeping, and Obed's gruff voice trying to soothe her, and the Sherman girl's voice, as she walked the baby up and down, up and down.

The Sherman girl. Mrs. Fanny scrambled out of bed, fumbled into her dress, and rang the bell for coffee. Mrs. Thomas came; she was the housekeeper, the only help they had in the house; help was very hard to come by in New Bedford. "Two coffees," Mrs. Fanny directed. "And send for that Sherman girl."

It had been a long time since Mrs. Fanny had greeted the day with such anticipation. She found life tedious; she contemplated the traveling she would have done, the books she would have penned, and the furor she would have created — if only she had not been lame. Mrs. Fanny was trapped in a halt body. Her only escape was the diverting company of the young.

Oh, the redheaded gals, she thought eagerly, and beamed when the Sherman girl came in. She was as bright-haired as remembered, with the perfect look of her mother.

Then, with a jolt, Mrs. Fanny saw that the girl carried the baby, and not only the baby but diapers. She grunted, "What did you bring her for?"

"She's not crying," Abby pointed out. "And I thought, I must admit, that was why you summoned me, to bring you your granddaughter."

"H'mp!" said Mrs. Fanny, confounded.

"And poor Victoria needs her sleep. She was awake all night," said Abby, plunking the baby on the sofa.

Obed was awake too, his mother thought. She grinned:

Obed hated it when females cried and got nervous, and Victoria, like the infant, had cried a lot. She said grumpily, "You were kept awake all night too."

"I did sleep and I was already awake when the baby cried this morning," Abby said. She untucked red flannel diapers and began to lay them out. Mrs. Fanny watched the nimble fingers and then, with wonder, saw that the girl's eyes were shining.

"The birds woke me," she said. "Birds!"

Mrs. Fanny was surprised, and enjoyed the sensation. "Don't you have birds in New Zealand?"

"Yes, of course we do, beautiful birds. They sing like bells in the bush, and some cackle like they are having a mad conversation, but none come near the house. And there was a bird on my sill that woke me this morning. A little bird, very drab and friendly. It cheeped like a chick, and twisted its head around in circles, watching me all the time. It had a neat little bib under its chin."

A sparrow? Did they not have common sparrows in New Zealand?

"And there was a larger bird," said the Sherman girl, "in the tree outside my window." She tickled the baby, who gurgled, and then deftly folded the napkins in corners. "It had a repertoire of several songs, very tuneful and cheerful to hear, and it had a cream-spotted breast."

It seemed incredible that this girl had never fed crumbs to a sparrow or watched a thrush demolish a snail. Mrs. Fanny said, "Don't New Zealand have slugs and snails, either?"

"Oh, yes." Abigail laughed. She was sewing the diapers carefully onto the baby with a big needle and white thread, the fingers of her left hand between the little belly and the flannel. "We have large snails of our own, in the bush, and little ones like the ones in Australia. In fact," she added, "I think the little snails came from Australia in the ships, maybe in the ballast."

Australia? She meant, Mrs. Fanny knew, the exotic continent of New Holland and New South Wales. Her blood stirred to think of what this girl had seen. "I once saw a slug on the water butt at home in Mangonui," said Abigail. "It had a pattern like a Maori tattoo, and it was quite six inches in length."

Six-inch slugs, Maori tattoos. Oh, this girl had tales to tell! Mrs. Fanny said jealously, "And you go to live with the Mitchells?"

The girl's face lost its radiance. Abigail broke off the thread and put the needle aside with elaborate care. She said tonelessly, "I go to live with my father's cousin, Mrs. Mitchell, to improve my demeanor."

This bright exotic creature in that cheerless household, this vivacity wasted in listening to twisted readings from the Old Testament and a stupid woman's whining? Mrs. Fanny shouted irritably, "Why does my granddaughter howl all the time?"

"She'll get over it," Abigail said, tears sparkling on her lashes. "She's normally the best of children."

"Then what in tarnation ails her now?"

"She misses the ship. She's terrified in a world that doesn't pitch and roll. You have to remember that she was born at sea and that this is her first time on land. I was born at sea and my mother told me the first time on shore I cried for a week."

A week? Obed, his mother thought, would go demented, and his reticent wife with her Boston upbringing would cry all the time. A week, while this girl who had walked the floor with the baby most of the night lost her bright game spirit in the cramped world of the Mitchells?

She rapped her stick on the floor, causing the baby to screech again. "Oh, take her away!" Mrs. Fanny shouted. "And when Obed rouses, tell him to come and see me."

After breakfast, while Victoria nursed the infant, Abby went exploring. She wanted to know where the water came from. There were levers on the pipes in the dressing room, and when they were lifted, fresh cold water came tumbling out to fill the marble basin. It was amazing.

Outside, the house looked even more palatial. It was made of gray stone, with a dark slate roof, and the lawn it stood in was dotted with great trees and formal flower gardens and even a marble statue of some man. The air was full of the smell of daffodils, and the ragamuffin birds hopped cheerily on the lawn. In the distance, down the hill, there was a constant rumble, the growl and rattle of New Bedford at work.

Close by, something was making a regular thump. Abby tracked it down to a well by the back of the house. Old Thomas was grunting asthmatically at a pump handle. He scowled and then did his best to ignore her, watching her from the corner of one disapproving eye.

Abby sniffed the smell of cold fresh water, a marvelous scent after three months of shipboard water in slimy casks, and then she offered to help. He was scandalized, but she insisted, and then outraged the old man again by singing a chantey while she worked the pump. "She was just a Maori maiden, with brown and dimpled cheeks," she sang. "And whee yay-ho, hey high-ho."

Eventually Thomas relented and told her what he was doing: every morning the water was pumped to a cistern in the attic, and that was where the miraculous water in the plumbing came from. Abby went up to the attic to look at this cistern, and there she found a ladder, which led up to a perfect jewel of a little room — the cupola. It had six sides and was full of windows, and was glorious. There was a bench built around the edge of it, so she could sit and look out in six directions at New Bedford and the bay and the river and the countryside.

Everywhere there were trees, scrubby trees in a

thousand shades of green. The hills were softly rolling—female hills, she thought, not like the bare, gullied, rugged masculine hills of home. Serried roofs lay before her on the city side, of slate or shingle, some with cupolas like this one, and down on the shores, large brick buildings, and chimneys—and ships. She could see the *Erasmus*. This, she realized, was how Obed's father had known his ship was in port. Her eyes couldn't open wide enough to take it all in.

Then a carriage rattled up the street and turned in to the entrance to the Cambridge mansion. A man climbed out. He wore black clothes, and he had a strange bent posture, so that all Abby could see was his chimney-pot hat, the black veil swathed around it, and black hair leaking from underneath the brim. It was Jezekiel Mitchell, she realized, Mr. Mitchell come to fetch her. The bubble of delight inside her shattered.

She felt cold and apprehensively sick. The man disappeared up the steps. Abby climbed down the ladder very carefully, and tiptoed across the attic and down the stairs. The wood of the banister felt smoothly greasy with beeswax and rubbing, cool and solid under her hand. Then, on the second-floor landing, just as she was on the point of turning into Victoria's apartments, she heard voices below her. She stopped.

Two men were crossing the hallway. She heard a high-pitched, womanish voice say, "My poor wife is extreme prostrated, sir. My household is in disarray."

"You have my condolences, sir." Obed's father sounded as smooth as the banister.

"The cursed sin of negligence has murdered my son," the other voice said viciously, "and the angel of vengeance will deliver up the transgressor, and he shall be destroyed, as Sodom and Gomorrah were destroyed."

The hairs on the back of Abby's neck rose. Her grip on the rail became convulsive. Mr. Cambridge made no reply as the footsteps moved on across the hall.

Then Abby heard the office door open, and Obed's voice said awkwardly, "Ah, Mitchell." Then he cleared his throat and said, "My regrets, sir. May a consolation sanctify the sad bereavement."

"A consolation?" Mitchell's voice held a spiteful snap. "Be ye also ready, Captain Cambridge, for such an hour as ye think not the angel of death cometh. I have called on other business, sir, the matter of Sherman's daughter."

Abby was trembling violently. Slow footsteps were coming up the stairs. There was no emotion inside her, just ice.

She waited. Obed's father came slowly onto the landing. He was alone. She had hardly exchanged a word with him, and found him intimidating. He had his face groomed in the New Bedford style, with clean-shaven upper lip and cheeks, and jaw-whiskers that should have made his face round and benevolent, but did not.

He said, "Miss Sherman. Your cousin Mitchell is here and requests the privilege of your company."

Abby nodded, her throat too dry to speak.

She felt empty and remote, as if this was happening to someone else. She walked down the stairs with the utmost care, holding her skirts in one hand, her back very straight. Mr. Cambridge opened the office door for her but did not go inside. The office was large and the shelves were full of boxes and papers.

Abigail stopped. Mr. Cambridge closed the door behind her, leaving her alone with Obed and Mr. Mitchell.

Mr. Mitchell was standing in front of the desk, facing the door; he was still wearing his mourning-draped hat, and did not take it off when she came in. He had a sallow pale face and flat, black eyes in gray sockets, and his hair straggled down about his tiny ears. Abigail nervously rubbed her palm on her skirt and then held out her hand to shake his. He ignored it. Biting her lip, she dropped it back by her side.

Jezekiel Mitchell stared at her. Then he said coldly, "You

are not wearing black."

Abigail swallowed. Her plain gown was dark blue. She said, "I have not had a chance to unpack, sir."

"And you have an extreme look of your mother. I remember her well, and how she neglected the God-given duty of true women. Your mother was Frances Brewster Sherman, who in her arrogance rejected the true path of keeper of the home and hearth, to take up the deceiving occupation of common adventurer. Are you of the same improper persuasion, miss? Are you a seeker after vulgar sensation? A seeker of adventure?"

It took a full incredulous moment for the words to register on Abigail's mind. She was trembling again, this time with rage. She exclaimed fiercely, "My mother sailed with my father because she loved him, sir! She believed she was doing her duty by doing what he wished, by staying at his side. And he loved her for it—and so did I!"

"Then what your father has written is indeed correct," Mitchell said coldly. "For your education in the seemly behavior of women is indeed deficient. Your mother was misguided and you must be schooled to understand it. A wife's rightful place in the eyes of God is not with her husband, but in the home, for it is a woman's God-given duty to guide the household and protect the hearth against her husband's homecoming. And if a woman do so faithfully indeed, and in the fear of the Mercy Seat, then will the angels rise and call her blessed, and at the time of the Resurrection she will be chosen as great."

His mouth snapped shut, and the blank eyes observed her coldly. Abigail's throat was too tight to form words. Then she heard Obed exclaim, "Do I understand you a-right, Mitchell? Do you preach against women who sail with their husbands? For I must inform you, sir, that my dear wife accompanied me on this very last voyage!"

"I was aware of that, sir," Mitchell snapped. "And my opinion is unaltered. And shame on you, sir, for carrying this child to New Bedford. For it is divine will also that a daughter remain in the place where she was raised, to prove the support of a parent in the declining years."

Obed barked, "I resent that!"

Mitchell merely shrugged, and turned away from him, and Abigail found the hard eyes fixed again on her face. Mitchell's expression was as dispassionate as any insect's: with his gray skin and flat, black, shiny eyes, Mitchell was like the cooked cricket on that awful day in Mangonui. His limbs were the same, dry and thin and crooked, and his abdomen was bloated under the tight buttoning of his black serge suit.

He demanded, "How long, pray, has your mother been dead?"

Hot tears stung her eyes. "Four years."

"Then the delay in sending you to New Bedford is remarkable. No doubt your father has learned in the meantime that he is not competent to the burden of parental responsibility, so he thinks to transfer the burden to others, so his daughter, who by divine ordinance is his sole responsibility, becomes a burden on another household. So why this belated decision to send you to New Bedford?"

Abigail looked apprehensively at Obed, terrified he was going to tell the shaming story of her fishing escapade, but instead, he was glaring at Mitchell.

He barked, "There is no burden, sir. Miss Sherman stops with us!"

There was dead silence, the only sound the baby crying upstairs. For a long moment Abby thought she had dreamed that Obed had said this wonderful thing. She gaped at him, and he stared aggressively at Mitchell. She could hear his angry breathing.

Mitchell said, "Then why the devil send for me, sir?" He stalked petulantly to the door, annoyed that he had been wasting his time.

Abby, dazed and magnanimous in her joy at this miraculous reprieve, said impulsively, "I could pay a call on my father's cousin, sir, perhaps one day, and present my father's compliments to Mrs. Mitchell and your daughter."

Mitchell stopped, and stared at her. "You forget our tragic bereavement, Miss Sherman," he snapped. "We are in no condition to receive callers. My wife has nervous health, and is at present utterly prostrated. Mrs. Mitchell will call — when she feels able." Then, with a curt nod, he departed. Abby heard the rattle of his footsteps outside, his dour snap at the coachman, and then the retreating rumble of the carriage wheels.

She didn't know what to say. She wanted to hug Obed but she didn't dare: she didn't even dare believe it. Mr. Cambridge was in charge of the household, and he might disapprove of his son's high-handed decision. She could find herself packed off to the Mitchells, after all. Mr. Cambridge would most certainly send her away when Obed and Victoria went back to sea.

Nevertheless tears of joy were streaming down her cheeks. She gasped incoherent thanks and, picking up her skirts, ran up the stairs to tell Victoria the wonderful news.

Mr. Cambridge, when he heard about it, said nothing to Abigail: in fact, he hardly ever spoke to her. He was heavily involved in commercial interests throughout New England, and there were pressing business meetings, too, because of the galloping craze for gold: all the talk, it seemed, was of California. Abby very seldom saw him, even at meals, for he was away so much of the time. Often, she only knew he had come and gone by the sound of carriage wheels in the dark.

Mrs. Fanny, on the other hand, was delighted that the girl should stay here. After all, it was logical. Victoria was an excellent model for polite manners, a paragon beyond price! How could anyone compare her fine Boston-bred demeanor with the whining of the Mitchell woman, or the petulance of her ill-treated sheep of a daughter?

Mrs. Fanny autocratically made sure that the Sherman girl spent at least an hour a day in her own company, and right entertaining she was, too, with her candid ways, her shining eyes, her amazement at all the new things she saw, and the tales she told.

And she listened, too—she was a wonderful listener; she seemed content to listen forever to stories of President Andrew Jackson, bless his name, and of that outrageous Cady girl who belonged next door, and of Mrs. Fanny's favorite nephew, that stiff-necked young pirate, Captain Seth Morgan.

As if there were any spare hours in a day! Mrs. Mitchell and her daughter, Charity, did not call for quite three months, and over those thirteen weeks Abigail almost forgot them, for the everyday bustle of the Cambridge household was so remarkably demanding. Despite the Cambridge wealth, everyone in the household—except lame Mrs. Fanny—had to bear a hand. Abby helped Victoria and learned as she went, and Victoria worked most astoundingly hard.

How had Victoria learned to run a household on such a tight rein? Abby often thought of the casual routine in her father's house, and felt extremely abashed about it. It was amazing to remember that Victoria and Obed had been married just weeks before they sailed on the *Erasmus*, for Victoria took over the organization of the mansion with such familiarity. How had Mrs. Fanny and the housekeeper, Mrs. Thomas, managed to muddle along without her? Help was scarce in New Bedford, but within two weeks Victoria had found and hired a maid, and the Cambridge house ran like a well-managed ship.

At six in the morning Thomas lit the fire in the kitchen, and at half past the hour the maid carried hot water to the dressing room, and Abby got up while Victoria nursed the baby. Then there was breakfast to be made, prayers to be held, and after that a commotion of dusting, sweeping, polishing and cleaning, the boiling of soap, the heating of the copper, the proving of bread, and the freshening of butter, lard to be chopped, raisins to be stoned, shirts to be mended, linen to be starched, stockings to be darned, curtains shaken, bedding aired, carpets beaten. Victoria made the lists and bought provisions and cooked and baked, and every day before the cleaning began she rationed out the black lead and soda. She was a perfect prudent New England housewife: Mrs. Fanny might sniff about her her Boston manners, but everyone, from Mr. Cambridge downwards, knew that Victoria was a jewel beyond price.

The sewing was not neglected. The first two weeks were a perfect orgy of sewing, for Victoria's wardrobe was out of style and Abigail's Sydney-designed gowns were too frivolous for New Bedford. Abby, under Victoria's expert eye, leafed through catalogues and magazines, and then the styles chosen were taken to the stores at Liberty Hall in William Street, and discussed with the energy commonly reserved for battle plans. Then came the business of choosing the fabrics. Once selected, the material was spread out on the counter and cut out by the assistants with constant reference to the picture of the gown, all without a pattern. The pieces of fabric were measured next and the amount bought calculated, along with the price. The cut-out pieces were carried home, and basted and pleated and draped and stitched, much of the time on the wearer's body. Abigail bore it all with patience—for none of the fabrics were black, the murder of her father's cousin's son being never mentioned—and was grateful, too, that her father had thought to provide her with a purse of money before she left New Zealand. Luckily Victoria ran out of ideas before Abigail ran out of coins.

Once the sewing was done and the wardrobes were complete, Victoria let it be discreetly known that she was At Home, and Abby learned further lessons, in the art of Calling. Victoria was acquainted with all the most important names in New Bedford, so that women of social standing came to call, splendidly dressed in silk dresses they called morning gowns, though they were invariably very tight fitting and never worn in the morning. Abigail learned how to shake hands and make correct introductions, to sing the right songs when Victoria played her little melodeon, and to pour tea and eat cake with the correct little fork, and to stand when people entered.

The callers had to be fed, of course, so the mornings became even busier, with the creation of dainties that Victoria, of course, created superbly. Abby even learned the different ways of making conversation: the society ladies talked of ships and shops and California, and discussed the sermons preached at the Unitarian church that they all attended; and in the hours that Mrs. Fanny claimed, the talk was of ships and islands and Women's Rights and Martha Cady.

Mrs. Fanny talked of Martha Cady all the time, and if Victoria was listening, she pursed her lips. The house next door was empty, and when Abby took the baby out in the garden she contemplated the shuttered windows curiously. The house was much smaller than the Cambridge mansion but substantial nonetheless, and it emanated an air of comfortable carelessness. The old trees around it had not been trimmed back for many a year. Mr. Cady was a widower, Mrs. Fanny said, and at present he and Martha were at an important place called Seneca Falls, at a meeting called the First Women's Rights Convention. Mr. Cady and his daughter, Martha, had been prominent in its organization. They had helped devise a list of eighteen grievances concerning the rights of women, and also assisted a woman called Amelia Bloomer who produced a paper called *The Lily*. Mrs. Fanny wrote for it, too. Despite Victoria's disapproval Abigail looked forward to the time when the Cadys would come home. She often wondered what Martha Cady's conversation would be like. Did she talk of the grievances of women all the time? Martha Cady, Mrs. Fanny said, spoke against the enslavement of Negroes, as well.

The two Mitchell women called in August. Victoria served them Genoa cake, of the *best* receipt—half a pound each of flour, sugar, and butter, four eggs, and a small glass of brandy—with a gelatin frosting. She also served oyster patties and Valencia nougats. Abigail poured tea, and then as the maid carried the plates around, she watched the visitors nervously from under her lashes.

Victoria was wearing superbly draped lavender silk; Abigail a lovely green delaine with a white ruching collar and bib. The Mitchell women wore black, of course. Both bonnets were heavily swathed in black crepe. Charity's bonnet framed a round pale face with large protuberant pale-blue eyes; if her eyes had not been so furtive and her mouth so prim, she would have been pretty. She was twenty-five, but worn-looking enough to be much older. Her mother was huge, a whale-like woman whose stays creaked like saddle leather. Her face was large to match her frame, and unhealthily flushed with dark red.

To Abby's discomfort there was a distinct resemblance to Nathaniel Sherman; it was obvious that her father and this ugly woman were related. Had William Mitchell been fat? What did Jireh look like? Consider West had called him "a dear boy for the girls," but, looking at these two women, it did not seem likely.

"My health," said Mrs. Mitchell, after munching much cake, "is exceeding bad."

"Poor Mama," said Charity dutifully, "is always poorly."

"Dr. Spooner has quite given up. He considers it a miracle that I continue to breathe. Even the thought of going downstreet is sufficient to lay me low with a sick headache."

"Poor Mama has a nervous disposition," said Charity, as she furtively studied the room.

Her eyes held envy, and no wonder, for Victoria's parlor was so very splendid. The furniture was substantial and grand. And everywhere, too, there were testimonials to Victoria's domestic activity—lamp-mats and tidies, table covers and embroidery. And there was evidence, too, of the exotic places she had visited—bunches of colorful birds' feathers, branches of coral faded to pastel, fans made of leaves and feathers, and painted urns.

"You have a maid," said Mrs. Mitchell jealously. "Mrs. Cambridge, I do declare I am astonished. Our servants keep on leaving. How to you contrive to keep one?"

"Our girls go to work at the cotton mills at Lowell," Charity said. "The wages are so much better. They live at the mill," she said, her pale eyes turned on Abby, "and receive a religious education in addition to their pay. It is an excellent scheme, but so inconvenient when it means you cannot hire a maid and keep one. Tell me," she said, "have you heard from your father, our cousin, Captain Sherman?"

Abigail mutely shook her head. Whaling vessels arrived from the Pacific every week, but she had not received a single letter, even though she wrote often—but that was not at all unusual. Letters went missing all the time, or went round and round the world without being received.

"So you do not know how he fares?"

Abby said quietly, "No."

She couldn't help the nightmares. Was he sick? Was Toria taking proper care of him? Wikitoria was so feckless— but then, there was loyal Tamati. She did not expect to hear from Tamati, because he could not read and write—but why had Broddy not written? How had Broddy felt when he arrived in Mangonui to find that his little Abby had been sent away?

She had been in New Bedford three months, and the *Erasmus* lay empty off Hillman's Yard—and all the time the ship lay idle she was wasting money. Obed seemed content to potter his days away in clubs and saloons, and his advice was often solicited on financial and shipping matters, but the time was surely near when Obed and Victoria would sail ... and if she didn't hear from her father, she would be left alone in New Bedford, at the mercy of the Mitchells.

Mrs. Mitchell ate more cake, brushed crumbs from her lap onto the rug, and said, "Is that Cady girl back from that scandalous business in Seneca Falls? The one who writes for that profane paper *The Lily?*"

Victoria paused. Then she said, "More tea, Mrs. Mitchell?"

The polite snub was obvious, but Mrs. Mitchell didn't seem to notice. She received the cup and saucer from Abigail's hands and said, "This Women's Rights movement is a-flying in the face of proper decorum and the God-given order of the world. It is an obscenity."

Charity dutifully pronounced, "Every woman buildeth her house, but the foolish plucketh it down with her hands."

Silence. Abby studied her clasped hands, wishing this dreadful visit was over, and Victoria said politely, "And have you report of our cousin Seth Morgan?"

Unexpectedly, Abigail's heart bumped. When she looked up, Mrs. Mitchell was smiling smugly. "Two and a half thousand barrels, at last report from Talcahuano, in June. Seventy-five thousand dollars, at present market. Mr. Mitchell is quite pleased."

Abby blinked—Seth Morgan's greasy luck had held. She said, "That's wonderful."

Victoria seemed equally astounded. "Excellent!" she said.

To the embarrassed puzzlement of both, however, Mrs. Mitchell heaved about in her chair, produced a handkerchief, and commenced to sob into it.

"It ain't right," she wailed.

Victoria stood, sat again, and looked about helplessly. "Mrs. Mitchell..." she said, and faltered to a stop. Abby had never seen her at such a loss.

Mrs. Mitchell wailed, "It ain't fair!"

"It ... isn't?"

"How can Captain Morgan be so fortunate, when our son Jireh fares so badly? He reports no oil at all!"

Victoria lifted a helpless hand. "'Tis the vessel, perhaps."

She looked at Abigail, mutely pleading for support. Abby said, "Some ships are luckier than others, and the *Pierrot* certainly seems to have good fortune."

"But the *Pierrot* was the ship where our dear son William was foully murdered! How can a cousin of our blood," Mrs. Mitchell said viciously, "say that a ship is lucky, when our son and brother was slain on that same ship?"

Oh God, thought Abigail. She saw Victoria shut her eyes.

"William met his Maker *unprepared*."

"God is merciful to the bereaved, Mrs. Mitchell," Victoria said, rather wildly, "if only they have faith."

"Next voyage," said Mrs. Mitchell, her tone spiteful, "Jireh must have the lucky *Pierrot*. Let Captain Morgan have the nasty *Lizzie Ann*."

Then it was autumn—and such a season. Abby had never dreamed that staid New England could be so colorful and exuberant, that the scrubby trees and the long salt meadows could be so vivid. Even the prim and proper trees of County Street abandoned themselves to bright red and orange. When she took little Emily out for her airings, the world was full of surprises—of grass that was intricately iced with gossamer in the mornings, and squirrels that flicked about with glossy tails in piles of brown and brilliant leaves.

There were huge delicate spider-webs spread between the branches of the elms, with dewdrops that dissolved when a chubby finger poked at them. Every day when the weather was good and Abby could steal an hour to herself, she and Emily wrapped up warm and took a walk along

County Street, down the hill, and along William Street to the pillared entrance of the customs house, to see if there were any letters. Abby enjoyed the shops and the bustle and the solid shuttered houses, and perhaps because she liked the city so much — or perhaps because there were never any letters — her walk was always meandering.

Centre Street, for instance: she had no right to be in Centre Street, for it was down by the waterfront, but Abby and Emily went always to this little street that was such a confusion of sail lofts and ship carpenter stores. The river was full of boats and ships, and whaleboats were moored to the piers. There were new whaleships in each time Abby came, some arrived all spick-and-span, with colors flying to show they'd done well; others, those with shameful reports, sneaked in grubbily, almost unannounced. Abby gazed at them all with impartial longing, and paid no attention to the men who thronged the wharves, hardly aware of their stares.

They were a motley lot, those men, as variously shabby or prosperous as the ships that brought them into town: gams of captains with heavy shoulders; restless-eyed mates with peaked caps and buttoned pea jackets; Chinese cooks with tar-tipped pigtails; loose-jawed green hands from hinterland farms; eagle-eyed Gay Head Indians; black Brava Portuguese; and tattooed kanakas from South Sea islands.

The Pacific Islanders made Abby feel homesick. She turned the buggy and went back to Union Street, pushing Emily with her head down. What would she do if she never heard from New Zealand? How would she get home if her father never wrote? Every time she came into town she couldn't help feeling a little hope that today, by some miracle, the clerk would nod and smile, turn to the rack, and find her a letter. Every time he shook his head, the disappointment bit more deeply. Her pin money was gone and if she never got a letter from home, how could she hope to raise the money to buy her passage to New Zealand?

Union Street was the main shopping street, and as she progressed westwards the crowd around her became predominantly female. Women crowded the pavements—females like herself, Abby thought apprehensively, who were trapped by men in New Bedford. They were just about all of them dressed in black and wore coal-scuttle bonnets, and many had the lonely eyes of women who were without their men, who were filling in the empty years while they waited for a ship to bring their men home.

When the men did come back, within four months they were away again, outward bound on a four- or five-year voyage. It did not make commercial sense to leave a ship or a seaman idle—and yet Obed had never mentioned any plans for sailing again. Every time she saw him now, Abby braced herself for Obed to pull his whiskers and beam at Victoria and jovially announce that he'd concluded to refit the *Erasmus*, and that he and Victoria—and Emily, of course—would sail for the Pacific in the spring. It was the logical thing for Obed to do; it was amazing that he had not sailed this fall.

And then, and then ... what? Would Obed fill her with joy by announcing that he would carry Abigail Sherman, too? Surely Victoria would appreciate Abby's company and assistance on the outward voyage to New Zealand? But what if Obed concluded to leave her? Mrs. Fanny liked Abigail, but despite her views, Mrs. Fanny had no say in the organization of the household. If Obed sailed and left her behind, Abby was doomed to be packed off to the Mitchells.

Then she stopped and looked up: she was on the corner of Second and William Streets, and the customs house lay before her. It was one of the busiest places in town and one of the grandest. The steps and the lobby inside were all of a bustle, for every captain, whether coming or going, had to clear his ship through the customs office, on the second floor of the building. The post office was on the first floor.

Captains paused in the midst of their business to look at

the pretty girl as she came in, but Abby hardly noticed them, Instead, with her usual sense of dreary pessimism, she pushed her way up to the counter. The clerk knew her: she did not need to say a word. She smiled at him apologetically and expected his headshake so fully that it took her quite a moment to see his grin. She had a letter—a letter! She was so excited she forgot to thank him.

The letter was a fat tiny package, folded and refolded and stained with travel dirt, and the seal had fallen off somewhere along the way—but the writing was her father's, and there was her name on the front. Miss Abigail Sherman, New Bedford. The words ran before her eyes. Her fingers trembled so violently that for a long moment she couldn't open it.

And it was a riddle. It was not a letter at all. There was no date, no salutation, not even a signature. If she had not known her father's writing, she would not even know who it came from. Her breath hissed in a gasp that was almost a sob as she turned it over frantically, but that was all there was: her name and the silly little riddle.

The number 5 was written near the top, circled. This meant that her father had made at least five copies and put each one on a different ship. So many letters went missing that this was common practice—with letters that were very important. *Important?* Abby had expected so much and waited so long, and there was such dread in her heart, and the awful homesickness—and all that had come was a *riddle.*

When she was small her father and Broddy had teased her so often, just like this, with silly little riddles and rhymes, to test and test her grasshopper mind. But this ... this was cruel...

With sugar and rice and apples I'm nice
Although I am wood, I taste very good.
When I am high, all sails fly.
When I am low, watch for a blow
What am I?

What? Abby had not a notion, and at that moment of fierce disappointment she didn't even care. She wanted to scream out her anger; she wanted to tear the stupid little message up and throw it in the street; she wanted to cry out her rage with this busy, complacent, uncaring New Bedford.

She did none of them. Instead Emily, her eyes round and puzzled, watched as her Aunt Abby broke down and wept bitterly, in a fury of frustration.

Seven

Two days later Mrs. Fanny summoned Abby into her sitting room. This parlor was disastrously over-furnished, crammed with furniture that Mrs. Fanny refused to give up, all of it hopelessly out of date. The settees and chairs were tightly upholstered and ornately carved, with sugar-stick legs and elaborate backs. Every piece was acutely uncomfortable. Nevertheless Abby liked it, for it reminded her of her mother's childhood stories. Today, Mrs. Fanny sat squat and foursquare as usual in her favorite chair with her knees well apart and her skirt well stretched. But Abigail stopped short in the doorway, for Mrs. Fanny had a visitor.

The visitor smiled, and said in a soft, warm voice, "Good afternoon to you, Miss Abby Sherman."

Abigail merely gaped. Who could this person be? Not Martha Cady, surely! Martha Cady, Abby was certain, was an aggressive woman with assertive views.

Abby had imagined her with sharp features and blazing red hair, tall and thin with elbows that were always akimbo. But this was a pretty girl, rounded and young. She had a soft mouth, and soft, amused brown eyes, and her hair was a dark auburn, like the autumn leaves of oaks. And the dress that she wore!

On her feet she had patent-leather boots with mother-of-pearl buttons, and above those boots she wore—trousers. Above the trousers was a sort of tunic, calf-length, and waisted in style, with a collar and tie. The scandalous trousers were gathered at the ankle and edged with lace.

Emily wriggled. Abby put her down on the floor, and said, "You cannot be Martha Cady."

Martha Cady laughed. "I am, I am," she declared, and curtseyed with the strange short skirt of her tunic. "And what do you make of my costume?"

Abby could think of nothing to say. Instead, she spread helpless hands and laughed, and Martha Cady laughed in return. "Mrs. Fanny loves it," she said. Mrs. Fanny scowled, her bemittened hand on her stick and—as always—her old-fashioned lace cap askew. "I do not," she said roundly, with an intimidating scowl. "It's a nonsense, and don't you go filling Abigail's head with a notion that it's not."

"But it's wonderful," Martha declared as she pirouetted. "So practical." Little Emily sat on the floor and gazed upwards with as much apparent fascination as Abby felt. The baby's cheeks were plump and red with teething, and she dribbled enchantingly. Martha swooped down like a dancer, scooped the baby up, kissed one round fat cheek, and set her down again. "This child," she said, and swept an eloquent arm, will grow up in a new age of female comfort and liberty because of the courage of females like myself!"

Mrs. Fanny didn't seem impressed in the slightest. In fact, Abby thought, if she hadn't heard Mrs. Fanny speak so admiringly of Martha Cady, she would not have believed that the two females were such close and loyal friends.

Mrs. Fanny sniffed, and said, "Where did you find it?"

"Oh, we wore this costume all the time, in Seneca Falls, Amelia Bloomer and Libby Miller and Aunt Elizabeth Cady Stanton and me. And how we made the citizens stare!" cried Martha. "And how envious some seemed, and how they wished they were equally daring."

"That's as well as well may be, but you ain't told me yet where you found it."

"Libby Miller brought the style back from Switzerland. The physicians prescribe the costume in the treatment of unfortunate souls who suffer from the effects of over-tight lacing. Amelia Bloomer reckons the costume will be all the rage — for, see, it is so very comfortable. With no petticoats to hold up, one needs no corsets!"

And on she talked — Martha Cady seemed to know everything and hold views on it all. Then, too soon, she left, still with that dimple, still talking, declaring that she must not leave her father to unpack, for if she did she'd be bound to find the shoes in the coal cellar and her nightgowns in the scullery.

Abigail could not stop thinking about her. Switzerland! And no stays! And who was Libby Miller? Next day, when she heard Martha's voice in Mrs. Fanny's parlor, she couldn't resist it: she put down her cleaning rag and took off her apron, and joined them.

Martha's dimpled smile was just as Abby remembered, and she was every bit as warm and friendly — and as willing to answer questions, too. Who was Libby Miller? And Amelia Bloomer and Elizabeth Stanton? Women's Rightists, of course. "Libby was raised as a boy, in dungaree pants," said Martha, and Abby felt an exhilarating sense of sistership with this unknown woman.

"Libby's father," Martha said, "believes that corsets are a symbol of the enslavery of women. He was at an occasion once where a lady's lacing gave way. There was a tremendous explosion, he said, and the woman collapsed.

Everyone thought that the unfortunate female had broken in half, he said. My father," said Martha, "declares that women will never experience liberation until the day they refuse to submit to the cramping styles that men design and think beautiful. And my aunt Elizabeth Cady Stanton declares that women will never make their true opinions known, even unto their fathers, brothers, and husbands, until the day they unlace their stays, heave a huge breath, windmill their arms, and let forth!"

Abby wondered if Mrs. Fanny would have been a Women's Rightist, too, if she had been born a bit later, and had not been so lame. It was difficult to imagine it, though, for Mr. Cambridge was undisputed master of the house. When Mr. Cambridge spoke, Mrs. Fanny always heard him. It was as if in the presence of her husband, Mrs. Fanny's ears leaped to full alert.

Next day, Martha was back again, and Abby made another excuse to go into the parlor. Martha Cady, she found, was only twenty, almost twenty-one. She was pretty enough for any man to want her, but she declared she would never marry. "Why should I?" she demanded. "I have a lovely papa who don't mind my awful housekeeping. He's more benevolent than any husband could be, and he's rich in the bargain! He don't mind if I read and write instead of cooking, if I improve my mind instead of scrubbing the floors. In my present unfettered state I can devote my energies to solving the great social problems around us, so why should I devote all that to the tyranny of some domestic Jehovah? Why, my papa don't even mind that I do no sewing!"

No sewing? Abby was most envious. "What would I sew?" demanded Martha. "Shirts? Lace? Pillow covers? Frills to make a man or a mantelpiece lovely? The pursuit of sewing is not even healthful!"

"Ruinous to the sight," agreed Mrs. Fanny.

"And develops no muscles!"

Abby laughed. "But other girls want husbands for their needles."

"They want whalemen, no doubt," Martha agreed. "Men who can be relied upon to go away for years at a time. But do those girls who marry realize that they are about to lose their souls?"

"That can't be so!"

"But it is! —for it has been decided by a body of men in their collective male wisdom. The Tennessee legislature has declared it. Married women cannot own property—and those who cannot own land cannot own souls, for slaves cannot own land, and they have no souls. Would you believe such logic?"

"Stop, stop," said Abby, laughing.

"This girl needs educating," said Martha to Mrs. Fanny.

"And you'll be the one to do it—for I knew that you two girls were bound to be friends."

Friends? Abby felt startled. Until she had come to know Mrs. Fanny and Victoria, she had never had female friends. She had had her mother, but shipboard life had meant that all her friends had been sailors. At school she had thought the little girls silly, with their giggling talk and outbursts of spite, and she had wanted to have as little as possible to do with them. Friends? It did seem strange.

After that, Abby saw Martha every day.

Usually, it was in Mrs. Fanny's parlor. Mrs. Fanny thought Martha's views wonderfully diverting, and in accordance, furthermore, with the philosophies of the late President Jackson, bless his name. However, Abby was just as welcome in the Cady house—indeed, the Cady house became her second home.

A very untidy second home. Martha had spoken nothing but the truth when she confessed her domestic inadequacy. The books and papers lay as thickly as the cobwebs and dust.

Martha's father was as prosperous as promised, too, with inherited wealth, and was elderly and extremely vague. His wife had been dead for over ten years, and Abby often wondered how he had managed to bring up Martha on his own. Occasionally he would peer foggily at Abigail and declare she looked reminiscent of someone, and inquire her name as if he had never met her before. Yet he was an editor and an essayist, respected highly by the intelligentsia.

Martha and Mrs. Fanny wrote all the time, too, and argued about what they penned. Martha wrote under the name Chrysanthemum, and Mrs. Fanny's penname was Wintersweet. Writing was necessary for the Great Work of Liberation, or so Martha told Abigail, for every instrumentality available had to be employed in the defense of downtrodden women. She did abandon the trouser costume, however, much to Victoria's relief. Martha had decided that the costume detracted attention from the Cause—always the Cause, and always with a capital C. Victoria, Abby thought, was amazingly patient with Martha Cady, for two more dissimilar women could never have been found. No doubt, Abby mused, Victoria conceived that it was her duty to be polite to her mother-in-law's friend, but Victoria even invited Martha upstairs when she was entertaining in her parlor.

"She is a whole-souled woman," Victoria told Abigail. "And, furthermore," she added, "joyful is the heart that sings." Martha could certainly sing, as heartily as Abigail and much more tunefully, and Victoria's visitors declared that it was heart-lifting to hear Mrs. Cambridge and Miss Sherman and that Cady woman all sing together. Martha had one more virtue, however, which went a long way towards endearing her to Victoria: Martha thought that Victoria's action in sailing with her husband on voyage was worthy of the most profound admiration.

"I commend her decision unreservedly," Martha declared. Victoria, blushing demurely, allowed herself to be interviewed for one of Martha's articles. "The presence of a lady on a whaleship must sober the most rambunctious of crews, for how they must respect the man in command," wrote Martha, "when they see him treating his wife with courtesy. And how homelike the ship when the firm but gentle feminine hand assists at the helm."

"The helm?" said Victoria, puzzled. "But I protest that I never..."

"It's a metaphor," said Martha.

"I steered my father's brig," Abby said proudly later, "and when I sail I'll do even more than that, for I'll navigate and keep the logbook."

"Of course you will," Martha agreed robustly. "When you have a brig of your own, you're not fettered by a domestic Jehovah."

Abby sighed and stared into the flames in Mrs. Fanny's grate, her mind many thousands of miles away. "I have to get back to New Zealand before I can do it," she said sadly.

Mrs. Fanny was in her bedroom taking her afternoon nap, and the girls were alone. Martha, Abby had found, was a warm and easy confidante. She had an attentive, sympathetic way about her, and was always reassuring. Abby said, "I have this most terrible fear that Obed will announce he's concluded to sail in the spring, and take Victoria and Emily, and leave me behind."

"That's ridiculous," said Martha. She smiled and patted Abby's hand. "Obed won't sail — he's far too comfortable — and anyway, if he does sail, Victoria won't let him go without you. How would she and Emily manage without your help? And, anyway, I hear tell he's thinking to sell the *Erasmus*."

Sell the *Erasmus*? Abby stared at Martha, filled with uneasiness. If Obed sold the ship and left the sea she might be safe from the Mitchells, she thought, yet she felt a nudge of grim premonition. Why? Then she realized that she had been banking on the idea that Obed would take her on the

170

Erasmus when he sailed, and that she would leave the ship in New Zealand.

It was a faint hope, but it was all she had. If she never heard from her father again, and Obed sold his vessel and gave up the sea, what chance did she have of getting home?

She said in a panic, "But Obed wouldn't sell—not his lucky *Erasmus!*"

"Well," said Martha with a shrug, "that's what I heard— that he would put the ship on the block in the spring, when he would get the best price."

It was snowing outside, and the world was muffled in a thin white blanket. Lucky ships sold quickly and well, Abby thought; she remembered Mrs. Mitchell and her whining that the *Pierrot* was lucky when the *Lizzie Ann* was not. To her discomfort, she found she was close to tears. She hid it with a forced, brilliant smile, and said lightly, "Perhaps I'll fall in love with a captain, and he will fall in love with me, and he will buy the lucky *Erasmus*, and we'll go together to sea."

"Love?" cried Martha, scandalized. "Fie on you, girl! Love is a delusion, a fable devised by men to trap women! Love gives a man the legal right to own and command another human being! Do you think your captain would allow you to keep your brig? And remember, young Abby, flogging is now against the law, but wife-beating is perfectly legal."

"And most commendable, too," said a lazy male voice from the door. "Particularly with a termagant o' the Cady variety."

Abby jumped with fright, and scrambled to her feet. Turning, she saw a deeply tanned sailor in a captain's sedate dark broadcloth gamming suit, slim and tall, with a white-bleached moustache above his curved mouth. A lock of yellow hair fell over his forehead, and soft brown eyes smiled into hers.

Mrs. Fanny was alongside him, hunched as always over

her stick, looking as if she was annoyed at being summoned from her nap. Who was he, this man who had arrived so casually? He had a hat and gloves in his hand, and snowflakes on his shoulders, and under his dark coat he wore some sort of waistcoat, which glittered with threads of gold and brightly colored silks.

Then, as Abby stared, bemused and enchanted, she heard Martha exclaim furiously, "Jireh Mitchell, you were eavesdropping!"

This Jireh Mitchell grinned. "Was I, pretty termagant?" he drawled.

Martha stormed, "Jireh Mitchell, you are not a gentle-man—and thirty-one months has not improved your manners!"

"And you were declaiming," he informed her. All the time, his eyes rested warmly on Abby's face. "Report did you much less than justice," he murmured. "You must be my young cousin, Abigail Sherman."

All Abby could do was nod, gazing at him without a word. This, her cousin Jireh Mitchell? The dear boy for the girls? How could this flamboyant, elegant man have sprung from the dreadful Mitchells? It seemed impossible that this debonair fellow was Jezekiel Mitchell's older son, or that the whale-like, whining Mrs. Mitchell was his mother.

"And," he said in an aside to Martha, as he smiled at Abby, "the logic o' women is past understanding. You deride men one instant, and bewail their absence the next."

"Bewail?" The echo was incredulous.

"Then why did you know the number o' months o' my absence so exactly?"

Mrs. Fanny snorted with sardonic laughter.

"*Months?*" cried Martha furiously. " I was counting the days—days of reprieve!"

Abigail shook her head in silent wonder. Didn't Martha realize that Jireh was only teasing? As if he had read her thought, Jireh smiled at her. He then looked at Martha and said, "My mother and Charity prevailed on me to bring them to town for Christmas shopping. I had time on my hands and thought I would come to see my pretty young cousin, and perhaps take two young ladies to Gosnold's in Liberty Hall for a dish of ice cream..."

Martha said coldly, "We're too busy. We have a paper to write."

Jireh heaved an elaborate sigh. Then he murmured, "But perhaps one day, *you* will come out with me, Little Cousin...?"

"Yes," breathed Abby. It was not until he'd been gone for five minutes that she realized that was the only word she'd said.

For days Abby's heart beat faster if she heard a step at the door or a horse in the street. She was reluctant to go out of the house, in case Jireh came while she was away. She thought of him constantly, and was constantly amazed that he really belonged to the Mitchells. Charity had the promise of prettiness, and perhaps Mrs. Mitchell had once been pretty. But Mrs. Mitchell and Charity never smiled, and Jireh ... Jireh had a slow, heart-breaking grin.

A week plodded by, and then the next one went faster. It snowed all the time, in sparse damp showers that disappointed, for the thin white blanket went brown and dissolved before the streets looked as magical as childhood tales had promised a New England winter could be.

Then one day it was finer. When Emily and Mrs. Fanny were both napping, Abby wrapped herself warmly in her fur-lined cloak and went out alone to see if any mail had come from New Zealand. The wind was sharp and the pavements were soggy: Abigail walked quickly, her cloak held about her as she dashed up the customs house steps. Then she had to wait in line. The Atlantic whalers were coming in, home for Christmas, and the lobby was full of captains. The clerk sorted out mail bags with interminable slowness while Abby waited, until all she was numbly aware of was the frozen state of her feet. Then the clerk looked up and held out the letter.

A letter from New Zealand. Her heart jumped, and she had to school herself not to grab. It had just come in from a late Pacific voyager, addressed just like the other, in her father's large black handwriting. She tore it open, stumbling down the steps.

It was the riddle again. Marked number two. The same stupid little rhyme. The disappointment tore so cruelly that she stopped dead. Her eyes blurred as the sharp wind yanked at the tears on her lashes. She hardly saw the man who stepped up and took her arm, until Jireh's warm voice said, "Crying, little Abby? Sad news?"

Her heart jerked again, and she gasped, "No!"

"What?" He frowned, and let go her arm at once.

She said, "No—no, I didn't mean that. I meant, that the news was not bad, not really. It's from ... from my father, one of his teases."

His brows tugged together as he stared down into her eyes. "Teasing? Why would he tease you?"

"It's a riddle," she said, and then, before she could stop herself, she had recited the rhyme.

"What the devil?" he said.

She smiled lamely, and repeated, "When I am high, all sails fly—and when I am low, watch for a blow."

His frown vanished, and he laughed. "Even I know the answer to that, and I know nothing of riddles!" Then he completed the old saying: "Long foretold, long last; short notice, soon past; first rise after very low, indicates a stronger blow."

"Of course!" she said. "It's a barometer! Why didn't I guess it earlier?"

"I have no idea," he returned. "But I do know that I am stranded again, and I do wonder if you will be a kind lass and walk with me a while. For if you do," he said with that heart-stopping grin, "we can both have ice cream — and I am very fond of the dish."

"Of course," she said again. The skies were gray and the wind was cold, but she felt as warm as if bathed in sun. She took his arm and they walked along Second Street as he talked and talked. The streets were crowded with Christmas shoppers — and Jireh seemed to know gossip about them all.

"There goes Captain Weeden," he murmured wickedly in her ear. "Perfect picture o' rectitude, don't you think?" He bowed at the dignified gentleman, and touched the brim of his hat. "First ship I shipped on was his, and me a tender boy o' fifteen. Chosen by my father in his wisdom, and to be sure we had Bible and homilies for the first few weeks, but once around the tip o' the Horn, his language would blister the paint off a Port Paita harlot. We called him Black Hawk. Aha," he said, and bowed again. "There goes another fine example of a whaling master. Pleased to meet you, sir, my compliments!" he cried, and got a dignified nod in return. "A first-rate commander, that one — o' holiday vacations. Shooting, fishing, and shaving the dog were the order o' the day. He would've been extreme put out if we had had the bad judgment to raise any whales. The first two weeks o' the cruise, he fitted out his boat for smuggling."

Abigail giggled, her hand tucked warmly in the crook of his arm, very aware of the girls in the street and their whispers and their envious looks. Jireh enjoyed his diverting gossip, she thought, but it was obvious New Bedford gossiped much about Jireh Mitchell, too.

Then, he said, "Why does your father send you riddles, young Abby?"

She had thought about it often. She shrugged and said, "My father and Broddy like to tease me."

"Broddy?"

"Captain Broderick McGhie, my father's partner in a shore whaling station. I have known him all my life."

"Ah." Then he said casually, "I didn't know your father

175

had an interest in a shore whaling station."

She sighed and said, "I think he may have been forced to sell it." Then, in an effort to change the uncomfortable subject, she said, "Could we go to the wharves instead of to Liberty Hall?"

"Yes, but why?"

Because she didn't want to run into Charity Mitchell and his mother, of course—but she couldn't tell him that. Instead, she said shyly, "I love to see the ships."

"Then why not?" he said, and turned their course to go down Union Street towards the skyline where the yards and masts of many ships were like pencil lines in the clouds.

"And I would particularly like to see the *Lizzie Ann*."

"That old tub?" Jireh shouted with laughter, and several passersby turned their heads. He looked down at this pretty red-headed cousin, and said, "You know I didn't take a drop of oil?"

She looked stricken. "Your luck didn't improve?"

"It did not," he assured her solemnly. Jireh had called at New York on his way home, and the full cargo of sugar in his holds had fetched a gratifying price, while the sixteen thousand pounds of tortoiseshell he'd had stored between decks had sold for twenty thousand dollars—but that was a secret he kept to himself.

He added, "Seth Morgan's report is amazing."

To his surprise, she scowled. Did she not like the stiff-necked pirate? The thought gave him some amusement. He said, "Three thousand three hundred barrels. The ship is full; he'll be home within the month."

"The *Pierrot* is the luckier ship, perhaps."

"You've been listening to my mother's superstitious nonsense."

"Well, I do know that lucky vessels fetch a better price, if sold."

They turned into Front Street, and before them lay the scruffy old *Lizzie Ann*. She was anchored off the end of

Merrill's Wharf, where casks stood in rows, draped with seaweed to stop the staves from drying out. Drays rattled back and forth, and men trudged about, hunched beneath the great sacks on their shoulders. Birds wheeled endlessly, drifting in and out of the pall that eddied over the river. Despite the scruffiness of the scene, Abigail's face was full of enchantment, utterly unaware of Jireh's intent gaze. Her eyes, he thought, were like the blue-green at the edge of sea-ice. What a deal he'd give to change places for an hour with one of the pins in her bright autumn hair—to recline there warmly, held in fire and caressed with the fur that lined her hood.

Abruptly her expression changed, becoming radiant. "Look, Jireh!"

He heard guffaws from the men on the wharf as he turned to look at his ship.

The sun must be shining somewhere, he realized, as a rainbow had flickered in the mist, nonchalantly irradiating the *Lizzie Ann*. The old box glowed in pastel colors. What a choice for a rainbow's favor, he thought, and laughed himself.

"There, see," she declared, "a pot of gold awaits. She'll have a wonderful report, next voyage, and you will be a lucky whaling skipper. Please, can I go on board?"

Jireh shrugged. "Why not?" He was distracted by a rider on a horse who hailed him, and when he turned back, Abigail was gone. Then he saw her on the ship, and strolled up the narrow gangplank to join her. The smell of bilge made his nose twitch.

Abigail was on the other side of the hurricane house. By the time he reached her she was perched on the larboard bulwarks with one arm stretched high to hold the mizzen shrouds. The light was behind her, and her cloak had fallen back, so he could see the outline of her slender body. Her stance pulled up her skirts, so Jireh could see shapely ankles in white stockings. She was leaning outwards with perfect assurance, balancing herself expertly as she studied the rigging aloft.

She was so dainty that Jireh's throat felt tight. Smiling, he stepped forward and put his hands on her waist. His fingers met at the back, under the warmth of her cloak. When he lifted, she came down lightly, her slight, warm body pressed against his, and he abruptly realized that she did not wear stays. The top of her tilted face was level with his chin. "Oh, Abby," he said softly, "you should see your eyes." And then he kissed her on the mouth.

Her soft lips quivered. She smelled sweet and clean. The warm fur-lined cloak fell around them both, encasing them as she leaned trustfully against him. It was her first kiss, he thought with deep pleasure. A purr of wicked gratification moved inside him, and he thrust one hand in her hair to cradle her head as he kissed her more deeply.

A steamer hooted in the near distance, and sense returned with a rush. Jireh slacked his hold and smiled down into her eyes. "Bad girl," he said, giving her a little shake, and when she looked puzzled, he laughed, "You must not lay aloft on my ship. Girls don't climb the rigging, you know!"

Abby took a long moment to respond. Her eyes were full of dreams, and he felt a pang of alarm, thinking that she was young enough to read too much into a kiss. Then to his relief, she burst into a giggle. But when he pressed her for a reason, she did not explain.

And, after that, Jireh was always around.

Whether Martha and Abigail were in Mrs. Fanny's parlor or the Cady house, or taking Emily for an airing, or even shopping at Liberty Hall, Jireh would somehow find them, materializing with his lazy smile. He and Martha argued constantly, often with disturbing passion, and he fought with Mrs. Fanny, too. He teased Mrs. Fanny by behaving as gallantly as any Elizabethan courtier, kissing the old lady's hand when she threatened to have him shown the door. He was good-humored even when Martha was at her sharpest—why? Why did he put up with her jibes?

Because of she, herself, Abby? Abigail wondered often if she was being courted. Sometimes, when she looked up suddenly in the midst of all that teasing and argument, Jireh's face wore a look of wryly helpless love. Did Mrs. Fanny see it, too? Her hooded eyes were often shrewd, and Victoria sometimes looked sentimental.

Then, at last, the moment came when she and Jireh were alone together. When he arrived, Abigail was sitting alone on the hearth rug at the Cady house, looking at the fire, surrounded by a clutter of papers and books. Obed and Victoria had taken the baby out calling, and Mr. Cady and Martha had gone to a meeting, while Mrs. Fanny was having her regular afternoon nap. Snow drifted gently outside, muffling the world.

The embers of the fire were the deep orange-red of pohutukawa blossom; the curl of the flames was like the intricate carving on the prows of Maori canoes. Abby heard a step behind her, but it took her a long moment to come out of her dreams.

It was Jireh. Squatting down to touch her cheek, he said gently, "Abby, why are you crying?"

She touched her cheek herself, surprised to find wetness. "I was thinking of home," she confessed. "It is exactly a year since I sailed from New Zealand. At home, it's high summer ... and there are peaches, and whaleships..."

He drew her into his arms, and she wept unashamedly into his chest. Muffled, she cried, "I haven't heard from my father at all."

"Letters often go missing. It don't mean a thing."

She pulled back, trying to smile. "Victoria says it's bad news that travels fastest."

Yet, all the time now, she felt that something was very, very wrong. Her father was old, sixty-one—he had had a birthday without her. If he died, she'd have no one. She bit back another sob, and said as bravely as she could, "It's the blues, just the blues. I'll have slept them off by morning. And he did send me that silly riddle."

Jireh paused, and then said, "You never told me the reason for the riddle."

"It's supposed to be the key to a secret fortune."

"Fortune? What fortune?"

Abby bit her lip. She had tricked herself into indiscretion. A clock ticked slowly, heavily, marking time. But what was the harm? Jireh's arm was warm and reassuring around her shoulders.

She said, "My father discovered something valuable in a valley near our house in Mangonui, but is secretive about it. I know where it is, but not *what* it is. The riddle, when I work it out, will give me the answer."

She heard him suck in a breath. "Gold?"

"Surely not," she objected—but why did she feel so surprised? Gold was the word on everyone's lips; there was another California tale in every edition of the papers. Men fought for berths to sail to San Francisco, and the harbor there was a forest of masts, because hundreds of ships that had been abandoned by their crews—men who were desperate to get up the Sacramento River to the mines.

She shrugged, and said, "You could be right—but what does it matter? The riddle has me beat. I'll never work it out, and if my father is … is…"

She couldn't get the word out. "Who will look after me?" she wept, and Jireh pulled her against his chest again. "Oh, Abby," he whispered into her hair. "Abby, you will never be alone, I promise. There will always be someone to look after you."

Abby stilled, the wonderful words trickling into her mind. Suddenly her heart lit with incredulous delight. She waited for more of this breathtaking reassurance that he— that he … but instead she heard him say, "Is Obed really selling the *Erasmus?*"

She drew away from him. "He needs the money to build his ship."

"Obed? A ship?"

"I heard about it for the first time today. It will be a clipper of revolutionary design, he says, and the keel is being laid at Hillman's Yard."

"Well, well," he said slowly, then abruptly let go of her, to rise to his feet.

She stood up herself, watching him head off for the door, feeling off-balance and uncertain. "Is something wrong?"

"No, not at all—but it could make things difficult."

"What? How?"

"My father is selling the *Lizzie Ann*, and I doubt if there'll be any interest in the old box, with a lucky ship like the *Erasmus* on the market."

"But I thought you didn't believe in that kind of superstitious nonsense?"

"I do not—but the merchants are like my mother, and far more likely to bid for the lucky *Erasmus* than the unlucky *Lizzie Ann*, believe me. In fact, my father may conclude to sell the *Pierrot* instead," he said as he opened the door. "Seth Morgan is back, and creating a great deal of interest with his gratifying report. My father would find the lucky *Pierrot* a good deal easier to shift."

Jezekiel Mitchell jutted out his chin. "Thou shalt not round the corners of thy head. And neither shalt thou mar the corners of thy beard."

Seth stared at him. He had forgotten how the man ranted, and never quite talked sense. He had also forgotten how chillingly Mitchell resembled his murdered son. Then, involuntarily, he stroked his beard, which he'd just had tapered in the Portuguese style at Thornton's barbershop in North Water Street.

"Leviticus," said Mitchell. His own beard was unmistakably square.

Seth said evenly, "And the exact same chapter, if I remember correct, says that thou shalt not defraud thy neighbor."

That got home, he saw to his satisfaction: Mitchell flushed a furious red. "You're getting your rightful share of the profits of the voyage!"

"I damn well am not, and neither are my men!" According to the paper Seth had signed before the start of the voyage, his lay was one-twelfth—which meant that his share was the value of each twelfth barrel of oil. By his calculations, he should have received nine thousand dollars, but instead Mitchell had handed over a draft for just five.

Mitchell sniffed. "All that oil on the market at once? What do you expect but a lowering of price? I have had to absorb losses, too! And there was shrinkage—the gauges did not agree with your reckoning. And you are discounting fourteen months of considerable loss at the start of the voyage."

Seth said flatly, "My God." Then he swung around and stared out the window. Mitchell's office was sited on the floor above his chandlery store in Front Street and the window overlooked the harbor, but Seth saw nothing, battling with frustration instead.

Sharks, he thought savagely; the sailors talked of crimps and pimps and boardinghouse-keepers, but they did not have to cope with canting owners. Jezekiel Mitchell was cheating him with barefaced hypocrisy, and Seth could not do a thing about it.

Mitchell said from behind him, "The money is enough for you to buy a ship of your own."

"What?" Seth, frowning, swung round.

"You could buy the *Lizzie Ann*." Mitchell paused and then said, as if it hurt him, "Five thousand—the exact amount of that draft."

Seth's eyebrows lifted. The price was very fair: he thought that Mitchell must have offered the ship around all New Bedford already, to have come down to such a bargain price.

Remembering the state of the ship as he had seen her at Capricorn Island, he inquired, "And who would refit her?"

Mitchell snapped, "The *Lizzie Ann* is sound in every plank! Oil acts as a natural preservative."

Seth laughed. "What oil?"

The thin cheeks went puce, and Mitchell snarled, "You do not command the *Pierrot* again, sir—be certain of that!"

Seth shrugged. A lucky captain carried a lot of weight in New Bedford. The owners would be lining up to hire him. Then, to his amazement, the merchant muttered, 'I've halve the offer."

"I beg your pardon?"

"I'll sell you the *Lizzie Ann* for two and a half thousand."

Utter silence, as Seth stared at him. The hull must be full of worms, he thought; the price was so absurdly low that for a moment he was tempted. He could borrow the money to refit and provision her; his rich Morgan relatives should look benevolently on his request.

Then sanity prevailed. It was obvious that every speculator in the district had turned down the chance of a share in the old box, and he had worked too hard to sink his money in such a chancy venture.

He said, "No."

Jezekiel Mitchell was white-lipped with fury. "Buying your own ship is the only way you will ever get another command!"

"With a report like mine?"

"With your reputation!"

"I don't know what the hell you are talking about."

"When you had foul murder on your ship?"

"You know I regret your son's sad demise. It was no fault of mine."

"No?" cried Mitchell. "When discipline was so slack that a murderous stowaway lurked undetected for quite six days?"

"The discipline on my ship could never be called slack. If anything, it was over-conscientious. And the stowaway was well hidden." In the recesses of his mind the trap of the forehold was around him again, Edmund hidden behind the casks with that enormous knife. He could smell rats and old oil. "He had help," he said. "Someone fed him."

Jezekiel Mitchell was absolutely still. Then he said in a whisper, "Fed him? Who fed him?"

Seth's nape prickled at the menace in the man's tone. He shifted his feet, and said, "A deserter was confined in the same forehold where Edmund was hiding. It seems they shared his food."

"Or someone brought down enough for two?"

Seth shrugged. "Anything is possible. I don't know."

"You had insurrection on your ship," Mitchell hissed. "Your ship was a serpent's nest of mutiny."

"There was no mutiny!"

"There was, Captain Morgan, and you think to conceal it."

"I concealed nothing! A full report was made and witnessed by an American consul."

"Report? I have seen no report."

Seth shifted again. Foreboding coiled inside him. "You have the report."

"I do?"

"Aye. The logbook." Seth pointed to where it lay on Mitchell's desk. His fingers itched to take it; he wished now that he had kept a log of his own. Many captains did that, to have their own record. Had Obed's advice been wrong—or come too late?Despite the cold, Seth was sweating. Mitchell said abruptly, "Buy the *Lizzie Ann*."

"No."

"It's your only chance of a command."

"I don't agree."

"My offer was confidential, mind."

Goddammit, the man had not only cheated him, but he was now casting aspersions on his discretion. Seth swung on his heel to quit the room. Then, abruptly, he remembered the letter in his pocket. Like most homebound captains, he had collected all the mail addressed to New Bedford at Talcahuano, the last port he had touched. He had delivered them to the customs house here—all except one. The one he'd kept back was addressed to Abigail Sherman.

He said, "I have a letter for your ward."

"My...?"

"The Sherman girl." Seth spoke impatiently, eager to get away. To his surprise, he saw Mitchell's expression become evasive.

Then Mitchell muttered, "The offspring of profanity."

The flat eyes were flickering everywhere to avoid meeting Seth's stare. At that moment Mitchell was so like his murdered son that Seth's skin crept.

"A mother's holy burden is her unselfish devotion to duty, and Sherman's wife was neither devoted nor dutiful. She took the way of unrighteousness and deviated from the ordained path. Even though the road be arduous, no truer happiness exists on earth for women than in filling the honored place of mother and homemaker. She did not. She did neither."

Seth frowned, oppressed with unpleasant memories of William Mitchell's mad ravings from the Old Testament. What the devil did the man mean?

He said, "Doesn't Abigail Sherman live with you?"

"I refused to accept the burden of an abomination before the Lord. The book ordains that a woman should do nothing that pertaineth to a man, yet Frances Sherman did so. She took up the way of the sea, which is the domain of men, and because of this the girl is motherless, and a tax on another's household. And that household, sir, is not mine."

Seth said blankly, "Then where the devil — ?"

"Thou shalt not bow down to profanity; the iniquity of the fathers should be visited on the children until the third and fourth generations to come, sir. You will find her at the Cambridge house."

Mitchell sounded utterly insane. Seth turned on his heel and grasped the handle of the door. The brass knob felt gritty, the workings rusty. Illogically, he felt trapped, but then he managed to jerk the door open.

"Also thou shalt not oppress a stranger," he snapped, and ran down the stairs to the street.

The air outside was full of dirty snow, but it felt clean in Seth's throat. After that appalling interview, he needed a brandy. He strode rapidly through the slush on the cobbles, past sail lofts and ship-smiths to the smoking saloon behind Thornton's barbershop on North Water Street.

The shop at the front was clean and smelled of soap and balsam. Seth nodded to the barber and strode on through, scattering the little piles of cut hair that lay by the chairs. The door to the saloon was at the back, and when he opened it he was engulfed in smoke and stuffy warmth and a sound of hearty male gamming.

How many saloons like this could be found in the whaling ports of the world? Rooms of creaky tables and creakier chairs, worn ragged with the weight of many captains? Out-of-date shipping lists cluttered every surface, and racks held private messages for visiting masters to collect. There were charts and timeworn cabinets filled with dusty curiosities. Here, hints were exchanged, and men talked of Hong Kong and New Zealand as if they were closer than Boston. In countless cabins of far-flung ships, captains thought of this particular room when they thought of home. Here, they were fully at ease, comfortable with their own kind, which they were not in the parlors of New Bedford.

It was no surprise to Seth to find his brother, Uriah, here, and not at the boardinghouse where their shiftless father might or might not be taking dinner. Here, both brothers felt more welcome. Uriah came over to join him, shouting for brandy and slapping Seth on the shoulder.

"Heard your report," he said. There was envy in his voice. "Thought that mine was acceptable—but when I heard of ship *Pierrot*..."

Seth took the glass, feeling soothed. His brother was a fleshy man, not as tall as Seth, and much fairer; his face went red easily, and was now flushed with comradeship. Other captains were equally jovial, offering cigars and congratulations. Some Seth had seen in the past few months, others he had not seen for years, but it made no difference to the hearty talk. Uriah was his brother by blood, but all the rest were brothers by profession. It was a grateful balm to his spirit to hear his report discussed with so much respect, and have others ask for details. Have trouble getting another command? Nonsense, he thought, and lounged back in his chair, feeling more and more relaxed as the brandy went down and the hours wandered by.

A man from Damons' confectionery came in with a tray of pies to sell, and found a good market. Seth ate as he listened sleepily to the gossip. When they had finished talking of reports and the oil market, the talk was all of gold: Gardner of the *Sylph* had sold his oil in Panama and gone into the passenger trade, carrying eager miners to 'Frisco. There was good money in it, they said—but there was a catch, too. "Gardner can count himself fortunate if he don't find his crew disembarking with the passengers," said someone. "Aye," said another. "Alleyn of the *Isaac Walton* lost all but two men when he dropped anchor there."

The harbor of San Francisco was choked with abandoned craft, the men all run to the mines. "We'll see more whalers stranded thus," said someone else. "And others altered to the passenger trade ... Did you hear that

Mitchell is selling the *Pierrot?*"

Seth sat up with a jolt. Brandy slopped in his glass, and he drained it. The *Pierrot* for sale? Mitchell hadn't mentioned that when he had warned him that the command of the ship was not available: all he had said was that the *Lizzie Ann* was on the block. But why sell both ships? Had Jireh Mitchell decided to quit the whaling business, leaving his father stranded without a whaling master in the family? Seth remembered the strange state of the *Lizzie Ann* at Capricorn Island, and Jireh Mitchell's ramblings about the advantages of the Oriental trade—and Jireh Mitchell came into the room.

Everyone except Seth hailed him. A glass was shoved into his hand. Jireh Mitchell grinned amiably, and winked at a few. Someone said, "Is it true that your father is selling the *Pierrot?*"

Jireh nodded. His eyes sought out Seth's, and his smile widened.

"Shouldn't have any trouble," someone commented, "considering Morgan's lucky voyage."

Jireh lifted his glass to Seth in a mocking salutation. "Of course you are right," he said to the other man. "But, on the other hand, my father will have great trouble shifting the *Lizzie Ann,* considering *my* report."

Silence. Some of the captains cleared their throats. Jireh twinkled, knowing perfectly well what was in their minds, but as placid as ever. Outside, icy sleet was slanting down, but in here it was warm and stuffy and cordial.

"Perhaps," one ventured, "your father would be best to stick with the old box, and hope she improves her report next voyage."

"No, no, he can't do that," said Jireh. "You see," he candidly went on, "my father needs the money—because he has bought the *Erasmus* from Obed Cambridge."

When Seth went out into the street, the late afternoon chill hit like a blow. He hunched his shoulders against the wind and sleet, striding along Water Street and turning left at Union, heading rapidly towards County Street. When he heard a shout from behind him, he stopped.

It was Jireh Mitchell. Seth wished he hadn't heard him. Capricorn Island was too vivid in his mind, along with Jireh's amusement at what he considered Seth's stuffiness.

Jireh said, "Are you headed for the Cambridge place?"

Seth nodded. Jezekiel Mitchell had told his son about the letter, he supposed — the letter he was carrying to Abigail, because this man's family had refused to take her in. He started walking again.

Jireh quickened his step to keep up. "I go there, too," he remarked. "My mother and sister are paying a call on Mrs. Cambridge."

It didn't surprise Seth that the Mitchell women would calm their consciences by eating Victoria's cake. He said nothing.

"You know Obed is building a ship?"

"What?" Seth hadn't seen Obed yet, and had not heard the gossip. How the world moved, he thought grimly; the Mitchells had the *Erasmus,* and Obed was a builder of ships.

"And you know my father plans for me to take command of the *Erasmus?*"

Seth shook his head, but was not surprised — though he did wonder what Jireh would do if the whales lined up to be killed and cut in, the way they had for Obed. Then they arrived at the Cambridge house, and Abigail came running down the steps.

She was wearing a gold-colored dress and her hair was a mass of copper curls, caught up with jewel-headed pins. Her expression was radiant. Seth stared, entranced. She was beautiful, so much more beautiful than remembered — and for a mad moment he thought the joyful welcome was for him. Something inside him moved hungrily. Then sense returned.

Her eyes were focused beyond him — at Jireh Mitchell. It

wasn't until Seth took a step forward that her gaze shifted to his face.

She blinked. Didn't she recognize him? He fingered his beard involuntarily, and she laughed, "You really do look like a pirate. A swashbuckling buccaneer!"

He frowned, affronted. She was like her cousin, colorful, frivolous, and flippant—and also like her cousin, she was casually insulting. He turned away from her, deliberately dismissing her from his mind, and a movement in the portico caught his eye.

"Ah," said Jireh's voice at his shoulder. "I'm late, for here is my sister awaiting."

A middle-sized female stood there, sedately corseted, dressed in decent black. She had a pink-and-white skin, and fine brown hair drawn back beneath a modest coal-scuttle bonnet. Seth met the questioning gaze of large pale-blue eyes—and smiled.

Eight

Abby's fingers were shaking as she struggled to open the letter that Seth Morgan had brought her.

She was in her bedroom, kneeling on the floor by her bed as if in prayer. The letter—thank God!—was not a riddle. It was too thick for that. Perhaps, she thought, it might even hold the answer to the silly little puzzle. She was tingling with joy and suspense.

She had thought that the Mitchell women would never leave. Victoria had invited Jireh and Seth Morgan to a dish of tea, and she had thought that the stilted conversation would go on forever, while Charity and Mrs. Mitchell had made sheep's eyes at Seth. But finally Mrs. Mitchell had heaved herself out of her chair, and Jireh had taken the women away.

Abby forgot them. She had the letter open.

My dear daughter

> *Do not think so hard of me for sending you to New Bedford. The day you sailed away was the hardest parting I ever had and no mistake, and the last thing I should want, I do earnestly assure you, is to know you to be unhappy, but, dear daughter, I had no choice. If only you would set your mind to it, you would profit from your stay in New England*

*and learn to be a decent American lady with some prospect
of a decent future.*

*Things is bad in New Zealand, and they are going to
get worse. Grey and his masters in New South Wales work
on with unblemished arrogance, despite the complaints of
the New Zealand natives. American ships are commanded
by men who insist on order, temperance and energy, and
British ships take one fourth the oil they do. And why?
Because the crew of English ships are characterized by
drunkenness and want of discipline. The foremast hands
desert in their dozens, and have to be replaced by men from
the New Zealand villages, which are emptying out so that
women and old men have to do all the work and if it
weren't for arrogance, the British would see that with these
policies of discrimination against the enterprise of
Americans, it is begging for war. It's only time before a
Maori will rise up and proclaim himself a leader, and incite
the Maori Sons of Liberty to rebellion! But it will come too
late for me, I fear. The British insist I sell my lands and my
holdings—everything.*

Abigail found she was weeping. Sell the land, the
house? Where would her father live? What would happen to
Wikitoria and Tamati—and Broddy? All her childhood
memories were of the brig, the school, and the big house in
Mangonui. When she was small she had sat on the stairs on
warm summer nights and listened to her father and Broddy
as they drank and sang and played fiercely fought games of
billiards. Later, after her mother died, Broddy had teased her
father into letting little Abby join them at the table. Would
the old billiard table be sold, too? Its oak bed was just a little
warped. One had to know a trick or two to pot a ball in the
southeast corner.

She had to scrub tears away before she could read more.

*I must sell to a proxy to save any profit for myself, a
man I can trust. It will be a paper sale only, and then when
he sells at the proper price we will share the money, only
half of what I expected, but half is better than none. And*

then when Te Wharenui and I have beat out a way to make our fortune we'll be rich again, little Abby, and you can come home.

BUT NOT YET.

The capitals were angry. *"Abigail,"* the wild black writing scratched:

> *I am most unhappy that you have not obeyed me and gone to our cousins the Mitchells. I have paid Mitchell and paid him well, and it shames me that you are presuming further on the kindness of Captain Cambridge and his lady. Your dear mother would be as distressed as I am that you have acted thus, and you must obey me now, on instant receipt of this letter, and remove yourself to the Mitchell house.*
>
> *I insist on it. I will not send for you until I have heard a good report from our cousin Mitchell that you have learned patience and obedience.*

Abby was shaking violently. He had paid Mr. Mitchell? He was ashamed of her? When it was Mr. Mitchell who was the cheat? The bed quivered in sympathy with her rage and disappointment. She had tried so hard ... so hard. She hiccupped, scrubbed her face with the corner of a sheet, and furiously jerked her writing desk out from under the bed.

She unfolded it and thrust aside the papers for the brig. Where was the *Pandora?* Had he sold the brig, too? Could he do that, when she owned it? Surely it was still hers.

She hauled out paper, and stabbed her pen in the ink.

Hon'rd father,

> *I take my pen to assure you of the health of your undutiful daughter. I rec'd your letter today, and you will*

193

never realize the pleasure it was to receive it, and the disappointment it was to read.

Father, I am NOT living on charity. It is news to me that you paid your cousin's husband, but no doubt it would suit him to take your money, while it does not suit him to take me. Father, I am certain that if you wrote to Mrs. Cambridge you would receive that favorable report you desire, for I work, Father, I work!

I can get three regular meals and clear them each day, I can sew and mend and wash and iron and starch all kinds and varieties of clothing. Please be assured that I have learned to school myself. All my dresses sweep the ground, I put up my hair, I can trim a bonnet, I can make polite conversation. Mrs. Cambridge has been the BEST of teachers, and you must try to be proud, for I can do all that is necessary to be a housewife, helpmeet and hostess.

BUT THAT IS NOT WHAT I WANT! Father, the brig is mine, and all I want in this world is to be on board of a ship, at the side of the man who commands her. I was born and raised at sea and that is where I belong. And fate ordains it, for...

She stopped, lifting her pen and staring into space. Yesterday Jireh and Martha had argued savagely, with so much passion that Abby had felt alarmed. When Jireh had left she had seen him to the door, and he had smiled wryly down at her, and kissed the tip of her nose and said, "Oh Abby, dear sweet-natured Abby."

He loved her. She was sure of it—as sure as she was that she loved him. She gripped her pen and wrote very firmly:

... for I love a man who owns a ship and that ship is none other than the Erasmus! Yes, Captain Cambridge has sold her and your own cousin's son Jireh will take her on her next voyage to the Pacific. Jireh is kind and handsome and greatly attentive, he dances attention all the time, and I

194

shall marry him, and we shall sail to New Zealand together,
and then I shall give him my brig, for my dowry.

Victoria called her from the parlor. Without re-reading it, Abby hastily signed the letter, and folded it in two one way, and three the other. Then she sealed the last fold with a hasty blob of wax, and put her thumbprint on it, and addressed it swiftly. She would take it to the customs house in the morning, and put in the bag that would go on board the first vessel headed for the south Pacific. She put it in her reticule, and then she slammed the writing desk shut, and shoved it under the bed.

Seth courted Charity Mitchell with businesslike haste. He took her to church meetings, to singing classes, and out on carriage rides—while he did not court her at Jezekiel Mitchell's home, he took her to Gosnold's for ice cream and to Damon's for cake. They went to the Lyceum to see a stereopticon and he helped her distribute hymnals at the Mariners' Home. In the mornings he saw owners and agents and read the papers for likely ships, but some weeks passed before he realized that while he seemed to be succeeding in one activity, the other was showing no promise at all.

Men were starting to avoid him. Agents looked embarrassed when he arrived at their doors, and owners were out when he called to see them. Men who had brought ships in after the *Pierrot*—and with much worse reports—had commands and were preparing to sail again, but there was not a single hint of a command for Seth.

Why? It didn't seem possible, for lucky captains were always sought after. Then, one noontime when he called in at Thornton's smoking saloon, the conversation stopped as he came in the door. He heard the awkward silence descend as he shut the door behind him, and his neck prickled. When he turned, no one spoke to him. Everyone avoided his eyes.

Captains turned their backs and continued conversations.

Seth took brandy from the tray and sat down. The coin, as he dropped it on the tray, made a loud rattle, and the chair creaked arthritically.

The door opened and Uriah came in. Seth's brother was smiling broadly. "I've done it!" he cried to one and all. "I'm an owner!"

Then he saw Seth, and his grin faded. His expression became embarrassed. When captains wanted to know what ship he'd bought, he coughed awkwardly. "The *Pierrot*," he said. "Mitchell met my price at last."

Silence. No one looked at Seth. Then someone slapped Uriah's back and gave him a cigar and the hearty boom of conversation resumed.

Seth drank his brandy and got up for another. When he and his brother were small, they had been very competitive. Their father had ignored them, so they had competed for their mother's attention when she was there, and fought when she was not. Uriah was four years older than Seth, so he had won the fights for long enough, but then Seth had grown bigger, taller, and stronger, which had annoyed Uriah extremely. Uriah had been married for quite five years now to a plump, pale woman without a hint of rebellion in her head. She had brought to the marriage a small farm in Dartmouth, and she lived there and kept it uncomplainingly when Uriah was at sea.

So Uriah had the lucky *Pierrot*. Jezekiel Mitchell kept on renewing his offer to sell the *Lizzie Ann*, but Seth steadily refused. That old box? Never, thought Seth, but then remembered that Mitchell's expression had become slyly knowing, of late. When Uriah left, he stood up quickly and followed his brother out of the saloon.

The air outside was cool and clammy, with a hint of spring, and there was mud seeping out between the cobbles. When Seth caught up with Uriah, he invited him to dine at the New Bedford Hotel. Uriah did not want to accept, but

Seth insisted, and when they were seated he started asking questions.

Uriah shifted unhappily. "Everyone is talking about how you shot and murdered to put down mutiny."

"What!" Seth half rose in his seat, his palms slammed down on the table top. No one looked around: more than two hundred men filled the huge dining room, eating and talking, and the din was deafening.

Seth said grimly, "There was no mutiny."

"Evidently you haven't seen this morning's paper."

When Uriah hauled it out of his pocket, Seth grabbed it and unfolded it. The story was on the editorial page. He couldn't miss it.

MUTINY IN THE PACIFIC
—While cruising in the New Zealand ground the crew of the whaleship Pierrot, Morgan, led on by a desperate stowaway, refused to do duty. Captain Morgan attempted to reason with the men, sending the first officer, William Mitchell, as ambassador. When Mr. Mitchell and another seaman were overwhelmed, Captain Morgan attempted once more to regain control of the ship, addressing the crew and stating his determination to maintain his authority, if need be at cost of life.

—The only reply was defiance. Captain Seth Morgan leveled his musket and fired. The ball entered the temple of the stowaway and passed out the other side of the head and he fell dead on the instant. Captain Morgan then informed the crew that he intended to pursue the same course with any other mutineer, and the crew determined that they preferred returning to their duty to being shot at, and the ship continued on her course.

"I'm in favor of flogging, myself," Uriah said. "It's better than coldblooded murder."

Seth's head pulsed with rage and consternation. He said, "Where the hell did they get that pack of lies?" He thought of the low rafters of the forehold, of slipping in blood, and of

Edmund slashing that great boarding knife at his belly, of Mitchell falling on top of the slimy pile of his intestines. How would Uriah have coped with that? He could wager, Seth thought furiously, that Uriah, like most men, would have been too yellow-bellied to go down that ladder, that he would have fired potshots down the hatch until Edmund was killed, even if it had taken weeks, while all the time the ship was gripped by terror.

He rasped, "I'll sue them." But how could he prove it? Cold panic seized him. Where had that story of mutiny come from? It was absolutely untrue, but he couldn't prove that, not unless a court of law forced Mitchell to produce the log.

Obed would be his witness, but how reliable was he? Obed, if he had done as promised, would have noted it in his own log. He must have it still, for the logbook belonged to Obed, as owner of the *Erasmus* ... but was it any good as proof? No wonder the agents and owners had been so evasive. How long had this libel been going the rounds? No wonder he had no ship...

His mind stopped dead.

He couldn't sit still a second longer. He knew now who had started the slander—and why. Without another word to his brother he left the table and strode out of the room and outside.

Jezekiel Mitchell was in the counting-house above his chandlery rooms. Seth shut the door behind him, turned and said grimly, "I wish to marry your daughter, Charity."

Mitchell showed no surprise. He said, "Well, you can't."

"And your reason?"

"A virtuous woman is as a crown to a worthy man, and I do not consider you a worthy man. You are a subject of gossip and calumny. You murdered to put down mutiny. How can my daughter marry a man of no reputation and no property?"

It was no less than Seth expected. He set his jaw and bit out, "The man I shot was your son's murderer—and there was no mutiny. The killing was to save both my life and your ship."

"So you say, but others say different and that is what counts. You have the arrogance, sir, to expect my daughter to share your ill repute. And I say no. If you had a command it would be different, but you don't. If you had a ship, it would be different, but you don't. Therefore, I say no."

Seth snapped, "And if I buy the *Lizzie Ann?*"

Mitchell looked cautious, his blank eyes moving evasively. It was as if he knew he had won but sensed nevertheless that he was not in control. He prevaricated, "You have seen that the ship is a bargain?"

"No, I have not. What I have seen, sir, is that you deliberately blackened my name in order to force me to buy your old tub. You were desperate for money to buy the *Erasmus,* so desperate that you stooped to libel to get your own way. I have been a fool—a fool to allow an officer to keep the only log, a fool to deal with a merchant like yourself. But you, Mitchell, have been a blackguard. So, I am forced to buy your old tub, for you have made sure that I will never be offered a command. I happen to need a wife and your daughter is willing, so I'll submit and take them both, or take neither. That's my ultimatum, Mitchell. I'll buy your tub, if you give me your daughter."

Silence. Mitchell had his head cocked to one side. "Very well, then," he said at last. "You have both my consent and the *Lizzie Ann,* on receipt of your five thousand."

"You said two and a half."

"Did I? Then that is very strange, for I don't recollect saying any such thing. Five thousand, or we'll forget the bargain."

Seth's fists clenched impotently. The *Lizzie Ann* would have to sail with the ship uninsured. He'd be going cap in hand to the Morgans again, but with more success this time. They would not fail to lend an owner the outfitting price, even if the owner possessed nothing more than a near-derelict ship.

He snapped, "Very well. Have two papers drawn up—the bill of sale and a marriage agreement." He was damned if he'd have any more dealings with Mitchell without a watertight contract.

Mitchell was silent. His mouth was set meanly, and his eyes were cautiously triumphant.

"And inform your daughter that we marry the moment the *Lizzie Ann* is ready to sail," said Seth, adding curtly, "and I've retrieved my good reputation."

"It had to be a mutiny," argued Jireh. "Someone had to get food to the stowaway."

Obed cleared his throat. "Seth told me the stowaway was down in the forehold with a boy who was in irons there at night. He reckoned the boy shared his rations."

"But at least some of the men must've known there was someone hiding on board—a man with murderous intentions. They must've had mutiny on their minds, seeing they kept quiet about it."

"I don't know about that," Obed said uncomfortably. He clicked his tongue and rattled the curricle reins. Privately, he was of the same mind, but after all, Seth was his cousin.

There had been too much talk of the nasty business, he mused. If the gory details were known, there would be even more chatter; folk asked him for those details all the time, for it was widely known that he had been the first to speak with Seth after the murders had happened. But all he could do was clear his throat and look knowing.

"The tale has even overtaken the talk o' gold," said Jireh. "Have you heard about Hussey o' the *Planter*? He shot to put down a mutiny, shot a man dead. Then he shot another one in the hand, shot it off. Next ship he spoke, he reported that he had lost one hand, and one of his men had lost another."

It took Obed some moments to work this out. Then he didn't laugh: he thought it was in very bad taste. Mitchell should be going about his proper business, he mused — overseeing the stowing and fitting out of his ship. The *Erasmus* would sail soon, within a month, and Jireh Mitchell was too casual about it altogether.

Obed concentrated on guiding the horses through the heavy spring mud, listening to the ladies chattering in the curricle behind him. His mouth curved indulgently as he thought that they would have to watch Emily, by thunder. The baby had discovered walking, and if they didn't look sharp, she would be head to toe in mud by the time they got home. But he wouldn't have countenanced the notion of leaving her behind, for today was special, an historic occasion, by Jove. Today the last plank completed the hull of Obed's new ship.

He had asked Seth to come, but Seth, as always these days, was a deal too preoccupied. Unlike Jireh Mitchell, he was busy outfitting his ship. The old *Lizzie Ann* — Obed couldn't understand why Seth had bought the old tub. She would cost him money and ruin him, in the end. But Seth didn't discuss much, these days; he had become grim and silent, perhaps because men took obvious pains to avoid him.

"You have to admire his guts," Jireh said. "Do you know he goes to Thornton's every morning precisely at ten? He has a shave and then a cigar and a brandy while he reads the papers, and then he leaves at precisely eleven. Everyone else avoids the place at that time, so he has the saloon to himself. What stiff-necked pride, eh?"

Obed was silent. He hardly ever went to Thornton's, but he thought he should go some morning at ten for family solidarity. Oh dear, he thought, he would be pleased when the *Lizzie Ann* sailed and the tongues stopped a-wagging.

Between Obed's boots a whiskey jug was braced, the contents sloshing against the stopper with a musical liquid sound. The grog was to be given to the shipwrights on this momentous day. The carriage jounced around a final bend, and there was Obed's ship, like a beached wooden whale set ponderously on bed blocks: stem, keel, sternpost and deadwood, keelson and ribs, all held firm in a scaffold of rough heavy timbers. Deck beams had been bolted from frame to frame, and then the garboard strakes and the planking nailed. Today that final shutter plank would be rammed into place, the last timber that, like the keystone of an arch, held and bound the forces of the hull together. Instantly, he forgot Seth and his problems. No other vessel would ever be as lucky and lovely as this ship!

The carriage slid to a stop and the baby crowed. The carpenters and caulkers paused to look around. The air stung cleanly, with the crisp piney scent of newly cut wood, of the salt pickle used to season the timber, of tar and oily rags. Then the men set to work again, with the squeak of ax on wood and pounding of hammers on springy locust trunnels and the rhythmic burr of saws on yellow pine and white oak timber. The long steam box hissed. Within it, the shutter plank was cooking.

Hillman's Yard was no grand affair, but it satisfied Obed's eye. Sheds stood about everywhere—low sheds where trunnels were carved, and sheds on stilts with saws underneath. The hull dominated all, thudding and echoing as if alive already, vibrating solidly as huge wooden knees were battered into place, framing corners. Obed's ship would have the strength of the whales he would capture. She would overcome everything the sea could throw— storms and ice and reefs, by thunder. Obed's lovely new ship would win over all.

He'd drawn no blueprints: the shipwrights needed none. The final shape was in the foreman's mind, and in the light wooden patterns he had made for the carving of the frames and knees. Great trees had been felled in the hinterland forests, each with a curve that fit the foreman's eye. They'd been trimmed roughly and hauled to the yard, and then the patterns laid on top, so that carpenters could chop them precisely to the required shape. And how the vessel had grown! Only weeks before, she'd been a gaunt skeleton of ribs and bends, but now she'd taken on flesh. They built so quickly, these New Englanders; the new ship would launch in the heat of high summer and sail in the fall.

Obed sighed with pure pleasure. He clambered down from the curricle bench and picked his way through the mud. The whiskey jug was under his arm, and the carpenters were eyeing it with anticipatory grins. Then they set to work. The shutter plank was ready.

The steam box growled with a savage burst of vapor as the front end was opened. Men gleamed with condensation as, in a line, they grunted and heaved, and the long heavy timber was slowly drawn out. "Huh," they said in unison, almost in a chant. Then the plank was braced on a line of hunched shoulders, and slowly and ponderously, boots sliding in the slush, men grunting with effort, the plank was hefted to the waiting gap in the hull.

The end was aimed, poised, and adjusted. Everyone waited, knees braced strongly. The foreman aimed his big hammer, took a breath, and—swung. Slam! The end of the plank shot into the gap. The men shuddered and braced themselves again. The foreman moved a pace along the plank. Slam! Another yard of timber creaked into place.

Obed stood very still. Every fiber of his body felt in tune with the timber. Then he became aware that someone had braved the mud to come and stand beside him.

He turned. It was Abigail. Her lips were parted, her eyes were brilliant, and she seemed enraptured. With pride, Obed pointed out the parts of his ship, and explained what the men were doing. Abigail listened intently to every word. "She's beautiful!" she said.

And so was Abigail lovely. Obed had become accustomed to her cheerful presence about the house, and when she and Victoria sang together—oh, sometimes his eyes stung with emotion. She was a credit to his dear Victoria, she was indeed, and he thought very highly of his wife for it. But it didn't seem right that a girl should be so radiant at the sight of a half-made ship.

He said gruffly, "I'll name her *Curtsey*."

"It suits her!"

"Not too romantic? Whalers are so ... functional, even clipper-built."

"Practical things that do their job well are always lovely." He could see she meant it. He looked back at his ship and the plank was in place; the hull was complete, so the *Curtsey* showed her shape.

Then Obed saw Consider West come towards him from beyond some sheds, and wondered what the young man was a-doing here. A couple of weeks back, Mr. West had come asking for a job, but Obed had had to send him away, as the young fellow would need to ship long before this autumn. Now, trudging over, West looked unusually uncertain, not at all like his jaunty self. He was mud up to the top of his boots by the time he arrived, his nose red, his wrists blue-white.

He said awkwardly, "She'll be a fine ship. She sails in the fall?"

"November, probably."

"And you haven't shipped a crew, sir?"

"No, of course not." Obed said patiently, "As I told you, I would take you on as third mate again, but you'll have found a berth long before then."

Consider West sniffed, rubbed his nose with the back of his glove, and looked unhappier than ever. "I've found a berth already. First mate, *Lizzie Ann*."

Obed was astounded—scandalized. Consider West was how old? Twenty? Good Godfrey, he thought, Seth must have been desperate for a first officer.

"It's a fine promotion, a grand opportunity," Mr. West

muttered.

Obed said dryly, "It is indeed."

"*If* the *Lizzie Ann* sails."

"What do you mean?"

"Cap'n Morgan's been arrested — for the murder of the mutineer what slaughtered William Mitchell."

Abigail hovered on the cobbles outside the shop in North Water Street. She felt horridly furtive. When a group of captains walked towards her, she hastily turned her back and stared in the storefront window.

ELISHA THORNTON, JR. declared the gilt letters. DRUGGIST & APOTHECARY. Inside the bow of the leaded panes an ornamental brass lamp cast light and shadow on the display. FRENCH CHEMICALS, DYESTUFFS, PERFUMERY.

Thornton's barbershop stood to one side. Abigail studied it nervously. It was five past ten in the morning. She had not seen Seth Morgan go in.

The group of captains was coming closer. Would they turn into the barbershop? She could hear their loud gruff voices. She leaned forward to peer with elaborately faked interest at Mr. Thornton's apothecary display, pulling her cloak close about her. FRESH FOREIGN LEECHES, MEDICINE CHESTS FOR FAMILIES & SHIPS. The hem of her skirt was sodden and dragging. A cold little wind blew up from the bay. Her feet felt frozen. The captains passed behind her, their voices fading round the corner, into Union Street.

The street was empty. Surely she would have seen Seth if he had gone to the barbershop? Abigail dithered, was abruptly convinced that this was a wild goose chase, that Seth Morgan was somewhere else. In jail, perhaps. But despite all that she ran to the barbershop door and shoved it open. A little bell tinkled above her head. The air inside was clean and warm, and smelled of balsam and soap.

There was only one customer, an anonymous figure with curly black hair and lather all over his face. He was shrouded in what appeared to be an enormous sheet.

As she shut the door, the little bell tinkled again and the barber turned. He was as bald as a billiard ball and completely clean-shaven. Abby had to bite back a hysterical giggle.

He said, "Yes?"

"C-Captain Morgan?"

"Yes?" said the barber again. The man in the chair was rigidly still. Then, to Abby's utter alarm, she heard voices outside in the street. She looked around wildly and saw a door in the back of the shop with SALOON written on it. She ran towards it. The barber yelped, "Miss!" Ignoring him, she shot through the door and snapped it shut behind her. The room was empty. She leaned her back on the door, panting.

Greasy leather armchairs were strewn here and about, and rickety wooden chairs were lined up by equally unsteady tables. Was this shabby place really the refuge of important captains? There was only one window, opening onto a narrow yard. She could smell old cigar smoke and the dregs of brandy. Books and papers lay everywhere, just as in Mr. Cady's house.

And there were curiosities in cabinets. Something was staring at Abigail from behind a dusty glass door. When her eyes focused, she saw the severed head of a Maori warrior, elaborately tattooed, shiny with varnish, glaring with frustrated fury. Abby gasped. She had heard of the barbaric practice of selling heads, but never seen any evidence of it before. Next to it: a wooden god with a phallus that sagged all the way to its feet; a Maori whalebone club with a dulled and stained edge; a spear edged wickedly with sharks' teeth, also stained with what had once been blood. What were these things doing in this place? Perhaps mariners who had collected them had belatedly realized that they were not fit to take home. In the primitive Pacific they had forgotten the rectitude of New England.

The door clicked open, and she straightened. She had forgotten how tall Seth Morgan was, how broad-shouldered he was, and how his eyebrows arched. The narrow blue eyes were arctic. He snapped, "What the devil do you think you're doing?"

"I had to see you. Were you the man in the chair?"

"What?"

"You have soap on your face."

For a moment she thought he was going to take hold of her and shake her, and she hastily stepped back. Instead, he wiped a broad hand across his face, removing half of the lather and none of the frown. He was clean-shaven; she tipped her head to one side, and said impulsively, "Why did you shave off your beard?"

"For God's sake, Abigail!"

"I liked it. Mrs. Fanny always said you looked like a buccaneer, and that beard did make you look so dashing — quite swashbuckling, really."

"Mrs. Fanny?"

She nodded. He seemed oddly confounded. Those eloquent eyebrows were slanted. For a moment, most disconcertingly, Abby experienced a most unanticipated desire to reach up and touch that clean-shaven jaw. She stepped back another pace. Then, in the barbershop, the little door bell tinkled.

Seth's hand shot out and grasped her arm. When she opened her mouth he shushed her. She heard the voices in the barbershop then, and her pulse jumped. Time crept by as they stood rigid and listened. Then the voices faded and the little bell tinkled again.

Abigail heard Seth's breath gust out. She pulled on her arm, but he held on. "For God's sake, Abigail," he said again. "Don't I have troubles enough with my reputation already?"

"It's a matter of life or death," she assured him.

"It's ... *what?*"

But he didn't wait for her answer. Still holding her arm, he opened the door and peered through the gap. Then, without another word, he hauled her through at a run. Her skirts rustled wildly, and she had to grab them with her unfettered hand. The barbershop was empty except for the bald barber, who was gaping. The door bell rattled agitatedly and then they were out in the street.

There were people hurrying along the pavements, but they were all hunched into their collars. A thin rain was misting down unpleasantly; winter had come back for the day. Seth dragged her into the doorway of the apothecary, so that she was trapped between the door and his large frame. He let her go and demanded, "What the devil did you say?"

"*Your* life or death," she said.

Utter silence. Seth stared down at her. Mist cobwebbed his thick black hair. Then he said, "Go on."

"What?"

"Put me out of my suspense," he urged. "Tell me what devious notion fills your pretty scatterbrain this time."

She scowled at him resentfully. "I only want to testify in your defense."

Seth paused, shook his head as if to clear it, and said, "Say that again."

"Con ... Mr. West informed me that you had been arrested for Edmund's murder, and I know you didn't murder anyone, not in cold blood. I know you killed Edmund to save yourself, and I want to give evidence to that."

"You want to stand up in front of a court and repeat the gossip you dragged out of that silly young man?"

"Gossip has nothing to do with it, Captain Morgan! I despise the chatterers as much as you do, so how dare you think I'd stoop to that! For all I care you can go to Gemini. But," she amended, "I don't want to see you go to your death when my testimony could save you—I wouldn't want it on my conscience. Edmund told me that he planned to murder you and William Mitchell, and that is what I am planning to stand up and say."

"And what do you think the gossipmongers would make of your testimony?"

She flashed, "I'm not over-sensitive about my reputation."

"Obviously not," he agreed. "You invade a barbershop and a smoking saloon at great risk of scandal and have evidently concluded to do the same in court. I can manage without that kind of help."

"You'd rather hang?"

"I have not the slightest intention of hanging—and I think I stand a better chance without your testimony."

"But I can tell them that Edmund swore murder because he was flogged so cruelly on your ship—and that he tried to kill you in Mangonui."

"During that struggle on the riverbank?" He snorted, "You're reading a deal too much into a single lucky blow."

"It's true!" she cried. "He had a knife, and he held it ready for the killing thrust, Captain Morgan. And I hit him with a lump of wood. I knocked the knife out of his hand and it fell into the river. And, if you don't let me testify, they will hang you. No one will credit that Edmund was a murderous madman who stowed away with the express intent of killing you and William Mitchell, not unless I tell them about how he tried his chance when you were lying at his mercy."

Seth's lips were pressed so tightly together that there was an angry white line around them. "If you stand up and deliver that in court, then I'm certain to hang. Is that your intention?"

She frowned, suddenly uncertain. "I don't know what you mean."

"I mean that I'd hang, most certainly—and that I would quit this earth with the reputation of a philanderer, a fool, a weakling, and a sadist."

"You ungrateful beast!"

"It's my life, as you pointed out. Pray allow me to take care of it."

"You'll be sorry when they convict you!"

"No doubt I would," he agreed sardonically. "However, that is very unlikely. I made sure of the best legal advice before I handed myself in."

"You ... *what?*"

"I handed myself in on the charge of murder," he said in a matter-of-fact voice. People were coming down the street, and he turned his head to watch them. "You see," he said, shrugging as he looked back at her, "I've been the subject of a deal of unpleasant tittle-tattle, and I concluded to clear my name — the proper way, in a court of law."

The passersby came closer, and Seth moved back, freeing her to step into the street. "And good day to you, Miss Sherman," he said with a wolfish grin, and was gone.

The fact that Seth Morgan had handed himself in on a charge of murder, as Abigail learned, did not necessarily mean that he would be put on trial. Martha and Mrs. Fanny, of course, knew which books to consult and were able to tell her all about it. Seth would first go in front of a magistrate, who, after hearing the charge and the defense, would decide whether there was probable cause to believe that a crime had, in fact, been committed. If he found against Seth, then his future would lie in the hands of a jury. To prevent that, Seth's lawyer needed to prove that the charge was baseless.

Abby had to attend the magistrate's court hearing — of course she did. How could she stay away? Victoria frowned and demurred, but Martha and Mrs. Fanny insisted on going, and Obed offered to escort the three ladies, to make their presence respectable, and Jireh Mitchell materialized to join them. They arrived early, which was a very good thing: the case had caused a great deal of excited speculation, and so the spectator benches rapidly became packed, mostly with men who shoved for room, and shouted at each other.

It was pouring rain outside, so the air was thick and steamy, and the din was deafening. Abigail had never seen such a crush, not even in Liberty Hall at Christmas. Where was the formality of justice? She had expected the careful silence of a church, certainly nothing like this. Why was so little respect being shown?

Martha assured her that people went to the law very casually in the States. The lack of awed respect for the formalities of the law was one of the benefits of being free. One man was as good as another, no matter what his birth or his wealth. Men gained or lost fortunes within a generation, so everyone felt free to sue everyone else. A landholder felt free to maintain his roads or neglect them, and the common drover felt free to sue the landholder if the axle of his dray broke on the ruts. How could Martha elucidate so calmly, when Seth Morgan's life was at stake? Jireh was laughing at a joke a man had just told him. Mrs. Fanny scanned the crowd with her ear trumpet.

Seth Morgan walked in and sat down. His lawyer went to a bench, and sat down, too. Then the magistrate arrived, and the sheriff banged for silence with his gavel. After the opening announcement, the prosecutor, a short, fat man, stood up and took a position in front of the magistrate's bench. Abigail hated him at once, even before he had cleared his throat.

"Captain Morgan," he said, and Seth Morgan stood up and nodded.

"I have a logbook in my hand, the official log of the ship *Pierrot* for your last voyage. Do you recognize the book, sir?"

Seth nodded again.

"Then pray allow me to quote. 'At three AM Edmund Davis seaman and Jack Rawlings steerage boy were put in the foremast rigging and flogged for insolence. I seized them up and striped their hides with three dozen to learn them their places so ends.'" The prosecutor waited until the gasps in the gallery had died down, and then said, "Is that a correct account of that punishment?"

"That entry was written by my first officer, William Mitchell. He carried out the flogging."

"And did you order that punishment?"

"I did not."

"And again, in Mangonui, a port in New Zealand, Edmund was flogged again. Still without your permission?"

Seth Morgan's lawyer stood up. He was so tall he made the prosecutor look unnaturally short. The magistrate put on a pair of metal-rimmed spectacles and said, "Yes, Mr. Lincoln?"

"I think it would be in order, sir, for that entry to be quoted in full."

"And your reason?"

"It will add a little light to this flogging business and the events that followed."

The magistrate hesitated, and then said, "I don't see how the details of such unpleasantness could help your client's case, Mr. Lincoln."

Mr. Lincoln said nothing, merely waiting, so the magistrate looked at the prosecutor and said, "Go ahead, Mr. Benedict."

Everyone looked back at the prosecutor, who studied the page for a long moment before reading aloud: "'At eleven AM Edmund Davis made assault on Mr. Mitchell the first officer and threatened my life, he not having learned his lesson He was put in the rigging and I stripped his shirt over his shoulder and made a net of his skin so that those which remain shall hear and fear and shall henceforth commit no more any such evil.'"

A hubbub of loud comment broke out, and the sheriff hammered on a desk with his fist and hollered for silence. Then the magistrate said, "And your reason for requesting this, Mr. Lincoln?"

"I merely wish to point out, sir, that Edmund Davis made a threat on the life of the first officer. A threat of murder," Lincoln repeated.

"And that is all?"

"Yes, sir."

"Oh, sit down, sit down," the magistrate said testily. "And will the prosecution please continue? We don't have all day to find if there is a case."

Nine

To Abigail's alarm, the prosecutor called Obed as a witness. He stood up reluctantly, and had to shove his way to the front. Mrs. Fanny was half standing, her hand gripping the back of the seat in front of her, her ear trumpet cocked alertly as she listened.

"Captain Cambridge, you presented your logbook for the defense?"

"I did, sir. I spoke Captain Morgan's ship and when I heard the account of the murders, I noted down what I had heard and signed it."

"Most neighborly, Captain Cambridge. But then, you are a cousin, are you not? Subject to the demands of family loyalty. And were you present, sir, when this series of crimes was committed?"

"Uh—no."

"Then your evidence is hearsay, Captain Cambridge, and hearsay is worthless in a court of law, particularly from such an interested source. But, while you are testifying, sir, perhaps you can inform me concerning a small fact that may hold some relevance. Would you agree, sir, that the master of a vessel is responsible for all acts of discipline on board of his ship, whether he is present or not?"

"Well..."

"Well?"

"Well, yes, sir, but I wish to point out that when a ship is in port the first mate—"

"That is all, Captain Cambridge. Please stand down."

Obed reluctantly returned to his seat, red-faced and rueful. The babble of comment had broken out again, and for the moment the sheriff let it be. The magistrate was talking with the prosecutor, who was thumbing through the *Pierrot* logbook as he listened. Seth Morgan was talking with his lawyer, whose expression was long and serious. Obed grumbled about flogging. "Softheaded lawyers! Put a lawyer on a quarterdeck with a crew waving fists and worse in the waist, and they'd drop their softheaded canting." Abigail thought tensely that this case was not about flogging, it was about murder, and why didn't they get on with it? Outside the rain was easing to showers, and it was growing hot. Men shuffled around on the benches as they shucked their coats and jackets.

Then the prosecutor cleared his throat and faced the courtroom. The hubbub instantly hushed. Mr. Lincoln sat at a desk, his long hands forming a steeple. It was time, it seemed, for the prosecution to state the case, and prove that the crime of murder had indeed been committed by Captain Seth Morgan.

"There is no doubt," the fat little man began, "that inhuman acts of punishment were practiced on the defendant's ship. Flogging is barbaric, and rightfully condemned by all civilized people. There is little doubt, furthermore, that the cruel punishments inflamed the mind of Edmund Davis, seaman, and caused him to secrete himself on board. Exactly why he did so will never be known, but perhaps he heard that his friend, his comrade in the hell that was the ship *Pierrot*, had been recaptured, and was held in irons."

Mr. Lincoln stood up casually, and said, "Really, sir."

"Yes, yes," said the magistrate. "Mr. Benedict, please confine yourself to facts."

Mr. Lincoln said, "Thank you. Quite apart from the extreme unlikelihood of Edmund Davis speaking to anyone from the ship, being a deserter on the run..."

The magistrate snapped, "Sit down, Mr. Lincoln! Your point is made!"

"But it is obvious," said the prosecutor, "that Davis, once he had managed to hide away on board, was given food by someone or other—that he had sympathizers on board."

Mr. Lincoln started to stand up again, and the magistrate waved him down. "Mr. Benedict," he said. "Do I need to ask you again to keep to known facts?"

The prosecutor inclined his head. "But it is certainly pertinent to give the *facts* of the murders, as written in the *Pierrot* logbook, and witnessed with the signature of Captain Morgan himself."

There was a rustle as everyone shifted, straining to hear every word as the fat little man read out the two entries:

Begins with fine weather Moderate winds from NNW, middle part shortened sail for the night, at brekkfast time a stowaway was discovered, and he murdered William Mitchell first mate and Joe Manuel seaman before being overpowered and Jack Rawlings steerage boy died of his wounds Captain Morgan shot Edmund Davis and killed him...

At Sunset we buried William Mitchell first mate and Joe Manuel seaman and Jack Rawlings steerage boy and Edmund Davis seaman with the usual burial service Captain Morgan read some verses from the bible and it was a very solem occasion after 3 greusom murders on board As Mr. Mitchell is dead I now keep the log, so Ends...

At the end, the magistrate asked him to read the entry again. Then he frowned and took the book and read it for himself, his lips moving.

Then he said, "This is most unclear, sir, most unclear, and yet, Captain Morgan, you signed it."

Seth stood, saying evenly, "I signed it after the event, on advice. I did not write it."

"And why not, sir—why not?"

"It is the first officer's job to keep the book."

"But your first officer was dead, sir!"

Mr. Lincoln stood in his slow unfolding way. He cleared his throat and said, "Murdered," and sat down again.

"Of course he was murdered!" the magistrate snapped. "We have murders a-plenty, too many murders! For it says, does it not, that Mitchell and a seaman called Manuel were murdered, and a boy called Jack died of his wounds? There were three murders, according to the logbook, three gruesome murders! So, according to this logbook, Captain Morgan, the third murder was committed by you, sir, for the steerage boy died of his wounds."

"Exactly, sir," said the prosecutor with satisfaction. "Captain Morgan murdered Edmund Davis, seaman, when he shot him down like a dog. I rest my case," he said, and sat down with the air of a man who had done a good job.

Mr. Lincoln spoke to the magistrate and then nodded at Seth, who took the stand. His lawyer looked at him, looked at the logbook, and said casually, "Captain Morgan, was Jack Rawlings murdered, or was he not?"

Seth seemed pale. His mouth was very straight. Abby watched him in suspense, and then he shook his head. He said in a low voice, "His death was accidental."

"You killed him accidentally?"

"I did not kill him at all. He fell onto Edmund's knife."

"A knife? Edmund had a knife?"

"He did."

"The same knife he had already used to murder William

217

Mitchell and José Manuel?"

"The same."

"Ah." Lincoln hesitated. He looked down at the logbook, frowning. "Jack Rawlings died of his wounds," he murmured. "H'm! That leaves us with a third gruesome murder, does it not, the theoretical slaying which this court wishes to investigate. When you discovered that William Mitchell and José Manuel had been foully done to death, why did you not act to overpower the mad killer?"

"It was not as easy as that—he was down in the forehold, with the knife."

"So you stood on deck and shot him through the hatchway?"

"I did not, sir. I went down the ladder with the intention of restraining him, if possible."

"If possible?" Mr. Lincoln echoed.

Seth Morgan nodded. "Unfortunately, it was not possible. When I shot Edmund Davis I had no choice. I shot him in self defense. He was determined to kill me."

"But you have no testimony to the fact that he was determined to murder you?"

Abby gasped. She was on her feet without premonition, her hands gripping the back of the seat in front of her. Seth's head jerked round and he stared at her; she gazed at him imploringly.

Seth shouted, "No testimony is necessary!" Mrs. Fanny's fingers circled her arm and hauled, and Abby sat down with a bump.

Seth said more calmly, "My fourth mate, Tom Kanaka, was with me. Edmund attacked us both. We were in the confines of the forehold. It was dark, and the floor was slippery. Edmund had that knife, and was rushing at us, swiping as he came. Jack Rawlings was already dead, having fallen onto that knife, and now Edmund was intent on killing me."

"Ah," said Mr. Lincoln, and smiled widely—and when

he smiled, Abby saw, he was suddenly beautiful. His lifeless eyes took on mischief, and he was like an overgrown faun. "A knife," he said. "And yet, Captain Morgan, you are a tall strong man. One would think sir, that you had spent your childhood as I did, in splitting railings! You had a gun; Edmund Davis was armed with just a knife."

Seth said grimly, "Mr. Lincoln, if you would kindly direct your eyes to the back of the room, you will see my fourth mate, Tom Kanaka. He is holding the knife that Edmund Davis used to slaughter William Mitchell and José Manuel—the same knife that killed Jack Rawlings when he fell on it. The same knife he was swinging about when he was trying his utmost to kill me."

Abe Lincoln stared. He put his hand to his eyes in dramatic fashion, and flinched back a step. "You call that weapon a *knife?*" he cried. "But it's longer than the longest fence railing! It's a chopper—a scythe, a halberd, an executioner's weapon!"

"We whalemen, Mr. Lincoln," said Seth, without expression, "call that a boarding knife."

The room was full of babble. Everyone had stood up, jostling to turn and stare. Tattooed Tom Kanaka glared back, as fearsome as the huge, long-handled knife he held. The magistrate and the sheriff had to hammer for quite five minutes before the crowd subsided.

"There is no case to answer," the magistrate said angrily. "It is a clear case of self-defense. And you, Captain Morgan, and you, Mr. Lincoln, should be properly ashamed of yourselves. You, sirs, have made a fool of this court."

Abe Lincoln grinned unrepentantly. Seth merely lifted his brows. "And someone has made a fool of me, sir," he said. "And that will be heard in court as well—after I have presented my writ for criminal slander."

Mrs. Fanny studied Seth with affection. "You're a rogue and a pirate, Nephew," she declared, and shook a finger under his nose. "And you, sir," she shouted at Mr. Lincoln, "are a two-faced scoundrel."

"Two-faced?" he said with ineffable charm. "Surely not, ma'am — for I most surely would not wear the face that I do, if I had another."

"And that, sir, deserves a libation," declared Jireh — who looked indecently entertained, considering that the flogging propensities of his brother had been openly discussed in court, along with his demise. "You will do me the honor of accompanying me to my ship, where I can promise you a fine French brandy."

Mr. Lincoln said regretfully that he was bound to travel. "Seth?" urged Jireh. "And you, Obed, too."

Obed was eager to accept Jireh's invitation: the *Erasmus* would sail within days, and Obed wanted a last look at his old ship. Seth hesitated but then agreed. He supposed a celebration was in order; he had not felt this good since he'd sailed into New Bedford with his fine report. His reputation was on the mend, thank God, and all because of a casual quest for a gun...

He had gone to Henry's workshop in Springfield, Massachusetts, and this lawyer from Springfield, Illinois, had been there on the same errand. They had struck up conversation as they narrowed down the choice to just one beautiful rifle, an exquisite piece of craftsmanship, finished with an elaborately carved and gilded stock. Then Abe Lincoln had concluded not to buy it, but to shop at Winchester's manufactory, instead. Seth had bought the Henry rifle, and was so pleased with his purchase that he had invited Lincoln to dine. And so they had talked, and he had confided his problems, and the marvelously devious lawyer had been hired.

Jireh, exhilarated by the prospect of a party, insisted that Martha and Abby and Aunt Fanny come as well, and the three women and Obed crammed into the carriage while Jireh and Seth clambered up onto the driving seat.

Then they rattled over muddy, steaming cobbles towards the squared timbers of the pier. The carriage wheels thundered, and watery sun lay kindly on the *Erasmus* as they approached. Seth's tub, the *Lizzie Ann*, was anchored out in the stream. The comparison was cruel, but nevertheless Seth abruptly ached to be away and at sea.

The decks of the *Erasmus* were as slippery as the cobbles, and they all stepped carefully as they headed aft. Jireh led the way down the stairs to the transom cabin, declaiming hospitality; everyone was infected with his mood, it seemed, because everyone was inclined to chatter. There was the promised French brandy for the men, and champagne—champagne!—for the ladies. Seth had been too tense to eat or sleep for days, and now the brandy went straight to his head. He was suddenly aware of his huge elation; with unusual benevolence, he watched Aunt Fanny wrinkle her nose as she sampled bubbles.

"Your ship," said Obed to Jireh, lifting his glass.

"My ship," Jireh agreed sunnily. He seemed intoxicated even without the liquor. "My ship, your ship—and even your ship," he said to Seth, and laughed. "And you have cleared your name! We have so much to celebrate—what can we do to suit this great occasion? How do we do it justice?"

Abigail Sherman said, "Run the rigging."

She smiled at Seth, but Seth did not smile back. My God, he thought, she could have ruined everything if she had opened her mouth in court. Then he heard Jireh echo, "Run the rigging?"

"My father and Broddy always did it, if they had something to celebrate—or were just merry-minded, for that matter. Blame the drink," said Abby, and laughed nostalgically. "For they did enjoy to drink together. Stem to stern," she remembered. She smiled at Jireh, a pretty red-head in a dark green gown with lace at the bodice. "Or stern to stern," she added.

Jireh laughed. "Why not? It must be—oh, Jehovah—

years since I last skylarked. By thunder, why not?" The ship rocked a little in the backwash from a steamboat, and the rigging creaked in invitation. Obed was looking very tempted. It was as if Abigail had thrown down a challenge that no red-blooded male could resist. Seth drained his brandy. Why not? He grinned at Obed and the three men turned as one, and went up to deck.

The air outside had become brilliant in the meantime, as if the rain had washed the newly blue sky. Grease lay on the decks, but the rigging and masts were newly scraped and slushed, the white tips of the yards gleaming and clean. Those yards were square, the sails tight in their gussets — and, oh God, the *Erasmus* was a lovely ship.

Seth sprang onto the bulwarks, and climbed hand over fist up the mizzen shrouds. When he set a foot on the spanker gaff he saw Obed following him, and Jireh on the roof of the house. The whaleboats were new, sharp and elegant in the cranes. They diminished in size as Seth climbed steadily higher. The *Lizzie Ann* bobbed in the stream, diminishing too as he reached the mizzen topgallant. He stopped, slid onto the stay, and bounced. He could see the three females far below him. There was a crowd gathering to watch on the wharf. Let them talk about him now! Agile as an acrobat, he shot down the stay, and thumped onto the maintop.

Gathering himself, he scooted up and up, all the way past the topgallant crosstrees, ninety feet above the deck. He could hear Abigail laughing, and Jireh chanting some disrespectful version of a Pacific war song. He turned, and with a yell he whistled down the fore royal brace, letting go, jumping, and catching the line again as he leapt the spreader. Then, thump!—he was in the foremast. A Yankee yell from behind him, and there was Obed in the middle hamper. Seth laughed, scrambled up to the fore royal shrouds, and paused to let Obed by.

Obed hit the foremast, and then down he dropped, by a

backstay, to deck. He was red-faced and sweating. Seth followed him, and then they both shook hands, roaring with laughter again. Where was the pompous citizen, the benevolent husband, now? Obed and Seth slapped each other on the shoulders and stood back with fists on belts to study Jireh's version of the performance.

Jireh cried, "Stand by!" Then, with a spring, he was up the mizzen. He ran up the shrouds as if Old Scratch himself pursed him—which was not unlikely, Seth thought with a grin. Then Jireh was at the topmast crosstrees, and "Watch out below!" he hollered, and, thump!—he was scrambling up the mainmast.

Seth heard a girl cry, "Oh dear God." It was Martha. He didn't look to see her face. He was grinning, still panting, watching Jireh, now a tiny figure in the main royal shrouds. Then, with a war cry, Jireh came hurtling along the main royal stay, to arrive with a thunderous wallop on the fore royal shrouds.

Abigail cheered like a high-spirited boy. Martha gasped, "Oh no," as with another exultant yell Jireh whistled down a jib-stay. Past the bow of the ship he skidded, over the water, and then with a thump he arrived on the jibboom.

Obed and Abigail were laughing uncontrollably. The folk on the jetty were cheering. Jireh swung a leg over so he straddled the jibboom, facing Seth and the others. He scrambled rapidly towards them, through a cluster of sheets and onto the deck; stood up with a triumphant whoop, took one step, put his boot in some oil—and whump!—down he went on his seat.

Seth's sides were aching with mirth. It was wonderful to see his future brother-in-law so consternated. He heard Abigail and Obed laughing, too—and Martha whirled past him. He blinked; her hand swung, and she slapped Abigail squarely on the cheek.

Abigail staggered; Seth moved instinctively toward her. Then he saw Martha again, running towards Jireh. The rascal was still sitting on the foredeck. As Martha stormed up his laughter stopped, and his eyes bulged with alarm. "Hey," he said, and ducked, but too late. With impeccable, furious accuracy, Martha slapped him twice, once on each cheek. "How dare you frighten me like that!" she shouted, and whirled and glared at Seth and Obed. "Call yourselves grown men?"

Jireh stood up slowly, looking dazed. He rubbed his face, shook his head — and grinned. He said, "You love me."

"You senseless ..." Martha stopped. "I do not."

"You do, Jehovah, you do!" Jireh jumped to his feet and shook an exultant fist at the sky. "She loves me, she loves me," he cried, and whooped. "After all these years o' courting, she loves me — and I'll sail a married man!"

Martha said, "You will not. My father will not allow it."

"He consented damn-three years ago, when I first told him I couldn't get the thought of you out of my head. We'll marry tomorrow, my beautiful termagant, and may the time go slowly until I have to sail from your side."

"That," said Martha crisply, "will not happen. I'll marry no man who don't care for my company. If you want me that much, then I sail with you."

"What?" There was horror in Jireh's voice. Seth thought of substitute stewards and pretty island girls, and had trouble not laughing aloud. "Your father," Jireh said quickly, "won't allow you to leave him. Your place is at his side."

"Nonsense," said Martha. "He will go to live with my Aunt Stanton. I will wait at home for no man, and certainly not a shiftless whaleman."

Whaleman? Seth thought of the bales of Chinese brocade, the chocolate and indigo and God knew what else, and had trouble holding back his guffaws. Then, to his further secret hilarity, he heard Obed pronounce, "The advantages of taking a wife to sea are manifold, the disadvantages few."

"Oh?" said Jireh sadly. "Then why can I think of so

many? But," he said, and heaved a sigh, "if the choice is Martha at sea or no Martha at all, Martha must prepare to sail."

Then Seth was distracted by Abigail's unusual stillness. The bright red of the mark where Martha had slapped her stood out on her pale cheek. Then he heard Aunt Fanny hiss, "For good Godfrey's sake, boy, catch that girl before she faints."

He moved without thinking, and Abigail Sherman was abruptly in his arms. Her eyes were shut; her lashes were very black against the red and white of her cheek, and her hair came loose and fell over his shoulder. He lifted her, and despite the dead faint she seemed so light that she was insubstantial.

"Champagne," said Aunt Fanny grumpily, and led the way down the gangplank.

When Abby came to, she was in the carriage, the wheels were jolting, and she was in a man's arms. For a dazed moment she thought it had all been a dream, and the man was Jireh, but then she heard Seth's voice and remembered. The carriage jolted round a corner and for a terrible second she thought she was going to be sick down his jacket. She pushed herself away, and after a moment her stomach settled. She sat up confusedly, pushing back her hair with a trembling hand. Jireh—and Martha—were not in the carriage. Obed was driving, and she was alone with Seth and Mrs. Fanny. Mrs. Fanny studied her with hooded eyes from the opposite seat. Seth Morgan was beside her, but he had moved away to the corner.

Oh, dear God, had she betrayed herself utterly? Did they all know that she had loved Jireh, and *he had not even noticed*? She stared miserably out the window as the carriage rattled up to the entrance of the Cambridge house, wondering if she would ever survive the awful shame.

Victoria came running frantically out, waving a paper,

her expression pale and stricken. "Oh, dear heaven, where have you been?" Obed jumped down and Abigail, seized with an appalling premonition, somehow fumbled her way out of the carriage. Victoria was in tears. She ran up to Abigail and put her arms around her, and said, "Oh, dear girl—oh, you look so bad—have you already heard? Did someone show you the paper? Oh Abigail, what happened? Did you have a fall?"

Abigail shook her head, and reached a tremulous hand for the paper. She knew what it contained before she even read the headline.

MASSACRE IN NEW ZEALAND

—-The New Zealand papers give detailed accounts of the dreadful murder of the American vice-consul in Mangonui, Captain Nathaniel Sherman, a former citizen of New Bedford, in September last.

—Captain Sherman was riding with a friend, Captain Broderick McGhie, when both men were set upon by a band of Maori rebels. Captain McGhie, though gravely wounded, managed to escape by throwing himself into a gully, where he remained hidden while the renegades sacked and burned Captain Sherman's vice-consular residence, which was less than half a mile away. The tragic sight so affected the wounded man that he swooned, and when he came to his senses, the rebels had gone, leaving the brutally abused body of Captain Sherman, whom they had hacked to death, and the ashes of Captain Sherman's home.

September. When Abby had written that last angry letter, he father had been dead perhaps five months. Everything inside her felt frozen; she couldn't see; her nails were biting into her hands, and she could taste blood in her mouth. The house gone—her childhood and her future both wiped out—Wikitoria and the other girls—where had they gone? Were they dead, too? And Broddy—Broddy was hurt.

And her father, her dear, beloved father...

It didn't seem possible that she could be so alone. "We must be submissive to the will of God," Victoria said. "With God's help we can learn to be reconciled."

Reconciled? To this? Abigail cried," Oh, no, God, no!" and turned and wept savagely, and didn't care that it was Seth Morgan she clung to, and hammered with her fists. She cried, "I can't bear it. Oh, don't look at me," and wept and buried her face in his chest.

Seth's expression was grimly determined as he rode to the Mitchell house along Boat Train Road. It was a lovely day. The goldenrod nodded in the grass of the verges and the yellow leaves of the huge old elms fluttered in a tiny breeze. Once, he drew the horse over, as a boat train progressed ponderously towards him. It was a procession of drays, each one loaded with a new whaleboat, the driver of each with a lifted whip like a lance. Dust fell and rose and eddied; when the dust had settled again, Seth moved his horse back onto the road. The Mitchell house was narrow, two stories high and two rooms wide, with paned windows each side of the central door. The door and windows were wreathed with black crepe. Seth's brows arched sardonically as he surveyed the sights of mourning.

The knock on the door was answered by Jezekiel Mitchell himself. The merchant was dour-faced, even more peevish than usual. "My wife is a complete hysteric," he declared. "Her cousin is dead, foully murdered, sir! Mrs. Mitchell was so overcome we feared for her life. And," he added as he showed Seth to his study, "our son Jireh has married that hellcat Martha Cady."

The office was at the front of the house, a prim cold place, with boxes meticulously labeled. The *Pierrot* logbook was aligned on the desk. Seth glanced at it and then away; it no longer held interest.

He looked with distaste at Jezekiel Mitchell and handed

him the writ, watching expressionlessly as it was shaken open, and Mitchells' face turned puce with incredulous rage.

He cried, "Sue me for slander? You wouldn't dare!"

"Then you, sir," said Seth, "are an uncommon poor judge of persons."

"You'd rise up before the hoary head and fail to honor the venerable face of age? You'd sue your own father-in-law for a slander you cannot prove?"

"Mr. Lincoln," said Seth, 'assures me that not only do I have proof, but also that I am certain to win. The editor to whom you communicated your libel is perfectly willing to testify."

"You would set this against me when my wife hovers between life and death, when our son is married to a bitch, a witch, and his mother's heart is broken, when her very own cousin met a brutal death, unprepared to stand at the Mercy Seat?"

"I would," said Seth inexorably. "Mr. Lincoln, however, advised me that you might want to negotiate, to keep your name out of the courts — and out of the papers."

Silence. Mitchell stared back, his expression becoming crafty. "Negotiate?"

"A settlement, and my silence, would spare your lady's sensibilities."

"How much?"

"Two and a half thousand."

"Bare-faced robbery!"

"It will reduce the price of the *Lizzie Ann* to its proper level."

Another silence. Then Mitchell said, "A thousand."

"I'm not prepared to bargain."

"You'd otherwise sue me and waste time in court action when your ship is lying idle? Extreme imprudence, sir!"

"The *Lizzie Ann* is mine — you made sure of that — so I can do what I like with her."

The flat eyes, which had been staring fixedly at Seth,

suddenly flickered around the room. Then Mitchell said, "You'll marry before you sail?"

"Of course," said Seth, wondering why he felt suddenly uneasy. "And I sail the moment I have your note for the money."

"Very well, then." Mitchell sat down and wrote the draft for the full sum of money, and sealed it. Then, viciously, he tore up the writ. Seth watched him tensely, with none of the triumph he had expected. Mitchell leaned back, and smirked, and said, "Before you go, we must discuss a further matter, the support of your wife."

Support? What was the devious bastard up to?

Seth thought of the watertight marriage settlement both he and Mitchell had signed, and said coldly, "That is none of your business."

"But indeed it is—and the amount will have to be substantial." To Seth's puzzlement, Mitchell began to write figures on a pad at his elbow. "Your voyage, no doubt, will exceed four years in duration, and a captain's wife must maintain the dignity of her position. Living in her father's household will reduce costs, granted. Shall we say a round figure of two thousand and a half?"

Seth's uneasiness turned into alarm: not only did he not taste the triumph he had expected, but somehow he had the sensation that it was sliding out of his reach.

Trying not to bluster, he said, "I don't know what the devil you are talking about. Charity sails, and it's no affair of yours what allowance I give her."

"Sail? But she don't sail, sir. How can she?"

Seth shouted, "We have an agreement—a signed marriage contract!"

"Exactly—and it's because of that agreement that my daughter stays here. Dr. Spooner has signed a certificate testifying to the precarious state of my wife's health—as he said himself, my wife requires a nurse if she is to see out the summer; he holds grave prognostications, sir, very grave indeed. And that testimonial, sir, is exactly as specified by that agreement."

Seth was shaking with rage and consternation. "There is nothing in the agreement that says Charity must stay here if your wife needs a nurse."

"There is, there is." Mitchell shook the document at him, at the same time babbling, "If death or other extreme family circumstance duly certified by a recognized practitioner..."

Seth roared, "You're lying," and found Mitchell's copy of the agreement thrust under his nose.

"Apparently," Mitchell smirked, "you failed to read the small print."

Seth snatched it, and read it, then scarcely bothered to glance at the physician's certificate. Mitchell had won. He couldn't believe it; after all his scheming and his *guts* in taking that court action, he had gained nothing but a leaky old ship. Without a word, he plucked up Mitchell's note for the two and a half thousand dollars, folded it, and put it in his pocket.

Mitchell watched, his expression suddenly worried. "You take my note?" he said. "You're refusing to support your wife?"

That, no doubt, Seth thought savagely, was covered by that goddamned contract as well. "I'll fulfill my part of the agreement when your daughter fulfills hers," he snapped. "I will not marry her until she is free to sail."

Mitchell's face went blank. "You will stay in port until my wife is better?"

"I sail tomorrow."

"But..."

"Charity will have to travel to meet me."

"That's outrageous!"

"It is not. Many captains' wives do it."

"Wives, sir, *wives*. You expect an unmarried woman to endure the privations of travel to some far barbaric port?"

"Sir, your daughter's impregnable virtue will be its own

protection."

"You will pay passage for a chaperone!"

"I will not." Seth's mind was working more clearly by the moment. "She can sail in a ship that carries a lady. The *Curtsey* goes to fish off Chile and Peru in the late fall or early winter with Mrs. Cambridge on board. My cousin, I am certain, will be happy to carry a passenger. Charity can help Mrs. Cambridge with the baby."

"That's heavy-handed and outrageous, sir! My wife's illness is a lingering and unpredictable complaint!"

"I don't give a damn about your wife's convenient ill health." Seth turned on his heel. "I'll call at Paita in March," he said over his shoulder as he opened the door. "If Charity has not kept the appointment by the end of the month, then I'll go north—and to the devil with our legal agreement."

"I do not agree with takin' wives to sea," said Mr. Allen.

Jireh sprawled back in his chair and surveyed his first mate thoughtfully. "I tend to that way o' thought myself," he admitted. Beyond the partition, Martha was vomiting again. He wouldn't have believed that anyone could be so seasick. The *Erasmus* creaked solidly as she forged her steady passage towards the Azores. The wind was fair and all sail was set. Sunlight slanted warmly through the skylight and the clutter left from dinner. Jireh reached out and took a piece of cold pie, and chewed slowly as he wondered how Martha would fare in a storm. He had enjoyed the calmest departure he had ever experienced and Martha had seem bright enough—for four hours after sailing. Now the absorbing pursuit of teaching Martha the arts of love had had to be shelved, apparently forever.

"So you were not happy that Captain Cambridge was accompanied by his wife?"

"Ah—but that was different, Captain. Mrs. Cambridge was never seasick. An exceptional woman, sir, she is one of the few ladies who form a taste for voyaging. It requires a special constitution."

"I'm sure you are right," Jireh said. In the stateroom, Martha sounded as if she was close to heaving up her boots.

"The crew is not reassuring, neither," said Mr. Allen. He chewed his pipe stem ruminatively, and Jireh realized that if Martha were being compared unfavorably with Victoria Cambridge, then he was being measured against Obed, and the results were not in his favor.

"Oh, the men will learn the way of wearing and tacking in time," he said with ill-founded confidence.

Obed's erstwhile first officer didn't deign to answer. The last time Jireh had been on deck, it had been just in time to see a staysail flap and plunge like a wounded bird to the sea. A slack-mouthed greenhand had been at the sheet.

It always happened. At least a third of every whaleship's crew had never been to sea before. Well, thought Jireh, with luck the worst ones would run away from the ship at the first port they touched — Fayal, in the Azores. Then he wondered if Martha would ever stop being seasick.

"At 11 AM all hands on board," wrote Seth. "Got under weigh with the wind from the west and rain with a heavy swell. Stood out under light sails, out of the Bay." He lifted his pen and held it poised, staring at the black impatient strokes of ink.

The light in the narrow transom cabin was dim, the stern windows scoured with salt, the skylight obscured with dirt. The barometer rattled on the wall above his small chart table. The *Lizzie Ann* pitched heavily and an evil stench rose from the bilges. Seth sighed: the ship was infernally down by the head. The anchor chains needed restowing.

It was as hot as the stoke-room of hell, and the air below was stuffy as well as evil. The cook was sick and green, the steward drunk and as dirty as Old Scratch.

Seth hunched his shoulders over the log. It promised to

be a horrible task, but, by God, Seth would never again make the disastrous error of not keeping his own record. He squared his jaw and wetted his nib.

"At 1 PM the wind light and baffling, sea and weather no better, at 5 PM left our Pilot."

Consider West had taken the *Lizzie Ann* out and anchored her in the bay the previous night, as was the custom. Seth had come out in the pilot boat to join his ship. An amazing number of friends and well-wishers had gathered to say farewell as he left the wharf; he had been touched and amazed. Uriah wasn't there, of course: the *Pierrot* had sailed to the Offshore Ground off Chile and Peru a long time since. One report had come back, a gratifying six hundred barrels. Seth's father had come, though. He, like many others, had been impressed by Seth's performance in court. For once his father had seemed paternal.

Mitchell hadn't come, and nor had Charity. Seth didn't know if he cared or not, but he knew that how he felt made no difference: Mitchell would undoubtedly claim that his daughter had been too busy in the sickroom. Obed had come, and Victoria, Aunt Fanny, and her husband, Seth's Uncle Cambridge, who had looked approving, too—and Abigail had come with them.

Seth had never seen her in black before. Her face was white, her eyes shadowed, and her expression had been desperate. When he had taken her hand she had gazed up at him with some enigmatic passionate appeal and said, "Seth..." She bit her lip and turned her face away. He heard her gasp, "The *Lizzie Ann* will be lucky," and she pulled her hand out of his and ran back to the carriage.

That old besom Aunt Fanny had been standing in front of him, leaning on her cane, peering challengingly up at his face. "She's the one with spirit," she shouted, to his embarrassment. "She'll warm some lucky man's bones for the rest of his life!" Then she had stomped away, as if he disgusted her.

Seth shifted impatiently in his chair and wrote in the journal, "Latter part all hands mustering for roll call." He could hear Mr. West hollering up on deck—"All hands assemble amidships—shake a leg there! You there, lay to the waist, *amidships*, man, amidships. Oh, Tom, for the sake of God and my sanity, point that fool in the right direction—"

How often, at the start of the voyage, had Seth heard officers with just such despair in their voices? Three quarters of the crew were green, slack-jawed yokels amazed at the sight of the sea. The first mate was not quite twenty-one, and Tom Kanaka was the most experienced officer on board. At twenty-five last Christmas and six foot three last measured, Seth was the biggest and oldest man on the ship. He stood up, shook himself irritably, and went up on deck.

The rain was streaming and the sea heaved with that nasty swell from the west. Seth pulled up his collar, and pulled down the brim of his hat. The men stood in a wet huddle just forward of the mainmast, scrabble-faced, lank-haired, and pallid. "All hands mustered, sir," said Mr. West with a martyred air. Water poured down his earnest young face.

Seth thrust his hands in his coat pockets and stood silent a moment, staring at the cluster of miserable humanity. Where the hell, he thought, had the agent found them? The crimps of New Bedford had been busy. They'd had an order to fill and a commission to earn, and they didn't hesitate to lie and bribe if necessary. Innocent farm boys and drunken students were victims alike to the land sharks' blandishments, and where promises didn't work, the cudgel often would. Every now and then a greenhand signed on willingly, with dreams of adventure filling his romantic head, but Seth was willing to wager there were none of that sort here.

A sulky wave rose, slapped at the bulwarks, and wet them with salt to strengthen the rain. The cooper staggered in a circle with the pitching; he was as drunk or drunker than the filthy steward. Seth braced his feet.

"That one there," he said to Mr. West. "Who does he claim to be, and how old?"

"Cotton, he says he is, sir. Willie. Says he's sixteen."

"If we're lucky, he's twelve. Bring him aft when we've finished—he will have to wait at the table." A boy to wait at the table where a woman should have presided. Seth said bitterly, "What a miserable collection."

"They're seasick—or drunk. Or both," said Mr. West. "And some are crippled in the bargain," he added. "There's one there—Peabody, says he shipped for his health. He's a lawyer's clerk, says he is suffering from consumption. And that one there, Tucker, he shipped for his eyes. He says the last voyage he took did them a power of good, and now they're bad again. Can't see an inch in front of his eyes."

"Tucker, the boatsteerer? You must be mistaken!"

"The whale he harpoons will have to be a monster one."

It was so terrible it was almost funny. "Any more cheerful news?"

"That one, Hunter, favors his arm. I suspect that it's broke."

"Then why the devil didn't you suspect it before the pilot boat left? Do we have any seamen at all?"

"Seven claim they've sailed before, and have papers to prove it, but when I sung out to that one, the Englishman, Pease, to overhaul the main topsail clewlines, he hauled the whole doin's into the maintop."

"Oh, God." Seth sighed. "Well, let's get on with it. We'll choose boats' crews and get below—not that there's much hope of dinner."

Consider West and Mr. Wood, the sly-looking second mate, and the third mate, Tom Kanaka, ranged up to the main hatch, and Seth joined them. There was a long suspicious pause as the officers and the crew stared warily at each other. The rain poured down and filled their collars and their pockets and the sea slapped hungrily at the ship.

The four of them chose men for their boats, one man at a time, in order, first mate first, captain last. The ones chosen by Tom stared in a kind of terrified hypnosis at his aggressively tattooed face—all except nearsighted Tucker, who merely blinked in a vaguely querulous fashion. The infant, Cotton, was the last to be picked, so of course Seth got him.

By the end of the awkward process, three of the men were heaving their guts out over the bulwarks and two were groaning in the scuppers. Seth ignored them, bracing his boots as the *Lizzie Ann* waggled her stern.

"Discipline," he said to the glazed faces of the survivors. "The safety of the ship depends on it. The officers are in charge. Obey them prompt and no questions or you'll be sorry. Unless ordered aft you stay forward of the waist. If you are ordered to come aft, you walk on the lee side, the larboard side if we are before the wind. Any complaints or queries go to the officer on watch, not me. They'll be relayed if important. Understand?"

They didn't, that was obvious. They returned his stare numbly, wet and no doubt wishing they were overboard and dead. With a gulp Cotton rushed for the rail.

"Food," said Seth. There was a flicker of interest. "Coffee at breakfast, six o'clock, tea at dinner, noon, and at supper, six. Hard biscuit every meal, soft bread once a day." From flour that was full of worms if he'd been cheated, Seth thought sourly, and at that moment he was sure that he had.

"Watches." The interest subsided. "Two watches— larboard, starboard. When one watch is on deck the other is below. You get your sleep in the watch below." If the men could, with the noise of the ship and the sea and the shouting of the watch on deck, the whining of the cooper's grindstone, and the hammering as the cook chopped wood for the galley stove. If they could, in the cramped space of the foc'sle, where men cursed and fought as they jostled for more room and the food that came down in a common kid, ate it voraciously with filthy jackknives and filthier fingers, and spat tobacco gobs, heedless of where they spattered.

"Sea watches are four hours; twelve to four, four to eight, eight to twelve, all around the clock except for the dogwatches. Dogwatch is four to eight in the afternoon, divided into two shifts so that watches can be changed about and all hands will get eight hours in their berths every second night. You will all be taught to keep the ship, steer a trick, learn the rigging, stand lookout, and watch aloft."

Learn the ways of a whaling vessel, which was a factory, as well as a ship—was it remotely likely, with this unhappy gang? Seth bit down a sigh as he turned to Mr. West. "Order the larboard watch below and hand over to Mr. Wood," he said, and without waiting for the "Aye, sir," he strode impatiently to the companionway stairs.

The dank heat of his quarters rose to engulf him. The bulkheads ran with moisture and mold. In the main mess cabin the table was set with cold food in dirty utensils. Seth surveyed it, rejected it, and went into the transom cabin.

Ten

Abigail had to get to New Zealand, and the key to getting there was Obed's new ship.

At night she dreamed of Broddy and the brig *Pandora*, and when Obed was home for meals she listened with intensity to his chatter about how his new vessel was progressing at Hillman's Yard. She had to get to Mangonui to claim her brig and her fortune and tie the strings of her life together, and then, perhaps, she would not feel so lost ... so alone.

Then one day, in a glorious September, Obed's new ship was given birth. She was launched. And all of New Bedford came.

The bay was sprinkled with sun shadows, and across the river Fairhaven lay in a demure assortment of spires and roofs. The pale sky was luminous above a thin pall of smoke. All the ships were flying house flags and ensigns in honor of the occasion, and the banners snapped to attention in the small stiff gusts of breeze. Abby's hair flipped about her face and her black gown rustled.

She was on the deck of Obed's new ship, her hands on the starboard rail, watching the crowd that milled below, in and out of the struts of the cradle. Emily crowed and danced beside her, chubby arms waving.

The ship smelled of seasoning wood and brine, a heady mixture that bit through the smells of dust and wood shavings. The deck vibrated to the sounds of many footsteps — the light inquisitive steps of all the young people who had been invited on board to view the launching from a privileged vantage, and the deliberate bootsteps of workmen. Voices chattered, and chains rattled in the bow. The ship seemed alive, anxious to quit the cradle and breast the waves.

A babble rose from the yard below, a commotion of comment from merchants, farmers, farmhands, lawyers, boardinghouse-keepers, crimps, pimps, runners and agents, carpenters, caulkers, and vintners. Rich or poor, respectable or definitely devious, they all had a stake in the *Curtsey*. New Bedford and her attendant villages were completely involved in the whaling trade. So much was required for a whaling vessel's outfit: charts of remote, little visited coasts and islands, goods like tobacco and drilling cloth to trade; navigational equipment, firewood, and food — tons of salt meat, flour, and hard biscuit, enough cheese and butter and molasses syrup to keep a whole village going for a year, enough grog for a month-long festival, hundreds of pounds of coffee and tea. And the *Curtsey* would not be just a floating village: she would be a whale oil factory, as well. For this, she needed line tubs, irons, lances, boarding knives, and at least six boats. And then there were the necessities common to all ships at sea: fresh water, rope, canvas, nails, boards, tar, vinegar, turpentine, paint, and lye. At the outset she would even carry oil: a six-gallon allowance to keep her lamps burning until the day she took her first whale. She did not just mean a profit to these watching men: for most, she represented their living.

Obed was striding about, the instigator of all this activity and potential. He was resplendent in a broadcloth suit with brass buttons, a living, walking credit to Victoria's

239

industry — his bosom shirt was starched and ironed to a state of luminosity, and his brass buttons glittered in the sun. His George Washington hat was set straight on his head, and his hands were lightly clasped at his back.

Behind Obed men were untying the guy ropes that held the ship in her cradle. Other men were coiling anchor chain about the windlass, making rough metallic sounds. On the deck, order was emerging from confusion. "Watch," Abby whispered to Emily, and Emily crowed with excitement. She was growing into a beautiful child, sweet-natured like her father, and with her mother's round hazel eyes.

"Ten minutes," said Obed. Ten minutes until the launching, when the ship would be set on the first few yards of her passage to the southern ocean. The *Curtsey* would not sail until the first week in November, but it was the ceremonial start to what would be a grand seafaring career. Abby watched Obed haul out his timepiece and thumb it open. The workmen who were stationed by blocks had sledgehammers hefted in readiness. The crowd around the cradle eddied back and forth. Most were consulting their watches.

"Four minutes," said Obed. The men by the blocks lifted their hammers.

"Three minutes," cried the shipyard foreman. The men with hammers braced their shoulders, and the men by the windlass spat on their palms.

"Two minutes!"

Twelve o'clock chimed. Obed tore off his hat, waved it high, and shouted, "I name this ship the *Curtsey* of New Bedford!"

Slam! A series of heavy crashes as the hammers pounded. The *Curtsey* trembled, quivering as the slope pulled her forward. Her hull creaked, vibrating on the brink of launch.

"Away!" cried Abby and Emily shrilled, "Away!"

Then Abby swung round, carrying the little girl with

her, running aft. The young folk on deck, when they saw what she was doing, ran sternwards, too. The ship vibrated with their steps, and then she lurched and—slid. Down the ways she grated, faster and faster, gathering momentum, grinding bed-blocks, gritting through sand and water until with a mighty crash she met her rightful element. A responsive wave surged up the beach and baptized the merchants and crimps with spray.

Abby renewed her hold on Emily, and ran forward again, weaving and stumbling with the *Curtsey* living and lively under her feet. She was laughing with joy, and Emily shrieked with delight. The ship bounced and rocked. They ran in little spurts, in a drunken dance of jubilation, and the small craft in the river bounced too.

Obed shouted, "Heave a breast line!" Anchor chains crashed and unwound, and the lines were eagerly snagged up by men on a jetty. The *Curtsey* rocked more steadily and slowly as she was restrained, and Abigail got her balance back. She stood still, laughing, but when she set down the little girl, Emily still weaved and lurched. Obed chuckled fondly, saying, "She's lost her sea legs, that girl."

"No matter," said Abigail happily. "We'll all get them back before we're even out of the stream."

Then she registered Obed's changed expression, just before he turned away. Her heart seemed to clench with a cold premonition. The nightmare of being left with the Mitchells was back.

After supper, Obed sent for her. He was waiting in his study. Abigail closed the door very carefully, and turned to face him. It felt hard to breathe, as if the fresh autumn air was the heavy air of summer, and she gripped her cold hands together just under her breasts.

Obed cleared his throat, and said, "No doubt, Abigail, you're wondering what will become of you when Victoria and I sail."

The dread of what was coming made her voice so high that it sounded unfamiliar. "I—I thought you'd take me with you, and return me to New Zealand."

Obed did not look surprised. Nevertheless, he asked gruffly, "Why?"

"B-Because it's my home." Why did her voice sound so squeaky and uncertain? It should have been vibrant with conviction. Abigail tried again, but all she managed was, "I b-belong there."

He shook his head, not quite meeting her imploring eyes. "Abigail, I know acceptance comes hard, but where would you go? Your home is burned down, and your father—"

She said swiftly, "There's Broddy—and the brig. You know I own the *Pandora*. I have to go there to claim my property." Wherever the brig might be, she thought in a pulse of panic. The *Pandora* could have been stolen, or confiscated by the English, or—wrecked. She had to bite down a sob. She said in a low fierce voice, "The *Pandora* is my home, not the house that burned down. Until I went to school, the brig is where I lived."

"And you would live on the brig now? An unmarried girl?"

Obed sounded so scandalized—but why not live on the brig? If she had been a boy, it would have been respectable for her to live on the *Pandora*, but because she was a girl...

She said in a low, shaking voice, "Am I expected to let other parties take the *Pandora* over, without paying a penny, just because I'm unmarried? Because I am a girl, do I have no right to my own property?" If she were Martha, she thought, she would have a logical and devastating argument to produce in her own defense. Instead, all she could do was try her hardest not to cry.

Obed barked, "It's impossible, and you know it."

"I can't stay in New Bedford!"

She broke off, trembling. Obed had brought her to this

city; she had worked hard and done her best, and he had no right to abandon her here. But how could she tell him that, when he and Victoria had been so very kind? Then she was saved by a memory, and exclaimed, "But I have a fortune to claim."

"A fortune?" Obed sighed, and said with the air of a man humoring a difficult woman, "Just leave the brig to me, Abigail. I assure you that when we get to Mangonui I'll make every effort possible to find your brig and either sell her on your behalf, or find a crew and bring her home with a cargo."

He'd sell the brig first, she knew that—and she didn't trust him to go to much effort to find her, either. She exclaimed, "I'm not talking about the *Pandora*. I'm talking about a fortune that my father discovered in a pumice valley near our house."

Obed looked blank. Abby gasped, "I'll show you," and whirled out of the room and upstairs. When she returned she was carrying her writing desk.

She set it down on a table and opened it. The papers for the brig were on the top, and she put them carefully to one side. Then she took out a copy of the riddle and gave it to Obed.

His lips moved as he read it, and then he looked up and said, "What the thunder is this?"

"It's a clue to what my father found in the valley."

"You'll know what it is, once you've worked out the puzzle?"

Abigail nodded, her hands clenched together with anxiety.

Obviously fascinated, he read the riddle out loud.

With sugar and rice and apples I'm nice
Although I am wood, I taste very good.
When I am high, all sails fly
When I am low, watch for a blow
What am I?

"What indeed?" said Obed.

"Well, there is certainly a reference to barometers."

"But you don't eat barometers," he objected.

Abby could have wept with impatience, but all the time he was here and interested, there was a chance to convince him to take her away from New Bedford. "The first part does seem to indicate something to eat," she agreed.

"Not food. A spice," he said.

When she looked surprised, he added complacently, "A good guess. The first time I read it I thought the word 'rice' was 'spice.'"

Abigail hid a sigh. Her father's writing was certainly wild and hard to decipher in parts; for the thousandth time she wondered with dread about his state of mind when he had composed this silly little puzzle.

"But that wood is a teaser."

Infuriatingly, Obed seemed to be enjoying himself. Abby said, "A barometer has a wooden case."

"True, that's true. And you reckon this puzzle points the way to a fortune your father has found?"

"Somebody..." Abigail's breath caught in a sharp little throb of misery that forced her to stop. Oh Jireh, she mourned, why didn't you love me? If Jireh had loved her, she would be at sea. If Jireh had loved her, she would not be pleading with obdurate Obed.

She said, "Someone thought it might lead to gold."

Obed's expression became alert. "There's a barometer on the *Pandora*, I imagine? A barometer in a wooden case?"

She had already thought of that; she nodded.

"Ah!" He was more animated than ever. "Give me the papers for the brig—to make things legal when I find her and claim her on your behalf."

He would certainly make an effort to find the brig now, she thought in a panic—but give him the papers? She cried, "I can't do that," and grabbed them up.

Obed looked angry and insulted, and she said quickly,

desperately, "We can make a copy and have it *notarized.*"

The word came out of a secret fund she didn't know she owned, and to her fervent relief it worked: he thought about it and nodded. "That's settled, then," he said, and to her horror he opened the door as if the interview was over, and she cried, "But you can't leave me here."

He frowned. "I beg your pardon?"

"There's the money to claim from the sale of my father's lands, and I have to turn up in person to do that."

He barked, "More nonsense, Abigail? You told me yourself that your father was compelled by the English to sell his lands to an Englishman, at the price he paid for them, with no profit to himself."

"But there's a proxy."Obed stared at her blankly, and she thrust her father's letter at him, "Oh, please, please read that, and you'll see what I mean."

Obed glanced at her doubtfully, and then he settled to read. There was silence as his lips moved and she tensely watched him.

He looked up. "English whaleships characterized by drunkenness and want of discipline? I quite agree — I'd rather be cook on a Yankee clam boat than the captain of an English whaler."

Abby could have screamed. She said, "Please read on, *please.*"

He rattled the page. "War?" he said. "Maori Sons of Liberty?"

"That was his belief. I think that's why the English — why Sir George Grey — were so hard on him." Oh, Obed, she prayed, pleased get on and read it. Obed was so *ponderous.*

He said, "It seems strange enough, don't you think, that renegade Maoris should have murdered a man what sympathized..." Then he saw her stricken eyes, and hurriedly returned to his reading.

"Sold his lands to a proxy?" he exclaimed. "But why?"

At long last he had got there. Abby sighed with relief

and said, "My father believed that if he could sell his lands to someone he trusted, that person could sell them again, at a fair and proper price, and then he and my father would share the money."

Obed, predictably, took a while to work this out. When enlightenment finally brightened his expression, she could have kissed him. He said, "So you wish to go to New Zealand to collect this half of the money?"

"Yes!"

He nodded. "And who is the proxy?"

"It must be Broddy; I can't think of anyone else."

"But you said he must sell to an Englishman—and McGhie is *Scotch*."

She felt a nasty jab of doubt. "Does that make a difference?"

He shrugged. "Could be. And if McGhie is such a trusted friend, why didn't your father tell you his name?"

Another jab. Every word Obed said was making horrible sense. She said desperately, "But I will never find out what really happened unless I go back to New Zealand."

"No." The word was flat, and came out with no hesitation. Abby stared at Obed in utter despair, and he said, "McGhie was wounded, badly wounded. That's what the papers said. And you've received no letter. You have to face it, but the sad fact is that he is dead."

Tears were running down her face. Even Broddy gone? She thought of all the times he had filled the house with his whiskey breath and his hearty chanteys; the times he had boarded the brig, preceded by his booming voice; she thought of the childish tricks he had played on her, and the games he had taught. He was like a well-loved, rather disreputable uncle; she couldn't bear to lose him, too.

Obed had picked up the letter again, reading it as if to avoid her eyes, and with abrupt horror she remembered what her father had written next. She said quickly, "Obed..." but too late. He lowered the letter, his face red with anger.

"Mitchell was paid for your keep?"

Abby said in a low voice, "So it seems, but I want you to know how very much appreciate your kindness..."

"You've been a good girl, Abigail, and I don't mind saying I would have written a warm testimonial to your father. You're industrious and kind, and a credit to dear Victoria. But if Mitchell was paid —"

Abigail cried, "Oh, please, couldn't I come with you?" She had been a fool, she thought, a fool to think up the idea of notarized papers for the brig, and a fool to forget what her father had written. She had trapped herself with her own impulsiveness. "I'd help with Emily, you know how I love her — and I do believe she loves me."

Obed stared at her, angry at her persistence, angry at being cheated by Jezekiel Mitchell. Obed had given his decision, and as a woman, Abigail should have listened, and not presumed to argue. Looking at his face, Abby knew complete despair. When she had said good-bye to Seth Morgan, she had so nearly begged him to take her along as his servant, to work her passage to Mangonui. She had not been able to avoid hearing the gossip, for everyone said it, that Seth Morgan wanted a woman on board to cook and clean and keep his cabins in order. Abigail could do all that and help keep ship, as well! And she had heard, too, that Seth Morgan had jilted Charity Mitchell, so the situation of a female steward was definitely vacant.

She had stopped just in time, before embarrassing Seth and herself. She said to Obed imploringly, "Please?"

"No," he said gruffly. "And even if it were wise, it would be impossible, for we carry Charity Mitchell, so she can join Seth Morgan in Paita in March."

Two weeks later Victoria spent a day sick in bed. She had a bilious night and was in bed when Obed left to oversee the stowing of the *Curtsey*, and was still in bed when he returned.

"I took an emetic," she said fretfully when he came up to see her. "I was hoping to remove something makes me feel half-sick all the time, but it didn't work."

"She's with child," Mrs. Fanny pronounced at supper.

Obed reddened. "Nonsense," he barked, and looked with embarrassment at Abby.

"Why?" demanded his outspoken mother. Her hooded eyes were derisive and amused. "She'd be half-sick tomorrow, and again the next day, and, what's more, she will not be able to sail on the *Curtsey*."

Abigail's heart jumped. If Victoria couldn't go, would Obed take her instead? Charity Mitchell would not be allowed to sail without a chaperone. Then the little bubble of hope dissolved—if Victoria was with child, Abby would have to remain behind to help. At most, it was a reprieve from the Mitchells.

Depressingly for Obed, his mother was right. When Dr. Spooner examined Victoria he produced the same diagnosis and the opinion that the rigors of a sea journey would be very dangerous so early in the pregnancy.

"He must be wrong," Victoria wailed. "I was perfectly fine with little Emily."

"We can't take the risk," Obed said gloomily.

The first heavy sea, the physician had predicted, would prove enough perhaps to lose not only the baby but Victoria as well. Come February, it would be a different matter. Come February, Victoria would be able to travel—but Obed couldn't wait that long. And it was unthinkable that his lovely new ship should sail under another master.

He took a deep, gusty breath. "Victoria, it can't be helped. You must stop home."

"Obed," she wept, and the tears flowed in earnest. Obed watched her in helpless despair. His big hands closed and opened ineffectually; he didn't know what to do to comfort her—or himself.

He loved her so much. He loved her more than anyone

realized, more than his ship or his wealth. He had loved her from the first moment he'd seen her. It had been at a grand occasion in Boston, and she had looked so remote, so beautiful, so unattainable. It had taken him two weeks of agonizing to work up the courage to approach her again. She had done him much honor when she had consented to become his wife.

He sat down carefully on the edge of the bed, and she cried into his shoulder. "You'll join me," he instructed.

"But how? Oh, Obed, when?"

"In March, when it is safe for you to travel." His big hand gently touched her hair, his fingers spread to cradle the cherished head.

"But the journey around the Horn can take three months!"

Obed winced. This counting of months was extreme embarrassing. Then inspiration struck. "The Isthmus," he said.

Her eyes widened with horror. "The road to Panama?"

"Aye. But they're building a railway across the Isthmus of Panama for the folks who go to California after gold." He was most gratified with himself for coming up with such a brilliant idea. "A steamer from Boston will carry you to Aspinwall, at the eastern end of the railway, and then you ride in the cars to Panama, taking but a day, I hear, and then from Panama a steamer will take but a week to carry you to Paita. I'll get my agent to book you tickets, and meet you there in March."

"But it's the Place of Skulls!" she cried.

Obed's eyes bulged. "I beg your pardon?"

"The Isthmus! You must have heard of it!" she cried, and to his total bemusement she struck a pose and began to recite.

Once more upon the land
O'er the appalling wilds of Panama
The Place of Skulls

They took their pilgrim way.

"You must have heard the poem," said Victoria. "It is all the rage."

"Good Godfrey," said Obed blankly. "Is it? But hundreds do it. Folks after gold cross the Isthmus all the time."

"Gold?" Victoria's tone was high with consternation. She let go of her husband and covered her face with her hands. "I can't go all that way alone," she wept. "Not without the caring presence of a man."

"Of course you can," Obed said bracingly, gratified and depressed all at once. "And you won't be alone, for you'll have Charity Mitchell with you."

The *Curtsey* sailed on November the fourth. Obed, impelled by a vague sense of guilt, invited Abigail on board for the hour or so of entering the stream. When the tug cast off and returned to shore, Abigail and little Emily would go with it.

Sirens wailed, hooters blatted, and hawsers were cast off. The deck of the *Curtsey* trembled beneath Abby's feet, and she clutched Emily's hand. The little girl was subdued despite the excitement; she had seen her mother and father in tears. Now Victoria was weeping at home, and Obed was gloomily pacing the deck. The third mate sang with a long-drawn wailing nasal note, and the men at the windlass provided a ghostly echo at the end of each line.

It's a cold dreary morn' in November ... November
And all of me money is spent ... is spent
Where it went to, damned if I can remember ... remember
So down to the agent's I went ... went ... went...

The wind was cold. Abigail shivered. The little girl huddled close, clutching Abby's skirt. The *Curtsey* gained momentum, tugged smoothly now, and all the ships in the harbor dipped their flags. Had New Bedford looked like this, all those long months ago when the *Erasmus* had made port?

Now Abigail knew the streets and shops and the names of the spires: the Baptist church in William Street, the Unitarian at Eighth and Union; there was the cupola of the customs house. She knew it all, and had come to love the city — but it's not my home, she thought passionately, it's not ... it's not.

The men were unfurling the sails, one by one, and they fluttered delicately in the following breeze. "Boys, be handy, skip handy," sang the chantey man. "For we're bound to Valparaiso..."

"... around the Horn!" came the grunting chorus. The Horn, thought Abby — Cape Stiff. Would she ever see the Pacific again? The sails spread, the tugboat cast off, and the *Curtsey* swayed, and lay aback. It was time to go. Obed grabbed Emily up and hugged and hugged her, and then Abigail stepped into the boat slung ready, and took the little girl as Obed handed her over. Then she sat still, cold inside, as the boat was lowered and pulled over to the waiting tug.

The smell of burning coal and hot steam surrounded her. She said nothing as she and the child were assisted on board, and did not turn her head as the whaleboat was pulled back to the *Curtsey*. She did not cry until the *Curtsey* bowed to the place that had given her birth, in imitation of her name, and then bore away in dreamlike splendor, on the first leg of her long haul to the Pacific coast of South America, to cruise for whales off the coasts of Chile and Peru.

It was a winter of cold hard mud and gray skies and a wind that bit to the bone. And then at Christmas Victoria was up and right smart, and the day after that a letter arrived from Jezekiel Mitchell summoning Abigail, so she could be taught to take over from Charity, before Charity went away.

A carriage was sent for her. It was driven by the same

hunch-shouldered farmhand who had brought the carriage when the Mitchell women paid their calls. As the wheels rattled viciously on the iron-hard ruts of Boat Train Road, Abby sat alone inside, looking out at grim winter-gray trees. With every jolt, her bags bounced up and down. Abigail felt numb, as if some vital spirit had fled. Emily had screamed when the carriage lurched away. Her father had gone, and now her Aunty Abby was leaving; her comfortable little world was breaking apart. Victoria had had tears in her eyes, and Mrs. Fanny had thumped her stick and mumbled to herself. Now, Abby felt like crying, too, but her numbed eyes refused to produce tears.

There were buildings scattered sparsely along the length of the road, surrounded by sere fields, but she didn't know which one was the Mitchell house. Jireh had brought her and Martha along this trail on sleigh rides one winter ago, but he had never pointed out his home. Why? Because he was ashamed?

The carriage jerked to a stop. The house was gray like the scenery, set in the middle of a square of frozen mud, not very far from the road. It was unpainted, and the walls looked mildewed, betraying that it was cold and damp inside. The windows were blank. There was no one on the step to greet her. Abigail clambered out stiffly and then stood looking at the shut front door.

The farmhand pushed past her to get at her bags. Then, with one bag on his shoulder and a second held in his other hand, he shoved past her again and trudged up an ill-defined path along the side of the house to the back. Abby followed him slowly. Condensation trickled down grimy shingles, and Abby cramped her movements so she wouldn't brush against the wall. Her chief emotion was discomfort because her feet were so cold.

There were outhouses at the back of the lot; Abigail could hear and smell pigs. A thin shivering dog cringed up to her and then cringed away.

The farmhand elbowed open a door at the back of the house, and Abigail went in after him, into a dim scullery. She could hear someone muttering in the kitchen beyond, and the sound of dripping water.

The mutterer was Charity. She was wearing a shabby washdress and was peeling potatoes that smelled bad. "So there you are," she said. She didn't smile, instead jerking her chin as she led the way upstairs. The house was very old, with wide uneven floorboards that creaked. "You will soon learn not to disturb Mother when she is lying down," Charity said. "She suffers from sick headaches."

She led the way to a bedroom at the back, a small prim room with a single four-poster bed. It was immediately obvious that until Charity sailed to join Seth Morgan, Abigail would be sharing that bed with her cousin. Charity's clothes were piled in trunks in a corner, or hung from hat-stands. There were no closets, for the house was so old that it had been built when closets were taxed. There was a fireplace, but the room was bitingly cold. Instead of kindling, a basket of dusty paper flowers stood in the grate. "You can help me in the kitchen when you're settled," said Charity, and left the room. The rattling of her shoes retreated down the stairs. When Abby had stowed her bags in the one spare corner, she changed, shivering, into a work dress.

Mrs. Mitchell did not come downstairs until the supper was set on the table. Abigail had a present for her, an elaborately frilled and beribboned pillow. "Smart may be as frivolous does," said Mrs. Mitchell, putting it to one side. "We have no use for frippery in this house."

Abby said in a low voice, "I made it myself."

"You will not have time here to waste on such nonsense." Then Mrs. Mitchell turned to her husband, who was reading his newspaper at the other end of the table, and said petulantly, "I thought I would die of the sick headache today. All that noise on the stairs..."

Charity set down cold plates.

"Poor Mama," she said. "Shall I brew an onion draft for your feet?"

Jezekiel Mitchell rattled the news-sheet. "The *Erasmus* reported nine hundred barrels in November."

"Then the *Erasmus* is truly lucky? I was right in my prognostications," said Mrs. Mitchell, as smug as if she alone was responsible for the good report.

"Prices are good right now," said Mitchell, just as complacently. "I'll send instructions for Jireh to ship the lot at the very next port he touches."

Oh Jireh, mourned Abby in her mind. It was summer in the south Pacific. This room was as cold as the rest of the house. The only warm room was the kitchen, with its wood-burning stove.

"And Captain Morgan?" Mrs. Mitchell asked. "How is his report?"

Abby watched Jezekiel Mitchell's expression become malicious. "Poor," he said with relish. "Shocking."

Then he put the paper down: Charity had brought in the food. If she had heard what her father said, her expression didn't show it.

The meal was dried salt cod, boiled and covered with a thick white sauce. As Abby helped Charity serve it, two men came into the room, the farmhand and a much older man whom Abby had not seen before. He peered at her through rheumy eyes and said in a high, quavery voice, "Who's this?"

Mr. Mitchell said, "She's the daughter of my wife's cousin, and will take Charity's place in the household when Charity is gone." Then, without bothering to say Abigail's name, he bent his head and prayed at length. "For God hath made the sea," he intoned, and, "God will take the ships of the blessed and so shall the sea be calm unto them, while unto the wicked and scheming the ocean will be wrought and tempestuous."

It made no sense — not unless he was indulging in more

malice towards Seth Morgan.

When at long last the oration was over, Mrs. Mitchell heaved about, hauled out a handkerchief, and dabbed at her mottled face.

"A shocking report?" she queried, just as if there had been no interruptions. "Captain Morgan does badly? Oh," she said, and began to weep. "Few can realize the aching of the maternal heart, when that accursed ship is destined to carry an only daughter across the seas to an unknown fate."

Abby looked quickly at Charity, but she had her head bent, her eyes lowered as she stared at her meal. Jezekiel Mitchell said impatiently, "Charity must go; there is no help for it."

"But my health is so precarious," wailed his wife. "That Captain Morgan is holding us to ransom, the cruel man; he pays no regard at all to my wretched state of health."

Abby was holding her fork very tightly. Why didn't Charity defend her intended? After all, she had consented to be Seth's wife, presumably of her own free will—unless her father had forced her to do it, as a means to his devious ends. She could see Charity's hand curled on the table, somehow weak-looking despite the cracked nails and work-reddened skin.

Jezekiel Mitchell was eating angrily, chewing in sharp little snaps. "What do you expect me to do about it? While Abigail Sherman is here to care at your sickbed, Captain Morgan will believe it a sufficient sacrifice on the altar of family responsibility."

Abby put down her fork, unable to eat another morsel. Mrs. Mitchell said in a sullen voice, "The grudging duty paid by an orphan is no substitute for the devotion of a daughter."

"You forget the Book," Mitchell said. He had a blob of white sauce on the end of his long, narrow chin. "The first book of Samuel records that Abigail was a handmaid for a servant—and you must resign yourself to that, Mrs.

Mitchell."

Abby's throat was cramped with threatening sobs. She thought savagely to herself, *Don't cry, don't cry* ... and with utter relief heard the old man say in friendly tones, "You be the girl from New Zealand?"

Obviously, he had been working things out during the interval. Abby looked up and mutely nodded, grateful for his grin. Who was he? He was hunched, like the younger farmhand, and he had straggling hair and tiny ears like Jezekiel Mitchell. His huge hands were cracked and knobbed. Then, as the dreadful meal meandered on, Abby found that he was an uncle. The family called him Uncle Henry. Though Mr. Mitchell treated him with a kind of habitual contempt, the old man did not seem to notice, or to mind, if he did. The younger farmhand said nothing, devoting his energy to chewing fibrous cod. After a while Abby deduced that he was Uncle Henry's son. Uncle Henry was a part-owner of the land and a widower of God-knew-what duration, and Fred had never bothered with finding a wife, no doubt because no one would have him.

At last Charity began to collect the dirty plates, and Abigail stood up and helped her. Mrs. Mitchell stopped where she was, in her chair: Charity, it seemed, cooked and cleaned and slaved for the entire household. Surely, Abby thought tiredly, it should make Charity feel friendlier, knowing that she was fated to take over that task — but it did not. She said nothing as she put the plates by the sink, and then walked out. Abby exhaustedly began to wash them.

The water was lukewarm and quickly went slimy. She had to struggle to keep the dishes from slipping out of her hands. Her eyes were stinging as she fought back tears, and she knew with despair that she was lonelier and more desperate than she had ever been before in her life. Then she heard footsteps on the flagstones behind her, and turned her head to Uncle Henry's grin.

The smile held stupidity, but Abby smiled back. He

might be senile, but his had been the only friendly face.

He came closer: she thought he was going to bear a hand with the dishes. Then, with a totally unexpected jerk, he thrust a knobby hand between her legs, his fingers poking hard.

Abby jerked back with utter loathing, biting back both an involuntary scream and the urge to slap him. "Don't you *dare,*" she hissed.

His grin merely widened. "Now don't yer git shy wiv me, me pretty, and pretend thee's a decent woman," he smirked. "Folks tell me how the New Zealand girls uncover their titties in the street."

Two weeks later Mrs. Fanny heard a tap at her sitting-room door. She dragged herself out of her chair and across the parlor, grumbling at the disturbance. Abigail was there, her face white and desperate, and Mrs. Fanny stood silent a long, long moment, schooling her heart not to break with pity for this child.

She was too old for such feelings of anger and despair at the unthinking arrogance of men, she thought. Her hand gripped the head of her stick. How could Obed have consigned this bright spirit to the mean world of the Mitchells … and how could her own husband have acceded so tamely to Jezekiel Mitchell's demand? If Martha Cady were here, they would write and declaim, and organize a protest, but what could one lame woman do?

She sighed and said, "Come in, girl, come in. You can brush my hair while you tell me about it."

For a while she wondered if Abigail had run away, but no, it seemed that the Mitchell women had gone downstreet a-shopping. Abigail had made a brief escape. She spoke hesitantly at first, as if she had learned to keep a careful silence, but then, as she brushed, the words started coming, faster and faster as Abby poured her misery out.

Mrs. Fanny's guess had been partly right: Abigail was

certainly plotting to get away.

"How far?" she barked. "All the way to the Pacific?"

"To New Zealand," Abigail replied. Her tone was dogged.

"Don't tug so, girl. I'm losing enough hair without your encouragement. And how would you survive there? On your wits?"

"I'll survive very well, once I find my brig."

"Without a man?" It was unthinkable.

"All I need is to get there," Abigail said obstinately. "I thought of working at the Lowell mills, and saving enough money for my fare to Auckland, but if I stay in New Bedford Jezekiel Mitchell will simply send for me again, and I will be in a worse plight than ever. So I have decided to work my passage. But I don't know how to go about applying for a job as stewardess, and that's why I want you to help me. Or perhaps," she said, sounding more tentative, "you would lend me the money for the fare. I would pay you back before very long, for I know there is money waiting for me in New Zealand."

"Money? What money?"

"There's a fortune waiting—once I work out what to look for."

"Child, you're not making sense!"

"My father was secretive about it," said Abby sadly, and told her about the riddle.

"So you will run off to New Zealand, just because of a puzzle?" derided Mrs. Fanny at the end. Like her son, she was intrigued, though, and asked Abigail to recite the riddle again. "Dreams and moon-dust," she mumbled; "barometers and a kind of spice." Her lively old mind tugged at the rhyme like a thrush with a snail. "You think it points the way to a fortune in gold, like all the California tales?"

"It's possible," said Abby. "They found gold in New South Wales, in great huge lumps—some convicts found them, and the soldiers accused them of stealing watches and melting them down, because they said it was impossible to get such big nuggets from the ground. And, if there is gold in Australia, it's perfectly logical that there should be gold in New Zealand, too."

"Like the pot of gold at the end of the rainbow?"

"Exactly," said Abby, and put down the brush. She stood up and fetched the long plait of hair that hung by the looking glass. It formed the base of Mrs. Fanny's back hair. Abby sat on the bed, the plait in her lap.

Mrs. Fanny stared at the girl's reflection in the mirror. Her mouth was set, and there was a determined light in the narrowed blue-green eyes. Abigail meant to go, she thought with alarm, and snapped, "What about your father's murderers? Aren't you worried about them — whoever they were?"

Abigail was drawing Mrs. Fanny's shed hairs out of the brush, frowning over the fiddly task. Then she wove the hairs into the plait. The braid held all the shed hair of a womanhood, dark brown at one end and steel gray at the other, fat near the start with the abundant shedding of several failed pregnancies and one successful one, and then growing progressively thinner. Watching her, Mrs. Fanny thought that Abigail might be reconsidering the mad idea, but then the girl said with spirit, "Why should I be frightened? My father was murdered for no reason at all, by dissident warriors. He just happened to be in the wrong place at the wrong time. Why would they want to harm me?"

"You're wrong," said Mrs. Fanny, and shook her head for emphasis.

Abigail looked up. "I beg your pardon?"

"It wasn't any warriors. The English did it. Why would a native kill a man who campaigned for Maori liberty? Of course it was the English — and they are the men you should be worried about. It happened often enough in the Glorious Revolt. Devious and underhand," she declaimed, riding a

259

favorite hobbyhorse. "The greedy tax-gathering colonialist English think they get their leaders ready-born, leaders when they pop out of the womb, folk born all natural to a life of wealth and leadership, but all they breed is arrogance! And if the English killed your father, my girl, then be sure your Scotchman is dead as well, for they'd never leave a witness."

Then Mrs. Fanny was engulfed with pity again, glimpsing the misery on Abigail's averted face. She sighed and said, "You have to face it, going to New Zealand would be plain plumb dangerous, and there'd be no profit from it."

"I'd stow away to do it!" Abby shouted.

"You would?" Mrs. Fanny winced. She shut one eye in lizardlike thought, and then grunted and rattled her stick. "Oh, go and see Victoria," she snapped in disgust. "She and Emily have missed you enough. And come and see me next chance you get; don't do anything bone-headed until we've talked again."

The only day of the week when life in the Mitchell household was remotely bearable was Sunday, for Sunday was a day of rest. The Mitchell women dressed in their best black gowns, and most of the day was spent at chapel. Abigail was very thankful indeed for the choreless Sabbath. During the week she and Charity worked in a hostile silence, to the accompaniment of Mrs. Mitchell's endless whining, but in the Sunday routine the mutual rancor was almost forgotten.

The pastor of the Mitchells' church was a relatively recent arrival, the Reverend Mr. Smith. A slab-sided, middle-aged widower in a drab brown suit, he reminded Abby more than a little of a sheep, for he had woolly mutton-chop whiskers and the same toothy, rather disdainful smile. He treated Mr. Mitchell with respect, and always escorted the Mitchell family to their carriage after the meeting. Then, as Sundays went by, it dawned on Abigail that Charity was in love with this man.

It was impossible not to miss it: Charity's prominent eyes were languishing in the shadow of her most becoming bonnet. Mrs. Mitchell was equally palpitating in the minister's presence, and the farewells were always protracted. Abigail stood quietly, content to be ignored and to watch the scenery, but she couldn't help wondering why Charity allowed the farce of her engagement to Seth to continue. Because she was so cowed by her dreadful father, she supposed.

The chapel was set on the crest of a gentle hill. Beyond the dainty white finger of the spire a multitude of slowly greening hills lay sprawled out for her contemplation. Marsh meadows sparkled beneath the silvery sky, and the silver coil of the river lazed its way in the distance, en route to Buzzards Bay. Then Abby heard the Reverend Mr. Smith say in regretful tones, "Only one more week, my dear young lady, before you venture to the Place of Skulls? How we will pray and how our thoughts and minds will be with you as you trace that tragic path."

Dead silence. Then Mrs. Mitchell asked in shocked tones, "Tragic?"

"I crossed that fearful spot just one year ago," the minister said.

Abigail stared at him: he was actually beaming, with no apparent idea of the effect of his words on his audience. "My dear wife expired," he informed them, "from the after-effects of that fearful passage."

Charity said, "*Died?*"

"Yes," said the minister. He took off his hat, bowed as some departing worshippers passed, and then return his mild gaze to Charity. "The poor woman died of intermittent fever, contracted in that awful spot."

"Oh, dear heaven," gasped Mrs. Mitchell. She turned to her husband and cried, "Mr. Mitchell, I protest!"

"There's no alternative," said Jezekiel Mitchell sulkily.

"But surely," urged the Reverend Mr. Smith, "can you not reconsider this decision in the light of the particular responsibility of a devoted father? My spirit fails me at the vision of your charming, susceptible" — he bowed to Charity and Charity quivered — "daughter across that awful shore?"

A pause as they all stared at him, and he said, "Send her around Cape Horn, instead."

Jezekiel Mitchell said sharply, "I have given my word to Captain Cambridge that my daughter will accompany his wife."

"But two ladies of refinement and culture..."

"Circumstances demand a sacrifice."

"Oh dear," said the Reverend Mr. Smith. "Oh dear, oh dear." He took Charity's hand in his own, gazing at her dolefully.

"That dreadful route lies through primeval jungle," he intoned; "through marshes alive with criminals of the most dangerous kind — it is truly the most dissolute of God's spots. A cacophony of oaths and imprecations assail the ears of decent folk, mouthed by the very worst kind of men."

Jezekiel Mitchell snapped, "The divine command says, Let not your heart faint, fear not and do not tremble."

"Yes, ah, yes, indeed you are right, sir. But I would consider it an honor, sir, if these ladies would bestow the privilege of their presence at tea at my house on the morrow. Time grows short, and I would esteem it a pleasure to have further talk, before your lovely daughter quits this place, perhaps forever. Come now, ladies, will you say yes?"

"Yes," sighed Charity. Her eyes were dumbly devoted.

The next day was beautiful, one of the warm, kind days that give false hope of an early spring. The Mitchell women wore their finest taffetas and the Reverend Mr. Smith presented Charity with a tiny china pillbox that had been his mother's. She received it with a languishing smile, and very obviously wished for the visit never to end.

Mrs. Mitchell, flushed and creaking in every lacing, was as reluctant as her daughter to leave. "You know not our trials and tribulations," she mournfully confided. "When I think of what my daughter must endure, my mind becomes inflamed with serious and unnatural imaginings. Is there nothing reassuring you can say, dear Reverend Smith?"

Abby, standing by the carriage, listened absently. The unaccustomed warmth of the sun made her drowsy, and she was only sleepily conscious of the rattle of harness as the horse shook its head, the smell of leather and drying mud, the annoying throb in a finger where a needle had pricked her, and the petulance of Mrs. Mitchell's voice. The woman was a fool, she idly mused; she would have given her soul to be in Charity's place. To get to the Pacific she would be prepared to hack a path through the jungle.

"And the *Lizzie Ann* report is *deplorable* ... I don't mind telling you, Mr. Smith that my husband is relieved that our name is no longer associated with that ship. I do not consider Captain Morgan trustworthy; we heard that his word as an honest man is no longer accepted."

"Oh?" said Mr. Smith, and put out a large soft hand to assist Mrs. Mitchell up the carriage step.

"He has had to sell what little oil he has got in order to raise the needful. After all," she said maliciously, "a man who has been put on trial for murder is bound to have no credibility with the merchants."

Jerked out of drowsiness, Abigail stared at her with distaste. Seth Morgan was acquitted, she thought angrily; he was not, in fact, ever put on trial, as the charge was dismissed. But she had learned too much over the past two months to be foolish enough to say it.

Mrs. Mitchell said, "When I consider that but for my delicate health my only daughter would already be wed to Captain Morgan, and sharing his privations on that unlucky ship..."

She broke off, letting the thought fade into the air as she

arranged herself on the seat, with much jolting and creaking of carriage springs.

Mr. Smith turned to Charity, and held out his hand. She took it caressingly, and the carriage swayed again as he helped her into it. Abigail watched her arrange her skirts, those yearning pale blue eyes fixed on the pastor's face.

"And when I think that by the end of the week..." Again, Mrs. Mitchell's voice faded away. There was an awkward pause as they all waited for her to go on.

She said nothing. Mr. Smith turned to Abigail. It was very quiet. The farmhand, Fred, cleared his throat, and the hacking cough seemed very loud.

When the pastor helped Abby mount the step, she said, "Thank you," and that seemed loud, too. The carriage rocked, and Mrs. Mitchell turned stiffly in her seat. Her whole torso revolved. Her eyes were wide open, and Abby froze. Mrs. Mitchell's expression was sulky and a little bewildered.

Abigail heard herself babble, "Something's wrong." Her skin, inexplicably, was crawling. Mrs. Mitchell sat bolt upright, the empty unblinking eyes staring right into hers.

The carriage was still rocking. Abby, poised on the step, held the door tight, for Mrs. Mitchell was slowly leaning, leaning, as if to overwhelm her with all that monstrous tightly laced flesh.

Abigail wanted to throw herself backwards, away from the descending weight, but she was paralyzed. Then, as she watched with gooseflesh creeping over her skin, Mrs. Mitchell leaned over, slowly, and slowly folded, and slowly fell with a thump to the floor of the carriage. Black taffeta rustled and then was silent. Charity screamed.

With the sound Abigail found control of her legs, and whirled in a blind rush into the garden. Then, at the foot of Mr. Smith's prize lilac, she was violently sick.

"Charity will not travel," said Jezekiel Mitchell as they stood in the graveyard after the funeral service.

Mr. Cambridge spluttered, "But your arrangement with Captain Morgan..."

"Captain Morgan can sail as far as the gates of hell, for my daughter does not sail with him. The marriage contract between us is perfectly clear on the matter. Also," Mitchell added viciously, "it is a statement of Holy Writ, verily, that the hoary face of paternal age be honored, so both the law and the Bible are explicit: the marriage contract says that my daughter stays behind in extreme family circumstances, and stop behind she will. I need a housekeeper, and cannot spare my daughter."

"But surely when you have Abigail..."

"The Bible says, ye shall do no unrighteousness in judgment, but I do find Abigail Sherman lacking. I do not choose to have her in charge of my domestic affairs."

"But my daughter-in-law cannot travel alone to Paita, sir!"

"Of course not," said Mrs. Fanny roundly. She scowled at Abigail as she said to her husband, "Abigail will have to go with her."

Abby's breath caught, and she stared incredulously.

Mrs. Fanny glared back, and thumped her stick. "It's vastly preferable to whatever other eventualities inhabit Abigail's mind," she snapped.

Mr. Cambridge looked suspicious. "And when Abigail and Victoria have arrived in Paita?"

"She won't leave Paita until she has found Captain Morgan," Jezekiel Mitchell said coldly. "I have a letter for him, with the news of the termination of the marriage agreement, and this must be given into his hand, by law, even if he be in prison for debt! Once it is delivered, Abigail will return, and then I will decide what to do with her."

Eleven

Come listen to me, Yankee boys, and a story I'll relate
That happened in the valley of the California state
'Twas down in the bottom lands where we fellows go so
*   bold*
To work like hungry tigers when we think about that gold
Oh, the gold, they say
Is brighter than the day
And when it's mine
Oh, won't I shine
And drive dull dare away—oh!

What a chantey for a ship! But then, Abby thought deliriously, the *Ocean Queen* was not a ship, she was a steamer, and doggerel was exactly what she deserved.

The *Ocean Queen* was an ugly, smelly, clumsy industrial invention. In place of towering canvas, the *Ocean Queen* had two miserable smokestacks; when she moved, her flags flew backwards. And who had heard of a ship that was owned by the passengers, even if only for the duration of the passage? The *Ocean Queen* was driven by a ridiculous little engine, and the actions of that engine were determined by the passengers, by vote at evening meetings. Those who'd paid a fare to fill the berths of the vessel, like Victoria and Abigail, were there by dispensation only.

"Soon all sea-going vessels will be driven by steam," Mr. Nicholas informed Abigail. Mr. Nicholas, like Victoria and Abby, was one of the fare-paying passengers, at the mercy of the evening meetings.

"Impossible! Where would all the steamers get their coal?" Abigail protested, enjoying herself immensely. "It would have to be carried to them. Nothing but coal would be freighted around the world, except perhaps for passengers, for the steamers' holds would be full of the coal they'd be carrying to each other."

On the inside, the *Ocean Queen* had proved to be even more fantastic than the outside. Decks were stacked above more decks, with ranks of square windows in their outside walls. The vast rooms inside the decks were called saloons. There was a general saloon for families, a ladies' saloon for ladies unaccompanied by men, and many men's saloons, for the *Ocean Queen* was almost entirely filled with men. They drank and they gambled and they spat tobacco, and all the time there was hearty singing.

By the banks of the river where we'll stop and bend so low
The flakes we'll find above the ground, the lumps are down
*   below*
But there's a spot where sometimes—or so we folks are
*   told—*
When the tide is 'way down low, we'll find great heaps of
*   gold!*
* Oh, the gold, they say*
Is brighter than the day
And when it's mine
Oh, won't I shine,
And drive dull care away—oh!

The men spent the time left over from drinking, singing and gambling in sewing overalls and tents and in fighting with the captain and the crew. They were all well-armed, for the state of lawlessness in California was beyond belief. Each of the gold miners had a two-barrel gun, a rifle, and one of Colt's revolvers. They practiced their marksmanship on the open decks until Captain Seabury took a strong stand and prohibited the open decks to everyone, without exception.

And how Abby enjoyed it all—after the prim rectitude of New Bedford and the horrors of the Mitchell house, she felt gloriously alive again, as if reborn into a world that promised adventure. She had abandoned her black gowns, leaving them behind for Charity, if she wanted them—and was wearing pretty, colored clothes that fitted her ebullient mood.

How Mrs. Fanny—and Andrew Jackson—would have loved the *Ocean Queen*, she thought—for here was the salt of common America personified, in all its cussing, sweating, fighting versions. One truculent miner had a tussle with the second mate, and the second mate got squeezed, so he turned round and gave the third mate a thump in the grinders that sent him off to his berth, and then the first mate and another miner had a duel.

"Choose yer weapons!" hollered the first officer. "Those what God gave me!" the miner yelled back, and next thing they were rolling about under a table. And the spitting! Victoria and the other ladies got up a petition for spitting to be banned, but the miners said they would stop spitting only if the captain and his officers stopped spitting too, so the petition lapsed in disarray.

"And," said Victoria, "the gambling is scandalous." She tried to get up a petition about that as well; it was as bad, she thought, as the gunslinging, but as the *Ocean Queen* sloshed steadily south, past Cape Hatteras and the Bahamas to Jamaica and the Caribbean, the gambling continued unabated, day and night, morning and afternoon.

Mr. Nicholas was a professional gambler. The gold miners, to him, were themselves a capital source of gold. He was not heading for San Francisco, however, but was traveling to Valparaiso, in Chile. His London merchant father, in a last effort to redeem his wayward son, had purchased Mr. Nicholas a commission, and he was on the way to join the English sloop of war *Dido*. But, in the meantime, he was taking the miners' money in games of poker.

And even the gambling had a song of its own. Abby used to lie awake in her bunk and listen, hugging her sense of release.

Treble, double, and rub.
Hulloa, there's a good hand.
Do you really think me pretty? Oh, flatterer.
You've gammoned me, by God!

Were they all escaping from something or other, these passengers on their hazardous way to the wilder parts of America? They were certainly dreamers. Why had the world so abruptly been embroiled in all this fierce dreaming of gold?

"It's the sun," declared Mr. Nicholas. His English education had taught him much about the solar body and its effects. "The sun casts rays and spots which determine the progress of evolution. And, what's more, the sun has a temperate climate."

"Surely not!" laughed Abby.

"But it stands to reason. For," he said earnestly, "the sun's warmth is dissipated in our direction, so there is little left to warm the surface of the sun itself."

"That's not so!" cried Mrs. Perry, who was an extremely ugly French woman with a mop of tightly curled gray hair and large prominent teeth permanently displayed in a broad smile. She had broad hips, too, and her gait was like that of a swan. Somehow, by some marvelous French alchemy, Mrs. Perry managed to radiate a confident aura of extravagant beauty, so that one instantly forgot her undeniable ugliness. It was the vivacious way she spoke, and the outrageous things she said. She and her husband were fare-paying passengers; they kept a hotel in Valparaiso. She played cards and gambled, like Mr. Nicholas, and her husband did too.

"The sun is not temperate," Mrs. Perry argued. "How could it be? It has variation, like all the other planets. The poles of the sun are cold, yes, as on our earth, the same."

Her husband was Yankee, and as long and thin as a whippy piece of whalebone, topped by a long, gloomy face. He was one of the few on board who did not live on dreams. "The sun," he said morosely, "is the reason for the troubles of South America; it is the fable of the cricket and the ant all over. In the warm sunny places industry means not the difference between life and death, while in lands with frozen winters the folks work hard through sheer necessity."

It made it very difficult for a man like himself, who was a hotelier in Valparaiso. "It is impossible," he declared, "to find reliable help."

"It's the same in New Bedford," said Abigail demurely.

But here there was the additional problem of the multiplicity of holidays. "Do you know that American workers give three more weeks a year of work than a South American equivalent? It is little wonder," Mr. Perry declared, "that it is fated that Americans will rule the world with their industry."

Across the saloon gold-mining dreamers were lining up to give Emily donkey rides. Victoria's sedate beauty and lovely gowns were universally admired, and sweet-natured Emily was hugely popular. What a shame, Abby thought, that the passage to Aspinwall, the gateway to the Isthmus, should take only ten plodding days—though Captain Seabury and his crew, no doubt, would be glad to get their ship back.

Land was in sight already—as soon as Mr. Nicholas and the Perrys returned to the gambling tables, Abby stole up on deck, despite Captain Seabury's strict prohibition, and hid in a corner between the bulwarks and the wall of a saloon near the bow. The steel-gray sea was washed with the swirling yellow mud of the Chagres River: South America, realized Abby, was on their lee.

The deck planks were steaming. An amazing downpour had drenched the ship ten minutes before, while they had been discussing the sun. Heavy vapor drifted up from the surface of the water, to join the mist that rose from primeval jungle, less than one mile from the starboard rail. Abby knew it was primeval jungle because she could smell it, a rich, damp, tropical stench of mud and mangroves, rotting leaves and burgeoning shoots, a cycle of life that was running wild, like nothing she had ever smelled before.

The *Ocean Queen* hooted, and the echo blatted back from the trees. Bright birds cried harshly, and rose into the air. The engine clattered, and beneath Abby's feet the deck vibrated as the ship turned ponderously toward the mouth of the river.

Odd, thought Abby. What had the miners' committee decided? She felt certain that the railroad terminus of Aspinwall was further south. She moved up to the rail, and held it tight as she watched to see where they were going. The steamer slowed, proceeding cautiously, laboring against the heavy seaward current. Then the river curved, and Central America engulfed the ship.

Great green clots of floating camalote weed bumped along the steamship's sides. The tops of creeper-laden trees hung like dense green clouds in the mist. The wash touched a log on a mud-covered bank, and the rotting timber crawled and turned into an alligator.

The river curved again and a huddle of miserable buildings bobbed into view. The *Ocean Queen* hooted over and over as the engine slowed still more. The bow reluctantly nudged a bank, and the ship came to a stop by a long, sodden pier.

The rows of hovels sat like chess pawns in the steaming heat. Yellow dogs cringed by mud-brick walls. Miserable horses stamped legs that bled with insect bites. Indians came slowly out of the houses and stood staring at the *Ocean Queen* with blank, unreadable expressions.

It was very quiet, the heavy air disturbed only by the tap-tap-tap of the engine. Then, in the distance—a rattle. A cart jounced around a corner and headed for the pier. It was laden with piles of wet sacking bundles. Leaves poked out of the tops. There were two Europeans on the driving bench; one wore a hat, the other did not. The one without a hat was stocky and half-bald; the hair that was left was like rusty wire wool. Abby leaned incredulously over the rail.

The men jumped down from the cart without looking at the steamship. The half-bald one waved at the Indians and shouted. The Indians moved slowly, and then began to haul the bundles off the cart and into the hold of the *Ocean Queen*, shoving them through a door in the steamer's side. Abby heard the bump as each one landed.

She was staring, afraid to blink. It wasn't possible—but that voice... A drop of sweat ran into her eyes and she was forced to close them for a second. When they opened the half-bald man had turned, and was looking up at the ship.

It was—it was—it was Broddy. It wasn't possible, but it was Broddy McGhie. Abigail shrieked, "Broddy!" and whirled around and ran along the deck and half fell down the stairs to the door that led to the quay.

Broddy McGhie was shorter than she remembered, and older and grayer, but indubitably, it was he. "Wee Abby!" he roared. His face went white and then bright red with astonishment. She sprang at his chest, and clung to him as his arms hugged her.

He hugged her and then held her out again, to look again at her face. "If Auld Scratch don't blind me, 'tis Abby!"

"Oh Broddy," she laughed, but was weeping at the same time. That was all she was capable of saying, his name, over

272

and over. It was the second miracle fate had bestowed on her, just in the space of three weeks — the kind fate that had saved her twice from the Mitchells had brought her Broddy. She was certain, now, that he was her father's proxy, that he had the key to her fortune and the brig — but South America! Of all places to find him, why South America? What in heaven's name was he doing here?

She opened her mouth, but Broddy beat her to it. "Abby, what the devil are you doing here? Eh?"

She was gasping with incredulous, joyful laughter, incapable of answering. Just about every one of the fifty gold miners who were temporary owners of the *Ocean Queen* had gathered to watch, nudging each other to see another's dreams come real. Then came Captain Seabury, who did not look pleased at all.

"Miss!" he barked. "I am certain that you are aware that the ocean decks are prohibited!"

"Oh, dear," said Abby, smiling tremulously. "I promise with all sincerity not to trespass again" — which was very easy, for the steamer was due to dock at Aspinwall that very afternoon. Right that moment, as the captain glowered at her, and Broddy blew his nose in the aftermath of emotion, the *Ocean Queen* trembled as the engine pattered into full-throated life. The gold miners, passengers, Captain Seabury, Broddy, and all, stumbled as the ship backed up and veered around to quit the river. With a final glare, Captain Seabury stamped off to direct the passage back to the sea.

Broddy put his handkerchief in his pocket, and took Abby's hand in one of his big paws, and it felt amazingly familiar. "Come," he said. "I need a drink tae settle me stunned intestines." Obviously accustomed to the ship, he led the way to a general saloon. He certainly needed a drink, Abby saw: he tossed down the first brandy, and immediately ordered another. Then he hauled out his handkerchief again, and mopped his face. "Well, young Abby," he said mock-sternly, "and what are ye doing in

Central America?"

"I'm on the way to New Zealand," she said deliriously, "to claim my brig."

"*What?*"

"My father sold me the *Pandora* — and I have the papers to prove it!"

Victoria rustled forward, holding Emily by the hand. Her smile was questioning. "Oh, Victoria," gasped Abby. "Oh Victoria, this is so wonderful!" Then, remembering her manners, "Broddy — Captain McGhie, this is my friend and kind hostess, Mrs. Cambridge. We're travelling together to meet her husband Captain Cambridge at Paita, on the coast of Peru."

"Paita!" cried Broddy. "Why choose that uncivilized place?" — just as if they hadn't found him on the uncivilized Chagres River. "Earthquakes," he warned. "And sand — great heaps of shifting sand, all of a yellow color, and not a tree or a shrub to be seen."

No trees? It didn't seem possible, not when one thought of the steaming jungle on the steamer's lee. But Paita was a long way south — it took a week for a steamship to travel from Panama to that place; Paita, it seemed, was a strange place for a port, being almost totally composed of dunes of sand.

"The water at Paita is brought from a spring in the interior, on jackasses," Broddy informed them. "Even the vegetable provisions come by small sloops." Paita, as he went on to describe, was both exotic and terribly dirty, but Abby didn't care. Up until this morning she had dreaded the thought of Paita; in her heart, she had known that her reprieve was only temporary, for Obed would find a way to send her back to New Bedford, but now, oh now, Paita held no threat for her. After Obed had collected his wife and daughter, she and Broddy would go to New Zealand to claim her brig, and then sail the broad Pacific.

Then her ebullient thoughts were interrupted by the

arrival of the chairman of the miners' committee, followed by the committee itself. He wanted to know the reason for the unscheduled stop. Why had the steamer made that detour and chugged up the Chagres River? The *Ocean Queen* was owned by the miners—until Aspinwall, at any rate—and their permission had not been solicited.

Said Broddy, "It's my arrangement with the company. The steamer always stops here for me goods, tae freight them back tae Boston."

"Goods? What goods?"

Broddy said teasingly, "Sir, ye would never guess."

The chairman looked infuriated.

"Orchids."

Orchids? Abby's mind went blank. Flowers? Surely not!

"There's a gey wee profit tae be made from orchids," Broddy informed them all, and the gold miners listened intently. "The grand ones in London will pay a fortune tae obtain a rare one, and the rich collectors what don't care tae travel? Ye've not a notion what they will pay!"

Broddy, as he went on to reveal, acted as the shipper for the other European, the one who had taken the empty cart away. He was the collector, a botanist who spent most of his time in the jungle, at great risk of disease and death, and Broddy organized the export of the plants to the agent in Boston, on commission. No wonder, Abigail thought, that Broddy looked so sweaty, grimy, and travel worn, leading a strange life like that.

Then, she abruptly forgot it. The *Ocean Queen* slowed, and ground to a stop, and the miners left the saloon in a rush, pushing and shoving in their race to arrive in Aspinwall first.

"What a comfort it is," said Victoria, "to arrive at such a foreign spot in the reassuring company of a man." It was a blessing, too, thought Abigail, that Broddy was so familiar with the landing.

With elbows, kicks and bellows, he forged a clear path for Abigail and Victoria, knowing exactly where he was going—Howard's Hotel, he said, the only hostelry fit for ladies, as the owner had a kind wife. He carried Emily on his shoulder, and the little girl crowed with delight—how it reminded Abby of her own childhood. How many times had Broddy carried her like that, taking turns with her father?

"Good bye, me lads, good bye," he sang, striding up the muddy street that led to the town of Aspinwall. "No one can tell me why, but I'm bound tae Californi-ay, tae dig the shining gold." The hook-tailed mongrels that slunk about the hovels in the alleys barked and whined, and the miners joined in the chorus.

Aspinwall was a miserable place, hot and steaming and overwhelmingly muddy. A big shed was set to one side of the street, with tracks leading out from it. Ahead, the town was a scatter of clapboard shacks and hotels, with rough planking sidewalks filled with shoving, cursing miners. Abby had two bags over her shoulders: the rest of the luggage would arrive by dray. She had everything she owned in the world with her—except for the black dresses—as she had hoped so fiercely that Obed would take her on board the *Curtsey*. But it didn't matter now, for Broddy was here! Abby joyfully joined him in the last chorus of the song.

The hotel was enormous, the entrance lobby a huge cavern that seemed to swallow them up. More than three hundred travelers were already in residence, their numbers suddenly augmented by the fifty gold miners and various paying passengers from the *Ocean Queen,* who surged in after Broddy as he shouldered open the doors. The din was deafening. Arguments and orders were bellowed, and delicate business was conducted at the top of men's voices. Abby was pushed to one side as the drays of luggage from the *Ocean Queen* arrived. Heavy trunks thumped down on valises, and Broddy and Mr. Nicholas and Mr. Perry had to fight to claim the ladies' bags.

"Mrs. Howard!" hollered Broddy, and crashed his fist on a countertop bell. The roar in the lobby faltered for one split second, just enough for the bell to be heard, and a harassed woman arrived behind the counter. "Ho!" cried Broddy, and reached over and gave her a smacking kiss. Mrs. Howard smiled tiredly. "The best rooms ye have!" cried Broddy. "And an usher tae the ladies' ordinary."

Mrs. Howard shook her head in despair. The hotel was full to overflowing. When the railway cars came in later that day, three hundred more folks were expected to arrive, and not all of them would board the *Ocean Queen*. Everyone in the world, it seemed, was either rushing to get to California, or rushing to escape from the place. Nonetheless, Mrs. Howard found Victoria and Mrs. Perry and Abigail a room. They had to share it with two other women, army wives who were joining their husbands on the coast, but it was a relief to get a bed at all.

The dining room was as immense as the lobby, a huge hot room with sweating bodies crammed at long tables, and insects swirling suicidally around the fizzing lamps. Abby was too excited to eat. Instead, she gazed at Broddy, indulging in many memories—of him playing billiards, and drinking, and yarning endlessly with her father, his endless teasing, and the ponderous way he had flirted with her mother. But no matter how he had teased and exaggerated, he had always been a warm, reassuring presence in the house—or on the brig.

There were so many questions to ask, but the dining room was too noisy to be heard. Then, at long last, it was time to take Emily up to bed. As soon as Victoria was absorbed in settling the little girl for the night, Abby ran down the stairs, found her father's old friend as he was turning into a smoking saloon, and gripped his arm. Broddy looked down at her, his jovial grin fixed in place but surprise creeping into his eyes, and she said, "Is there someplace quiet we can talk?"

The smile faded, and his deep-set eyes became brooding. Then he nodded, and led the way to a parlor. The room was noisy — in the lobby, on the other side of the door, bells rang incessantly, and men shouted for keys, rooms, drinks, shoe-shines, tobacco, whiskey. In the street, outside the windows, horses and carts rattled back and forth. The windows had wallpaper blinds, which slapped back and forth whenever doors crashed open or shut. Most of the chairs were occupied, but there was nowhere more private, or so Broddy said.

Broddy found two spare bentwood chairs and Abby sat down and looked around, very conscious of the other people in the room. One man snored and his head lolled. Two others quarreled over some papers that one of them held. When she looked back at Broddy he was staring down at his hands where they dangled between his spread knees. He looked defeated, she thought with a pang. His hands were calloused and spotted with age, and the fingernails were dirty.

She said impulsively, "Is there really that much money in orchids?"

He shrugged without meeting her eyes.

"Broddy, why did you leave New Zealand and come to South America?"

"I had nae choice. And when your father was ... was gone, there was nae left to stay for, anyway."

For the first time he looked up. His face was haggard, reminding Abigail of her father's expression when Sir George Grey's secretary recited off the list of his holdings that were in dispute.

"Did you write to me about my father's death, Broddy? I only ever received one proper letter from my father. He wrote it in July, just six months after I left Mangonui, but ... but I didn't get it for nearly a year." She swallowed, and said with difficulty, "He must have written it just days... just days before he died."

"And what did he say?"

"That he'd sell his lands to a proxy, someone who would share the money when they were sold again at a proper price." She swallowed again, very scared of Broddy's reply, and said, "I thought—I thought it was you."

He said nothing. The silence dragged, and she said in a rush, "What happened to the shore whaling station?"

"Lost." His voice was bitter.

"But I was so certain that—that a Scotchman would be secure from the English."

"Is that what your father told you—that I was the proxy, and a Scot was safe?"

"No, but..." She stopped in dismay, because she couldn't think of anyone else her father would have trusted enough.

She asked desperately, "Who bought the whaling station?"

"The English. Who else? Ye ken their rules and regulations, how they decreed that none but English can own New Zealand property. Just like your father, I was forced tae sell—at the same price we paid Te Rauparaha for the island. The bastard English," he added in a low savage tone, "ruined us both, me and your puir dead father. And after he was murdered..."

Outside in the Central American night thunder rumbled. When Abigail spoke her voice was small and remote in her ears, "How did he die, Broddy? Why was he killed?"

Lightning stabbed outside the window. For a second Broddy's head was grotesquely backlit with a pulse of blue fire. The thunder cracked with a cataclysmic noise right over the hotel. The man who'd been snoring woke with a yell. Abby's ears popped, and a clammy chill seized her. Broddy shouted, "He—and I—were coming tae the house from the *Pandora*—and—natives—screaming—"

The words were disjointed by jolts of thunder. Then the sky opened in an unthinkably violent downpour. Broddy's mouth moved but Abby heard not a word. Water sprayed in the window behind him, and the blinds rattled deafeningly.

"Tamati!" Broddy shouted. "Tamati killed him!"

Tamati? That was *impossible*. Impossible! Abigail shouted the word. Broddy's face was convulsed with emotion. Then he jerked down the neck of his shirt and Abby saw the dreadful furrow in his left shoulder. The scar was ridged with the healed edges of cut sinew, and there were lumps where bone had splintered and healed badly.

She said in a horrified whisper, "How did that happen?"

"Tamati did it."

"No. Not Tamati! Tamati would never hurt my father. He loved him."

"A man never forgets the moment when he gets a wound like this, Abby. I put up a gey fight, I did my best, but I lost, and he killed your father, with his friends, and almost killed me."

"His friends? What friends?"

"Renegades like him!"

"But it wasn't logical for Maori renegades to murder my father!" She shouted it out, and Broddy shouted back, "I was there! There! And when I fell, I fell into the gully, and when I came to my senses, the house was burning!"

"Is everything gone then, everything?" she cried. "What about my brig? *What happened to my brig?*"

"They seized the *Pandora*. Tamati and his friends took the brig. That was how the murderous thieving pirates made their escape."

So where was the *Pandora* now — the brig that was the key to her future? Abigail shut her eyes to contain the pain, then opened them and asked evenly, "So what did you do after you buried my father, Broddy?"

Broddy was silent a long moment, his expression haunted. He said heavily, "Once I was fit to go to sea, I shipped as master of a fine clipper ship, *Rainbow*."

Rainbow. It was such an evocative name. Dreams and

wishes, she thought ironically; moon-dust and rainbows.

"Only eight hundred tons, but och, she was lovely. I was tae take her tae Glasgie with a cargo of oil and flax—but I was unlucky enough tae also have passengers for 'Frisco." She saw his throat throb as he swallowed. "Thirty-five days from Auckland tae California, a record passage—and she lies there still."

What? Had he wrecked her? Then she understood. The bay of San Francisco was a forest of masts, full of ships abandoned in the rush for gold.

"I discharged my passengers—and the crew left me, too. I lost them all. Those that didn't race to the mines shipped on other vessels that could afford them. D'ye ken how much the other masters offered? A hundred dollars a month! The owner of the *Rainbow* could not meet that, not in a thousand years. I had tae take tae the mines myself, and try my own luck."

His luck needed no describing; it was grimly apparent that it had been dreadful. Broddy heaved a shuddering sigh, and said, "So, wee Abby, here I am, trying to make a fortune from stringy plants."

She could have wept. Instead, she braced herself, and said as reassuringly as she could, "It will all come right, Broddy, when we get to New Zealand, because there's another ray of hope..."

He was staring at her, his expression aghast. Then, just as she opened her mouth to hastily reassure him by describing the secret fortune and the riddle, Victoria came running frantically into the room.

Emily was missing. Victoria was incoherent with distress. The little girl had been asleep, and one of the army wives had offered to watch her while Victoria fetched water for washing. But, when Victoria had returned, both the woman and Emily were gone. Then, when she had found the army wife, the woman was alone. Now, she followed Victoria into the parlor, wringing her hands and weeping. The child was not her responsibility, she said as she wept; she would not harm the mite for the world; she had looked such an angel as she lay asleep, so quiet and peaceful that it had seemed quite safe to leave the room for a bite to eat.

Abby and Victoria and Broddy rushed off in different directions, dividing up the search. It was a nightmare. How would a tiny girl feel, wandering lost in this great crowded building? Abigail shoved through great clots of humanity in the lobby, and invaded saloons, crying Emily's name. Every now and then she could hear Victoria's voice, calling out for Emily, too.

The cars from Panama arrived, and the big doors at the front slammed open and shut, open and shut, as the lobby became even more packed as people eddied about, both coming and going. The Indians who carried luggage did not understand what Abigail said, and neither could the Spanish servants. Gold miners from the *Ocean Queen* responded to her pleas, though, and search parties were set up. She could hear men shouting as they searched rooms and closets and crannies, but there was no triumphant yell of discovery.

An hour went by, and the thunder came back, growling around corners and threatening more rain. Abigail's waist was wet through with sweat, and her hair fell down. "Come here, little pretty," said a drunken man, gripping her arm. Abigail kicked viciously at his shins. The man swore and hopped, and she ran in another direction—outside, because it had become obvious that Emily was not in the hotel.

Lightning cracked as Abigail ran out the front doors. Dogs barked, and horses galloped in the dark. The *Ocean Queen* hooted, ready to depart now that the railroad cars had arrived. Oh dear God, thought Abigail, could Emily have wandered back on board? After a week of living on board, the steamer would seem like a home, to her.

She picked up her skirts and ran towards the quay, passing the big train shed on the way. Inside the shed, other whistles echoed the steamer—the train, she thought. She ran faster, tripped on a wet, slick rail—and there, incredibly, was Emily.

The child had her thumb in her mouth. Abby gasped her name, and scooped up the hot solid weight.

She was weeping; Emily seemed merely annoyed. "Oh, you bad girl," said Abby, sobbing and laughing all at once. She hugged the little girl, luxuriating in the warm familiar feel of her, the trusting way Emily put her arms around her neck. "Why did you wander away?" she demanded. "Your mother is crying. We must hurry and tell her you are safe."

"Man wake me," said Emily. "He wake me and frighten me." She gave Abby a wet comforting kiss and said, "I wanted my daddy."

Her daddy? Had she thought that the man who woke her up was her father? Or had she dreamed it? Emily had been told they were to meet Obed, of course, but how could she understand that he was still many miles away? Who or what the man had been didn't matter, though, because Emily was safe, thank God. Abby stumbled through the hotel doors, calling out for Victoria.

In the fuss and tears and scolding and laughter as Victoria regained her daughter, Abby forgot the mystery of the man who had woken Emily. But then they arrived at the doorway of their room and saw the mess and disorder that the opportunistic thief had left. All the bags had been torn open. Clothes were torn and papers strewn and linen thrown on the floor. The broken pieces of Abigail's little writing desk were lying on top of the mess.

And the papers for the brig were gone.

Twelve

The railroad cars were long and red, with many pairs of wheels. The train, as Abigail mused wearily, was yet another contraption. The engine had a tall smelly smokestack that was streaked with rust like those on the *Ocean Queen*, and it made an unpleasant noise that did not ease her throbbing headache. But the train did leave on time, at exactly nine in the morning.

An official wearing duck pants and a dirty shirt paced the plank-way outside the carriage windows, importantly surveying the big shed. He had no uniform, but he did have a whistle.

"All aboard!" he shouted. "Tumble in for your lives!" He blew his whistle, and the engine answered. Gritty black smoke billowed through holes in the shed roof. Men stumbled down the length of the cars, bowed under bags and bundles, clanking with pots and short-handled shovels. Abby recognized many of them from the *Ocean Queen*, and some, as they passed, wagged their eyebrows at Emily, and said how glad they were she'd been found. Which one of them had been the thief? Little Emily, questioned again this morning, had remembered that a man had wakened her, but she wouldn't say a name. She probably didn't know it, thought Abby.

"Go a—head!" bawled the official, and swung aboard with a final blast of his whistle. The engines hissed and the wheels stiffly turned. The cars all lurched against each other, and with a series of clangs they were off. Victoria and Abigail bounced shoulders, and Emily let out a squeal that was half delight, half shock.

Broddy had organized their seats and the stowing of their luggage, handling the bags himself. "How could we have managed without his supporting presence?" Victoria sighed. Abigail silently agreed. Neither she nor Victoria had had any rest the previous night, even after Emily had been coaxed back to sleep. The fright had been too bad and the shock of finding their baggage ransacked too horrid. Much more than the brig's papers had gone, including rather a lot of clothing, and Victoria had wept as she found the wreckage of her best bonnet, as if it had been the last straw. When they had finally blown out the lamps, rats had scurried across the floor. So the lamps were relit, and mosquitoes had danced and whined in the shimmering shadows throughout the long, hot night.

Victoria sat by the window, Abby at the aisle with Emily in her lap. The car was lined with ranks of double seats, with the aisle down the middle. The seats could face either way, and Broddy and Mr. Nicholas sat together, their seat-back tipped so they were facing Mr. and Mrs. Perry. They had a valise balanced on their knees and Mr. Nicholas was dealing out cards. The cars clattered over a gap in the rails and the cards fell to the floor, and when Mr. Nicholas swore, Broddy laughed.

How could he be so cheerful when his life had taken such an awful turn? Perhaps he was a little drunk, Abigail thought sadly; his laughter was that bit too loud. She had not had a chance to talk with him again; there had been too much panic, and too much bustle as men rushed to make the next step on the journey to California. So many people, she brooded, all dreamers, all frantic to get to the gold. A cheer echoed from the cars behind as they chugged out of the shed and into the blinding sunshine.

And Broddy was singing:

My creditors sued for what was due
I did 'na know what I should do
So I shipped away with a Chinese crew
To work upon the railway!

Mrs. Perry clapped her hands in time to the jaunty tune. Outside the window the sun blazed down on a vista of mud and green, impossible jungle. Emily was hot and heavy in Abby's lap, her head lolling. Chinese coolies and pale Irish navvies stood in miserable huddles by the side of the railroad, waiting for the train to pass so they could resume their sweaty labor. They held shovels and picks as if they were too dejected to drop them.

The railway, I 'm weary of the railway
Ohh-h-h, poor Paddy works on the railway!

Half the men in the car had joined in Broddy's chorus. From the car behind, the competition was roaring, "Oh-h, the gold, they say, is brighter than the day," and Abby's head ached fit to burst. And when it's mine, she thought; she felt sick. The *Pandora* – where was she? And how could she claim the brig, if she did find her, now that the papers were gone? She supposed they had looked valuable to the thief – like bank drafts, or bills of exchange, perhaps. He might even have thought that they were the stake to a claim in California.

"Poor bastard coolies," said someone behind her. "They do say one has died for every sleeper laid. They live in hulks on the crocodile-infested river, you know."

Abigail shivered, despite the humid heat. The train rattled into a world of green, and it was impossible to think; it was only possible to feel.

"Poor Paddy works on the railway," sang Mrs. Perry in her French accent. "Poor sods," said someone, and when Victoria leaned forward to look out the window, cutting out the sunlight, Abigail unexpectedly nodded off.

She dreamed to the rhythm of the wheels, of her father and Tamati, and then of Mrs. Fanny, who shouted, *The English killed your father, my girl, and they wouldn't leave the Scotchman alive, for he'd be a witness!* In her dream, Broddy was the witness; she saw Tamati running to the brig with blood on his hands, and the Maori renegades making sail, to escape to ... where? Then the broken rhythm of the train became the clatter of carriage wheels, and in her dream Mrs. Mitchell was dying again, toppling slowly to suffocate Abigail with her dead weight. Jireh was there, but he turned his back. Abby woke up with a stifled scream.

A full-scale Central American storm was in progress. Lightning spat and thunder crashed and rumbled, and under an incredible onslaught of rain the jungle bent and tossed like the sea. The train was moving slowly, wheels sliding in gathering mud. Victoria, huddled in her corner, was asleep. Abby stared at the vista with a sense of utter unreality. She felt sick. Her hair stuck to her cheeks and forehead, and her camisole was pasted to her skin. Then, with a lurch of horror, she realized Emily was gone. But as soon as she stood up she saw the little girl with Broddy and Mr. Nicholas, chattering with them, confiding who-knew-what.

Abby sat down and looked out the window again. The storm passed over, and everything steamed in the sudden sunlight. Such trees, she thought groggily; she wondered if she knew a fraction of their names. Some were medicinal, like the Peruvian bark that made quinine; it was a crazy, riotous quilt of medicinal plants, twisting lianas, spice trees.

Spices — *although I am wood, I taste very good.*

Cinnamon. The word popped into her head and stayed there. Of course, she thought dazedly. Cinnamon, the spice that came in little sticks, which were kept in a special jar. Every good housewife had a jar of cinnamon sticks in her pantry. *With sugar and apples and rice I'm nice.* Then the cars slowed even more, and the sound of the wheels became a hollow rumble. The blurred green outside the window was replaced with sky-blue. The train was carefully and vertiginously rolling across the narrow bridge that spanned the Chagres River.

The coolies and the Irish navvies were still building it, and the bits they built kept falling down. Tense silence, as everyone wondered if it would stay up today. The gorge seemed a mile below; the cars were suspended precipitously in space — but still Broddy sang:

My creditors rendered me so damn poor
I made port on Panama's shore
I had a pickax and nothin' more
Tae work upon the railway.

The train wheels dawdled creakily. Thunderclouds were boiling on the horizon beyond the river. Abigail saw another group of miserable Chinese as the train approached the end of the bridge, heads down as they waited for the cars to go by.

Then, no sooner were they out of sight, than the train abruptly stopped, its rumble turning into a hiss. What was wrong? Listening to the commotion of questions and answers, Abigail found that though Obed had been right — the journey to Panama City from Aspinwall did indeed take only one day — he had also been wrong, because the railroad wasn't finished, yet. A trek through the Place of Skulls lay ahead. Was it going to be as bad as the Reverend Mr. Smith's prognostications?

No one stayed behind to tell her. All the men, including Broddy, Mr. Perry and Mr. Nicholas, left the car in a rush, shoving and shouting as they fought to get through the doors.

Victoria said in dismay, "Where have they gone?"

Mrs. Perry smiled with the confidence of the seasoned traveler. "For mules. There are mules for hire."

Abby shook herself free of her stupor, stood up stiffly, and went to where Emily was perched on one the seats. She had been popped there by a thoughtful miner so she wouldn't be trampled underfoot in the rush. Abby tied her bonnet strings under her chin, and picked her up. "I hope Broddy is a good judge of mule-flesh," she said, and led the way to the nearest door.

In the jungle clearing outside, it was even hotter than in the carriage. Hundreds of people milled about. Indians in motley European clothing led strings of bony mules, shouting in excellent English. When the track was completed they would be out of employment, Abby supposed, fated to sink once more to the hand-to-mouth jungle existence. She wondered what would happen to the mules.

Two miners suddenly fell to the ground, throwing wild punches. A raucous crowd gathered around them, shouting encouragement and laying bets. Butterflies danced over their heads. Insects in the undergrowth scraped and sang in rhythmic waves of sound, and the men's shouts, by contrast, seemed impermanent and puny. Then Broddy emerged from the crush, red-faced and sweating, leading four mules and an Indian guide.

The guide wore buckskin trousers and a lady's pleated camisole, and strings of silver dollars hung from his ears. Abigail thought of their missing garments, and wondered if Indians were wearing them now. The lower part of his face was painted black. After taking a horrified look at this apparition, Victoria allowed Broddy to assist her onto one of the mules. Abby hopped onto another, and Broddy climbed onto the third, holding Emily before him. Then, once the fourth animal had been loaded with their bags, they set off for Panama City.

The trail was reassuringly wide and clear, evidence of many comings and goings. Abigail's mount, however, gave her trouble from the start. She drummed her heels on the animal's side, urging him to lift his hooves at more than a snail's pace, but he merely turned his head and grinned at her in toothy derision. Abigail, feeling hot and irritable, watched Broddy and Victoria disappear around a bend in the distance. Then, gradually, she was overtaken by most of the company. The gold miners nodded or smiled; some seemed disposed to keep her company, but the slow pace of her mule discouraged even them. Mrs. Perry waved a large white hand and shouted, "'Allo, 'allo," as she passed.

Then Abby was alone. She shifted about, hauled up her skirts, and swung a leg over to ride astride, revealing that she was wearing dungaree pants in place of a petticoat. The mule whickered on a startled note and began to move faster. Evidently it had learned the difference between male and female riders over the past mad months, and had more respect for the former.

The pants had become shorter over the last two years, and slender ankles in dusty white stockings protruded from them. Abby waited for someone to come alongside and lift a scandalized eyebrow, but she remained alone. Huge ferns loomed overhead, while beyond them the jungle waited to reclaim its territory. Insects danced shrilly in the unmoving air, and monkeys shrieked both near and far. Mud sucked at the mule's hooves every time he reluctantly lifted them. The air was hot and clammy, and the noise of the monkeys and the insects was very foreign, but she did not feel frightened; the forest was enough like the bush of New Zealand to seem familiar. If a tattooed Maori face poked out from between two great ferns, would she be surprised? Abby thought not — but she jumped a foot when Mr. Nicholas materialized beside her.

He lifted his hat, and said, "Good afternoon, Miss Sherman," without even a glance at the pants, managing to look urbane and elegant even in the saddle of a mule. "They tell me that they are optimistic that the railroad track will soon be completed," he smiled.

"In Aspinwall, I was informed, champagne is laid down for the great occasion. It will, of course," he added, "signal the end of the passage around Cape Horn."

"Surely not," said Abby.

"But indeed it will. It is obvious, with thought. A train will be designed that is strong enough to carry ships across the Isthmus, from one ocean to the other. 'Tis the alternative to a canal—and building a canal in these fever-stricken regions is, of course, impossible. It has been tried already, with daunting lack of success. So—the railway. How ingenious is the mind of man!"

"Perhaps," said Abby demurely, "it's the effect of the sun."

"Miss Sherman, you display remarkable perception! At times the rays impress with stimulating effect, preparing human minds for an era of invention. Have you noticed how inventions, like wars, come in batches? The sun in certain phases brings a passion for novelty. The common folk begin to insist that the inventors set to work. Thus, when the Panama railway was only eight miles long, the common folk not only insisted on using what had been built, but they insisted that the work continue, whatever the difficulties. Before the railroad, travelers took canoes, and stopped in tents and taverns, and walked or rented mules, at uncountable risk of thieves, murderers, disease, alligators, and drenching in the river. Many died," he added. "Do you feel nervous, Miss Sherman?"

"Oh, no," said Abby. With the fresh air, her headache had cleared, and she felt a great deal more cheerful, her mood helped by the solution of the first part of the riddle.

"Do you think there might be cinnamon trees in this forest?" she asked.

Mr. Nicholas pursed his lips. "Good question, Miss Sherman. May I ask the reason for your interest?"

"A fortune might depend on it."

"In the Panamanian jungle?"

"No, in New Zealand."

"A fortune?"

"In gold, I think," Abby said, and told him all about it, finding this conversation with Mr. Nicholas a very pleasant way of passing the time. Indeed, the time went very fast, and she was surprised when they rounded the last bend in the track.

Unexpectedly, the Gulf of Panama lay before her, shimmering blue. The Pacific Ocean. There were sudden tears in her eyes.

When Abigail arrived at the American Hotel, Victoria was waiting in the downstairs lobby. Her dove-gray gown was uncrumpled, her collar and cuffs quite spotless, and Emily, who was holding her hand, looked equally pristine. Evidently, Abby mused, they had been fortunate enough to escape the drenching downpour that had enlivened her own mule-trot through the streets of the city. The Indian guide who had waited at the entrance of the hotel to reclaim his property looked wet enough, and Abby's dress was literally steaming.

"Our rooms were already booked in anticipation of our arrival," Victoria declared. "And there are staterooms reserved for us on the steamer *Bolivia*, leaving for Paita tomorrow evening."

"That's a coincidence," said Abby. Mr. Nicholas had confided that he was traveling to Valparaiso on the steamer *Bolivia*. Instead of explaining, however, she said, "Where's Broddy?"

Broddy, it seemed, was supervising the stowing of their

baggage in their rooms. "Captain McGhie," said Victoria, "advises me that a walk over the Battery is rewarding. How pleasant that there will be time enough to walk out tomorrow —"

And the door opened, and Obed walked in.

Obed was looking all about him with an anxious smile, which instantly broadened when he sighted his wife. So delighted was he, he seemed bereft of words, standing in front of her like an awkward bear, hands opening and closing at his sides. Oh, kiss her, for heaven's sake, thought Abigail, but he didn't move until Emily ran to him and grabbed him around the knees. Obed, with obvious relief, scooped her up and hid his face in her hair, while his daughter hauled at his whiskers.

"Safe and sound, eh?" he barked at last.

"Yes, Obed," Victoria said sedately, not looking at all surprised that he was here, and not in Paita.

"And Charity Mitchell..." He swung around. Abigail silently watched his eyes bulge. "Abigail!" he cried. "What in tarnation ..?"

Victoria explained. Obed said, "Oh dear, oh dear. My sympathies on the sad loss of a cousin," he said to Abby, "but what Seth will say..." Then he broke off and coughed. "Not, of course, that I am ungrateful that my dear wife had the support of your company."

"We were robbed," Victoria complained. "And we could not have coped without the reassuring presence of Captain McGhie."

"Captain McGhie?" Obed's echo was blank.

"Oh, you will like him," Victoria assured him, and — of course, as Abby thought a little ironically — she was right. No sooner had they shaken hands than the two men disappeared into a drinking saloon, and when they arrived at the supper table they were both very flushed and jovial.

Obed did all the talking, being full of gossip. The *Curtsey* was laying off and on at an island in the Gulf, and his first mate was loading fruit; the ship had been there two weeks while Captain Cambridge had waited in the city, expecting Victoria daily. It was a testament to his devotion that he was here, instead of Paita.

His own report was good; and the *Erasmus* had been confoundedly lucky. Every time Jireh gammed with another ship, that other ship raised whales. So, by whaling custom, he sent over men to help with the cutting in and boiling out, and then appropriated half the oil. It happened every time! Wasn't that the luck of the devil? Martha, however, had never got over being seasick. *Seasick?* Abby couldn't believe it. She had never been seasick herself. How did Jireh feel about having a seasick wife?

And then, of course, there was Seth Morgan. The *Lizzie Ann* report was dreadful—according to Obed's agent here, Seth had taken no oil at all. His ship was clean!—and next week, when he met the steamer *Bolivia*, he would be even more disappointed.

Abby silently contemplated the dinner she did not want to eat, and heard Victoria say, "I was wondering what we should do with Abigail?"

Abby looked up and said quickly, "Please..."

"We cannot send her to New Bedford on her own, and of course it is equally impossible that she goes to Paita by herself."

"Please, I must..."

"It's all arranged," Obed said complacently. "Abigail goes back to New Bedford. Captain McGhie made the offer himself. He needs to see his Boston agent, he says, and he has very kindly offered to make himself responsible for Abigail. They go on the cars to Aspinwall the day after tomorrow and from there will take the next steamer to Boston."

"No!" Abby cried. She stared pleadingly at Broddy, but he refused to meet her eyes. She said desperately, "Please, I must get to New Zealand."

Looking annoyed, Obed said, "Do we have to have that conversation again? There is nothing for you there."

"But there is!"

"You've had another letter, telling you exactly what your father planned? Or have you received another copy of the puzzle?"

"No, I never heard from my father again, but..."

"That's settled, then," said Obed, and then added on an afterthought, "That reminds me, I did have a letter for you, Abigail—but only briefly. I put it on a homebound ship, of course, believing that you were in New Bedford."

"From my father?" she cried. "Telling me the name of his proxy?"—but no one answered, because someone had knocked over a glass of wine, and there was a fuss while the mess was cleaned up. When she saw Broddy's glass being refilled, she realized it was his glass that had tipped, and said to him desperately, "I have a right to go home!"

But Broddy refused to answer, merely looking away, and Obed firmly changed the subject by bragging about his ship. "She's a sailer, my *Curtsey*—sweet and responsive, just needs a touch on the helm when full and bye. Spoke a merchantman out of Callao, but he wouldn't haul aback to take our letters, so we sailed round her stern, read her name. Showed her captain a lesson, eh? *Majestic* of Boston, she was."

There was blatant envy on Broddy's face. "I commanded such a sweet sailor myself," he said. "Ship *Rainbow*, eight hundred tons. In storm or calm, she always showed her skirts to the rest."

Abigail stopped listening. It was a dreadful echo of the day in Mangonui when Obed and Victoria had taken over her life with their arbitrary arrangement to carry her to New Bedford. The two men had forgotten her; Abigail Sherman's affairs were all arranged, and she didn't count any more—it was as if Abigail Sherman wasn't a shipowner, too.

Angrily, she interrupted, "I have a ship, remember—a

brig, and I have to go to New Zealand to find her! I'm not afraid of the English. I'll go to them and report the theft of my brig, and they'll find her — they have to, for I am the legal owner, and then they will have to give her back to me."

There was dead silence as she stared challengingly at them all. Emily's mouth was open wide with surprise at her passion. Victoria had her hand over her eyes. Obed had never looked angrier. Then, slowly, Abigail became aware that Broddy's face held grief.

"Oh Abby," he said gently, "that ain't possible, I'm afraid. When Tamati and his friends stole her they wrecked her. The *Pandora* foundered on a reef off Rarotonga."

Next day the party walked out to the ruins, at Victoria's request, before the Cambridge family took a boat out to the *Curtsey*. Abigail's head was throbbing again, and her eyes were gritty; she had lain awake all night devising new arguments. She had Mr. Mitchell's letter to deliver to Seth Morgan in Paita, and Mr. Mitchell had strictly enjoined her to hand it over in person, as otherwise it would not be legal. And, anyway, Seth Morgan deserved an explanation for the non-arrival of his intended.

"The situation could be adequately communicated tae Captain Morgan in a letter," said Broddy. "That's legal enough, I am sure."

"Victoria will write it," decided Obed.

But, argued Abby, she could be so useful on board of the *Curtsey*, and if Victoria's time came on the way to New Zealand...

"We do not go to New Zealand," Obed said impatiently. It was obvious he heartily disliked having to divulge his plans because of Abigail's intransigence. He had concluded to fish the ground off Chile and Peru until early next year, when he would whale along the Line. Mrs. Cambridge could be set ashore in due course, to await her time in a boarding-house.

"Perhaps there'll be tidings of your father's legacy in the letter that's on its way to New Bedford," he said.

Had it been written by her father? With the name of his proxy? Abigail's thought was dreary. It was more likely that it was from Broddy, with the sad news of her father's murder; Broddy just hadn't got around to mentioning it.

Now she lagged behind the others. As if the weather mocked her, it was a heavenly day. There were banana palms planted among the old stones, and the sky and the gulf were a tropical blue. The *Bolivia* wisped with steam in the distance, readying for her departure that evening. A schooner scudded across the bay, in and out of the variegated shipping in the roads, and beyond that a whaleboat tacked lightly into shore. From the *Curtsey*, Abigail realized; she watched it achingly. It looked like a hummingbird with its blue-and-white sail.

She leaned her arms on a rough wall, and rested her chin on top of them. Narrowing her eyes against the glare of the sun, she stared through her lashes at the sea. The Pacific. She could imagine New Zealand lying beyond the horizon, waiting like a quiet string of fish. She could hear Obed and Broddy laughing, and she hated them for being so cheerful. Emily was crowing as one of them swung her about. The little girl would love the sea — would she ever see her Aunt Abby again?

Abby didn't hear the man's step until he was at her shoulder, and when she spun around, she was unsighted for a moment.

Then her eyes focused. "Mr. Nicholas!" she exclaimed. "Exactly the person I need! But don't talk," she said rapidly, as his expression became puzzled, "I don't have much time, so just listen."

The weather came in thick off the coast of Peru. It was early morning. The *Lizzie Ann* had been laying to all night as the weather deteriorated, struggling under close-reefed main topsail and staysails. Seth was on deck, and the watch was in the act of wearing ship when Dutchie at masthead called out, "Blow."

Everyone stopped short. The wind kicked up the sea, and the *Lizzie Ann* pitched with a groan. Dutchie called out more loudly, "Blow!"

Seth stepped to the after companion door, and reached around to where his spyglass was stowed. He watched Dutchie all the time. The distant figure had one hand holding his hat secure on his head, and was obviously straining to stare at the heaving sea. The *Lizzie Ann* rolled, uneasily sharp on the wind. Something wooden rolled across the deck. A wave flicked up and hissed into the scuppers.

Seth's fingers touched and grasped the glass. Then Dutchie's figure stiffened and he yelled, "Blow, blows, blow, dere she blows!" Seth ran to the mizzen mast; the wind tugged his hair as he surged over the maintop. He took one look and came scrambling down again.

A pod of whales, sperm whales, on the lee bow and not three miles from the ship. "Get ready the boats!" he cried. His boots made a hollow sound on the deck as he ran. He was filled with wild impatience. "Move!" he roared. "Put in your lines, fix your craft! Mr. West, get those lubbers moving and prepare to lower larboard and waist!"

Consider West looked odd enough. He'd instructed Willie Cotton, the cabin boy, to sew rows of patch pockets down the legs of his whaling pants, and now he rattled with various bits of equipment as he scurried. "Brace full and down tacks for the whales!" roared Seth, and heard Mr. West shout, "Aye, sir!"

"Clear away larboard and waist!"

"Aye, sir!"—and all the time Dutchie was hollering in his thick accent, "Blows!"

Then the two boats were gone, splashed down and away.

Seth skimmed up the rigging again, watched, watched, and —

"Prepare to lower starboard and bow!"

"Aye, sir!"

Seth could see the other boats in snatches as they crested waves. Not the best weather for whaling. He shrugged tense shoulders and shouted, "Keep her on the nor'east tack!" and, "Shipkeepers aloft!" Peabody promenaded up the mainmast shrouds. "Keep a sharp lookout and keep those signals running." Nearsighted Tucker, now the steward, pushed by to his post of lookout in the bow, where he would be as little use as ever; Dutchie had been shipped in Fayal to take Tucker's place in Seth's boat.

"Breaches!" shouted Peabody, and then, "Flukes!"

The whales had sounded. Would they run straight? As if anything was straight, in this sea. "Lower away!" roared Seth, and the last two boats rattled down.

An hour later the empty, heaving ocean was abruptly specked with whales. They breached all at once, well apart and running for a dirty horizon. The four boats were scattered too, all on different tacks, appearing and disappearing on far-apart waves. Seth's eyes were slitted and his face felt raw with wind and salt water. The whales were small with distance, blunt heads all going in the same direction, their spouting hidden in the spray. Mr. West's boat was closest to a fish; Seth altered course to meet him.

They were still two ship's lengths away when Mr. West's boatsteerer stood up. He was a Fayal man called Silva. Seth saw him heft the iron. The stocky frame poised — and with a toss the whale dived. Silva lowered the harpoon.

Seth's boat sank in a trough and all he could see was gray waves. He leaned his weight on the sweep, bracing himself for the lift and surge to the top — and Mr. West's boat popped into view. For a ghastly second Seth couldn't comprehend it. Then he saw the powerful flukes that had hurled it up into the air.

Oh God, he thought—and the boat rose higher, every man stopped short in his place. Seth could see them all, like frozen toys. Then the boat exploded. Men, gear, tubs, lances, irons, and lines went hurtling all over the whipping surface of the sea.

Seth clenched his teeth, set his shoulders, and brought his boat about. Men and wreckage were strewn everywhere. In the distance the whales were fleeing. The other boats faltered and then put about as they gave up the chase. The horizon was black and bruised with purple thunder clouds, and the sea was growing savage.

Three of the mate's boat's crew were swimming. Mr. West held up another against the floating mast and was gulping water himself. His pockets and the water they trapped had almost killed him. Dutchie, in the bow of Seth's boat, gripped Consider West's collar and hauled him in with a mighty heave and then grabbed the other man. The boat shipped half a wave and Willie Cotton, the cabin boy, baled madly with his hat.

The sixth man was screaming as he threshed about and tried to grip the surface of the sea. They couldn't get to him; he kept on splashing and floundering just out of reach. Then, just as Seth touched his hand, he sank, leaving a terrible impression of feeble fists groping at the foam. Seth kicked off loose seaboots and dived; thrusting the steering oar at Mr. West as he quit the boat. A wave instantly overwhelmed him. Something bumped against his leg. He felt about but couldn't reach it. When he came up, his chest felt tight and sore, and a wave filled his open mouth. Dutchie hauled him in and Willie baled with his hat again.

They beat up to the wreckage and took all they could on board. The other boats came up and helped them. Everyone was silent. The drowned man had belonged to Boston. He had hated the sea and had died because he was so gallied. He had killed himself by wasting his strength in useless struggling and panic.

At sunset they saw the whales again. The sky was a canvas of streaked angry black, the horizon a streak of bloody red. The spouts of the whales were like tiny distant dandelions against it. Seth ordered the ship made snug for the night, and trudged below. The next day they steered for Paita. It was the middle of March.

On Thursday there were more than twenty whaleships at anchor in the bay of Paita. Seth stood on the beach and watched the steamer *Bolivia* sail slowly around the headland. His fists were thrust in his pockets and his shoulders were braced. He had no way of knowing if Charity Mitchell was on that steamer, as arranged — but she had to be. Of course she was — the agreement had made sure of that.

The steamer chugged slowly, threshing the water, setting whaleships to bobbing. Then the *Bolivia* eased to a stop, half hidden behind a sturdy hull. She hooted once, and Seth heard the distant rattle of chains. When the ensign rose jerkily on the faraway signal mast, the customs house boat put out from shore.

Seth watched its slow progress to the *Bolivia*. Two white-uniformed figures clambered up the side and disappeared into the paddle box. Then he turned and scanned the town behind him. The *Lizzie Ann* liberty men had been swallowed up within minutes of their arrival. Paita was a maze of walls — some white-washed mud brick, others made of thatch — that hid alleys that led to secret courtyards. Where the village stopped, the dunes began, without a scrap of greenery. Sweet potatoes and onions and exotic fruits and fresh water could be bought here, but everything was carried in by sloops and strings of plodding jackasses. Paita didn't look like South America, or even the tropics, but like some fabled place from the Arabian Nights. Only the mosaic promenade on the foreshore was Spanish, and that from the Spain of the Moors.

Seth turned and scanned the bay again, from one sandy

301

bluff to the other. There was no movement on the steamer; her ensign sagged lifelessly. But of course Charity Mitchell was on board—of course Seth had won his tortuous battle with the stringshanked merchant. He found a cigar in the top pocket of his jacket, set it between his teeth, and smoked slowly and evenly while he waited.

With a sudden noise a gang of young caballeros galloped by—siesta, it seemed, was ended. They trotted their horses up and down the waving mosaic of the promenade with much flamboyant jangling of over-embellished harness, but their steeds were stiff-legged and insect-bitten and as starved as their owners. Their manes were hogged to the middle of the nick, with a hank left dangling for mounting. Gaily patterned ponchos alternately flipped and sagged as the riders trotted back and forth, but the high-cheeked faces above them were gaunt with the realities of life.

A trio of ragged half-breed urchins squabbled as they watched over two of the *Lizzie Ann*'s whaleboats. It was whalemen like Seth's liberty men who kept the town of Paita alive—and runaway whalemen, like the two hands who had deserted the *Lizzie Ann* the day before, who kept the local American consul busy. If he lingered here, Seth knew he would lose more, hidden by locals, or stowed away on luckier ships—and today was Thursday. By midnight tonight Seth had to quit this place, or risk more bad luck by sailing on a Friday.

Charity might not like the hurried ceremony he had arranged, but she would be too obedient to make a complaint. She'd be grateful he'd organized a proper preacher—Mr. Premble, the missionary from Valparaiso. If Mr. Premble had not been so conveniently visiting Paita, Charity would have had to make do with a South American priest. Premble stuttered most distractingly, but who cared? Seth had the wedding ring ready in his pocket.

There was movement on the *Bolivia*. Several figures

were exiting from the door in the paddle box and dropping into the customs house boat. The two officers first, distant, but identifiable by the white of their uniforms—and then, a woman. She was wearing a sort of dark-golden color that stood out against the hull and the sea, with a matching bonnet.

It was impossible to see her face, but she must be Charity Mitchell. Seth wondered if she would be sulky because he had not come to Panama to meet her, like that devoted husband, his cousin. He certainly could not afford to recruit in Panama; the California trade had made prices there far too high—and anyway, with his foul luck, he'd be windbound in the gulf.

The boat pulled for shore. There were eight or nine other passengers, all male. The female watched the shipping, not the shore, so she had her back to Seth. Was she looking for the *Lizzie Ann*, to check that he was here? Seth dropped his cigar, heeled it out, and waded into the surf.

Abruptly a yelling muddle of urchins surrounded him, boys who had come from nowhere to lay hands on baggage and earn a tip. He cursed under his breath and barged his way though. Spray hissed as they kicked out at Seth and each other. The boys grabbed the side of the boat and hauled. It tipped, beginning to ship water. Seth cursed again, and reached out for the woman. She had ducked to miss the spray. Still, he couldn't see her face, but it had to be Charity. He lifted her clear of the boat, into his arms.

She came up easily, much lighter and more agile than he had expected. He had to take a quick step backwards to keep his balance, and her weight fell against him. He felt a startling stab of physical excitement, which was so unexpected that he stumbled again. Then, when she clutched him around the neck to save herself from falling, her bonnet fell off, and he saw her face.

He saw her face. Not a woman—a girl. Abigail Sherman. Her eyes were wide. *Abigail Sherman*. He heard her quick voice, brushing his ear. "Seth, I'm so sorry. Charity isn't coming."

He said, "Oh my God," softly and savagely. Trembling with rage, he carried her ashore.

He dropped her more abruptly than he intended, but Abigail landed on her feet as neatly as a cat.

She watched him nervously as he took an angry step away, and then her eyes flickered past him and she said in a gasp, "My bags!"

For an instant Seth thought she was going to dash into the water. He pushed her aside, waded out to the boat and grabbed bags indiscriminately until she called out that he had the right ones. To his relief, there were only three. Lugging them, he came out onto the beach and set off at a rapid pace to the promenade and across it. He could hear the crunch of sand and the rustle of Abigail's skirts as she hurried to keep up. The caballeros were dashing back and forth with renewed zest, showing off for the pretty girl, which made Seth angrier than ever. Jerking his chin for her to follow, he swerved into the alleys of Paita.

Mud-brick and bamboo walls immediately enfolded them. Drunken singing echoed from behind whitewashed courtyard walls. The air in the alleyways was close and dusty, and sand slid with garbage down the central channels. Sailors staggered from one house to another. They all goggled at Abigail—and Abigail insisted on dawdling. It infuriated Seth beyond endurance. "Come on," he snapped, and strode faster, not really caring if he left her behind. Charity was not coming; for some inexplicable, humiliating reason Abigail Sherman had come instead. Jezekiel Mitchell had won. "Hurry," Seth barked.

"I am hurrying," Abigail panted, but she lagged behind, missing her step because she was gazing all around. Twisted iron gates barred the way to courtyards where whaling men caroused. A drooping branch of scarlet bougainvillea seized the eye. Behind tubs of dusty tropical plants sailors were perched on a bench like parrots, rocking back and forth as they swung tankards and hollered:

> *Seraphina's got no drawers,*
> *I bin ashore and seen her*
> *Seraphina! Seraphina!*
>
> *She got no time to put them on*
> *That hard sweat' Seraphina!*
> *Seraphina! Seraphina!*

They turned a corner and Seth shouldered through the entrance of the hotel that Captain Hillman had established for the lodging of whaling captains. Two servants stepped up. Thrusting the bags in their direction, Seth snapped at Abigail, "Follow them." She met his stare warily, and then she nodded. He nodded back sharply, and went into the smoking room, slamming the door behind him.

Two brandies made him feel no calmer. He strode up the stairs to his bedroom and to his irritation the door was locked. There was a pause when he tapped, and then he heard a rustle. Abigail's expression, when she opened the door and let him in, was very cautious indeed.

She was wearing the same gown but had freshened up. He could smell the castile soap she had used. The copper lights in her brushed hair glistened in the bright sunshine. He went to the window, stood with his back to her, and listened silently as she told him about Mrs. Mitchell's death and how she had accompanied Victoria and Emily across the Isthmus. He felt remote, as if this convoluted tale was being told to someone else.

When Abigail's voice drifted into silence Seth said nothing. So, he thought coldly, Jezekiel's wife is dead. By dying she had provided Mitchell with the excuse he needed. Mitchell, he thought, had probably never intended the marriage to take place. Once the ship was sold, here had not been the remotest possibility that Charity Mitchell would

305

ever come to Paita.

Sour luck and a comfortless vessel, he thought savagely, were fated to be his lot. It didn't matter that he could hardly remember what Charity looked like. She had become a symbol of orderliness and comfort.

He swung round at Abigail, and shouted, "And why the devil did you come here? Your job as Victoria's companion stopped when Obed left you in Panama!"

Her eyes widened. Then she said virtuously, "Coming here was the decent thing to do."

"Decent?" he said angrily. *Decent* to come and watch his humiliation?

"I thought you deserved more than a letter."

"And by coming you saved Obed the trouble and expense of packing you back to New Bedford?"

"That's not fair! Obed had nothing to do with it. It was Mr. Mitchell who gave me strict instructions to find you and give you his letter in person—even if I had to search the debtors' prisons—as otherwise it wouldn't be legal."

It took an incredulous second for her words to sink in. Then he shouted, "*What* did you say?"

"Mr. Mitchell says that you have trouble getting merchants to accept your paper."

"My God," he said flatly. The slimy bastard was back to his slandering. He roared, "And what the hell am I supposed to do with you?"

He saw Abigail blink. She said, "I beg your pardon?"

"I presume that Mitchell didn't provide the wherewithal to pay your passage home, for all that he declares me such a pauper?"

Her eyes flashed. "That, Captain Morgan, is not your problem. I assure you I can take care of myself."

"Oh, yes?"

"And I am *not* going back to New Bedford."

"Then what the devil *are* you going to do?"

"That's no concern of yours!"

"Is it not indeed? Paita is not the place for a young girl, you know. It's not New Bedford, or even Mangonui!" The black fury filled him again. "I can't sail away and abandon you here, goddammit!" he shouted. "Not if I want to live with my conscience — and you bloody well know it!" And he had to sail that night, he thought savagely. "What do you expect me to do? *Marry* you?"

Then he stopped short, appalled at the words that had spilled out of him. He made an apologetic movement towards her ... and she was blushing.

His diaphragm clenched. It was as if something had clicked. Abigail was blushing, the very picture of guilt, her confusion plain in her sea-colored eyes. "My God," he said softly. "You did mean to marry me."

"No! That's not true! I thought..."

"I think it is true." He was staring at her, strange thoughts in his mind. Abigail Sherman, a substitute for Charity? A grunt of sarcastic laughter escaped him, but his mind kept on working. Abigail loved the sea; she had declared that the *Lizzie Ann* would be lucky. Well, he thought cynically, she was the only one in the world to think that. Perhaps he should marry her for the old tub's sake.

What other virtues could she offer? His eyes flickered over her slight body. None of the curves and bounteous hips that Charity had promised — but Abigail was undeniably pretty. Excitement stirred inside him. He stepped up close to her, frowning down into her face.

"I think you did mean to marry me," he said softly. When she started to shake her head, he put out his hand to hold her chin still. Her jawbone was fragile in the cup of his palm, and her skin was smooth and cool. "So what would you bring to me?" he murmured. "Can you work hard? Do you promise loyalty?"

She flushed again, trying to look away, and he saw tears of humiliation in her eyes. Then, in a flash that almost shamed him, he thought, the girl was certainly loyal. She had come to the trial; she had come to say good bye. At one time she had been the one person in all of New Bedford who believed he was right. Even Obed had cleared his throat and looked embarrassed. He had held her when she fainted. Aunt Fanny's voice echoed in his mind: *She's the one with spirit!* She would warm a man's bones for the rest of his life.

That physical excitement stirred again. He said softly, "How old are you?"

She blinked warily, put off balance by his caressing tone. "Almost eighteen. Why?"

Seth was silent, thinking. Almost with his realizing it, his thumb was stroking the line of her jaw, caressing the smooth, taut skin. Seventeen was young enough to be adaptable: maturity would give her commonsense and make her less impulsive. She loved the sea, and knew the ocean in all its moods. She would never complain in a storm.

His thumb moved to her mouth, brushing her trembling lower lip. "By God, I'll do it," he whispered. He felt her gasp, and try to pull away, and remembered how she had pushed away from him when she came out of her faint. She had fainted because Jireh had announced that he was going to marry Martha, he was sure of it; he remembered her running out of the Cambridge house when he had arrived with Jireh, and how her whole being had radiated delight. Seth kissed her more roughly than he intended. Then he took her arm, and said, "Come on."

She pulled back. "Where?"

"To get married." He felt galvanized. A new man, he thought. He wanted to get it over and get back on board the *Lizzie Ann.* "You have no choice," he told her harshly. Her eyes widened, and he was suddenly afraid that she would prove intractable and he'd lose her. "If you don't agree to marry me, then I'll send you back to New Bedford. I'm not leaving you in Paita to your own devices, Miss Scatterbrain! God alone knows what crazy scheme you'd get up to next. And I must sail tonight, so..."

He watched her closely as she looked away, looked back at him, and bit her lip. "Well?"

Abigail took a deep breath, shut her eyes, and nodded. A surge of elation filled him.

"Excellent," he said, and hauled her in a whirlwind rush to the door, down the stairs, and into the hall, to confront the stuttering Reverend Mr. Premble in the front room ordinary.

Thirteen

The tide turned at nine; Seth wanted to be gone by ten.

Two captains witnessed the short wedding ceremony, and jovial witnesses they were indeed, but Seth was aching with impatience as they drank their toasts. It was growing late, and dark.

There were only nine men on board the *Lizzie Ann*. The third mate and his boat's crew had sailed a whaleboat down the coast after provisions, and the whole starboard watch was on liberty. They had orders to be on the beach by seven, but a large merchant bark had come in during the afternoon, and sailors from the bark were in town. Merchant sailors and whalemen had little liking for each other, and with grog, rivalries could explode.

Abigail was pale and ate her supper very slowly. Seth had to stop himself from snapping at her to hurry up. When Willie Cotton, the cabin boy, came to report, Seth strode urgently into the lobby. Abigail, to his irritation, immediately left the table and joined him.

Willie stared at her, and grinned stupidly — all the crew knew that the captain had come here to fetch his wife, but had no idea what she looked like.

By his expression, he was surprised by her prettiness. Then his oafish smile faded as he returned his gaze to his captain. "Ah ... the starboard watch, sir, ain't on the beach, and ... and the boat's crew what went after provisions have come back with their bellies full of grog, sir. Mr. West wants your assistance real fast, sir."

Then Willie added, "There's a first-rate fight going on, sir, on the marina."

Seth said, "Oh my God." To his relief Abigail's bags were ready, but then Captain Hillman took long moments to work out how much money was owed. At long last the bill was paid, and Seth was free to sling Abigail's third bag over his shoulder, grip her arm with his free hand, and urge her outside.

Willie led with Abigail's other two bags, dashing like a terrier. The alleys were rowdy with sailors who pushed and shoved towards the waterfront, drawn by the sounds of battle. Abigail's skirts brushed against Seth's legs, slowing him as he hurried. Lamps flickered in blurred halos in the courtyards. Harlots, drawn by the commotion, leaned in the gates and stared at Abigail's gown with naked envy. Behind the bawds, stubborn drinkers swayed and shouted, determined not to be distracted from their spree.

Seth glimpsed Gustavus, the Swede, with the cooper of the *Lizzie Ann,* and let go of Abigail to dive in and nab them. When he came back, Abigail was fighting off a drunken sailor. She kicked at his shins, Seth roared, the seaman hastily made himself scarce, and they hurried on.

There was a full-scale battle on the Paita marina. Sailors swung at each other with fists, bottles, clubs, stones, and jackknives. The groups of battlers staggered in and out of the darkness in bloodthirsty little rushes. Caballeros galloped around at the fringes, not participating — yet. They shouted in Spanish and the sailors roared in a profane polyglot. Horses reared and screamed with excitement, and men hollered unforgivable insults as if the world were

311

coming to an end.

It was almost eight o'clock. Seth dragged Abigail at a run, dodging the fracas. All over the mosaic of the promenade merchant sailors were hammering whaler boys, and the whalemen were giving as good as they got. He saw Hunter, Dutchie, Manuel, and the other Fayal men, but because of Abigail he couldn't stop to haul them out of the mess. He could hear Dutchie roaring, and the crack of huge fists. Even a lowly guano carrier, the merchant boys yelled, was superior to a stinking spouter! Dutchie's reply was incomprehensible. Willie hesitated, and Seth urged the boy along with a touch of his boot. Abigail's steps pattered, and Seth could hear her fast breathing. "Hurry!" he barked.

"I am," Abigail gasped. The two beached *Lizzie Ann* boats loomed out of the night. They were in a clear space on the gravel. Tom Kanaka was sitting cross-legged on the middle thwart of his boat. He was studying the stars with his arms folded and his pipe in his mouth, the picture of proudly tattooed virtue, an image spoiled only by a rapidly blooming black eye.

Seth rasped, "Look after my wife," and shoved Abigail in Tom's direction. Seth heard Tom say blankly, "Well, bugger me, eh?" but didn't wait for the rest. He dropped Abigail's bag and barged his way into the battle.

A new war was developing. The crews of several of the whalers, disdaining combat with merchant boys, were battling one another for the honor of their individual ships. To his disbelief, Seth heard a holler of "*Lizzie Ann!*" The man must be very drunk, he thought, and shoved towards the sound.

It was the near-sighted Tucker. "*Lizzie Ann!*" he cried, and he and his opponent hurled themselves to the ground. When the writhing heap stabilized Tucker, miraculously, was on top. He aimed great blows at his enemy's skull but missed myopically each time, crashing his fist on the stones and howling with pain and mortification. Seth slapped him into some sort of sense and rushed him towards the *Lizzie Ann* boats. Time was running out. He could hear the disciplined hooves of a police guard arriving, and the crack of whips. He cursed and shouldered into the battling mass again.

Eight men were still missing. Where were Gustavus and the cooper? Helping to retrieve his hands from the melee, Seth hoped. The caballeros were dispersing with prudent speed, hallooing off into the night. Seth tripped over a prone body and stumbled several steps before he caught his balance. He ran back, and when he turned the unconscious man over, it was Tom's boatsteerer, a Gay Head Indian. One eye opened blearily and the man belched a spray of rancid rum. Seth reached down, grabbed his collar, and began to haul. "Tom!" he shouted as he neared the boats, and Tom roused himself from his interested contemplation of Abigail, and came forward to help. Then the Gay Head Indian was in the bottom of the boat. "Get her launched and ready," Seth instructed, and ran back to the battle.

Despite the commotion, his sailor's ear could just pick the chuckle of the turning tide. *I have to sail,* he thought. He saw the consumptive clerkish Peabody standing to one side, smirking righteously at the free-for-all. Seth irritably hassled the fellow to the boats, then headed back to the fray. Policemen cantered and shouted orders in Spanish. Sailors hurtled past into the darkness, intent on escaping arrest.

Seth found Hunter defying one of the mounted force. He had grabbed a whip in his half-crippled hand and was flailing it unsteadily, hollering rebellion and advancing step by step on a wary policeman. Two other militia had lost their steeds and were struggling to hold the battle-intoxicated Dutchie. As Seth arrived at the run, one policeman was lifted from his feet and hurled two yards off. As he landed with a thunderous crash, Dutchie bawled, "Come und get me!"

Five policemen and six sailors descended in a rush, and

the whole conglomeration collapsed in a pile of waving legs.

Seth grabbed the flailing whip and tweaked it out of Hunter's hand. Tossing it to the mounted policeman, he slapped Hunter into subjection, and rushed him back along the beach. He was wearing a trail, he thought tiredly. Tom Kanaka and Tucker were pushing the boat into the water. Abigail hovered uncertainly. Seth shoved Hunter in their direction and ran back for Dutchie.

The mass of struggling men heaved and flew apart as he arrived. Dutchie reared up, bloody and roaring, and Seth stepped out of the darkness and slammed a fist into his jaw. It hurt his arm and wrist and vented his pent-up rage most wonderfully. Dutchie swayed, roared, swayed again, and fell with a thunderous crash. To Seth's relief Gustavus and the cooper bobbed out of the night and helped him haul Dutchie at a staggering run to the second boat.

Jim Pease, the Englishman, and the Fayal men were there. They were bloody and bruised and not at all sober, but at least they were there. Seth ordered the second boat launched, tossed Abigail's bags inside, and scooped her up. Her petticoats frothed, and all the men gawped. He roared, "Move!" and they snapped out of their amazement and tumbled into the boats. Seth dropped Abigail on the stern thwart and jumped in behind her. After a moment of confusion the men all found their places, and began to pull for the ship. The noise of the chaos on the beach gradually faded. Seth leaned on the steering sweep and watched the nearing ship, wondering what conditions were like on board.

Then he could hear shouts and thumps on deck. Urgency filled him again, and the instant he touched the hull he scrambled up the side. Four men were groaning in the scuppers, smelling of rum and a great deal of salt water. Somehow, Consider Fish had managed to get the others to their work; Seth could hear the tipsy singing as they heaved on the windlass and hove the ship short.

Oh-h-h—she's the queen, me lads, of Paita girls
That work in the old cantina
Seraphina! Seraphina!

She uster kiss for monkey nuts
But now she fucks for vin-ah
Seraphina! Seraphina!

"Stow it, you little buggers!" bawled Tom Kanaka. "Don't you know there's a lady in the boat?"

Dead silence. All movement froze. Then Seth heard Abigail hiss, "Seth! Captain Morgan!"

He looked over the side. Abigail was standing on a thwart, swaying neatly with the bobbing of the boat, and was holding up her hand for him to help her on board. Instinctively, he bent and grasped her hand and pulled, and in a froth of skirts and petticoats up she came, as neat as paint on a wall.

The awed silence all about decks was palpable. Seth said softly, in a shaking, rage-filled voice, "Don't you dare ever do that again." She stared at him, her face pale, and he met her stare challengingly.

He said, "*Ladies* wait to be hoisted up in the boat." To his disbelief, her lips twitched, and he abruptly remembered that she had been raised at sea, and was undoubtedly as capable of scrambling up the side as he was; by extending her hand for his assistance, she had probably thought she was being ladylike. If she dared to laugh ... He could hear Dutchie coming to with a groan in the bottom of his boat, while one of the third mate's men moved feebly in the scuppers, and was acutely conscious of the conscious men's stares. He shouted furiously, "Get back to work!" Consider West ran up, his eyebrows very high as he sighted Abigail, and Seth snapped, "Oblige me by lowering main and forecourses."

Consider West ran away again, shouting as he went.

Men, moving as stiffly as puppets, edged up the rigging to loose the headsails, and slowly the decks began to take on a more normal appearance.

Seth turned to Abigail. "And *you* will oblige me by going below." She flushed, but turned and went aft without a word. He sent Willie after her with her bag.

Gustavus took the helm. The Swede was reliable even when half-drunk. The off-shore wind had a dirty feel about it but Gustavus was strong.

"A-l-l hands! Up anchor ahoy!"

"Aye, sir — man the windlass!"

Dutchie was conscious enough to set the rhythm at the windlass with a chantey.

O-o-h, leddy, hev you a dotter fine?
Slapundergosheka!
Fit fer er sailor vat's crossed de Line
Slapundergosheka!

Feet stamped, and reluctantly, link by clattering link, the anchor chain writhed up the hawse pipe. Battered ruffians snagged up the links with chain hooks.

"Brace the yards, there!" The canvas snapped hollowly as it dropped. Tom Kanaka and Consider West had their heads tipped backwards as the headsails rose jerkily to the masthead. Then the canvas was sheeted home, with much infuriated exhortation. The *Lizzie Ann* heeled slowly as she took the damp dark breeze, and then nosed out towards the open ocean, a ripple spreading from her blunt prow. A heavy sea awaited them: Seth could hear it and smell it. The old ship would pitch and toss when they met the cross wind and the northerly current outside the bluffs.

The *Lizzie Ann* hesitated, seemed on the verge of balking, and then a ground swell took them smoothly over the bar. Seth sniffed the wind and breathed out slowly, in a long gust of relief.

There was bad weather to come—but they'd sailed. He'd forgotten for the moment that he was married.

The *Lizzie Ann* slatted and banged about in the dark, but for Abigail, it was a blessed reprieve. Seth would not take in canvas until he had a good offing: the coasts of Chile and Peru were studded with the remnants of ships whose captains had been overeasy about this shore and the remorseless northward current. Until then, he would stay up on deck.

She sat a little while on the sofa in the transom cabin, listening to the sounds: orders shouted and echoed, the trampling and stumble of feet, the creaking of blocks, and the groan of rope and timber. Here, below decks, it was equally noisy—every particle of the ship was on the move. Along with the squeak of straining planks she could hear plates and cutlery clashing in the after cabin, forward of the partition. After a while, she stood up and went to the door, braced herself against a lee roll, and opened it to survey the after cabin.

The plan of the afterquarters was the same as on the *Erasmus*, but the circumstances and conditions were very different. As on the *Erasmus*, the after cabin was where the captain and his officers ate, and the table was the same, a massive affair with one end built around the base of the mizzenmast, with benches along each side, and an armchair at the other end where the captain sat. The cabin itself, though, was much smaller, barely eight feet by ten, and the table was a disgrace, stained, dented, and spotted with old grease. The fiddle boards were up, fencing in food-encrusted plates and spoons that slid clamorously about. One mug skidded back and forth miraculously upright, a scum of coffee still within it: the weather pitch caught it just as the lee pitch threatened to tip it over. The walls seemed to dash back and forth in the light of the wildly swinging lamp. To her left, the doors to the two mates' staterooms banged, left

317

off the latch.

She peered cautiously inside the first one. There was a single berth and a little writing desk. The room was untidy but reasonably clean. She recognized Consider West's shore-going clothes: the last time she had seen the outfit was in New Bedford.

In the second stateroom a stranger snored disgustingly in sodden sleep. The third mate, she guessed. He was in the upper of two berths. There was an overwhelming stench of old rum and fresh vomit. How could she share the meal table with a man like this? The lower berth was neat, with a tidily tucked in blanket, and, incredibly, a pillow in an embroidered case. Tom Kanaka's? She thought he might be the second mate.

Abby backed out and looked about the slovenly mess cabin again, feeling both revolted and shocked. The stench of mold was becoming more foul by the second—the bilge was being shaken about in the nether regions of the ship. The transom cabin and Seth's stateroom, which were the captain's private quarters, were spartan but reasonably clean, so no doubt the after cabin had got into this state while Seth was on shore, waiting for Charity Mitchell to arrive. She remembered the times her mother had had to cope with a dirty, surly steward, and thought with some trepidation that she was bound to do the same.

The steward's domain was the pantry, which was forward of the cabin, with a door leading into it. The sink was full of filthy dishes and the racks above it held scarcely cleaner ones. Every single plate and cup was stained and chipped.

No wonder, Abigail thought, Seth Morgan had been in desperate need of a wife, and pressed her lips together. It would prove a challenge, but she was certain she was equal to it. As soon as breakfast was over she would send to the galley for hot water, and make the steward help her wash every dish and every fork and spoon.

She turned and stood in the pantry doorway, holding onto the door frame to keep her balance as she looked about the cabin again. There was another door by her shoulder, but she knew not to open that one. It led to the steerage quarters, where the boatsteerers and the cook and carpenter and cooper and steward lived. She would never go there, just as she would never see the foc'sle. That was a rule that had been taught when she was just a baby—and, anyway, she had plenty of plans for the after quarters.

The bulkheads needed washing, with lye and hot water and then strong vinegar in the rinse. That would take care of the bilge mold, for a while. A coat of whitewash—or even varnish—would be even better. The table certainly needed a scrub—and a revarnishing, too. The panes in the skylight, she was certain, would prove filthy in the light of day. All of a sudden she was alive with plans. Her knees had shaken throughout the brief wedding, and her mouth had been almost too dry to whisper the responses; she had hardly heard a word the pastor had stuttered—but she was at sea, at sea! Her own daring had terrified her, but now she was at sea, and Jezekiel Mitchell could never govern her life again. At the dawn of this day she had been on the steamer *Bolivia,* defiant and nervous about the coming confrontation, and now she was at sea—on her husband's ship. An excitement gripped her—she couldn't resist it. She ran across the cabin and up the companionway steps.

A dramatic scene lay before her. The rugged seas were rolling in from the south with the mighty force of the southeastern Pacific behind them. The waters astern rushed in mad confusion, slashing at the quarter bulwarks while an invisible hard rain flattened their tops. Seth and Gustavus had their shoulders to the wheel, and the canvas in the tops slapped and roared full and then slapped again as the *Lizzie Ann* pitched into troughs and slammed her bow at the crests.

Despite the squalling rain, the moon flashed at intervals from behind scudding clouds, setting men and decks to gleaming. Abigail recognized Consider West, his round face shiny under his tarpaulin hat. He saw her and grimaced silently. Then her hair whipped forward, over her face.

A sea slapped over the taffrail and water foamed towards her. Abby hopped, hanging onto the companion doorway, but nevertheless her stockings got soaked. Spray slopped past her down the stairs.

"All hands ahoy! Bear a hand to take in sail!"

It was Mr. West's shout. The wind was hauling east-southeast, and Seth had spoken in his ear. The *Lizzie Ann* had gained her offing, It was now safe to shorten sail.

"Take in fly' jib!" The heavy sea banged on the bow as the *Lizzie Ann* changed tack. Men stamped and stumbled and grunted at lines, drunken with motion as well as drink. Abby craned her head to watch those aloft, edging precariously as the wind whipped at their clothes. Spray flew the length of the decks and there was a high whistle of wind in the rigging. "Haul out to leeward!"—and Abby could picture clumsy fingers snagging at points and bunts. The great sheets of canvas slatted with a deafening bellow, fighting the men for every inch, but "Haul out to leeward!" the men cried and slid hastily to deck. Another sea slapped. Seth began to turn, looking about as if he sensed her watching him, and Abigail fled quietly back down the stairs.

She went to the captain's stateroom, past the small privy and sink. There was no quarter berth like the one on the *Erasmus* where she had spent a hundred nights—the *Lizzie Ann* was not big enough. A lamp swung wildly in the stateroom over the big swinging bed. Drops of dank condensation ran down the walls and flicked out onto the bedding. Abby shoved her bags into a corner and opened one with stiff fingers.

Her nightgowns had been stolen in Aspinwall, so when she undressed, she kept on her chemise. She folded her gold gown and petticoats and put them away; as of tomorrow she would wear the shortened washdresses that were shipboard clothes, with dungaree pants underneath. Then she lay down in the bed, the bed she would share with Seth. Her husband.

She lay tensely, looking up at the pitching deckhead in the feeble light of the lamp she had left lit. Undoubtedly it was filthy, too. The state of the quarters was far worse than she could have imagined—but the *Lizzie Ann* would be lucky. She had seen her illuminated by a lucky rainbow. If she worked hard, the *Lizzie Ann* would turn into a home—a home like her lost brig *Pandora*. If she worked hard, Seth would realize what an asset he had married: she could keep ship, steer a trick, run aloft, keep the log, work the navigation, rate the chronometer. He didn't offer love, or even tenderness, but she didn't need that. With time, and hard work, the *Lizzie Ann* would be neat and clean and lucky, fit to rival the *Erasmus*. Jireh's ship.

Jireh. There were tears on her cheeks. After a long, long while she curled up under the quilt, sliding down to the bottom of the bed as she relaxed, finishing up as a sleeping bundle at the foot, just where storms had sent her in her childhood berth on the *Pandora*.

Abigail slept longer than she had intended, exhausted by the long, eventful day. There were no small birds to hail the dawn and wake her. The seas were still rugged, and the ship pitched briskly, but the gimbals on the swinging bed had given her a peaceful rest. For a groggy moment Abigail thought she was still on the steamer *Bolivia*, and that Mrs. Perry and Mr. Perry and Mr. Nicholas would soon tease her to play another game of cards. Then she heard the working of the pumps, remembered where she was, and scrambled out of bed to get dressed.

When she burst into the transom cabin, she stopped short. Seth was asleep on the transom sofa. He had taken off his oilskins, but was otherwise fully dressed. She tiptoed over, and looked down at him.

He had not been lying down long; she could see droplets of moisture in his hair. She remembered the times her father had been on deck for many hours on end in bad weather, and how he had come down and stretched on his back on the floor, to ease the ache in his bones from standing so long on a pitching deck. Seth's black eyebrows were tilted wryly at whatever dream flitted through his sleep.

Her husband; the thought made her feel strange. He was so hostile—and yet his eloquent eyebrows fascinated her. By turns, they expressed amusement, derision, irony, and anger. A pirate, Mrs. Fanny had called him, and he certainly looked like one now. Abby shook her head. She had married a tough, competent, professional sea captain—who looked like a dashing buccaneer. Once, he'd had a tapered beard, but he had shaved it off. Had Charity made him do it? Abby wondered what their relationship had been like—had he kissed her tenderly, and whispered endearments into her hair? She shied away from the thought, wondering instead what Charity would have made of the state of this ship. Had vapors, undoubtedly. And she would certainly have been seasick.

Seth had stubble on his cheeks and jaw; she could see the crisp short blackness against his tanned skin, and she wondered what would happen if she touched it, very lightly with the tips of her fingers. She could imagine what it would feel like, for her, but not what it would be like for him...

Her fingers were curled into her palms, and she was abruptly scared of what would happen if he woke up. She turned quickly, and opened the door to the after cabin.

The smell was as bad as it had been the night before. Consider West and Tom Kanaka were sitting at the table eating, while the steward—Tucker?—served them. Tucker had a sulky expression, peering eyes, and a bandaged hand.

They all stopped short when they heard the door open, and stared without expression. She smiled rather nervously.

Tom Kanaka smiled back, his cheeks creasing his facial

tattoo, but then he hurriedly grabbed a fistful of food and made himself scarce. Why had he done that? Polynesians had always been her friends. Abby started to protest, but the steerage door shut.

Puzzled, Abby looked at the other men at the table. Consider West was eating single-mindedly, and the steward looked downright bad-tempered. No one said a word, and the silence was very intimidating. She and the officers were fated to be constant companions for the next few months or even years, and she and the steward had to work together — and it was becoming obvious that her presence was resented.

She understood their reasons, because of things she remembered her mother saying. The captain's wife had no status, because she was not a member of the crew, but was also powerful, because she had the captain's ear. The mates and the steward could make her life miserable, but it was very easy for her to have her revenge. Those fears, if they had them, were groundless, she thought emphatically, and forced herself to smile brightly and say, "Good morning!"

The steward grunted, and went into the pantry with a slam of the door. Consider West smirked, and said, "Why you — and not Charity Mitchell?"

"That's none of your business."

His grin never wavered. "The whole crew knew that Captain Morgan's woman would join him in Paita, and have been as sour as a chip basket about it."

"What? But why?"

"They don't relish the prospect of a woman on the ship. They think it's unlucky."

"Nonsense! You had wonderful luck on the *Erasmus*."

"And they think it unnatural. They say a ship with a woman sports two captains on the quarterdeck."

When their captain was Seth Morgan? Abigail laughed.

"It's no laughing matter," said Consider West. His mug went sliding across the table top, and he caught it with an experienced grab. "There'll be a deputation to the captain, you just wait and see."

By ten that morning the *Lizzie Ann* was running free in a rugged sea and a brisk gale of wind from the sou'sou'east. Seth was on deck, ordering the fore topsail set and the reefs shaken out of the foresail. Abigail, in the after quarters, was arguing with the steward. Tucker considered himself a seaman, and strongly resented that he had been demoted because of his near-sightedness, so was bad-tempered, anyway, and now was doggedly uncooperative when Abby insisted on cleaning up the quarters.

By the light of day, the pantry had proved even more disgusting than expected. Her clearing out uncovered shoes stuffed in cupboards, dirty pipes in the dish racks, and old chews of tobacco stowed under mugs. The floor was dark brown with tobacco spit. Abigail thought Tucker was filthy, and told him so. He thought she was interfering, and was equally candid.

"You would oblige me, Miz Morgan, if you would let things alone in *my* pantry!" he muttered.

"So you can continue to wash the plates with the same rag you use to mop the floor?"

He had no answer to that, simply muttering about complaining to the captain, before retreating to the haven of the steerage. She shouted in his wake, "Do it!" and sent Willie Cotton for another tub of hot water. Then she set to scrubbing the table, while Willie shyly helped her. Together they swept and washed the floors of the cabins and stateroom; then they cleaned and trimmed the lamps, and after that they washed the stairs, while all the time she wondered what Seth would say if Tucker carried out his threat.

At noon the third mate stumbled to the table. He ate very little and said nothing. He looked, Abigail thought, like the last three days of a misspent life. When he glanced her way, which was seldom, he seemed as hostile as Tucker. She didn't even know his name, but gathered from Willie that he had been shipped at Talcahuano when the second mate had run from the ship, and Tom Kanaka had been promoted to the runaway's post.

In the afternoon the sea was still rugged. The *Lizzie Ann* ran nor'nor'west under flying jib, topsails, and courses. Abigail, in the unrecognizably clean pantry, made bread and a plum duff for the cabin supper. The cook, when she took her pans to the galley, was as uncooperative as Tucker, so she didn't dare leave, strongly suspecting that her bread and duff would end up overboard if she didn't keep an eye on him. The watch stared at her as she hovered in the galley door, but when she looked at any man, he looked away, avoiding her eyes.

She couldn't believe it: never, ever, had sailors not been friendly. If anyone had ventured an opinion that she might be unwelcome on her husband's ship, she would have laughed. When she returned to the after quarters with her baked bread and steamed pudding, she went to the transom cabin after setting them in the pantry, to be alone and come to terms with the unpalatable reality that Consider West was right, and her presence was strongly resented.

She was fated to be foiled in her quest for solitude, even: Seth was sitting at the little chart table and writing up his log. He didn't smile when he looked up, and she wondered if Tucker really had complained about her interfering ways. He was silent, though, so she impulsively said, "I can write up the log, if you like."

He said curtly, "I keep my own log."

"But I do know how to do it—how to get the position from the slate by the wheel, and write down the details of the sails and the weather. My mother used to keep the log on the *Pandora*—and she navigated, too."

"And your father allowed it?"

"Of course. It gave him time to do other things."

"And how did the crew feel about that?"

Tucker, Abigail thought with a wince, had indeed complained. She bit her lip, choosing words, but was forestalled when the ship gave a horrible lurch and an urgent shout rang out on deck.

The ship had been caught aback by a contrary squall. Seth shoved past her, running up the stairs. Abigail followed in an impetuous rush, then stopped short in the doorway, gripping the frame. The ship was pitching wildly, sinking into troughs as the canvas slapped and fluttered. The topsail halyards were flying free and the yards were rattling. The *Lizzie Ann* groaned in every plank. Rain thundered on the decks and flattened the sea; every man had to turn his back to the force of the wind.

"Take in tops'ls!" Gangs fumbled up the mainmast and foremast shrouds, the slow ones trampled over in the rush to get aloft. Sheets and sails were stiff and wet, and fingers obviously panicked. Abby's skirt flapped about her legs, and her hair tore free from its pins.

"Haul out tops'l reef tackles!"

Men worked feverishly, hunched over yards, stumbling to lines. "Get moving!" Seth roared. "Prepare to wear ship!"

The foresheet whipped about the deck. The cook, traditionally the man to that rope, was rolling about in the scuppers. The *Lizzie Ann* lurched, and water rushed across the waist. Seth roared, "Bear a hand to those clewlines!" Abby saw him throw his shoulder to help the man at the helm. Her face was streaked with rain and strands of wet hair. "For God's sake get a hand to that sheet!" Seth roared, and Abby, with no thought or premeditation, dashed out into the wet.

The gale took her as she came out from the small shelter of the house. Hair and skirts whipped and she stumbled. Then, miraculously, she had a hand to the rope.

Supper was a silent and stilted affair.

Seth and the officers ate the bread and pudding without comment. Abigail, dressed in dry clothes, merely looked at her plate. The weather was getting worse. The *Lizzie Ann*, now before the wind, was pitching wildly under close-reefed fore and mizzen topsails and double reefed courses. Seth and the others ate quickly and went up to deck as soon as they had finished.

Abigail, left alone at the table, listened with her head down as Tucker sniffed and slammed down plates. Willie cleared away silently. Everything was going wrong. Her husband was angry with her; all the crew hated her. The *Lizzie Ann* had been an unhappy ship before she had arrived; the seamen had been dreading the arrival of the captain's wife, and they had seized on her presence as another grievance.

With a sigh, she stood up and helped Willie, Tucker muttered in a resentful undertone all the time she washed the dishes, while she did her best to ignore him. Then, wearily, she went to bed. Blessedly, she was not interrupted. As on the night before, Seth stopped up on deck, and then napped on the transom sofa.

Abigail slept the concentrated sleep of the exhausted, and got up early, determinedly smiling. She was not, she decided, going to be beaten by a set of surly sailors.

The weather was still thick, with east-sou'east gales and a heavy running sea. At noon, when Seth wrote up his log, the *Lizzie Ann* was lying to under close-reefed main topsail and staysails. When he finished the entry he noted the ship's position in impatient ink-strokes, and then stretched and sighed. He hated this job. He had almost been tempted when Abigail had offered to take over, but he didn't trust her; he didn't trust anyone to keep a precise record that would stand up, if necessary, in a court of law. He would never again have his future and fortunes rest on what had been hastily scrawled in an ill-kept journal. Then he was hauled out of his thought by running footsteps on the stairs.

It was Abigail.

She said urgently, "Seth," and then whirled and ran up again. Startled, he followed her.

And it was a whale, a large bull sperm whale, right by the side of the ship, spouting slowly. The lookouts were silent, no doubt with their heads hunched into their collars.

"I saw it breach," Abigail gasped. "It was so close I didn't know what it was, at first, and then I didn't like to shout."

A shout would certainly have gallied the whale. Seth's eyes were narrow as he considered what to do. When would the whale see the ship? He didn't even dare to order a change of course; they would have to stay as they were and overtake the monster fish.

He said softly to the helmsman, "Ease her down slowly—handsomely, now." Consider West came up on deck, whistling. He had just done dinner. He stopped whistling when he saw Abigail. Then he saw the whale.

"Aye," said Seth. For the first time for weeks, he was grinning. "A whale, all set to board us. We'll help him, shall we? I'll lower my boat," he decided. His boat was on the other side of the ship, and one should be enough. "My wife," he added, "gets the bounty for raising the whale."

Abigail whispered, "What is the bounty?"

"A box of cigars," he said, and her eyes laughed into his. Then he turned his attention to the whale. The bull lay quietly in the troughs of great waves, as if stunned. Had he knocked his head on the ship when he breached? There was no attempt to run away. Tom went as Seth's boatsteerer, and when he planted two harpoons the whale continued to lay still. After Seth changed ends with Tom and lifted the lance, he belatedly realized that the whale was dead. Perhaps he had chosen that moment to die of old age—but his blubber was half a yard thick, so who cared?

But it had been too easy.

They secured the huge carcass to the starboard side of the ship—the weather side, the side towards the vicious wind, so that the gale and marching waves would pin the body against the ship, holding it still so that it would not thud against the side. Its seventy-ton weight was chained by the flukes, with its head to the stern.

As the men lowered the cutting stage over the great carcass, Seth watched the sky. It was two in the afternoon, but as dark as early evening. The wind was whipping tufts of spray from the wave-tops. Then the stage was in place. Seth, Tom and Consider West scrambled out onto it, and stood suspended over the other side of the pinned whale, with long-handled cutting spades in their hands.

No sooner had they started work, than a nasty cross-sea started, and the whale began to slam rhythmically against the side of the ship. Dear God, thought Seth as he hung onto the slender waist-high rail with one hand, if this kept up the *Lizzie Ann* would break apart. He shouted to the men on deck to secure the whale more firmly—and just as they were hauling on a fin chain, the lashing of the stage gave way. It crashed down to the bottom extent of its hinges, throwing all three men into the water.

Seth grabbed a breath in a whoop of salt and blood and went right under. He was wearing heavy jean whaling clothes. His boots were heavy rawhide. He was still holding the razor-sharp cutting spade. The two mates thrashed alongside him, as blinded as he was.

Men and spades floated and sank in a murderous clutter, taken down by sodden clothing, crashing into each other and thrusting free again. They were trapped in a maelstrom of sea and blood and grease between the stage and the ship, in a space mostly taken up by a huge bobbing carcass.

Seth gulped, spat and struggled. His nails sank into the whale's side and clawed free. His heart was thudding with panic; his chest seemed to be on fire. A wave seized him, seized the whale, and slammed them together. Seth went under, threshing through the muck that washed into his mouth. He was drowning. Perhaps, he thought, he was cut with a spade, for his legs and arms felt shockingly heavy and weak. He sank and came up again.

Then he heard the shouting all about him. West's voice was hoarse with terror. A rope fell and hit him. Seth grabbed at it, went under with the slack, gripped higher, and was roughly hauled out.

He arrived on the deck on his belly, vomiting water. When he got blearily to his feet, water poured down on him in an endless stream; it didn't seem possible that his clothes had absorbed so much. Then he realized that rain sheeted down from an increasingly hostile sky. And then he heard the slamming, and understood that the carcass was likely to destroy his ship.

It hurt to shout. His throat felt as if he'd swallowed copper wire, but he managed to rasp, "Secure that goddamned whale, for God's sake get that fluke chain tight!"

Consider West and Tom Kanaka were lying on the deck planks, retching. West struggled to his feet, and began to bellow, too. The *Lizzie Ann* shuddered as a gust caught her. It was too dangerous now to cut in on the weather side; the ship would have to be brought around so the starboard side was on the lee. "Wear ship!" Seth cried. It was a desperate move, in the growing storm, but he was damned if he was going to lose that whale. "Bring her about!"

Consider West's face was white with fear, but Seth saw his mouth move obediently as he repeated the order. Men stumbled to weather braces and spanker sheets, and the helmsman already had his shoulder to the wheel, ready to put it to weather.

Another hand was with him, giving him the assistance he needed. Men stamped, blocks squealed, and the spanker was taken in. Officers hollered—and the bow turned to lee, as the stern came round. The *Lizzie Ann* jerked in every plank, taking a sea over the taffrail.

"Brace round foresails!" cried Mr. West. Men ran in staggering short bursts, timing their rushes to the lurch of the ship. "Set spanker!" Lines and braces squealed and canvas flapped.

Seth's neck cracked as he stared fiercely from foresails to spanker and back. Don't catch aback, he prayed. If the sails didn't draw, he could lose his ship. He stared in suspense at the mizzen staysail. Would it draw in time? The two hands at the wheel heaved at the spokes.

The *Lizzie Ann* creaked, took another sea on the beam—and with a crash the fluke chain parted. The whale swung free, held only by the mainmast tackle. It swung in an arc, sluggishly at first, then faster and more powerfully, in a giant pendulum motion. The entire timber of the mainmast sang.

God! Seth could see the whites of Tom Kanaka's eyes. Every man on deck stood rigid despite the lashing rain, every eye fixed with dreadful fascination on the straining mast.

Seventy tons of fish swung out, seventy tons of inertia, powered by the heaving sea. The mast could go any second now, pulled out like a rotten tooth. Seth opened his mouth to roar at the sky and spiteful fortune, and he heard Consider West's scream: "Cut the falls! Release the whale!"

The cooper skidded as he ran for his ax. Elemental terror held the rest.

Then Seth heard a fierce shriek. "No, don't do it!" shrieked Abigail—and the *Lizzie Ann* heeled and creaked, then came to the wind like a courageous little terrier, and lay easy.

Abigail was the second hand at the wheel.

Her soaked hair was plastered to her shoulders, and her skirts snapped, showing the dungaree pants she wore underneath. Every man was staring not at her, though—but at Seth. The cooper had his mouth open, and the ax in his hand. Seth said nothing for the moment; he was speechless with rage. Abigail, his wife, a woman, had countermanded the first mate's order. She had saved the whale and made Mr. West look gallied, and Seth himself a fool.

Seth had made a grim vow that he would never have his authority undermined again. William Mitchell had done it with his sadistic rages, and Mr. Leonard had done it when he introduced prostitutes to the *Pierrot*, and Seth had made that vow that it would never happen again.

Consider West suited him, for Consider West was just a boy, and would never question or defy him—but now there was a snippet of a girl on board who had done what he dreaded most. Moreover, she seemed determined to behave like a common seaman.

Seth said curtly, "Get the flukes forward and put another chain on the whale. And hawsers," he added, but knew that the ropes would not be needed. Abigail had saved them from losing the whale.

"Commences with cutting in the whale," Seth wrote in his journal the next day. They had cut in all night, with the weather moderating just enough to make the job possible. "Strong winds from the east heading to the north and west," he wrote.

His eyes were gummed, and his whaling clothes stank and were as sodden as when he'd crawled out of the sea. "Finished cutting in the body at two o'clock and shortly after the carcass broke away again, and separated away from the head. The whole affair sank like a stone, carrying with it sundry irons, straps and other articles. God forbid," he wrote, "that we ever have such a job again."

In the blubber room, the watch was cutting up fat as it came in the hatch, and sending it up again to be boiled into oil in the tryworks furnace, grimly enduring the whaleman's hell, his penalty for capturing the greatest fish in the sea. Seth did not go up to deck to supervise. Instead, he called for Abigail to help him undress and wash. Then he took her to bed.

Fourteen

When Seth woke up, Abigail was gone.

Once he realized he was alone in the bed, he lay still, listening to the placid sounds of the ship. Now that the whale was cut in and the most valuable part — the head, with its store of fine spermaceti — was lost, the wind had moderated. Of course, he thought sardonically. Soon they would be in the calmer waters of the Callao ground, fishing off the peaceful Galápagos Islands.

Then he heard his wife moving about in the transom cabin, and he got up, and washed and dressed to join her. He wondered if she would look any different. She did. She looked shockingly ill. Guilt nudged, and he said sharply, "What's wrong?"

Abigail was leaning over his desk, studying the chart he had left out. She didn't answer, or even raise her head. The early sun was slanting through the stern windows behind her, and her expression was hidden from him. He walked up to her and tilted her white face with his palm, and saw her tears just before she flinched away.

The rejection hit him hard, with unexpected pain. He said harshly, "You're crying."

"The sun was in my eyes."

Seth reached out and turned her to face him again, but still she refused to meet his stare. She stood rigid in his light grasp, looking heartbreakingly young and lost and forlorn and ... damaged. He wanted to comfort her, and try to explain, but instead he stepped back and said, "What are you doing?"

"I just wondered where we are going, that's all."

"And you hoped it would be New Zealand?"

She shrugged. Her lashes were obstinately lowered, very black on her white cheeks, and sharp regret moved inside him. That damn chemise, he thought savagely. Why, for God's sake, had she not worn a decent nightgown? Only sluts wore shifts to bed.

Horribly, he had remembered seeing her before in a chemise. By the river in Mangonui. When he had hauled her out of the river, he had asked her if Edmund had raped her. Edmund had been filthy, ridden with a vile disease ... and then his muddled thoughts had brought back the memory of Abigail running out of the Cambridge house to greet Jireh. There had been such / open love in her face, and her slim body had been vibrant with welcome — and he had wondered if Jireh Mitchell had got there first.

He had been too tired and angry to think straight. He had taken her swiftly and roughly, before his confused thoughts unmanned him. He had hurt her, and when she had cried out, he had been stricken with awful regret. He had even tried to draw back, with the confused notion of starting over in a kinder fashion, but nature had intervened, demanding instant release. Then, instead of trying to comfort her as she lay stiff and shocked beneath him, he had collapsed into an exhausted sleep.

Oh God, he felt dreadful about it. He remembered how he had held her as she wept so passionately after learning about her father's murder. And now she was crying again — because of him.

His tensely folded arms began to unfold; he was on the

verge of reaching out to try to make up for his cruel and clumsy blundering, but then she looked up and said, "Do you remember the day my father took you to the pumice valley, near our house in Mangonui?"

He stilled, taken aback. He remembered the excursion vividly. Nathaniel Sherman had led him along the river to the inland hills, babbling of some mysterious fortune, trying to sound impressive but just sounding like a rambling dreamer.

He said, "Why do you ask?"

"I wondered if my father had shown you something — or told you what the valley held."

The valley had held nothing but hot rock and steaming mud and a nauseating smell of sulfur. In the bush there were hot pools of water and mud, and Sherman had taken him to see the chieftain, Te Wharenui. The old fellow had been naked, lying in mud and coated with mud, with bare-breasted girls piling more mud on him. Sherman had said it was a kind of medical treatment.

Seth snapped, "There's no fortune there, if that's what you want to know."

His voice was louder than he intended, and he saw her wince. The guilt stabbed again, and he wondered what she would do if they did sail to New Zealand. Run away from him? It seemed very likely, and he didn't think he could bear it.

He demanded , "Is that the reason you married me? For a passage to some theoretical fortune in Mangonui? Well," he went on with savage irony, "I am sorry to tell you this, Miss Scatterbrained Sherman, but we do not sail south!"

She gasped, "My name is Mrs. Morgan," and ran out of the room.

"The songs of Zion are sung in a thousand churches at home," declared the consumptive Peabody. "But the echo to me comes only from remembrance. I held great hopes that

336

with a lady on board divine service would be held on the Sabbath, but life is indeed a journey of disappointments. Mrs. Morgan has learned a deal of storm and wind and the mighty deeds wrought by the lord of the waves, but she has also learned of the Godlessness of the men who sail in ships, even to her very own husband."

It was a fine Sabbath, with a brisk fair wind, and because it was Sunday and the weather was good, the men had no work to do, apart from keeping the ship in trim. They had washed and hung their clothes out, and now they were gathered about the fore-hatch, having a gam.

"A woman's got no place on board of a ship," said the Englishman, Pease. He hawked and spat. "Nothin' but a soddin' encumbrance. A parasite. Eatin' good grub and rationin' the foremast men to keep the books straight. Our luck's been soddin' bad enough, and what happens now, eh? It can't do nothin' but get worse still, because she's so bloody interferin', on deck when she's no right to be there."

"Aye," said the steward, Tucker. Then he lowered his voice and looked around before saying with the air of a man who had privileged access to the afterquarters, "It has made trouble in the after cabin, I don't mind tellin' you. The mates is all of a mutter about it. It's a poor state of affairs when the captain is shamed by his very own wife. A lady should not be about the decks at such a time. I mean to say, what if she had of went overboard?"

"Aye," said Hunter. "She put the whole bloody ship's company at risk."

"And she had no right to call out agin the mate," said Pease. "Who is the first officer of this ship, I ask yer? Mr. West, or the captain's woman?"

"But she knew what she was a-doing!" Willie Cotton cried.

"Aw. You," said Hunter. "You didn't see the mast a-going. It put the fear of Old Scratch in me, I tell yer."

"It was an awesome sight," Peabody agreed.

337

"Our survival,"he orated,"was a testament to God's mercy, in view of Mrs. Morgan's headstrong nature."

"Aye," said Hunter. "How can we bear a hand in a soddin' storm, if there's a bloody female running about the decks? Only God knows, and He ain't tellin' any of us."

"It's the Sabbath," cried Peabody. He threw up his hands. "I am so heartily tired of cursing and reviling talk — even the captain takes the name of our Lord in vain!"

Dutchie had arrived just in time to hear this. "Vat be wrong wit' de cap'n?"

"A man in his elevated position should disdain to take the name of our lord so lightly, even in the presence of his wife."

Hunter said, "She don't care, depend on it, Peabody, a-cause she had an English eddication, and the English take profanity for granted. Godless race, they are."

Pease bristled. "What yer say?"

"Strange habits, Englishmen 'ave," Hunter smirked. "And you should know, for aincha got the English disease?"

Pease gobbled with rage at this, while the men crowed. Even Dutchie grinned as the meaning of the coarse innuendo seeped in, and Pease aimed a spiteful kick at the massive belly. "Dutch disease, more like," he cried.

Dutchie frowned, said, "Vat der?" and began to rise ponderously to his feet. Hunter, who had appointed himself as the thick-witted giant's caretaker soon after he'd been shipped at Fayal, pushed him down again. "Shut it," he said to the prancing Pease. Dutchie grumbled with frustrated wrath, and Hunter said, "Oh, go and blow off steam in Gustavus's ear. Pease is too dim to mean a thing. Gustavus talks your Dutchie lingo, not this soddin' Lime-oh."

There was a sixth man in this group, a short, sturdy seaman with a weathered face and grizzled hair, who had scarcely opened his mouth since coming on board at Paita.

Now he lowered the book he was reading and said, "Gustavus is a Swede, and Dutchie is Deutsch—a German, not a Dutchman. And it is as ridiculous to assume that a Swede and a German speak the same tongue as it is to expect a Spaniard to understand a Fayal Portuguese."

Silence, bemused silence. The others all stared at him with blank faces that gradually took on insulted expressions, while the speaker calmly stared back. Then Hunter said, "You got a lip, for a man who I don't even know his fuckin' name."

The seaman merely shrugged, and went back to reading his book. It was called *David Copperfield,* and was written by a man called Charles Dickens.

"What is his name?" Pease demanded petulantly. No one answered. Their expressions were aggrieved: it was as if they felt somehow bested by this man who had been shipped in Paita to take place of one of the two runaways.

"Anyways," the Englishman finally said, "I won't have the *Dutch* disease for long. A man on the *Erasmus* told it ter me. If I spunk a virgin, right young to make certain, and give it to her hard, then she takes the disease away with her, filthy whore."

"Oh you," said Hunter, and spat. "You're bloody disgustin', and it ain't even true."

The man who had been reading the book by Dickens was even more disgusted. Silently and deliberately, he stood up and walked to a private corner by the carpenter's bench. Then he sat down again, keeping his back to the men about the hatch.

The roughest and toughest seaman of any merchant vessel, he decided, would blush at the talk on a whaler. He had heard it was a filthy trade, but had not expected this. Not for the first time, he wished he had waited for another berth.

However, he had been on the beach, out of money, and reasonably desperate—so here he was, on the whaleship *Lizzie Ann.* Amazing are the ways of Providence, he mused.

In many ways, life on the *Lizzie Ann* was a lot like life in the Cambridge house, and became even more so as the weeks went by.

Sunday was the Sabbath and a day of rest. Seth read in the transom cabin, and posted the entries in the ship's books, and Abigail made ginger cookies for all hands, according to Victoria's receipt: one pint of molasses, boiled and *skimmed,* one cup of sugar, one cup of butter, half a cup of water, a teaspoon of ginger and another of saleratus, the whole mixed with *sieved* flour. She even managed to sing while she did it. Tucker, the steward, sniffed with contempt, but at least it made the ship more cheerful — and the baking made the ship smell better, too. The men ate the cookies with suspicious looks and not a word of thanks, but she noticed that they were not thrown overboard, either.

Monday was the day for laundry. Even if no rain fell to be collected for the job, Monday was the allotted day for washing. It was hard enough, on a rolling ship, but Abby was used to the task. Seth's grease-soaked whaling clothes were not in the pile of laundry to be done, and she was thankful for that. And Willie Cotton was friendly.

She clambered on top of the roof of the house and stood and looked around while Willie shoved up the wooden tub of clean washing. The ocean was gloriously empty. It was as if the *Lizzie Ann* was sailing across an endless blue saucer, and the humdrum world and its petty affairs were wonderfully remote. They were on the Callao ground: the men in the mastheads shaded their eyes as they stared out and about at the sunlit sea. She had a coiled clothesline in her hands, and she looked about for somewhere to hang it.

Willie said, "I thought all ladies were seasick."

"Well, I'm never seasick, and I guess I am a lady."

His grin was approving. "Mrs. Mitchell of the *Erasmus* is sick a-constant, they say. She never left her cabin all the time we gammed her ship."

'Gammed the *Erasmus*?" Abby echoed. Seth hadn't told her that—but then, he told her very little. If they were on the same ground, she thought rather nervously, sooner or later they would speak Jireh and Martha—and the *Curtsey*. Oh lord, she thought, what would Victoria and Obed say when they heard about her latest adventure?

She turned to hide her face, slinging her line between the larboard quarter davit and the mizzen shrouds. Willie said, "We were only one month out from home when we spoke. The captains had brandy with their dinner, and they got merry and raced their boats."

"Good heavens," she said inadequately. This was a new aspect of Seth, she thought, but then remembered how enthusiastically he had run the rigging of the *Erasmus* to celebrate his win in court. He had looked so dashing, back then. She threw a wet sheet over the line, and threaded a big needle, saying, "Who won?"

"We did, of course. Captain Morgan had them all beat."

Abigail gathered from his smug tone that Willie was in Seth's boat's crew. She said gravely, "Congratulations," and sewed the sheet to the line. When she finished she was close to the hole in the roof that allowed the helmsman to watch the sails, and when she looked down at him, she could see that he was listening, because there were wrinkles of amusement around his eyes.

"The *Erasmus* boat beat in pulling," said Willie, "but our boat beat the whole crowd in sailing. We sailed past the rest and then sailed around the ship's head, which none of the rest could do. But then," he added, aggrieved, "when we came aboard the *Lizzie Ann* no one would allow that we had beat them, and then they said that something was not fair or something was wrong. Both captains stayed on board of us to supper and after supper their boat's crew and our boat's crew had a dance on the waist deck until past nine o'clock at night."

Abby wished she had been there.

She said, "But Mar... Mrs. Mitchell was seasick and confined to her bed?"

"Aye." Poor Martha, thought Abby, and remembered Martha announcing to Jireh, *If you want me, you don't sail without me.* Did she regret that, now?

Willie confided, "I'm in Captain Morgan's boat."

"I guessed that," said Abby gravely.

"And Dutchie," said Willie, handing up a wet petticoat, "is bow oar. He's strong, you see—has to be, to pull the boat up to a harpooned whale. We shipped him in Fayal."

"And what was a Dutchman doing in Fayal?"

"He's not Dutch, he's German, or so Ike says. He says that when Dutchie was asked his nationality he said *Deutsch,* and everyone thought he said *Dutch.* And the others say that the mate of a Bremen whaler cracked his skull and left him for dead on the beach. He's slow," said Willie. "He don't even recollect his name, so that why we call him Dutchie. Then there's Hunter—he's stroke oar, and takes care of the whaleline. And there's Peabody, who's about as useful as a preacher in a whorehouse."

Abigail said, "Willie!" She thought she heard a hastily smothered laugh, and peered down the hole in the roof to look at the helmsman again. His face was tipped up as he studied the sails with an air of concentration. She began to look away again—and stopped. He looked familiar.

Then she forgot it. Willie nudged her and pointed—and there was a sail on the horizon, like a moth at the edge of the sea. Its silhouette was clear and clean, and like the helmsman, tantalizingly familiar.

By noon the ship was very familiar indeed. Abigail's moment of reckoning had come faster even than dreaded. It was Obed's ship, *Curtsey,* and Obed Cambridge was determined to gam.

The *Lizzie Ann* was the windward vessel. The *Curtsey* hauled aback and waited for Seth's ship to run down and speak.

342

Consider West, resplendent in buckskin trousers tied below the knee with leather thongs, was the officer on the quarter-deck, and sang out orders to head *Curtsey*-wards with such dramatic fervor that for once the *Lizzie Ann* functioned with a snap. In fact, Seth thought with barely hidden alarm, the maneuver was downright dangerous. The *Lizzie Ann* swept up to the *Curtsey* in full-bellied splendor and then slowed with a hiss as she sheered past the other ship's stern.

Seth was standing on the roof of the hurricane house. He had never seen the *Curtsey* before. He ran a professional eye over decks and hull and hamper and then looked at Obed, who was standing on the other house.

Obed said, "*Curtsey* of New Bedford."

"*Lizzie Ann.*"

"Flamboyant piece of sailing."

Seth undug his nails from his palms and nodded. Then he thought that Obed sounded rather awkward, and looked somewhat red in the face. He coughed and said, "You received our letter?"

"What letter?"

"The one my agent put on the steamer *Bolivia,* to get to you in Paita."

Seth said grimly, "No, I did not."

"Ah." Obed cleared his throat again, and said, "Better come on board."

Seth said sharply and very clearly, "I'm married." The ships were passing each other rather fast, but nevertheless he had a very good view of his cousin's thunderstruck expression.

"Bring her on board," Obed hollered. "I bought a hoisting chair — it'll be a first-rate chance to try it out!" Then the ships were sliding away from each other, and Obed was out of earshot. Seth, frowning, went below.

When the *Lizzie Ann* hove to, the two ships were about a half-mile apart. The weather was fine, with a balmy little breeze, and the sea was as calm as a clock.

Abigail was wearing blue-sprigged white muslin, and was very pale. She sat in the stern thwart of Seth's boat, against his knee as he stood at the steering oar, and he looked down at the neatly brushed copper curls and the flat blue bow that held them in place. He wore formal broadcloth. She had said nothing, and he wondered if she was nervous. Then, as the hoisting chair bobbed down and swung over the boat, he decided she was *scared*.

They all dodged and ducked as the chair came down. It was made out of a cask, with a board to sit on inside, and it was lowered from the mainmast by the cutting falls. It spun round and round as it came down, and two men had to grab and hang on to it as it twirled in the air over the boat.

By the time they had it steady Abigail looked so horrified that Seth wondered if she was going to mutiny. She stepped into it and sat down, however, and the whaleboat dipped and splashed with the movement. Then the men on the *Curtsey* heaved it up with a jerk of the falls, and the cask, revolving, swerved upwards. Abigail was clutching the sides. Seth scrambled up the side of the ship, in time to steady the chair as it swung giddily to the planks. It landed with a crash, and Abigail, visibly trembling, stood up.

Obed's eyes bulged. "Abigail!"

Abigail took one step, and collapsed in a heap of muslin. Seth bent and scooped her up. He thought she had fainted, like that day on the *Erasmus*, and waited for her to push him away. Instead, she grabbed him around the neck, and he realized she was merely helplessly giddy. She clung to him like a leech, and something warm and amused and unexpectedly protective moved inside him.

Obed cried, "You married *Abigail?*"

"Yes," Seth said stiffly, his nose in Abigail's hair. "Abigail came to Paita and did me the honor of becoming my wife." Then he became aware that Abigail was gulping, that she was fighting not to be sick, and he hastily put her down.

She stood this time, but hung on to his arm, leaning against him for balance, and he put that arm around her.

"But she's supposed to be on the way to New Bedford!"

"Well, I am not," said Abigail indignantly. "Obed, where did you find that terrible machine?"

"You eloped, and married Seth? Oh dear," Obed said gloomily. "What Victoria will say, I have not a notion." He frowned at Seth, and Seth frowned back. Then Obed visibly roused himself. "Come below," he said. "I need a drink, and I'm not sure that you don't, too."

As he led the way to the after companionway, he said with revived smugness, "A capital thing, that chair, don't you think? I bought it from a captain in Valparaiso when I first arrived on the coast. He had it for his wife, but only used it once, because after that she stopped on shore."

"I'm not surprised," said Abigail.

But instead of listening Obed was looking awkward again. He muttered, "Just a moment." They all stopped on the stairs. Abigail was still holding onto Seth, warm in the dimness. "I'd better go ahead, and warn Victoria. H'm! — in her condition, it could prove disastrous."

He disappeared down the companionway, and Seth heard him humming and hawing. Then with a shriek of "Aunty Abby!" a small girl came tearing up the stairs. Emily demanded to be lifted, covered Abigail's face with ecstatic kisses, and knocked off her bow.

When they arrived in the transom cabin, Victoria was sitting on the sofa looking as sedate as ever, but her brow was wrinkled.

She said, "But what happened to that nice Captain McGhie?"

Abigail blushed. "I ran away from him."

Seth scarcely noticed when Obed thrust a glass in his hand. He said coldly, "Would anyone care to inform me who this Captain McGhie might be?"

But the moment the words were out of his mouth he

remembered.

Nathaniel Sherman had talked on and on about his partner in the shore whaling station in Cook Strait. "McGhie is a fine man, a first-rate fellow," Obed said, pouring brandy for himself. "Terrible luck, though. Left New Zealand in command of a clipper ship, *Rainbow,* and had the shocking poor judgment to take on passengers for San Francisco. Well, you can guess what happened. He lost his crew and the ship lies there yet. Probably beached on the mud," he added in ghoulish tones. "It'll take the owners a bit of money to get her fit for sea again."

"But the poor man." Victoria looked reproachfully at Abigail. "How must he be feeling?"

"Pretty bad, I should think," Obed answered her. "Trapped in South America until he finds another command. He must be pretty desperate."

Seth shook his head bemusedly, and then realized that Obed, Obed-like, was stuck on his own conversational track.

"Shocking judgment," Obed repeated, and gulped brandy. "He trades, you know, up and down the coast. In orchids."

"*Orchids?*"

"Aye, Seth. And he's a runner for the agents, makes a commission recruiting for the ships. He'll never get rich, that's as plain as the nose on your face, I've seen in happen before. Folks come along to the South American coasts, see the natural possibilities, think what a little hard work and ingenuity can accomplish — Yankee style, you know — and then everyone of them, each and every manjack, they lose their money and off they go, sore enough for certain. We left Abigail in his care," he went on, wagging his eyebrows at Abby. "Said he'd take her back to New Bedford and hand her over to Jezekiel Mitchell, right neighborly, I thought."

"We met him in Aspinwall," contributed Victoria. "Abigail, how *could* you have run away from him, after all his kindness?"

346

"It was easy," said Abby, and dimpled. "The berth was already booked for Charity Mitchell on the *Bolivia*, and Broddy was drinking. I don't think he noticed for hours that I'd collected my bags and gone. At the time, though, I was dreadfully scared that he'd follow me and make a fuss."

"A *fuss*?"

"Well, it might have been more than that, but it doesn't signify, because he didn't notice. And we had such an exciting departure! The steamer left exactly on time, only backwards by mistake, right into a schooner moored behind us. The captain was drunk—or so everyone said. There was a tremendous crash, and everyone fell over. Then when the passengers had got to their feet, the steamer went forwards, and crashed into the pier, and everyone fell over again."

"But Abigail," Victoria expostulated, "people will talk!"

Obed cleared his throat and said severely, "Victoria."

"There will be trouble from *tattlers*."

"Victoria!" Obed scolded. "It's a romance—a romance! But the little minx, eh?" he said indulgently to Seth. "I knew all along that she was desperate to get to the Pacific, but I never guessed the real reason."

"Desperate?" Seth echoed. Then he remembered the day he had sailed from New Bedford. Abigail had come to say goodbye, and she had almost begged him for something. She had certainly looked desperate then.

For supper they had warm bread and butter, whortleberry preserves, cold boiled ham, plum cake, cheese and coffee, and Seth and Obed drank more brandy. "I feel greatly for poor Captain McGhie," Victoria said severely to Abigail. "Female virtue is like a tender and delicate flower. Let but the breath of gossip mar its petals, and it will wither and perhaps perish. The poor man must feel responsible for your unthinking damage to your reputation."

"Victoria!" barked Obed.

"But Captain McGhie was so good to us, so *supportive*, particularly after the robbery."

347

Seth was only half-listening, relaxed and sipping brandy as he watched his wife. The atmosphere was cozy, he thought. Despite Obed's rambling and Victoria's dismay, it was obvious that they were fond of Abigail and she was fond of them. It was like a family: he felt an unexpected jab of envy. Now, abruptly registering what had been said, he asked Victoria, "What robbery?"

"In the hotel in Aspinwall. Our belongings were ransacked. Abigail lost her ... nighttime attire, and the thief made off with my gray delaine and completely crushed my best bonnet."

"Man wake me," said Emily from Abigail's lap.

They all looked at the child. "But two years old," said Obed indulgently. "Bright as a buttonhook, and I must confess it, I'm half-dead about her. It has virtues a-plenty, this carrying of one's family to sea, I can attest to it Seth. An excellent choice, to carry your wife!"

"Man wake me," said Emily, determined to finish her story. "Carry me out-street, and I run and look for my daddy."

"Cunning as a little pig, eh?" said Obed fondly. Then the silence got through to him. "Man?" he said. "What man?"

"*Carried* you out into the street?" said Abigail. "You didn't say that before."

"And when he put me down, he push me, and I run."

"But who?"

Emily merely smiled; as in Aspinwall, she didn't have an answer. "She was sound asleep," said Victoria, reliving the horror. "Oh, the sheltering ways of Providence—and when I think that all the time we were searching for her, some horrible opportunistic thief was going through our belongings at his leisure—and for what? For women's clothing!"

Seth saw Abigail open her mouth as if she was going to add something to this, but Obed took over the conversation with hearty whaleman talk.

"Mitchell is doing as well as ever from his gamming with others," he said, shaking his head. "Every ship he speaks catches whales while in company with the *Erasmus* — amazing, ain't it? But," he added, "Martha is as seasick as ever."

Abigail said, "Have you seen them?"

"Nope. I haven't spoken anyone who's seen them in the last six weeks — but I have it on authority, she's as seasick as a dog. My own wife," he said smugly, "has the constitution of a true mariner — and Seth, I can vouch for your lady, too. Some folks reckons that it's the smell of trying out that gets Martha a-going: she should've been with him on the *Lizzie Ann,* eh?"

Abigail straightened in her seat, and looked at him coldly, and Obed buried his face in his glass. By the time he escorted them to the rail, though, he had recovered his bonhomie. "A romance, eh?" he said, and chuckled indulgently. "And I don't mind saying, Seth, you have gained yourself a treasure — she's a real hard worker, and cheerful in the bargain; I remember often how she sang about the house. But the little minx, eh? She had us all gammoned she was set on going to New Zealand for her one-dollar brig."

Seth's brows snapped down. "Her — *what?*"

"H'm! Hasn't Abigail told you?" Obed was looking awkward again.

Abigail wasn't listening. Her entire attention was on the hoisting chair that stood waiting on the deck. "I am not going down in that," she said. Her tone was aggressive.

Obed barked, "You won't?"

"I'd rather jump," she said, lifting her chin. She and Obed had a short battle of wills, and to Seth's satisfaction, she won it. At that moment it gave him pleasure to see his smug cousin bested.

Abigail was lowered in a boat and then crossed from that boat to Seth's with an agile step and the assistance of his hand. Then she settled on the thwart in front of him, and he watched her broodingly as the boat pulled back to the *Lizzie Ann*. It was moonlight, and the two ships, lying so gracefully aback, were like luminous gulls. The pale stuff of Abigail's dress was insubstantial, and her hair gleamed. Seth felt a little aching tug inside him, thinking that her nightgowns had been stolen, and that was why she wore those damned shifts to bed.

He stayed in the boat with her as the men hoisted it up, and when they stepped onto the roof of the hurricane house, they were as alone as they were in his stateroom. He stopped her by holding onto her upper arms, and demanded, "Is that why you were desperate to get to New Zealand ... for a brig?"

She hesitated. Then she admitted, "Yes, it was for my brig. My father sold her to me for one dollar, so the English couldn't take her away."

That fitted in with what Nathaniel Sherman had told him. Seth said, "So that's why you came to Paita—so I would take you to New Zealand, to claim your brig?"

She shook her head. Her upturned face was earnest in the starlight. "It had nothing to do with the brig."

Seth studied her for a moment, wondering why this gave him such pleasure. Then he said slowly, "Abigail, do you remember saying goodbye to me when I sailed?" She nodded, and he went on, "You were going to ask me something—you said my name."

"Oh yes, I was going to ask you to take me with you. I wanted to work my passage, and I thought you needed a ... a steward."

"Passage with me to New Zealand? So you could claim the *Pandora*?"

She nodded, and the disappointment hit hard. Then she said, "But that was back then. It's different, now. The brig doesn't signify any more."

Seth paused, feeling puzzled, thinking that there was a

great deal he didn't know about her, and wishing that he had sought out her company in New Bedford, instead of wasting his time with Charity Mitchell. Then, remembering her hesitation in the transom cabin of the *Curtsey*, he said shrewdly, "Did the thief in Aspinwall take something more than your nightwear?"

"He stole the brig's papers—but they won't do him any good. The *Pandora* was wrecked."

"Wrecked! How do you know that?"

"Oh, Broddy told me, when we were eating supper in Panama."

She had known it before she had traveled to Paita. The realization gave him such relief that he felt reluctant to believe her, for fear of disappointment again. He barked, "Is that the truth, Abigail?"

"Of course it's the truth," she snapped. "I'm not in the habit of telling lies."

She turned and flounced to the ladder, but he caught her up and went down first. Then, standing in the shadow of the house, he held up his arms. She scowled angrily down at him, and for a moment he thought she wouldn't jump, but she did, landing warm and agile and light against him, and he gathered her up to his chest. She smelled clean and sweet and felt intensely alive. When he kissed her she wriggled to get away, but he was determined, and when he teased her lips apart she tasted clean and fresh and sweet, too.

Like his ship. The difference she had wrought was amazing. He whispered softly into her hair, "I never imagined that a pretty scatterbrain would turn out to be such a good housewife."

She said nothing, but he sensed her pleasure. She was blushing, he thought; she had blushed when Obed made her a compliment.

"I like your gingerbread too," he said.

"Well, thank you, kind sir."

"For a young minx, you've done very well."

"Not so young," she said pertly.

"Oh?"

"It's my birthday."

"Eighteen," he remembered. "Remind me in the morning, and I'll give you that box of cigars."

"Oh, how generous," she derided. He chuckled and led her down the stairs to their stateroom, and that night, for the first time, she did not sleep in a huddle at the bottom of the bed.

In the morning the *Curtsey* and the *Lizzie Ann* had been joined by other ships, gathered on the cruising ground to meet the twice-yearly migration of whales. And, while they waited for whales, they gammed. Seth spoke all the captains, and many of the captains came on board to meet the new Mrs. Morgan. Abigail baked for her visits, and behaved with the propriety that Victoria had taught her, and bloomed with Seth's approval. The visiting captains seemed equally impressed, but none had heard of the *Erasmus* or Jireh Mitchell.

Then one morning when Abigail came on deck with tins of gingerbread mixture for the galley oven, the sails were all to the weather quarter, and the *Lizzie Ann* had topgallants set. In her preoccupation with the sails, she hardly noticed the cook's more friendly nod as he took the tins. Then, on the afterdeck, as she passed the helm, the helmsman said softly, "Hello, Miz Abby."

She stopped short. Her mind went blank as she stared at him, and then everything fell into place and she laughed and exclaimed, "Ichabod Jones!" The seaman ducked his head, nodding, looking at the sails, smiling to himself. "You sailed with my father ... Heavens, nine years ago!" Seth was in the transom cabin, and she called down the skylight, "Seth— Captain Morgan!"

Seth came up quickly, frowning, and she laughed and said, "This man is an old friend—Ichabod Jones—he sailed with my father on the Auckland-Sydney run when I was nine years old." Mr. Jones ducked his head, looking embarrassed. "He was so good to me—he taught me to knot macramé. And read me stories out of a book called *Pickwick Papers*."

She stopped, run out of memories for the moment, laughing as she looked from one man to another. Seth was still frowning. Surely he wasn't cross because she had found an old friend—a friend from her distant childhood? Then she remembered the flogging. Ichabod Jones was the first man she had ever seen flogged. Nine years ago, but she would never forget it. Mr. Jones still had great dignity—and a dry and pedantic choice of words, no doubt.

She slipped her hand into the corner of Seth's arm and leaned against him a little for reassurance, and felt him relax. It was almost as if he had been jealous, she thought, and had now got over it—but that was ridiculous, of course. She forgot the strange notion, listening to Seth ask Mr. Jones about his seafaring past. Ichabod Jones had joined the ship in Paita, just the day before she did.

She said, "What were you doing in Paita?"

"I was escaping from California," he said; his expression was wry.

So he was another who had tried his luck at the mines. First Broddy and now Ichabod Jones, she thought. "Before that I was wrecked," he said. "I was first mate of brig *Chatham*, which was wrecked at Penrhyn Island."

"Wrecked? How?"

"Taken by a current onto the reef. There were ten on board and ten survived, due to the captain's good judgment. We were taken prisoner by the natives, though. Then we stole one of the brig's boats and escaped to Rarotonga. Amazing are the ways of Providence."

"They are indeed," said Seth. "And how did you get to California?"

"That is what is amazing, sir, for I shipped as mate of a

Rarotongan brig, which sailed all the way to San Francisco, where I left her."

"Rarotongan owned?" said Abigail, puzzled.

"Aye, Miz Abby, beg pardon, sir, Mrs. Morgan. The captain was the owner, a young kanaka who was terribly battle-scarred and at times entirely out of his mind. He raved of revenge, which made us nervous enough, but he knew where he was a-going, and was determined to get there. We got to California and as far as I know, he still sails along the Pacific American coast, seeking the man he intends to kill."

"Kill?" Abigail exclaimed.

"Aye—and I pity the man when that kanaka catches up with him. But what is amazing, Miz Abby, Mrs. Morgan, is that the brig was none other than the craft your father used to own, the one I served on when I shipped with him. She was none other than the brig *Pandora*."

Fifteen

It was May Day. A highly unusual May Day, Jireh brooded. He had never spent the holiday at Capricorn Island before, and he'd never been windbound, either.

Six weeks—trapped in the lagoon for six weeks! He felt a fool for coming inside the reef at this time of year, but Martha's seasickness had got him down to the point where he would have dropped anchor at the doors of hell. It had been bad enough when Jireh had been forced to admit to the king's minister that he was carrying a wife, and that trade in girls was banned on his ship, but then he had been punished still further by the onshore wind that had almost instantly sprung up to trap him in the anchorage. It was little comfort that he had company in his predicament—the *Java*, Captain Lawrence.

Jireh limped into the thatched house the natives had built for Martha, saying bitterly, "You'd never have guessed..." His voice drifted off. Martha was asleep on her cot, soothed by the rustling palms that overhung the roof.

His mouth curved. Martha was sprawled sensuously, the light wrap thrown over her upper body revealing one round, pouting breast. She was like a delicious nymph, he thought: six weeks windbound had restored her to her lovely self.

Her delicate skin was flushed, and he could see tiny droplets of moisture above her upper lip. If he moved quietly, he could part the two legs of her lace-edged muslin drawers, find the inviting damp warmth between, and join her in her lascivious dream...

He moved, winced, and cursed under his breath. Then he carefully sat down on the edge of a chair, listening to the thunder of the surf breaking on the reef. The fifty-foot sprays it threw in the air were spectacular, but he was tired of watching them.

Then Martha moved. He watched her blink, yawn and turn her head.

She said, "Why does the sea sound different?"

Different? Jireh thought it sounded the same as it had done the last confounded forty-two days, with the wind blowing smartly and directly up the single narrow passage in the reef, setting the surf curving like a rooster's tail, and trapping his ship inside.

He stood up stiffly and went out to survey the lagoon. The *Erasmus* swung on her anchor chain like a hound on the leash—swung, when she was normally still?—but the lagoon was calm. The sound of the surf, though, was unusually muted.

There was a sail approaching, a whaler, close enough for her topgallant sails to be seen from the beach. She was tacking for Capricorn Island. Tacking! The wind had veered, Jireh thought with a jolt.

If he moved fast, he had a chance to get his ship out to sea. The seamen were on the other side of the island, doing what they had done all the six weeks—collecting sea-slugs and gutting them and boiling them and smoking them to make the cargo of bêche-de-mer that was going to profit him well in the Manila market ... if he ever got there. Jireh shouted out to a nearby cluster of native men, who ran up eagerly, inspired by his bribes.

A couple dashed off to fetch his men, while others thrust

canoes into the water. Within minutes several dozen had leapt aboard, and were lithely scrambling up the masts.

As Jireh watched from the beach, sails began to loosen and drop and wrinkle. Then his crew arrived in a rush—not all of them, but plenty for the work of weighing anchor. Whaleboats lying upside down on the sand were righted and launched, and Jireh jumped on board the first of them.

The wind was light, the wind was gusty, the wind was variable—but to move with purpose was intoxicating. Up the side of the hull they clambered, and quickly sorted themselves out. Men to the footropes, men to the windlass, the third mate beginning a jubilant chantey:

"Gimme heave ho—gimme high ho—"

"And wallop me ass with a razor!" sang the men. The king's minister was promenading importantly about the quarterdeck, earning his ten dollars by piloting them through the reef. Jireh cried, "Heave short, Mr. Allen!" and the men pumped with a will at the windlass.

And the sails filled with wind! Martha was still on shore, and the third mate was missing, along with a dozen men, but it didn't matter: the *Erasmus* sailed! Jireh shouted, "Take over, Mr. Allen! Set jib and foresail and wait for me outside the reef!" He dropped back into his boat, and some natives helped him pull for shore. Martha was waiting there, looking rather bewildered, and the third mate was with her.

"The wind is aye-variable," the third mate said. His tone was anxious.

"But we'll be fine," Jireh said. He had absolute confidence in Mr. Allen. The first mate and the native pilot would get the ship through the gap in the reef and then lay off and on, waiting for him to board with his wife and the rest of his men.

But—just as he turned to see how the *Erasmus* was negotiating the channel, the wind flicked on his other cheek. He blinked—and in the space of that one blink his lovely ship went onto the reef.

His ship was *on the reef.*

He couldn't believe it. It had happened so *fast*. The *Erasmus* was perched on the coral like a mighty bird; her jib and foresail were set as if she were about to take flight; her yards were braced clean and graceful, but she was pinned immovably to that bitch of a wall of coral. As he watched incredulously the men on board leapt into their boats and canoes – they were all, damn them, abandoning the ship.

Mr. Allen had tears running down his seamed cheeks as he arrived on the beach, and the king's minister was looking furtive. Jireh was convinced that the bastard had done it on purpose because he had been cheated of his trade in girls, and it took four of his men to hold him back from killing the old warrior and starting a war with the natives. Finally he regained sanity. The tide was running at its peak. The wind had died. One hard gust and the *Erasmus* would sink like a stone, as the water rushed through any holes in her bottom. Furiously, Jireh ordered his boat's crew to take him out to his ship.

It was utterly calm, a calm filled with the noise of the running tide. They had to pull, but when they neared the passage the current took them along with it. Then, just as they reached the beginning of the gap, the wind freshened.

It came in a sharp gust. Jireh heard the distant agitation of palm leaves. His hair whipped abruptly, while the wind flicked and flurried. Tensely, he watched his ship. The sails looked like eager wings, filling with the gusting wind, stretched and luminous as they lifted the *Erasmus*. The broad canvas wrinkled, filled with another gust – and the *Erasmus* lurched.

Jireh heard the scrape of hull on coral. He thought his ship was gone. Canvas rattled and stretched, and the *Erasmus* moved – but instead of filling and sinking she *sailed.*

"By Gemini!" he roared.

There was not a living soul on board of her. Before his incredulous eyes the *Erasmus* filled and took her departure with magnificent disdain, commanded only by her wayward spirit.

The masts barely quivered as the coral scraped on her coppered hull, and then the ship lifted as the open sea welcomed her. With royal dignity the *Erasmus* set off, completely unmanned, for the horizon and South America.

"Set the bloody sail!" Jireh shouted. The mast was stepped in a hurry and fidded, and then the lugsail snapped and filled and tugged at his fist. "Catch her!" Jireh cried, and they set off in frantic pursuit of his ship.

The *Erasmus* sailed as if her heart were in the race. In fact, for a time, she appeared, most disconcertingly, to be gaining. Then, when the approaching whaler changed tack to intercept her, the *Erasmus* seemed to pause, as if debating whether to speak the stranger or not.

Stranger? It was the confounded *Lizzie Ann!* Jireh recognized his old ship at once. Bluff bows, too wide for her length, single tops'ls, ship rig on a butter box, indubitably the old *Lizzie Ann*. "Pull!" cried Jireh, suddenly exhilarated. "Or that pirate Morgan will seize the *Erasmus!*"

It seemed that the *Erasmus* identified the visitor too, for he saw the rudder move with a transitory swing of the wind and the offshore current. It was if she were avoiding the old tub with regally proper disdain. The *Lizzie Ann* tacked to intercept, yards sharp to catch the hint of breeze. Jireh glimpsed a figure on the roof of the house, pointing at the decks of his ship. Then the *Lizzie Ann* luffed and hove to, and a boat rattled down the side.

Seth was in that boat, racing him for the runaway ship, by thunder! Jireh yelled, "Pull! There's a bottle o' grog on it!" The wind was variable, then the wind dropped. They sweated at the oars. "Spring to it!" Jireh roared. and leaned on his steering oar like a man demented, while his oarsmen sweated and hauled.

The wind flicked up, the *Erasmus* fled on. Jireh could see Seth's face now, and the white teeth in his creased-up grin.

The *Lizzie Ann* was making sail, pacing them in their race for the ship, and Jireh could hear men cheering their captain on. And then both boats caught up with the *Erasmus*, and the *Lizzie Ann* hove to again, a bare ship's length off.

The boats were so close as they ran alongside the fleeing *Erasmus* that Jireh could have reached out and touched Seth Morgan's shoulder. "My ship!" Jireh cried, and Seth shouted with laughter.

"Your ship?" he demanded. "When you were so uncommon careless as to let her quit your side?" He wasn't even sweating, damn him. "No, no," he said. "She belongs to the first man to board her."

"You just try." Jireh leaned on his oar and looked at his ship, and Seth Morgan was doing the same. The *Erasmus* had set them a most remarkable challenge.

The green water rushed and swirled along her hull. One unwise bump and a boat would be stove. The boat falls dangled just out of reach. Jireh jumped, grabbed and missed. The boat swept outwards and he seized his balance by a hair.

He heard Seth say to his oarsmen, "Pull three, stern two." His boat swerved perilously close to the ship, and danced along the curl of water running past her hull. Seth launched himself into space. A wildly flailing fist hit the rope, gripped and hauled. Seth bounced against the side and scrambled upwards. His boots kicked powerfully; with a heave he was over the gangway.

"My ship!" he declared at the top of his voice. Then he looked over the side. By thunder, Jireh thought, the man was a magnificent figure. Where was the stern and righteous citizen who had defended his name in New Bedford? Seth's black curls whipped about his face with a new gust of wind, and his brilliant blue eyes were slitted with laughter.

"Be damned to you," Jireh retorted. Seth's boat's crew had completed the dangerous job of hooking on to the running ship, and one by one they scrambled on board.

Jireh could then hear them hooting around the decks, and wild clucking as the resident poultry scattered. A hen came squawking overboard, and Jireh grabbed her legs in full flight and tossed her back to Seth.

The *Erasmus* was slowing. Seth's crew had sobered and hauled her aback. Jireh reached out, grabbed a boat fall, and the boat clicked smartly against the hull. "I'll keep this ship," Seth decided as he hauled Jireh aboard. "You can have the old *Lizzie Ann*. How the devil did you get in this pickle?"

"From a different pickle," Jireh sighed. He went forward, and swung out on the jibboom and surveyed the damage where the cutwater was shattered and some copper sheets had started. But an inspection of the forehold confirmed what the pumps were telling already: the hull was undamaged. It was a miracle.

"Old Scratch," said Seth, "looks after his own."

"I'm fortunate," Jireh acknowledged. The rigging and bulwarks of the nearby *Lizzie Ann* were bustling with animated men, and they were preparing to lower another boat. Canoes were putting out from the island. By Gemini, he was lucky! It would make the papers — give Martha something worth writing about, for once. "Did you see her?" he demanded of Seth. "Did you see her sail across the reef? Like a goose in the frenzy o' mating?" He clapped Seth on the shoulder. "Come below, and I'll send up a pail o' grog for your men. They deserve it, by thunder, and so do we."

He led the way down the stairs with a rapid limp. Then he sobered a little: he'd forgotten how frowsy the cabins had become while the ship was trapped in the lagoon. When they were at sea, the steward did the work, but while they were windbound, the steward had lived on shore, and Martha hadn't bothered to take over.

Seth was looking about, too, but his eyebrows lifted when he saw that Jireh was watching him. "Tell me," he said, "where you got that rather spectacular limp."

Jireh passed him, fetching a pail and a mug and the doings for the hot buttered rum from the pantry. "I've had the devil of a trying time. Windbound is the very blazes. Lawrence o' the *Java* was windbound with me, and though he is a fine good fellow, he's fond o' vicious hounds." Measuring rum and sugar into the bucket, then adding butter and steaming water, he added, "Lawrence reckons the dogs retrieve, because he spent his weeks windbound in teaching them. We went a-gunning this morning. I shot a pigeon, and Lawrence ordered the bitch to fetch."

"And she did?"

"She did not. She turned about on the word o' command, and bit me in the bum."

Seth couldn't help it: he roared with laughter. Then he heard Jireh say casually, "Do I call you brother-in-law yet? Is Charity on the *Lizzie Ann*?"

Seth sobered, thinking, Goddammit, why should I be eternally the one to deliver bad tidings? This time, he did not feel up to doing it kindly, so he simply said, "Jireh, I regret to inform you that your mother has expired."

There was only silence. For a moment Seth wondered if Jireh had not heard him. Then Jireh said in a high, shocked voice, "My mother is dead?"

Seth shifted uncomfortably. Mrs. Mitchell had doted on Jireh, he remembered. "It happened in February," he awkwardly said. "I heard the news in March."

"From Charity?" Then he saw Jireh think again. "No, of course not. She would have to stop home to look after my father. My God, Seth," he said, and shook his head.

He sent the bucket up to deck and then poured brandy for Seth and himself. Carrying the glasses, the two captains went into the transom cabin. Jireh sprawled on the sofa and Seth sat more sedately on the chair by the chart desk. It was reminiscent of the time he had sat in the *Lizzie Ann* cabin and seen the substitute steward, Seth ruminated. Even the squalor was the same. This time the *Lizzie Ann* was the tidy, homelike ship—and the *Lizzie Ann* belonged to Seth. What a difference Abigail had made, he thought: she had, indeed, done well.

Brandy and bereavement made Jireh philosophical. "God, Seth," he ruminated, "what strange lives we seafaring men lead, and how the world moves on while we're a-pottering about the ocean. And windbound," he added broodingly. "And married. Carrying a wife, Seth, is not recommended."

"No?" said Seth.

"I have to admit I've enjoyed the pretty girls' favors—but I took them for granted, like toys. And my mother, bless her departed soul, indulged me. But," Jireh sighed, "Martha is different."

Seth raised an eyebrow.

"When I first saw Martha, she was speakin' at a rally, in the street, Seth, in the street! All that glorious hair and delicious form wasted in mindless ranting. But I couldn't get her out of my mind. I was bored when I was away from her."

From the sounds of bumping on the deck, another boat had arrived, but Jireh paid no attention. "Martha's tongue," he continued broodingly, "will be the death of me. Have you heard the saying that love and hate are bedmates, Seth? Well, I tell you in all sincerity that it's absolutely true. Martha flies into rages and we fight and then we fall into bed. It ain't natural," he said virtuously. "It ain't right. When Martha is in a rage the poor *Erasmus* is likely to founder, simply because of the extreme inattention o' her captain. Martha," he repeated, "is passionate, particularly in a rage—and I should not have come to Capricorn Island, though I must confess there are few other islands where I would not be running the same risk. Do you remember Mary?"

The substitute steward? Seth lifted his glass.

"The moment we dropped anchor she came on board to show me the pickaninny I gave her last time I was here."

"My God," said Seth. He paused to control the shake of laughter in his voice. "And ... ah, Martha?"

"Was wild. I still bear the scars on my back to prove it. Oh, Seth, count yourself lucky you don't carry a wife."

And with a patter of feet on the stairs, Abigail ran into the cabin.

Seth stood up as soon as she burst into the room. She was wearing a light brown gingham that was one of his favorites, and her expression was radiant. Seth was instantly transported back to the day she had run out of the Cambridge house to greet Jireh ... and Jireh was here. The jealousy hit hard, like a jolt in the chest. She was glowingly lovely—because Jireh was here? Oh God, Seth thought hungrily, was this the response for Jireh, while he, Seth, her husband, had to be grateful that she didn't flinch when he touched her any more?

She said, laughing, "Was I right? Was the *Erasmus* unmanned? How in heaven's name did it happen?"

Jireh was standing, staring at Abigail. His voice was numb as he said, "If someone would kindly explain?"

"Abigail is my wife," said Seth. He put his arm around her in a possessive gesture, and Abigail leaned against him a little, in the confiding way she had lately adopted. "Abigail came to Paita," Seth went on, his tone challenging, "and did me the honor of marrying me."

"But ... Charity..."

"As you pointed out yourself, your sister stops at home."

Of course, thought Jireh; his father would demand it. He was staring at Abigail as she stood in Seth's embrace. Abby... little Abby, grown up and beautiful. He felt an emotion that was disconcertingly like the grief he had felt when he heard that his mother was dead. He had kissed her, this girl... he had been the first man to kiss those soft lips.

With a flash of spite that was purely Mitchell, he smiled and said, "Congratulations, Seth, your luck is unbounded!

This girl was determined to marry a shipmaster and go back to sea, and you're the lucky captain who won her! But it amazes me that you're here and not in New Zealand, solving the riddle and finding that gold."

Seth was staring at him, his black brows curled down; Abigail had gone red and then white.

Seth said grimly, "What riddle?"

"Didn't Abby tell you about it?" said Jireh. His smile was apologetic.

Abigail said tentatively, "I heard that you are a martyr to seasickness?"

"I am, I am." Martha was sprawled moodily on the divan in the little room on the deck of the *Erasmus* where Abby and Victoria had spent many hours sewing. They were alone, because Jireh and Seth had taken gangs of men to help Captain Lawrence warp the *Java* through the gap in the reef, the wind having died to dead calm.

"Jireh has tried everything," Martha said. "It makes me ill to think what I have eaten and drunk to try to fix the ghastly complaint—oranges, lemons, champagne, brandy, and bromide of soda, seawater, plain water, coconut milk, and shark's liver oil. I've eaten dry bread, wet bread, salt tack and chocolate. No one," she said fiercely, "who has not been seasick can have an inkling of what it is like. The condition is indescribable. Seasickness is sufficient to render a moron out of a philosopher. Your tales of the sea, young Abby, were a gross misrepresentation. For land's sake, Abby, I should sue you!"

"Oh dear," said Abigail. She felt embarrassed that she had never been even the slightest bit squeamish.

"To think,' Martha ran on fiercely, "that I—I, who always swore I would never be subjugated by a man, should be a slave to two of them! Old King Neptune, and my very own domestic Jehovah, who both keep me shackled to the bed."

Abigail was looking about, so it took her a moment to register what Martha was saying. Victoria had taken such pride in this little room, and she despaired to think what Victoria would say if she saw it. The dust and clutter made it almost unrecognizable. The Cady house had always been a mess, but she had thought it was because Mr. Cady liked it that way. Now she realized that Martha was lazy.

"I'm not jesting," Martha exclaimed. "I'm shackled to the marriage bed! My husband takes pride in his goatish virility, and demonstrates it too confounded often, by day as well as by night. Making love can be enjoyable, I admit; indeed, it can be *most* enjoyable, and the weeks I am seasick must be frustrating for him—but sometimes I wonder if he will ever clamber off me, and let me get on with my own life!"

Abigail stared. Then she blushed.

Looking at her, Martha's smile became more gentle. "Now that you have found your captain, are you happy, young Abby?"

Abigail didn't even need to think. She still hankered to help more with the routine of the ship, and the first few days of her marriage had been dreadful. She had blundered in her over-eagerness, and Seth's disapproval and disappointment had hurt. But Seth had turned into a much kinder husband than she had any right to expect, and it was easy to sing as she worked.

"Oh yes," she said.

"You'd marry Seth again, given a second chance?"

"Of course." Abby studied her friend. "And you, Martha? What would you do, given a second chance? What about when you get back to New Bedford? Will you choose to stay on shore?"

"I'll come back to sea, of course."

"Even though you're so dreadfully seasick?"

"Even though I die," Martha exclaimed. "I will not—I repeat, will *not*—be left on shore to live with Jezekiel

Mitchell and his browbeaten sheep of a daughter."

Abigail was startled: she had assumed Martha would live with Mr. Cady. Then she realized that of course Jezekiel Mitchell would extract due subservience from his daughter-in-law.

Martha expostulated, "You have no idea whatsoever what living with the Mitchells would be like!"

"Don't I?" said Abigail, with an incredulous laugh. It didn't seem possible that Martha did not know that she had lived with the Mitchells, because it seemed as if she had endured life in their house for an eternity.

Martha, as always, was a wonderful listener. "For land's sakes," she said at the end. "This man you call a *friend* — Captain McGhie — was determined to take you back to that? No wonder you ran away! But how did you manage it?"

"Seth's agent had booked a berth on the steamer for Charity Mitchell, and Mr. Nicholas — a man I met on the *Ocean Queen* — was travelling on the *Bolivia*, too. Luckily, I had a chance to talk to him privately, so I asked him to help me — and he did. He met me at the hotel and carried my bags, and escorted me onto the ship so gallantly and attentively that the purser didn't ask any difficult questions at all."

Martha's expression became alert and inquisitive, as if she sensed gossip. She paused, then probed, "And the passage to Paita took how long?"

"A week."

"And ... how did you fill in the time?"

"Played poker," said Abby.

Seth and Abigail returned to the *Lizzie Ann* a long time after sunset. Jireh Mitchell had insisted on celebrating the miraculous escape of his *Erasmus* from her coral trap, and the eating, drinking, dancing and singing had gone on and on.

The sea was black silk, shot with phosphorescence, and

water drops fell like diamonds from the blades of the oars. Echoes of fiddling and singing drifted from the decks of the *Erasmus* and the *Java*, but all was quiet on board the *Lizzie Ann*. Water rippled and splashed as the men hauled slowly. Some had pipes in their mouths.

Seth was quiet, and Abigail was silent, too, lost in contemplation, turning over her conversation with Martha. She sat on the stern thwart by Seth's knee, and listened to his quiet breathing and felt his strength as he stood behind her at the steering oar. He had looked magnificent as he boarded the *Erasmus* after racing Jireh's boat...

Making love was enjoyable? *Most* enjoyable, Martha had said. Seth had slept on the settee for a week after that first night, and when he had finally come to their bed he had possessed her with desperation, as if he couldn't resist her any longer. Despite his urgency, he had been considerate, and she had gradually relaxed, because it hadn't hurt. Now she liked the close connection, and was glad that her body gave him such obvious pleasure ... *enjoy* it?

The *Lizzie Ann* bobbed sedately with her mainyard aback. She might be an old box, but she smelled and felt like home. Abigail went down the stairs first, and Seth caught up with her in the transom cabin. She turned when she heard the door shut, smiling rather shyly, and then saw him standing there with his legs braced apart and his arms folded. With a jolt, she realized he was angry.

He snapped, "What's this about a riddle?"

She blinked, taken off balance. "What?"

"The riddle that Jireh seems to know so much about, but I know nothing."

Abby couldn't understand why it made him so cross. For a second she wondered if he was jealous, but of course that was quite ridiculous.

"It's just a silly rhyme," she said.

"And gold?" he demanded. He looked as if he was going to unfold his arms and shake her, so she took a quick backward step, and he went thin-lipped with rage.

"Is that why you married me, Abigail—for passage to some gold mine in New Zealand? Have you been lying to me?"

"I don't lie! I told you that, and I meant it."

"Then what have you been keeping from me?"

"There was a riddle, yes, but it means nothing—it was just another of my father's impractical dreams! He was scared that the English would find the fortune first, so he sent me a silly rhyme so I could recognize whatever the valuable stuff might be when I found it. But I haven't worked the stupid puzzle out—and you told me yourself that there is no fortune in that valley!"

Seth looked most taken aback. "I told you?"

"Yes! In this cabin, right here! And I never believed there was any fortune, anyway, for I knew how my father romanced." She paused to take a deep breath. "Look, Seth, there were three reasons for me to get to New Zealand. One was the fortune—which I didn't believe existed. The second was the money from my father's land—as you know, my father told me he was selling to an Englishman who would return him half the profit when it was sold on at its proper price. But Broddy assured me that there was no proxy! The third reason was to claim the brig—but Broddy had told me that the *Pandora* was wrecked. When I agreed to marry you, Seth, I had no reason to get to New Zealand."

Seth's expression was strange. "You didn't care if you went there or not?"

"That's what I am trying to tell you!"

"Yes," he said. "Yes." He shut his eyes, and when he opened them he was smiling. To Abby's relief, he looked his warm, familiar self. She moved closer to him, her lips parted.

Instead of pulling her into his arms, however, he spoke up with lively interest. "A riddle, eh?" he said.

His expression was uncannily reminiscent of his Aunt

369

Fanny's. "Tell me what it is," he urged, "and let's see if I can work it out."

Early in June Obed's ship *Curtsey* was raised. No sooner had the *Lizzie Ann* laid aback than Obed lowered a boat. He arrived in a rush, saying could Abigail please come on board at once. As Obed took her off in his boat, Seth could hear her berating his smug cousin for his carelessness — "I thought you promised to leave Victoria on shore in good season!" Seth stood at the rail and watched them go, feeling warm amusement as he listened to Abigail's cross voice fading with distance.

When Abigail came back in the evening, Seth was sitting at his chart table, posting his books. "Well?" he said. "What is it?"

"Another girl." She dimpled. "And Obed fainted."

"What!"

"He swooned. He did make an awful crash, and nearly scared me out of my wits. Then, when he came to his senses, he tried to pretend it hadn't happened. He hemmed and hawed and said very gruffly, We'll call her Abigail."

Seth watched her, entertained. She looked very pretty with the animation of her yarn. "And?"

"No of course they won't. Don't you know that Abigail means servant? No, no, they call the baby Frances, after your Aunt Fanny."

"The poor unfortunate infant," said Seth. "And no doubt Obed will want to celebrate. When do we expect him?"

"Soon," said Abigail. "The baby is a screamer, and Emily is jealous. Would you mind very much if we offered to have Emily for the night? It would make things on board there so much easier."

Seth sighed. The last thing he wanted was a fractious child scrambling about his apartments, but Abigail loved the little girl, and Obed was his cousin. "Of course," he said.

Obed arrived as soon as supper was done, bringing his

older daughter with him. Emily sat on his lap with her thumb in her mouth while her father drank brandy as if he needed it. "I was mighty grateful to raise your ship, Seth," he said. Seth lifted an eyebrow, and Obed grumbled, "The physician had said there was no urgency and—well, the weeks slipped by without me noticing, and then—well, a hundred-barrel whale delayed me, I must confess it, and I was making for Valparaiso with all expedition, but things— well, they went off at a rate unexpected."

Seth thought that Obed could count the months as well as any man when huge whales didn't get in the way. Since he had left Jireh Mitchell loading some mysterious cargo at Capricorn Island, the lookouts of the *Lizzie Ann* had raised nothing, not so much as a sunfish. With what patience he could muster, he listened to Obed's report of what seemed to have been an endless procession of whales begging to be cut in and boiled, and all the time the child on Obed's knee stared at him with her thumb in her mouth. The unwavering gaze, from round hazel eyes so like Victoria's, was peculiarly disconcerting.

Then all at once the child moved. She jumped off her father's lap, ran the two short steps to Seth, and scrambled onto his knee without so much as a by-your-leave. She was surprisingly solid and heavy as she made herself comfortable. Seth would never have believed a small child could be so confident. She patted his cheek, said happily, "Aunty Abby," and appeared to go to sleep.

"See," said Obed, paternal and delighted, "she knows you."

"So it seems."

"Powerful fond of Abigail, she is, and cunning with it. You just wait until you have one of your own, Seth. Godfrey, how I feel for all those benighted mariners who leave their wives and children at home; think of what they miss! Not," he added, "that I wasn't a little worried before we raised your ship."

371

"I'm sure you were."

"I wondered if you might be south, on the way to New Zealand."

Seth paused, set his jaw, and said curtly, "Why?"

"The riddle, of course! I know it's a nonsense, but it kinda tugs at the imagination, don't you think? I was the first one to guess the spice clue," he bragged, but added, "Though I must confess it was because I found Sherman's writing on the wild side. In fact, I do wonder about the poor fellow's state of mind. And barometer... What do you reckon, Seth? Do you think it leads to a fortune in gold?"

"I'm certain it's not gold." Seth's tone was crisp and final: he did not want to discuss it.

"There's that letter, of course."

"What letter?"

"A letter from New Zealand, for Abigail. At least, it's something in an envelope, addressed to her in New Bedford. Didn't she tell you about it?" Obed waited, but then the icy quality of Seth's silence got through to him, and he abruptly cleared his throat. "She had other things on her mind, no doubt," he mumbled. "I told her about it the night before she ran away, eloped to marry you. Oh, she's a lovely gal, you've done right well for yourself—but wouldn't it be first-rate if she brought you a fortune as well?"

The door opened and Abigail came in. She started when she saw Seth with the little girl on his knee, and smiled, looking delighted. She was holding a banana, and she sat on the sofa beside him, peeling it to give Emily, who woke up and wriggled.

Obed beamed too. "I was telling Seth about that letter."

Abigail was absorbed in feeding the banana into Emily's birdlike mouth. "What letter?"

"The one from New Zealand in an envelope that was addressed to you in New Bedford."

She shrugged. "It won't be anything important, just another copy of that confounded riddle. Though it might be

372

from Broddy, with the news of my father's death. I am sure he would have written to me."

"But it could have the answer to the riddle."

"That's ridiculous," said Abigail.

Seth opened his mouth to agree with her, but then he had the abrupt thought that the letter might name the proxy—if Captain Sherman had indeed sold his lands to an intermediary.

"Anyway," said Abigail, "it's in New Bedford and out of reach, so what does it matter?"

"No, it can't be in New Bedford." Obed mused aloud, "Let's see—I put it into the hands of Swain, ship *Catawba*, as he told me he was homeward bound, but I hear they concluded to stay out here another season, so they'll either put it on another ship, or leave it at some customs house for forwarding."

"Which customs house?"

"Dunno. It would be at some port on this coast, but I don't know which one. But I was right glad you were still in these waters," he confessed.

"I should think you would be."

"I don't know what I would have done if we hadn't raised your ship."

"Neither do I."

"And I'd be extreme grateful if we could sail in company for a few days, so you could come on board and help."

She lifted mocking brows. "You still can't manage without me?"

"I'm real obliged to you, Abigail," he said, and finished off his brandy with an air of relief.

Abigail bit down a sigh. Then, all at once, she became aware that Seth had stiffened. And when she looked at his icy blue eyes, she realized that he was furious.

The next day Seth retreated to the masthead, to brood over

his quarrel with Abigail. His wife was now on board the *Curtsey*, and no doubt she was singing as she settled Victoria and the baby, and kept the child entertained. He had demanded to know how she dared *think* of making decisions that affected his ship—he, Seth, had not married her so that she, Abigail, should be available every time his smug cousin got himself into a family fix! She had snapped right back that it was not her fault that Obed had deliberately misinterpreted her: she had only meant to be sarcastic, and if Seth had any perception at all, he would have understood that! And, if he *had* understood that Obed was taking advantage of her careless words, it was up to him to set Obed right.

And so the quarrel had continued. When Obed had sent a boat for her that morning, she had flounced off to the *Curtsey* after packing a bag, and Seth had done nothing to stop her going—though he had every right, as her husband. Why not? Because he couldn't, goddammit, Seth brooded now; because Obed was his cousin; because—

He glimpsed a single dandelion puff, three miles to leeward. Raising his spyglass, he studied it carefully, and then turned to look at Obed's ship. The *Curtsey* lay quietly, with no discernible activity on the decks or in the rigging. Had the *Curtsey* lookout seen the spout? Or was everyone asleep?

This whale, Seth thought fiercely, was his. His. Obed had had his share of luck, and this was a single bull. He slid down a backstay and hit the deck as softly as he could. Tom Kanaka, at the head of the foremast, suddenly called out, "Blows!" and Seth was illogically anxious that he would be heard on the distant *Curtsey*.

He ran aft, and snapped to the helmsman, "Hard a-port." Consider West came hurrying up. "Stand by to brace sharp," Seth said. "No signals." Mr. West looked at the *Curtsey*, and grinned with quick understanding. Then he ran forward, calling out for all hands, and the crew came tumbling up from below.

The cooper was in the mainmast hamper. He abruptly shouted, "Blows, two points off port, headed to leeward!"

Damn it, thought Seth, the *Curtsey* was positioned in the whale's path. Surely they would see the spout soon? "Steady," he said to the helmsman. "Sharp on the wind — keep her sharp." The cooper and Tom were silent: the whale had sounded. Most of the crew had joined them in the rigging. Surely Obed or his mate would guess what was up? Seth sprung up onto the roof of the hurricane house — and saw movement on the other ship.

Goddammit, he thought: the *Curtsey* was putting on canvas. Where would the whale rise? He ordered a main topgallant set. The cooper was as still as a statue, and Tom was shading his eyes.

Time limped by, then — Cooper cried, "Blows!" Seth saw the puff the same second. So close! Off the lee bow. He shouted, "Ease down — handsomely now. Four boats, prepare to lower!"

Straightening, he saw the whale breach and spout again. The bull was huge, an old and powerful warrior — a hundred barrels, at least. The rigging of the *Curtsey* was full of gesticulating men. The devil take it! Seth ran for his boat.

The men pulled a few strokes to windward and then set the lugsail. The *Curtsey* had luffed to, and was lowering. Seth's boat was in the lead, then the other three *Lizzie Ann* boats, but the *Curtsey* boats were in the chase, setting sail. The whale lay low in the water, spouting placidly, and then he lifted his flukes a little, swishing from side to side. Close, close, but not close enough to heave a harpoon...

A flurry of presumptuous movement. A *Curtsey* whaleboat was sneaking in between Seth's boat and the bull. "Take their wind!" Seth roared. "Get the jib tack clear and pull!"

The whale lay still. "Pull three, stern two!" The boat danced sideways, forcing the *Curtsey* boat to dodge, and then they were in place! Seth shouted to his boatsteerer, the harpooner stood, aimed, planted his iron, and they were fast.

The fight was short and hard. Dutchie at bow oar pulled the boat up to the bull, and Seth finished it off quickly. Then the four *Lizzie Ann* boats linked together to tow the huge carcass to the ship. It was hard work, but cheerfully done; they pulled their oars with wide grins on their faces, jeering at the *Curtsey* men. Then they sang as they got the cutting falls attached to the windlass and set the stage on the starboard side, ready for cutting in their whale.

But then, as he ran out onto the stage with his cutting spade, Seth saw two boats heading their way from the *Curtsey*. Obed was in the first one, and boarded with a jovial grin. He was full of congratulations on the first-rate capture — and he had twelve men with him, to help with the cutting in.

And it was then that Seth remembered that because the two ships were in company — because Abigail was on board the *Curtsey*, damn it! — any whales taken had to be shared. He now knew how the captains who'd been forced to share their luck with Jireh Mitchell had felt.

"Never mind, it will halve the work," said Obed, rubbing his hands together. "My men would have helped with the towing, too," he added, aggrieved, "if your fellows hadn't been so insulting."

As it happened, it was fortunate that the cutting in and boiling out was speeded up, as the weather turned for the worse. At the end of the next day, when the tryworks fires were out but still warm, and all the oil was still on board the *Lizzie Ann*, a squall spun onto them from over the horizon. The night was wild and storm-wracked, and in the morning the skies were racing with clouds.

And the *Curtsey*, with Abigail on board, was nowhere in sight.

Sixteen

It was the Fourth of July, a Sunday, and the *Curtsey* lay at anchor in the port of Valparaiso.

Abigail was close to weeping with frustration. She said to Obed, "You told me that the *Lizzie Ann* would be here — and she isn't! How can you possibly be sure that Seth is coming to Valparaiso? That he'll ever find me, if you leave me here?"

"Abigail," he exclaimed, as angry as she. "Why do you never listen? He told me he would recruit for provisions on the coast, and I'm heading south to whale on the Line. If I keep you on board we mightn't meet up for months, or even years."

"But he could be in trouble — the ship could be wrecked!" If she were a man, and the master of the ship, Abigail thought furiously, she would have mounted a much better search. She would have never left the ground before she found Seth — "You gave up too easily!" she shouted.

"I did not!" he roared. "No man could have searched more thoroughly — Seth has my share of the oil on board!"

Abigail stared at him with something like hatred. "That whale was Seth's."

"Mating's a good custom," he blustered. "It spreads good fortune around the fleet."

377

"But it wasn't fair. The ships were only together because I was doing you a favor."

"Oh, for good Godfrey's sake, stop plaguing me, Abigail!" And Obed stomped forward, where Abby couldn't follow him.

At dinnertime, though, he couldn't avoid being at the same table. She looked at him challengingly, and said, "I want the papers to my brig."

"The *Pandora*? But why?"

"Because she's mine—and Seth's."

"But she's wrecked!"

Abigail paused. Broddy had been definite that the brig was wrecked, but she was inclined to believe Ichabod Jones. Mr. Jones had served on the *Pandora*, and knew her well, and if he said the brig was afloat, she was sure he was right.

However, instead of protesting, she said craftily, "Well, if she's lost, there's no reason I should not have my copy of the papers." Obed growled, but he got up and went into the transom cabin, and when he came out he had the notarized papers in his hand.

In the afternoon they landed in one of the *Curtsey*'s boats, and walked up a cobbled terrace to the boardinghouse where Obed's agent had found Abigail a room. Obed was carrying Abby's bag, she had Emily by the hand, and Victoria was carrying the baby.

There was dancing and music in the streets. Victoria said, "I don't find that very pleasant viewing, on the seventh day of the week."

"It's their fashion," said Obed.

"I know it is, poor deluded souls. Kept in darkness by their priests."

Abby wondered how many of the folk who thronged the alleys could understand English, for she and the Cambridge's got a lot of attention from the exotic Spanish throng. However, there were no frowns, just smiles, many of them melting, and cast in her direction by men who were dressed showily, in short coats that skimmed their narrow hips, open-necked frilled shirts, and red silk sashes. Their narrow black trousers were trimmed with gilt, and their spurs struck sparks from the cobbles as they strutted.

The melting smiles were easy to ignore, because there was so much to see. Everything was colorful—soldiers in bright uniforms, like an army from a children's tale, ladies in splendid flounced dresses. Men in multi-colored rags massaged the brilliant plumage of fighting cocks, hunkered down in groups at corners. Many of the houses had elaborate balconies with brightly striped awnings above them, and multi-colored blankets were thrown over the rails, while vines of red and purple bougainvillea trailed up the whitewashed walls.

The street wound upwards, with many shallow steps. Abby walked slowly, partly because she was gazing raptly around, and also because Emily's legs were rather too short for the job. Then Obed turned into an entranceway; they had arrived, it seemed, at the boardinghouse where Abigail would wait for Seth to get the word to come and collect her.

The hotel was called the House of the Ewer. It was plain from the outside, with small barred windows in the thick walls, but inside it was as colorful as the rest of the city, with a big central courtyard that rioted with plants. The guest rooms on the upper floor were reached by a stairway that spiraled up the inside of this courtyard, leading to an interior balcony. It was not at all private, as anyone could see who was going from one room to another, but it was definitely beautiful, in an exotic kind of way.

Abigail's room had an outer balcony as well, so she could lean over the balustrade and watch the ships come in. The harbor was a bustle, with several men-of-war moored in the merchant shipping, but the *Curtsey* was the only whaler. What would she do if Seth did not come? She missed him desperately; she missed him with a passion that scared her. Staring unseeingly at the harbor, she thought that she would never have believed that she would miss her husband so much. It took several long moments before she came back to the present, and realized that Obed and Victoria had left the room and gone back down the stairs.

Emily was still there, sitting on the bed and clutching a handful of mosquito netting. The expression on her round face was sulky; she was still jealous of her noisy little sister. Abigail contemplated her for a moment, then sighed and lifted her off the bed, took her hand, and opened the door of the room.

The courtyard seemed even more exotic when looking down from the inner balcony. There was a fountain rippling in a little tiled pool, and orchids hung like waxen birds among the more brilliant flowers. Abigail could hear dishes clattering in a dining room somewhere on the lower floor; male laughter from a smoking saloon, and the click of billiard balls from beyond yet another door. Obed and Victoria were in the open part of the courtyard, talking to a man and a woman, and a white-coated servant was offering them drinks from a tray.

Abigail's eyes focused—and panic hit. The man and woman were Mr. and Mrs. Perry. The House of the Ewer, apparently, was their hotel. Oh lord, she thought, what was the garrulous Mrs. Perry telling Victoria? Then Emily cowered behind her, whimpering.

"I frighted," she whispered.

"But why?" said Abby, puzzled. "You know Mr. and Mrs. Perry. They were on the steamer *Ocean Queen*."

"Man." Emily buried her face in Abby's skirts. "Man frighted me, carry me into the nasty street, and I tried to find my daddy."

"What!" Abigail remembered the terrifying search at Aspinwall. Had *Mr. Perry* been the man who carried Emily into the night? It was impossible—what possibly could be his motive?

She stared tensely down at the little group.

Obed had taken a glass from the tray the servant held out. He laughed at some joke Mrs. Perry had told, and the servant went away. Then Mrs. Perry looked up, sighted Abigail, and let out an exhilarated shriek.

"The little!" she cried. "The romantic!" She kissed her fingers and beckoned imperiously. "Come, come!"

Emily, evidently remembering her at last, detached herself from Abigail and scampered down the stairs, her fright quite forgotten. Abigail warily followed.

"They tell me you are married!" cried the Frenchwoman. Her grin was full of the large white teeth that Abby remembered so well. "All the way to Paita on the steamer *Bolivia* I suspicioned that you harbored a secret, yes, for so little of your attention was on what you were doing." Mrs. Perry clasped soulful hands while Abby held her breath, waiting for terrible revelations, but instead the woman merely cried, "I was right; you were in love and embarked on an elopement. How old?" she demanded.

Abigail had not a notion of Seth's age. "Twenty-five?" she hazarded.

"No, not your husband's age—you, yourself, you!"

"Oh. Eighteen."

"Aha, I knew it. At eighteen a pretty girl marries a captain, a leader of men, for that is the most perceptive of all French proverbs. At twenty-one," she added, "she marries an equal. At thirty—pouf!—she marries what she can get."

Abigail could think of nothing to say. She wondered how old Mrs. Perry had been when she married, and stole a look at the eternally gloomy Mr. Perry. Had he really taken Emily out of the hotel in Aspinwall? It didn't make sense. Emily had completely forgotten her fright; she had her arms wrapped around her father's leg as she gazed at Mr. Perry with no trepidation whatsoever. It was unreal—so unreal that Abby watched Mr. Nicholas walk out of the billiard room with no sense of surprise.

Mr. Nicholas, like the Perrys, had not altered one iota, as

urbane and willowy as remembered. "Good heavens," he said, and shook Obed's hand as Mr. Perry introduced them, and bowed elegantly to Victoria and Abigail.

Abigail said, "Is the sloop *Dido* in port?"

"I'm now attached to the man-of-war *Nympha*."

"But I thought—"

"My term on *Dido* was short-lived, I fear... The small matter of a gambling debt." He smiled, seeming perfectly serene.

"And on *Nympha*?"

"We are a British presence in the Pacific, constantly prepared to go to the assistance of our nationals at the notice of merely a moment! Hourly we expect to be summoned to deal with colonial uprisings, but in the meantime we are the upholders of the law, officers of support and sustenance for Englishmen all over the world! We also search out pirates, and look out for vessels that pirates have seized," he added. "And to this end we have annotated lists of missing ships, schooners, barks, and brigs, with affidavits of their ownership, and in this way we repair the fortunes of those who have been robbed."

Abby stared at him, riveted. Affidavits, she assumed, meant ships' papers, like those she had for the brig. She said, "I meant, what do you, yourself, do, Mr. Nicholas?"

He smiled forgivingly. "It's Lieutenant Nicholas, actually, and my days are occupied most pleasantly, for I am the aide to Captain Mara, the commander of *Nympha*. I am his amanuensis. I keep all his files in order."

Files, thought Abigail. It was fortunate indeed that she had asked Obed to make notarized copies of the brig's papers. Otherwise, the theft of the documents that night in Aspinwall would have been a disaster. Her gaze returned to Mr. Perry. He looked the same as ever, tall and whippy and miserable. Had he taken Emily out, to clear the scene for the burglary? It was unbelievable. Why would he do it?

For a tantalizing instant something nudged at the back

of her mind. Then Obed cleared his throat, ready to say goodbye, and the notion vanished before she could pin it down.

Next morning Abby stood on her outside balcony in the House of the Ewer and watched the *Curtsey* beat her way out of the harbor. The ship looked insubstantial, like a dream of luminous canvas slowly breasting the wind. She watched until her eyes stung, belatedly regretting her quarrels with Obed. Then, shaking herself into reality, she put on a bonnet and went to the customs house.

She had to wait in line, as the lobby was full of captains. Only the heat and the flies made it different from the customs house in New Bedford — that, and the fact that the clerk had very little English. He was a fat man, with stubbled cheeks and a long black mustache, and if any captain couldn't make him understand, he merely waved the frustrated mariner away.

With Abigail, however, it was different: she was a pretty girl. He twirled his mustache, smiled meltingly, and took her into an inner office to meet his superior, who spoke excellent English. That man, too, was helpful and attentive, declaring himself quite desolated that he had no news of the whaleship *Lizzie Ann* of New Bedford. He assured Abigail most earnestly, however, that if Captain Seth Morgan was reported at any port on the coast, he would certainly be informed that his wife was waiting in Valparaiso.

Vastly relieved that Obed's gruff assurances had turned out to be right, Abby asked about letters for Miss Sherman. She didn't bother to explain that she and Miss Sherman were one and the same; that, she sensed, held too many pitfalls. The two men looked baffled, but conversed in rapid Spanish. Then the superior translated. There had been a letter, yes, put here by a whaling captain ... when? They both looked at the ceiling and the flies and cogitated on the date, while Abby waited in suspense.

Then they both shook their heads. They couldn't remember, but it didn't matter, because it was gone.

Abby sighed, but smiled. It was no less than she had expected. Then, to her surprise, the superior was looking severe.

"It belonged to New Zealand," he said. "So we sent it back."

"To New Zealand?"

"*Si.* That also is what we told the captain who made the same inquiry; we told him, too, that we had returned it."

So Obed had asked after it, she mused, but hadn't bothered to tell her. It was ironic, really: the letter had tacked back and forth about the Pacific, just to be returned to sender. Then she forgot it, because otherwise it had been a most rewarding expedition. The officials had assured her most earnestly that there were no reports of any wrecks, so the *Lizzie Ann* must be safe. She smiled as she stood, and the two men stood too, with flattering gallantry.

Then, on an afterthought, she asked, "Is there any report of the brig *Pandora?*"

"Of New Bedford?"

"No. Of New Zealand—or maybe Rarotonga."

"Rarotonga! The one with—h'm! —the mad native in command?"

Abigail's mind was abruptly full of Broddy's story, and the way the thunder had rattled the blinds in the Aspinwall saloon; she also thought of the tale Mr. Jones had told. Her mouth was too dry to speak, so she merely nodded.

"Ah yes, *Pandora.* Poor fellow, yes, he trades up and down the coast."

She said huskily, "And the captain's name?"

"Sherman," said the superior. "A coincidence, no? He calls himself Captain Thomas Sherman, but I believe his native name is Tamati."

Abigail had her head down as she trudged back to the House of the Ewer. Tamati had been part of her childhood, since even before the day his mother had given him to her mother. He had ignored her loftily most of the time, being an unimportant girl ... but he had taught her to ride, and had scolded her when she neglected her horse. He had been silent but stalwart company when he had been told to go along with her on fishing excursions, and he had been totally Sherman, totally loyal. Abigail had changed greatly since then, and it seemed evident that Tamati, tragically, had changed a great deal, too. Now he was a murderer and a pirate, with arrogance enough to keep the Sherman name.

But, she thought angrily and emphatically, she knew how to make sure that he was arrested by the proper authorities, and how to get back possession of her brig. After she had returned to her room, she collected the copies of the *Pandora* papers she had collected from Obed, and spread them out on her bed. The notary's seals and signature looked most impressive. Thank heavens, she thought, that she'd had the inspiration of getting these copies made. Obed had been insulted, and at the time she thought she had blundered, but if it weren't for these copies, the theft of the brig's papers would have been a disaster. All hope of reclaiming the *Pandora* would be lost...

Her thoughts stopped short. Had the robbery been as opportunistic as they had all believed — or had the thief known exactly what he was looking for? Was it common knowledge on this coast that a madman who commanded a brig had no papers for the vessel? Mr. Perry was an agent for the ships, so he would certainly know ... and Emily had been terrified when she saw him again, for he was the man, she said, who had carried her out into the dark. So he could return to the room and search for the papers? It was possible — and would be proved beyond doubt, if she could find the stolen papers in his possession.

The courtyard, at that pre-dinner hour, was full of

gamming captains. Several nodded benignly as Abigail came down the stairway, and pushed back their hats as they turned to watch her. She smiled vaguely at them all, and kept on walking. Then, as she reached the billiard room door, she hesitated.

Lieutenant Nicholas was inside, playing pocket billiards with two other officers and Mr. Perry. There were plants in pots in the billiard room, and motionless lizards on the walls. The door to Mr. Perry's office was at the far end, beyond the billiard table. It was open. Abby could see a big desk, and wooden boxes with names painted on their sides, and unsteady heaps of dusty papers. Someone bumped against her, a sea captain who looked preoccupied. Intent on getting his ship provisioned and back to sea, he called out Mr. Perry's name, and all four billiards players looked up. Seeing Abigail, Mr. Nicholas looked surprised, but Mr. Perry merely nodded and then invited the captain into his office.

When the office door shut, Abby smiled diffidently from the billiard room doorway. "Mrs. Morgan," said Lieutenant Nicholas, and with his usual flair introduced her to his two companions, each of whom clicked his heels as he inclined his head over Abigail's hand. Then, as she turned away, feeling awkward, she heard him say coaxingly, "Perhaps, Mrs. Morgan, you would not be averse to learning this game?"

He gestured at the billiard table, and when Abigail hesitated, he said, "Come now, you might even be good at it—it demands quite a different skill to playing a hand of poker!"—which Abigail thought rather unkind. "It's perfectly proper, I do assure you! In the highest of London social circles, it is common for ladies to play billiards. Even duchesses play it!"

Abigail couldn't imagine Victoria ever permitting herself to play billiards. "I'm not sure," she said.

"But billiards is played by all the smart set!" cried one of the young officers.

Abigail couldn't remember either of their names, and had trouble telling them apart, too, as they both had languishing eyes, and a very gallant bearing. "It is the ideal recreation," this young gentleman declared. "It can be played day or night, by lamp or by sun, winter and summer, rain or shine, so why not by both sexes?"

"Billiards is a moral and hygienic occupation," urged the other. "No one can smoke and play billiards, no one can chew tobacco and play billiards. It eliminates all kinds of decadent habits! So why not let us teach you?"

"Well," said Abby. "As a matter of fact..."

How many times had she stolen out of bed to sit on the stairs and listen to her father and Broddy as they knocked the balls around? They had discovered her, eventually, but instead of scolding her and sending her back to her room, they had taught her how to play.

"But," she said firmly, "I will not contemplate playing for money."

"Of course not," agreed Lieutenant Nicholas—which was very fortunate, as Abigail mused with chagrin twenty minutes later, for her game was disconcertingly rusty. She muffed more shots than she would have thought possible. However Mr. Nicholas and his friends declared it a most promising performance, and made an appointment for another game next day.

Then, to her further chagrin, they all went off together.

She had had no opportunity for a private chat with Lieutenant Nicholas, or even another look through the door of Mr. Perry's office. She was certain that the papers for the brig—if indeed Mr. Perry had stolen them—must be somewhere in that room. It was logical that he would keep them with similar documents, that being the best hiding place.

So, at three in the morning, when the hotel was quiet at long last, she crept out of her room and down the stairs to the patio.

The air was cool with the sprinkling of the fountain. The only illumination came from the dim lamp in the billiard room. Abigail stole through the courtyard with a wildly beating heart. The billiard room was quite empty. She tiptoed inside and carefully shut the door.

The door to the office was open. The light from the billiard room fell inside in a golden rectangle. Lizards flickered on the walls, and rustled in papers. The billiard table was still set up, as if some players had left it in the middle of a game. A cue lay slantwise across one corner.

Abigail went into the office, and studied the names on the boxes. As well as the names of ships, there were some labeled with the names of captains. None were familiar. She opened a box at random. The paper she unfolded read, "1500 of pork at 6 cts. 90.00; 4000 oranges 24.00; 2 sheep 6.00; 12 bunches bananas..." All the others in the box were the same kind of provisioning account. Abigail grimaced, put them back, and opened another box.

The one held bills. There was nothing that looked like ownership papers. Then a footstep sounded in the courtyard. Cramming the papers in the box, she shut it quickly and whirled into the billiard room. There was a click as a hand landed on the knob of the outer door. Abigail grabbed up the billiard cue, and bent hastily over the table.

The door opened. Abby saw Mrs. Perry. The Frenchwoman's mouth opened soundlessly with surprise.

Abigail put down the cue. She was shaking too much to pretend to hit a ball. She said in a rush, "I—I'm sorry. I didn't want to disturb anyone, but I couldn't sleep."

Silence, as Mrs. Perry stared at her. Then, with disbelief, Abigail watched the large teeth appear in a very knowing smile.

"Aha," said Mrs. Perry, and made one of her all-inclusive gestures at the room and the table and the office door. "Oho," she said. "I know what you do."

Abigail swallowed. "You do?"

"Yes. You pine, yes, you pine." Mrs. Perry looked roguish, coming further into the room. "So young and just conversant, yes, with the activities of love. You find the solitary couch no longer to your liking."

Abigail said blankly, "What?"

"To sleep alone is impossible when the pleasures of ardent virility and languorous response are so new."

Abby slowly went red as the words sank in. Mrs. Perry surveyed the blush with vast satisfaction, and said, "But take heart! Your husband is pining, too. How could he not, when the memory is so warm of his pliant young wife?"

"Mrs. Perry..."

"But I know it!" Mrs. Perry cried. She kissed her fingertips and threw them into the air. "There is a French saying of course, for what every man desires of his bride."

"There is?" said Abby, curious despite herself.

"Of course! Every man wants a lady in the parlor, yes, a gourmet in the kitchen, so. But, most of all, *ma petite*, he craves a harlot in his bed. Surely you have discovered that, yourself?"

Abigail mutely shook her head.

"But it is of the most essential!" Mrs. Perry's eyes were sparkling with animation; she was enjoying this improper conversation most enormously. "And now I tell you the secret of seduction," she said, barely lowering her voice. "First you ensnare with your melting smiles, then you caress with your seeking hands, and then you entrap with your lower extremities, you twine your limbs about him."

Most disconcertingly, Abigail found herself trying to imagine Mr. and Mrs. Perry in bed. It was impossible. She had to bite down a hysterical giggle.

"And that is the ritual of seduction—the rite you must remember," Mrs. Perry instructed. She briskly put out the lamp and ushered Abigail into the courtyard. Then she locked the door to the billiard room. "Remember," she repeated imperiously, and stood and watched Abigail go up the stairs.

Abby climbed slowly. At the top she turned, and said, "Ah—good night. I'm sorry I disturbed you."

"It is nothing," said the indulgent lady. "I go in there to put out the lamp and lock up every night. But remember the rite," she said with mock severity. "And furthermore, to keep the knees well bent. That is of the most essential."

Seventeen

Within a week, Abigail's game of billiards was vastly improved.

But, apart from that, she had gained very little. The siesta times during the hot, early afternoons, she had found, were the best opportunities for going through Mr. Perry's papers, but sneaking into his office in broad daylight was suspenseful in the extreme, and so far she had had no success. Otherwise, when she was not playing billiards, she worked at making a copy of the notarized papers for the brig, and plotting ways of getting Lieutenant Nicholas to help her to claim it.

The copying took hours, but she did not begrudge a moment. She was determined never to be without papers for the *Pandora* again, but, if Mr. Nicholas was to help her, he would need a set for his files. At the end of the seventh morning, she had finished. She spread the sheets of careful copperplate writing on her bed and admired her work. Apart from the lack of seals, the papers looked most impressive, she thought. She needed a notary to make them legal, but though she did not know of any notaries here, she did know the name of the American consul, Mr. Melvin. At the end of siesta, she put on her bonnet and walked down the street to find his residence.

Mr. Melvin was a short, tubby man, He greeted her with caution, inquiring politely about her health and her lodgings. Keeping an eye on captains' wives who were waiting for their husbands seemed to be a common task, for him. When she handed him the papers and asked him to sign and seal them, however, his manner became much less polite.

Indeed, he was affronted. Women, he informed her, did not involve themselves with legal matters or shipping affairs.

"The brig is mine," she insisted.

"But you are a married woman, Mrs. Morgan! What your husband will say is what concerns me, ma'am! I doubt he'll be pleased. No, he can bring them in when he arrives in Valparaiso."

She said very firmly, "Mr. Melvin, Captain Morgan will be much too busy, and this is of the greatest urgency."

"But what are you going to do with these papers?" he demanded. Abigail did not deign to answer, and finally he gave in, and signed and sealed the documents, muttering all the while that he did not approve or like it a bit.

Abigail thanked him, and walked back to the hotel, putting her mind to the next step in the plan, which was to persuade Mr. Nicholas to help her. The problem was getting Mr. Nicholas on his own. She played billiards with him every day, but he was inseparable from his many friends. They all looked the same, these young officers from the naval vessels in the harbor, courteously amazed that a girl should play billiards so well, and very complimentary about it. They all remembered her name, and she could remember none of theirs. They talked of wars and places and people she had never heard of, and were very interested in the state of affairs in New Zealand, seeming to know more than she did. But the problem was that they were *there*.

Lost in thought, Abigail walked slowly. Then she had to stop altogether, as she almost bumped into two white-clad women. Coming out of her preoccupation, she looked around, and saw there were more women than usual in the crowded street. They were all wearing white dresses. Some clutched white flowers, while others had flowers in their hair, and they were all either going in or coming out of a large building with an entrance that was set back from the street in an alley. From inside the building came a kind of rhythmic swishing sound, and the doleful plunking of guitars.

As Abigail watched curiously, someone just behind her said, "Yes, I agree it is very odd."

It was Lieutenant Nicholas. He smiled benevolently, and said, "It's an *angelito*—a small dead boy. The little corpse is arranged in a seated position on a chair, while men take turns playing guitars, and the females dance to celebrate the entry of a pure soul to heaven."

Mr. Nicholas was alone. The duplicate papers that Mr. Melvin had signed and sealed were in her reticule, and Mr. Nicholas was *alone*. Abby instantly forgot the women and the guitars, saying quickly, "Lieutenant Nicholas, I would be very grateful if you could see your way to doing me a favor."

"Again?" His tone was indulgent.

"Yes!" She looked about. The street was too crowded for private talk, so she took his arm and set off down the terrace again, towards a low wall that overlooked the foreshore. Mr. Nicholas came along cooperatively, and when she came to a place that was quiet, and sat down on the wall, he sat down beside her.

She said, "I want to see Captain Mara."

"But why?"

"I want him to claim a brig for me, a brig that was stolen by a pirate."

"Good lord," he said. For once, his urbane expression was taken over by surprise.

"I have documentation," she assured him.

"In fact," she added, eagerly opening her handbag, "I have papers right here."

She hauled out the copies she had made and gave them to him, and watched his face go completely blank as he read the name of the brig. It was as if he was assessing a hand of poker.

Then he read the documents slowly and carefully. She watched him, feeling proud of her work. With Mr. Melvin's seals they looked most official, she thought. Silent moments went by. One of the huge old carriages the people of Valparaiso used for public transport rattled at breakneck speed on the street below, driven by a yelling Yankee sailor. Drunken seamen were always commandeering the vehicles and careering about at risk of public life and limb. It jolted around the far corner, and four sailors fell off, waving arms and legs.

Papers rustled as Mr. Nicholas turned them. On the foreshore straggling caravans of mules and donkeys were carrying provisions for the ships; they had come all the way from Santiago. When would Seth learn that she waited in Valparaiso, and would he come quickly? Had he missed her as much as she missed him? Was Mr. Melvin right—would Seth be cross when he learned she had gone ahead with filing the claim for the brig? Surely not. He'd be delighted, Abby was certain, to learn that the brig wasn't wrecked. She had saved precious time by copying the papers, and now she wanted to make the claim as soon as possible, in case Mr. Perry had the original papers, and made a claim before she did...

A thought nudged, and then fled. Mr. Nicholas had finished reading the papers and was looking at her. He had the documents in a neat pile, and she could see the Bill of Sale on top: she could see her name, and her father's signature.

She said, "Do you think Captain Mara will help me?"

"Of course he will."

"I'm American, not English."

"I assure you that makes no difference." He hesitated. "Your father sold you this brig—for one dollar?"

"That's right."

"He would not have conducted a ... ah... similar sale with any other person?"

"Of course not!"

"And you haven't sold the brig since then?"

"Lieutenant!" Then she felt contrite, for she saw that Mr. Nicholas was only doing his job, and checking her case.

He smiled understandingly. "Pirates, you say? When did this happen? And how?"

"My father was murdered." It was still hard to talk about it. "The man who stole my brig killed my father and then escaped on the *Pandora*. It was over two years ago."

"Two years? Then I must ask you why you didn't report this earlier."

"Because I thought the brig was wrecked! When Broddy McGhie told me the sad story of the murder, he also assured me that the brig had been lost on the reef at Rarotonga."

"Captain McGhie? The agent who boarded the *Ocean Queen* at the Chagres River?"

"Yes—but I think he might be in Boston."

He looked startled. "Boston? Certainly not. At the moment, I think, he's in Talcahuano. He does work for shipping agents there, dispatching sloops with provisions to the recruiting ports."

So Broddy was still on the coast, living hand to mouth, Abigail thought. Had he given up on orchids? It didn't matter—she put it out of her mind, trying to think of other details that would help her case for claiming the brig.

She said, "The men at the customs house know about the brig—not that Tamati is a pirate, but that the *Pandora* sails in these waters."

"Then it should be easy to find her." Then, to Abby's consternation, Mr. Nicholas took the Bill of Sale in one hand

and made to give her the rest of the papers with the other.

"Don't you need those" she asked. Surely all the copying had not been a waste of time?

"I need the Bill of Sale to start off the process—but surely you want to keep the ownership papers?"

"No—please add them to the file," she said. After all, she had the other copies.

To her relief, Mr. Nicholas tucked the papers away in a pocket before he stood up. "I'll begin proceedings the moment I'm back on *Nympha*," he assured her, and helped her to her feet with a polite hand. As they turned the corner she cast a look back at the shipping. There were no whalers in port. Where, she wondered, was Seth?

The next day was shadowed with a sense of anticlimax. Searching Mr. Perry's office seemed pointless, now that she had filed her claim. At siesta time, instead of sneaking into the billiard room, she pulled a shawl over her head and shoulders, and wandered out into the street.

The rites for the *angelito* were still in progress. Abigail paused to watch the white-clad women go in and out to the sound of tired guitars. Grimacing, she moved on. Every tall broad-shouldered man in the street reminded her of Seth, and she wondered much about the state of the *Lizzie Ann*. No doubt Tucker was back to stowing tobacco chews under cups. Were the men pleased that they had got rid of Mrs. Morgan—or did they miss her gingerbread?

As she walked down to the foreshore, sailors called out to her, but it was easy to ignore them. Avoiding the mule trains, she crossed to the beach. There were grogshops on wheels there, gaily painted like showmen's wagons. When new ships made port the grogshop owners shoved their wagons out into the surf, to snare the sailors' money before they even stepped on land.

The afternoon drew on. The spill of towers and terraces of Valparaiso became golden with late light. A new sail was beating up the harbor, followed by another. A cool breeze had got up, and Abigail adjusted her shawl. When she looked at the bay again, the newcomer ship was a plain silhouette — a whaler; she could see the boats and the tryworks chimney. It was the *Lizzie Ann*, she was sure of it — the topsails were loose and men were working on the yardarms. Her heart was jumping. Then she saw the second sail anchoring. It was two-masted. A brig.

Her hands clutched the edges of her shawl. The customs house boat was putting out — to the *Lizzie Ann*, not the brig. The brig was silhouetted now, and sun slanted on her rigging and hull. Her shape was plain, and Abigail was sure of it — the brig was her brig, *Pandora*. She whirled and ran headlong across the beach and up the terrace.

The cobbled streets were surprisingly empty. She could hear faint sounds behind the thick stone walls: people getting meals, babies whimpering, children demanding. Inside the *angelito* house the sad guitars were still strumming. Abigail's way wound upwards, and her skirts rustled in rhythm to her running steps. She was panting, her breath harsh in her ears. Lamplight fell in murky squares from tiny barred windows. A donkey brayed in the distance and another answered. Two streets away a water-selling boy cried out with ghostly cadence, *"Agua-a-a."* Abby dashed through the courtyard of the House of the Ewer and burst into the billiard room.

Mr. Nicholas and three of his friends were playing. For a moment Abigail didn't have the breath to speak, but then she gasped, "My brig is in the harbor.!"

His eyes widened. "The *Pandora?*"

"Yes! Oh, please, send a message to Captain Mara."

"Are you absolutely certain?"

"Yes! And I saw my husband's ship arrive!"

He paused, his expression becoming careful. "But if Captain Morgan is coming, surely — "

Oh God, thought Abigail.

He would refuse to do anything until Seth was present. She had made a mistake in telling him the *Lizzie Ann* was here. She gasped in frustration, "Damn!" Whirling, she dashed out of the billiard room and out into the street again.

As she ran, she could hear Mr. Nicholas and his friends tearing after her, calling out her name. She ignored them, dashing headlong back down the terraces towards the shore. The echoes of their shouts and her steps rattled back from the walls, and then, in the distance, she saw two men striding towards her.

One was tall and broad-shouldered and vividly familiar and the other was ... Broddy McGhie. Abby stopped short, disturbed that they were together, foreboding inside her. She was by the alley that led to the entrance to the *angelito* house. Through her panting she could hear the strings and the swish and Mr. Nicholas shouting her name. Seth and Broddy saw her and quickened their steps. Broddy had something — in his hand. Abigail stood still, frozen — and a wild figure ran out from the alley.

He had a musket in one hand. With that other he grabbed her arm and hauled her into the mouth of the alley, and then let go and shoved her up to the door of the *angelito* house. Abigail stumbled, crying out in fright, but kept her balance. He shrieked incoherently, and shoved her again. Her shoulder hit the door; it slammed open.

Light sprang out of the opening, falling on her assailant's face. It was ... Tamati. His face was dreadful, a shattered mask. Again he pushed, his elbow shoving her hard as he brought up the musket, and Abigail fell backwards. A shot rang out — a close and deafening explosion — and then another. Two shots. The two shots were almost simultaneous.

Abigail staggered to her feet. She was in the *angelito* room. Women in white had stopped short in the middle of their dancing. The bright yellow light came from the lamps and candles arranged around the little corpse.

The *angelito* had been seven or eight years old. He was sitting on a chair and wearing embroidered clothing. His face and hands were greenish. Abby gulped, and ran back into the street.

She was crying out Seth's name, terrified that Tamati had shot him. Broddy was standing there, a pistol in his hand, with blood welling out of his sleeve and trickling down his fingers. Tamati was dead, his poor mad shattered face pressed into the cobbles. Broddy had killed Tamati. Then she saw Seth—he was unhurt. She gasped, "Seth, oh Seth," and threw herself into his arms, clutching at his familiar warm weight.

She could feel his heat and the pounding of his heart, and for an instant his arms tightened around her. Then she dazedly heard Broddy shout out Mr. Nicholas's name, and pounding footsteps as the lieutenant ran up. Seth let her go so abruptly that she nearly fell again. With a wordless roar, he swung at Lieutenant Nicholas with a furious fist.

Lieutenant Nicholas fell sprawling. Abigail screamed, "Seth, what are you doing?" The lieutenant scrambled back to his feet, shaking his head groggily. He looked at Seth towering over him and put up a trembling hand as he backed away. Then he and turned and ran. Broddy McGhie was visibly shaking, blood dropping from his fingers. He called Nicholas's name again, and stumbled after him, still shouting.

A crowd was gathering. Abigail dropped to her knees by the corpse. Tamati? Now, in death, he was Tamati indeed, dreadfully familiar. There were tears running down her cheeks, of grief as well as shock. Tamati had been utterly loyal ... and what had happened to his face? What had caused those dreadful furrows? Had Broddy done it during the murder at Mangonui? Broddy had said he had put up a fight, and now Broddy had killed him. If Tamati hadn't wasted time pushing her into the *angelito* house, he would have shot Broddy first...

Abigail stumbled to her feet and gripped Seth's arm and said desperately, "We must go down to the harbor and board the brig."

The police had arrived. The noise of the crowd had become a babble. Men were ripping down the door, to carry Tamati's corpse away. Women gaped from inside the room. The waxwork-like body of the dead little boy sat stiffly in his chair. Then she realized with a lurch that Seth looked ill. He was very pale; the dark stubble stood out on his face, and there was a white taut line about his mouth.

He said harshly, "What brig?"

"The *Pandora!* Ichabod Jones was right, she still sails! She's down in the harbor and Tamati is dead and if we don't get there soon the natives on board will hear the news and sail away. It's perfectly legal!" she cried at his unmoving expression. "I filed the claim with Lieutenant Nicholas!"

Seth said grimly, "Is that so?" Then he took her arm in a hard grip and urged her up the street—up, toward the hotel. She tried to stop him, crying, "Seth!"

He spoke through gritted teeth. "Perry's place, is it not?"

"Yes, but ... Oh!" she wailed. "We have to get to the brig, oh please!"

He moved implacably, impelling her along. Then they were in the hotel courtyard. It was crowded with the usual mob of captains.

Seth said tersely, "Which is our room?"

She cried, "Seth!"—but he urged her up the stairs. She whirled into the room and turned to face him, alarmed at his pallor in the light. "Oh Seth, please listen to me, oh Seth, are you all right?"

He shut the door and leaned his back on it, grimly facing her. His arms were folded. He said, "What is this nonsense?"

"It isn't nonsense! The men at the customs house confirmed that the brig sails this coast and I made copies of the papers. Then I persuaded Mr. Nicholas to give them to

400

Captain Mara of the man-of-war so he can..."

She broke off, and cried, "I can tell you the whole story later, Seth. But it doesn't matter now, for we must get down to the brig."

"Doesn't matter?" he echoed. He took a furious step forward. She backed away, and anger and pain sparked in his eyes. He shouted, "And I suppose exactly how you ran away from McGhie in Panama City doesn't matter either!"

"What?" She was bewildered. "What are you talking about?"

"Captain McGhie," he said coldly, "had the goodness to inform me that you eloped in the company of a common gambler called Nicholas."

She shook her head incredulously. "But it wasn't like that at all! And though Mr. Nicholas might be a gambler, no one who knew him would call him *common*."

For a horrible instant she truly believed he was about to throttle her. She flinched back again, and the netting of the bed brushed her shoulder. Seth's eyes were tightly shut. He opened them and shouted, "And you're a common little adventuress!"

"Broddy told you *that?*"

"You deny you spent the voyage playing poker?" She bit her lip, and looked away. "For money?"

"That I did not do. How could I play with money? I had none."

"Then Nicholas really did make a fool of you, Abigail. You can't play poker without a stake, so you played with his money, didn't you?"

"But Mr. Nicholas made no profit—I play poker very badly. I—I only did it to be pleasant."

"And men came to the table to watch the pretty girl lose her protector's money," he sneered with terrible jealousy. "And they stayed—to lose to Nicholas."

Abigail would never have believed that words could hurt so much. She said numbly, "Oh God, I was a fool."

Then, desperately, she said, "Seth, can we talk about this later? The brig—"

"To hell with the brig!" He was shuddering. She took another involuntary step. The bed hit her behind the knees and she collapsed in an undignified heap on the mattress. He stood towering over her and she put up her hand pleadingly.

The expression in his eyes flickered, and for a tiny moment she thought she saw his hand move towards hers. Then he stepped back. "I'll attend to the matter of the brig in the morning," he said icily. "In the proper manner, with the proper authorities. And in meantime, good night to you! The day after tomorrow you head back to New Bedford."

"What!" She frantically struggled to her feet. "Seth you can't mean that!"

"You can go and live with my Aunt Fanny Cambridge, and the best of luck to you both. And if she won't take you, your cousin Mitchell will."

"No—no, I won't leave you, I won't!"

"I assure you that you will. Captain McGhie guarantees it. He still has to get to Boston—and this time he'll make damn certain that you don't get away."

The door slammed as he left. Abigail stood frozen, waiting for him to come back, so that she could explain, and tell her story properly. Surely if he had a glass of brandy and calmed down and thought about her protestations of innocence, he'd return in a more amenable frame of mind?

An hour dragged by. When Abigail opened the door Seth was down in the courtyard, but when he saw her he turned his back.

Drearily, unable to think of anything else to do, she went to bed, and waited. But though she waited all night, he did not come to join her.

Finally dawn touched the windows. Abigail ran out onto the balcony, and stared desperately out to sea. And the brig *Pandora* was gone.

Abigail washed and dressed, and went down to the billiard room. Because it was so early, the courtyard was empty. She tapped the balls about idly, brooding, and then jumped with fright when the door abruptly opened.

It was Consider West, as baby-faced as ever. He was wearing black trousers that were fastened with gold buttons down the sides of the legs. He said, "Hey, Abby."

She snapped, "Mrs. Morgan to you."

He ignored that, shifting from one boot to another, and then said, "Abby, scuttlebutt has it that Cap'n Morgan has concluded to pack you off to New Bedford, that you won't be with us when we sail tonight. Surely that ain't right?"

"It surely isn't right," she glumly agreed. "But unfortunately it's true."

"Some of the men ... well, some say it's our fault. We didn't make you welcome. Back when you were first on board, the men sent a deputation to the cap'n, and my watch complained to me, too. The fact is, we all feel bad about it. We — well, we've missed you."

"Cupboard love," she said with a sniff, but there was a touch of warmth inside her.

To hide it, she sighted down the cue again, aware of Consider bobbing around. Then she heard him say, "Can you play that game?" She nodded, not looking at him, and tapped a crisp cannon with a neat flick of her cue.

He said, "Would you learn me?"

Abigail turned and stared at him. "You want to learn to play billiards?"

He nodded eagerly, and she said, "Well..." Then she shook her head and said, "No, it's impossible." She studied his downcast look from under her lashes, and then pensively, "But if you did me a favor in return..."

"What favor?"

"I'm not telling you until the lesson is over."

"That ain't fair!"

"Then go away."

She turned her back and played another shot, very conscious of being watched. Then he grudgingly capitulated.

She demonstrated, they practiced, they played a trial game, and then they played in earnest. Abigail won so narrowly that Consider demanded another bout. She said, "That favor."

"What is it?"

"I want you to get me on board of the *Lizzie Ann* tonight, just before she sails."

"Abigail!" He was horrified. "You want to stow away?"

"No, I want to be a female sailor. You gave me the idea yourself, a long time ago on the *Erasmus,* so don't argue."

"You're jesting!"

"Mr. West," she said firmly, "I jest not." Mr. Perry came into the room, looked about, nodded, and then passed through to his office and shut the door.

Consider West was looking hunted. "You're gallied," she jeered.

"I'm not!"

"Then say you'll do it."

"Oh, lord." His expression was more cornered than ever. "I'll see you later," he muttered. "I've got ship's business to do. I'll think on it."

"Do that," Abby instructed sweetly, and he escaped.

Seth had ship's business as well, but because it was siesta, Perry was not in his office. Both the courtyard and the billiard room were empty. Seth rubbed his forehead where the headache nagged and then concentrated on knocking balls about the table.

He was lining up for a cannon shot when he heard the footstep in the doorway. It was his first officer. Consider West, Seth thought tiredly, was undoubtedly bringing more bad news. Six men — including the hard-drinking third mate, damn him — had deserted in Talcahuano and had not been replaced. Now Perry had been given the job of finding more men, which was bound to prove expensive.

He said, "What is it?"

Consider West shifted from foot to foot, and then said, "Could I have a word, sir?"

"Yes?" Seth returned his attention to the billiard table. His teeth were set lightly in the cigar he was smoking, and he squinted. He shifted his stance, leaning one long thigh along the table as he angled for the knock.

"It's about Mrs. Morgan."

The cue skidded at the instant of impact. The ball rolled wildly past the red to a wobbling stop. Seth swore under his breath. Then he took the cigar out of his mouth, stared at his first officer, and said forbiddingly, "I beg your pardon?"

Mr. West, infuriatingly, was studying the vibrating cue ball with his head on one side. He looked like a sparrow. He said brightly, "Would you like a game, sir?"

"I didn't know you could play."

"Someone learned me how to do it."

Seth was silent. He was certain the boy didn't know the game, but anything was better than stewing in jealousy. Damn the minx, he thought: why couldn't he get her out of his head? He had missed her so, she brought color to his life. *She made me feel bored when I was away from her.* He nodded curtly, palmed the two white cue balls, and held the two fists out to his first mate. The tendons stood out on the backs of his hands. Mr. West hesitated, and then touched the right. It was the spot ball. Seth gave it to his first officer and they set up the table.

Seth said, "Mr. Perry will get us four seamen by tonight."

Tom Kanaka was on board, in charge of the larboard watch while they took on provisions. The starboard watch was on liberty until sunset. The tide would turn at eleven.

Mr. West said diffidently, "What about a third mate, sir?"

Seth shrugged. "The new man—Ichabod Jones—is a good seaman, and has been mate at times in his past. He'll make a fine steady officer. I'll send Willie Cotton forward; he's big enough to cope with the foc'sle now." Then, with a decisive movement, he lined up his cue.

Mr. West tried hard and had a natural eye, and he seemed very surprised that he was doing so badly. He kept on giving Seth little sideways glances as he chose his shots, which was probably putting him off his form. Then, at the end of a break, he said tentatively, "I was wonderin' if we could talk about Mrs. Morgan."

Seth straightened and stared at him. Then he leaned his cue against the table, folded his arms, and said, "Yes?"

"I've had a deputation from my watch."

"About what, this time?"

"They want her back on board, sir."

"They ... *what?*"

"True grub," Mr. West assured him earnestly. "They're right upset about her leavin', and they wish they had been kinder when she was first on the ship."

"Well, that's their problem, not mine."

To Seth's angry bemusement Mr. West shut his eyes and seemed to brace himself. "I think it would be wiser, sir, for you to reconsider."

"You're being impertinent!"

Consider went bright red and mumbled an apology. Then he said in a mutter, "I sure hope you won't be sorry." Seth glared at him, and went back to his game. Then he heard Mr. West muse aloud, "You're sending Willie Cotton forward?"

"That's what I said."

"But even with him, we'll be one man short in the boats."

"Tucker can pull an oar. One does not need the sight of a vulture," Seth sardonically informed him, "to heave at an oar in a boat."

"But he's steward, sir! We have to have a cabin boy, if the steward goes down in a boat."

Seth frowned. Mr. West, he thought, was far too fond of his stomach. Then the alignment of three balls caught his attention. He aimed along his cue, braced his stance, and made his shot. The wood knocked the cue ball with a crisp thud, and then he heard the clean double click and felt an instant of pure aesthetic pleasure.

It had been a lovely shot. Seth sighed and said, "My game." He hoped he would have another game that evening: the Perrys had invited him and McGhie to supper. Then he looked at Mr. West. "Your game shows promise," he said. "I would enjoy a bout with your tutor."

Mr. West's expression, he thought, was strange. Was he still worrying on about having no cabin boy to prepare food for the cabin table while the steward was down in the chase? Seth said tolerantly, "If you're so keen on having a cabin boy, you can hire one, if you can find one. But he must talk English!" He shook his head, and said, "An impossible quest, I think."

Mr. West's expression was odder than ever. He said, "Would you care to put a bet on that, sir?"

Abigail thought the supper meal would never end; she felt sick with nervous excitement, unable to eat or make sensible conversation. Seth was as silent as she was, and she kept casting worried glances at his face. He looked ill, and was sweating even though he had his coat on, as if he felt cold. Every now and then he rubbed his forehead as if it hurt, and he was drinking far too much. Perhaps she should call everything off, and nag him into seeing a physician—but what kind of medics did they have here in Valparaiso? Dirty, she was certain. The clean sea air would be best for him, she thought. And, anyway, Seth was in no mood to listen.

Cabin boy ... could she possibly get away with it?

Tucker being near-sighted would certainly help. If only she could keep up the pretense until the *Lizzie Ann* had a good offing, surely Seth would not bring her back to Valparaiso... But could she get away with it for that necessary twenty-four hours? She pushed her food about with her fork.

Luckily Broddy was noisily garrulous, and was three sheets in the wind, as well. He was drinking as if he had something to celebrate — though he made it plain he was very angry with her, too. He glowered when she wasn't looking, but if she lifted her head his eyes flickered away at once, refusing to meet her stare.

He looked old; his hair was woolly gray all over now, and there were large liver spots on the backs of his hands. Flirting ponderously with Mrs. Perry, he undoubtedly fancied himself young and lively, but all he looked was undignified. How could the Perrys have told him about that voyage on the *Bolivia* — Mrs. Perry had played poker too! — and how could he have ratted to Seth, and twisted the facts so cruelly? *A common little adventuress...* How could Seth have listened and believed him, when he wasn't willing to listen to her side of the story?

She could see Seth's hand on the table. His fingers were long, the palms very broad; the back of his wrist was flecked with black hairs. She badly wanted to lay her hand on his, but didn't dare. Then the hand moved as Seth drank more brandy.

Broddy was maundering on and on about that clipper ship he had lost, *Rainbow*. Her accommodations, it seemed, had been magnificent. "Black walnut," he rambled. "Nicely carved, and och, the fancywork! Steamboat fixings in the captain's stateroom, with lead piping to take the water off, and green Brussels carpet, like a parlor. And she was a bonny, bonny sailor, oh, in a storm and calm, whatever."

She had heard it all before; Abigail stopped listening, thinking impatiently that if he was so obsessed with the ship, he should go to San Francisco and retrieve her. But he didn't have the money, she supposed. Broddy was flirting again; she heard Mrs. Perry's roguish laughter. Then at long long last the dreadful meal was over. The men stood up, talking about a game of billiards.

Abigail stood up too. Suddenly, it was hard to breathe. Consider West would be waiting in her bedroom, as arranged, and for an instant her courage failed her. Then she looked at Broddy. Go back to New Bedford? Never!

To her alarm, when she walked away from the group and to the foot of the stairway, Seth came with her. She stopped and looked up at him. Surely he could hear the hammering of her heart? She was shivering with suspense. Seth looked ill, and she was riven with anxiety.

He said in a low voice, "We sail at eleven."

"I know." Then she wondered with a jolt if she should not have known that. She said lamely, "Mrs. Perry told me."

He was frowning deeply, with something bleak in his eyes. "Abigail..."

"Yes?"

Seth paused, almost as if he were waiting for her to go on. Then he shook his head, and said sadly, "It doesn't matter." Without another word he turned and followed the others into the billiard room. Abigail stood still for a moment, watching his broad familiar back, thinking her heart would be breaking now, if she didn't have other plans. Then she roused, whirled, and ran up to the bedroom.

Consider West was waiting like a canary on her balcony. She gasped, "Do you think cabin boy is such a good idea? Seth — Captain Morgan — will see me too often for me to get away with it."

"You are not," he said masterfully, "goin' to sleep in the foc'sle."

"I should think not!" She tipped her head on one side, trying to remember where Willie had slept when he had been her cabin boy. "Where *am* I going to sleep?"

"Any spare corner," he shrugged.

Then, when she looked about the empty room, he said, "Willie's taken your bag on board."

So her bridges were burned; the die was cast. She pulled her hair out of the pins and yanked it into a single bunch. Then she turned her back and said, "Cut it."

"I can't!" His tone was horrified. "Cap'n Morgan would have my intestines for a bandanna!"

"For heaven's sake! — cut it."

Muttering and grumbling, Consider West produced his jackknife and sawed away. Abby hopped from foot to foot as the hairs tugged, until at last he held a fistful of ringlets. The nape-long hair that was left sprang about in wild curls as if alive. "Hey, Ginger," he said, and guffawed. "You look like a marigold."

She darted to a looking glass, and winced. Then she said, "Get out. I'm going to change."

"Such modesty, in a female sailor," he derided, but retired to the balcony, to shin down the rope she had left there.

Abigail tore off her gown and dragged a shirt over her dungaree pants. Dirt from the balcony was roughly smeared on her face, and then she dragged a woolen cap over her curls, and scrambled down the rope herself. Consider West was waiting at the bottom, and she followed him to the shadowy entrance of the hotel.

To her great dismay, Seth and Broddy came out of the billiard room just as they arrived; worse still, Seth called out Mr. West's name, and both men walked towards them. She quickly bent her head, and studied her dirty bare feet, listening to them coming.

Seth stopped just a yard away. He shoved his hands in his pockets, swayed a little, and said to Consider West, "Well, well, I would never have believed it, you've found a cabin boy — but he has to speak English, remember."

"It's an American boy, sir."

"Good God," said Seth. "What's its name?"

410

Abby swallowed, and made her voice as gruff as she could. "B-Bill Butler, sir." It was the first name that flew into her mind.

"And how the devil do you come to be in Valparaiso?"

Abby could smell the brandy that Seth had been drinking. "On the ... *St. Bernard* of Boston."

"You deserted?"

"Took my discharge, sir. Cap'n carries his wife, sir, and her and me didn't suit."

Seth laughed in a short, harsh sound, and said, "Well, Mr. West, you've won your bet."

Bet? Abigail shot Consider West a very sharp look from under her lashes.

Then she heard Broddy say in a slurred voice," Shipping boys is ill-advised, Seth. Lazy wee devils, sogers, they are. I would'na take him on, if I was you."

Abigail waited, not daring to breathe. She saw Seth rub his hand over his face, and stagger a little. He said, "Are you a soger, boy?"

She shook her head fervently.

"Have you eaten?"

"Aye, sir," she said, and then regretted it. Boys were always hungry. It would have been more convincing to have pretended to be starving.

Seth, however, merely said, "Don't go away," and turned and went into the billiard room.

She didn't dare feel relieved. Broddy was still there — Broddy, who knew her better than any living person, perhaps. Broddy, who had been listening to her voice since babyhood.

She could feel Consider West's tension; he, too, stood very still. Broddy was weaving a little, frowning, and the silence dragged on ... and on. Abigail desperately wished Consider would say something to fill it, just to break the tension.

Then, all at once, Broddy muttered, "Bloody little sogers,

boys," and turned and went into the billiard room in a stumbling shamble.

The instant he was out of sight Abigail sank to the edge of the fountain, too weak with nerves to stand any more.

"I have to go," Consider West whispered. "Perry's got some men for me to ship—but I'll be back."

Before Seth, Abigail fervently hoped. But there was no need to worry. Seth did not emerge from the billiard room until after ten, and by that time Consider West had arrived with four silent Spanish greenhand seaman.

And Seth, most providentially, was drunk.

The stars were shining brightly when Mr. West herded his little squad to the beach. His shoulders were aching. Captain Morgan had leaned on him all the way—and had been nervewrackingly reluctant to leave the hotel. He had mumbled about going up to the bedroom—the bedroom that was empty except for Abby's discarded gown!—and Consider had had to drag him bodily out into the street.

The new cabin boy was nervously quiet. The four Spanish greenhands trailed along unhappily, perhaps regretting the bargain they had made. Gustavus was waiting with a boat. Captain Morgan passed out completely on the way to the ship, so Mr. West ordered the boat hoisted with the captain still in it. The *Lizzie Ann* crew, he saw to his relief, were so riveted by the unusual sight of their skipper dead drunk that they paid scarcely any attention to the new men. The Spaniards and Abigail clambered onto the deck and then stood about in an indecisive group.

There were chickens running about all over the deck, and a bullock was lowing sadly in the pigpen. The foresail and topsails were loosed, and the ship was hove short. Consider West looked around, nodded approvingly at Tom Kanaka, and said, "Man the windlass."

"Wait," said Ichabod Jones. A guard boat was coming off from shore.

There were Chilean soldiers in the boat, with an officer who wore dingy regimentals and had a serape folded over one shoulder. He had come, he announced, to search for deserters from the Chilean army.

The four Spanish greenhands looked nervously at one another. Then three of them moved, disassociating themselves from the fourth. Abigail stood by the solitary man a moment, then visibly started and moved away. She had caught the officer's attention, however, because he beckoned with a dirty finger.

Mr. West stood frozen. He knew he should respond to this emergency by doing something inspired and dramatic, but his brain refused to respond.

Abigail took one step forward. The Chilean officer was a short officious man, with the wide bottom of a man who spends much of his life on horseback. He sent the soldiers about the ship, but remained where he was, staring at Abby. Then he lifted one hand and snapped his fingers.

Abby looked apprehensively at Mr. West—and Consider was sent below, with a soldier, to fetch the ship's papers.

He forced himself to move at a normal pace. Below, the soldier looked at Seth, snoring where he was sprawled on his swinging bed, and smirked. When Consider heard shouting on deck, he had to force himself not to run.

As he arrived, the soldiers were slapping the fourth greenhand about, while the unfortunate fellow sobbed, then coughed in a sound like spitting. He was kicked in the belly, then in the face. A tooth flew out, and rattled to the deck. Pease and Hunter were grinning, while the rest of the *Lizzie Ann* crew silently stared.

Then, to Mr. West's horror, Abigail said very clearly, "Please don't do that."

Consider was convinced at the second that his heart would never beat again. The officer pointed a finger at Abigail, and snapped, "You!"

The soldiers came out of their stupor and dropped the wretched Spaniard over the side into their boat. Then the deck was very quiet, as everyone stared at Abigail.

Consider West said desperately, "It's only an ignorant American lad, sir."

The officer smirked. "Runaway boy," he said. "Runaway from home."

Abigail said firmly, "Sir, I am a seaman."

The officer grinned evilly. "Prove it," he said.

"Sir?"

The pointing finger moved upwards, aimed like a carbine at the main topgallant crosstrees, eighty feet above the deck. "You climb there," he said.

Consider West blinked, and Abby was poised on the bulwarks. Another blink, and she was halfway up the mainmast shrouds. He would never have believed that she could climb so fast: she moved like a lizard. The men began to guffaw. Then she reached the futtock shrouds, and they were silent.

Mr. West heard a very odd little noise, like nothing he had ever heard before. He looked round, it was Willie Cotton, standing beside him with his freckles standing out in his white face, and his teeth audibly chattering. Abigail would never make it over the futtock shrouds—she wasn't tall enough to reach over the rim of the maintop, and here in the harbor, she didn't have the roll of the ship to help.

She hesitated—and threw herself bodily outwards. Consider West waited with horror for the scream and the thud as she hit the deck. Then he saw her in the topmast shrouds. It was magic.

Once in the topgallant crosstrees, the cabin boy stopped up there, hanging onto a lanyard and looking about. It was as if that distant figure owned the whole confounded ship. Mr. West turned and looked at the officer. They exchanged curt nods, and the soldiers dropped over the side.

The boat pulled away. Consider West sighed a gust of

huge relief, and nodded at Tom. "Man the windlass," he said.

From Valparaiso we sailed away
Heave away, Santy-ana!
To the north'ard yet our course we'll set
Heave away, hurrah, for roll and go!

Eighteen

Seth had never imagined that it would be possible to feel so vile and yet still be alive.

He seemed sunk in an endless fever, trapped in a nightmare of sodden blankets that twined around him like reptiles. He head rang like a cracked bell, and all the time there was that dreadful anxiety.

He knew he had vomited until there was nothing left to heave. Someone cleaned him up and cared for him. Medicines and sweet arrowroot paste were spooned into his mouth, and he drank sugared water and laudanum, and all the time he dreamed of the grotesque visage of the dead Maori, Tamati. He tossed in his sodden nightmares and saw Abigail shoved aside over and over, and all the time *the pistol was ready in McGhie's fist.*

Seth opened his eyes and sat bolt upright and shouted, "We have to go back!"

Tucker, the myopic steward, peered at him. "Pardon, sir?"

Seth winced. The *Lizzie Ann* was round him, but the dream was still there. He said huskily, "What the devil is wrong with me?"

The threadiness of his whisper was horrifying.

Tucker said, "You have a fever, sir, contracted in South America. Your condition when you arrived on board," he added with a sniff, "weakened your constitution." Then he plumped a pillow.

Then why the hell wasn't he back in Valparaiso, under the care of some filthy Chilean doctor? Seth shouted, "Get me Mr. West!"

Consider West arrived, looking very wary. Seth snapped, "Where are we headed?"

"Nor'west, sir, to the Callao ground, as you said, sir."

"Well," said Seth, "we have to go back." The consternation on his first mate's face was infuriating. Seth shouted, "Do it!" Weak and fuming, he dropped back on the pillows, and then while he was still struggling to keep awake and impress the urgency of the situation on Mr. West, the nightmares reached out and grasped him again.

Once he half-woke, grunting with terror, and a bundle of gray blanket unrolled from the floor by his bed. It was the new cabin boy, and my God, he was a filthy little hound.

Seth rasped, "Are we at Valparaiso yet?"

The boy shook his head. The ship felt easy, forging gently on a calm sea, and he was disgusted that the boy had to help him out of bed. When he returned from the washroom the bed had been remade with fresh linen. Seth didn't want to lie down again, but the state of his legs and head forced him to submit.

He said weakly, "We have to hurry, boy." The boy silently fed him mashed yams. Seth could have killed him. Instead he ate the paste and went back to sleep.

He dreamed vividly again, of Abigail. In his dream, she said, *It is perfectly impossible that Tamati killed my father.* He said urgently to the cabin boy, "Are we there yet?" but there was no reply. He staggered to the privy and staggered back to bed, so groggy that all he was aware of was that time was passing and he was too weak to do anything about it. Frustration and guilt ground inside him. He dreamed that

417

Abigail was with him. She sat on the edge of the bed, and washed him all over with tingling cold water and she said, "It's all right, Seth, it's all *right*," and he went back to sleep and for once he didn't dream.

When he woke up his nightshirt and bedding were dry and clean and the fever had gone. Tucker was standing by the bed. The *Lizzie Ann* creaked as easily as a child's cradle.

Seth struggled up against the pillows and said, "How long have I been sick?"

Tucker said uneasily, "Two weeks, sir."

Two weeks. Oh, God. Seth shut his eyes. In the space of thirteen days McGhie would have taken Abigail up the coast and across the Isthmus; they would be in Aspinwall, or even on the way to Boston. His wife was on the Atlantic seaboard now ... when would he see her again?

That last night in Valparaiso, at the bottom of the stairs, if she had asked him to forgive her, he would have altered his mind. Oh, God, she only needed to smile and tilt her head in the coaxing way she had and say please, and he would have given in with humiliating speed.

Too late. Seth opened his eyes and swallowed on a dry throat. Too late. "Get me Mr. West," he said. "We'll head back to the Callao ground."

Later he slept, and the nightmares touched him again.

Three days after that, Seth was gnawing on the bone of frustration. His officers mollycoddled him and foiled him in his efforts to take up the reins of the vessel again, and his residual weakness infuriated him beyond bearing. He didn't even know their position, or their course, or how far they had been out of Valparaiso when he'd ordered them to turn back.

Now the feel of the ship told him that they were on the Callao ground, but he didn't know precisely where. He snapped at Tucker, and the steward sniffed and sulked.

He snapped at the dirty little fiend of a cabin boy and

threatened to have the cooper put him in a tub and scrub him all over, and the cabin boy kept well clear of him after that. Even sleep eluded him. He'd slept too much for the past two weeks, and when he slept he dreamed miserably of Abigail.

At three in the morning he finally found his log, where someone had hidden it. It had been kept conscientiously, in a careful rounded hand. "Middle and latter part light trades and fine weather," he read. "At 10 AM sent down FTG mast backstays repaired them and sent them up again. Captain continues to improve So Ends This Day."

Seth's eyebrows were arched very high. Then he turned back pages and his scowl became thunderous. The damn ship had never steered towards Valparaiso. His orders had been deliberately ignored—unless his orders had been part of his delirium.

He stood up, frowning, took a cigar from the box on his table, and padded barefooted up to deck in the duck pants and loose shirt he was wearing. Hunter was at the helm. He looked at Seth uneasily, and then looked away. No doubt, Seth meditated, everyone on board was acutely aware of the skipper's bad temper.

He walked out from under the house, stood surveying the sails and the sea for a long moment, and then climbed the ladder to the roof. The *Lizzie Ann* was clean and shipshape. The air held a deceptive freshness, belying the heat it would radiate when the sun was fully up. Seth clambered into his slung boat to smoke his cigar while he watched the sun rise. The boat rattled in the davits, and to his amazement a groggy figure lurched to a sitting position and rubbed bleary eyes.

"Good God," said Seth. "It's Bill Butler. Are you sogering, boy?"

The boy stuttered a bit, and said, "It's too early to make breakfast, sir."

But he was acting as guilty as the devil; Seth wondered

419

what was up with the lad. He puffed a pensive cloud of smoke and said, "Do you make a habit of sleeping in the starboard boat?"

"No, sir." The reply came fast. Then the boy got ready to clamber out. He seemed very awkward and very much in a hurry.

Seth said indulgently, "As you said, it's early. Stay there." The boy froze. Seth said, "Don't you have a berth?"

"N—Not really."

Seth nodded. Then he wondered where Willie Cotton had slept, when he had been the cabin boy. On the floor of Mr. West's stateroom, perhaps, or maybe with the steward. Then Seth remembered that this boy had slept on the floor of his stateroom when he had been ill. Now that the captain was recovered, he was reduced to the captain's boat for a bed.

Seth said, "Be sure you don't get moonstruck." The boy said nothing, and all at once Seth felt chagrined that the youngster should be so scared of him. Was he really such a tyrant?

"Moon blindness comes from waking with the moon on your face," he said. "And being moonstruck means that you're fated to be at sea forever."

"Is that so, sir?"

There was a quiver in the boy's voice, and Seth fell silent. His benevolent moment was over—for he was struggling with the impulse to put a reassuring arm around the boy's shoulders. A dirty little villain of a cabin boy!

He stood up abruptly, and quit the boat. The davits rattled. The sun was on the rim of the horizon. "Since you're so fond of my boat," he said harshly, "you can pull an oar in it."

With the utmost consternation in his voice, the cabin boy exclaimed, "*What?*"

Seth frowned. The low light shone in his eyes. He turned and pitched his cigar butt into the sea, shaking himself free of weird imaginings, and said, "I'm short a man." Consider West had reported that the Chilean army had reclaimed one of the greenhands. "You'll pull stroke oar, right under my eye, my boy, and we'll lower for practice today. And clean yourself up!" he snapped.

"Stroke oar?" echoed Willie Cotton in horror. "In his boat?"

Abigail sighed and nodded, and listened to him bobbing about in consternation while she stared moodily at the pattern her toes traced on the deck.

"Oh, crumbs, Mrs. Morgan, oh, crumbs," he moaned. "That really spits it, it really do"—and Peabody at main masthead called out for whale.

Abigail's heart jumped, apparently right up into her throat. For a second it was as if she were the only person who had heard the cry, and then Peabody said angrily, "Blows!" and Seth came running up to deck.

He looked as galvanized and vital as if he'd enjoyed superb health the whole of his life. He shouted, "Where away?" and was halfway up the mainmast before Peabody could reply. Then he piled down a backstay, shouting orders.

Abigail stood frozen, with not a notion of what to do. The mates were running up and down, yelling orders to clew up courses and square the main yard. Seth strode past her, shouting, "Prepare to lower starboard, larboard, and bow!"

Ichabod Jones, it seemed, was to be left in charge of the ship. Willie grabbed Abby's arm. She jerked out of her paralysis, and looked about wildly. Peabody was descending the shrouds with mincing dignity, and Mr. Jones was scrambling aloft.

"C'mon!" Willie hissed. Numbly, Abigail followed him up to the roof of the house.

Hunter and Dutchie were already there. Hunter said, "The cabin boy? Jest our soddin' luck."

She silently helped them as best she could, saying nothing when Hunter growled at her ineptness, tossing down boat davit falls, hoisting the boat a little to free the craft from the cranes, swinging the cranes back against the side of the house, freeing the boat so it swung from the davits.

The boat swayed with the movement of the ship. The weather was perfect, the sky a beautiful blue. Seth shoved past her and clambered into the head of the boat. Gustavus, his boatsteerer, ran up and jumped into the bow. "Get her down," Seth snapped. The boat lowered in jerks as the men held the ropes, let them slide, choked them, and then the boat hit the water.

"C'mon," urged Willie again. She followed him in a flustered scramble down the side of the ship, to land with a thump on a thwart. Dutchie and Hunter followed her. Seth gripped her shoulder and shoved her into the place nearest his legs, and, trembling, she took hold of an oar. It was years since she'd last rowed a boat.

Seth was directly in front of her. If she put out a hand she could touch his knee; it was the first time she'd sat in the boat facing him. He seemed titanic, rearing up against the sky with the massive steering sweep firmly wedged in his leg armpit. His legs were powerfully braced. He had his head thrown back as he yelled orders to Ichabod Jones.

"Brace forward main yards and keep to wind'ard!" Then she saw him look down at her. The narrow blue eyes flickered past her, looking at the others. He said, "Pull ahead." Despite the stubble of his growing beard he looked magnificent: tough, fierce, and very dangerous. "Follow stroke!" he snapped. He was staring at her. Abigail jumped with consternation as his right fist shot out and grasped the handle of the oar right up close to her own two hands.

"Put your back into it!" he barked, and heaved. Abby could hear the men grunting behind her. She worked gamely with Seth as he helped her heave at the oar. She was sweating, and spray flicked across her face. She stared up at him as she leaned back with each stroke, mesmerized, unable to look anywhere else. Her hat blew off, and she felt her hair whip back as the boat worked to windward of the whales.

Seth was staring past her, to where the whales spouted. "W-a-ay enough," he said, and the men slumped over their oars. She could hear their panting but numbly tried to keep on rowing until Seth held the oar still and she realized belatedly what had happened.

She heard the mast stepped, and then the sheet was in Seth's fist. When she tried to look behind her Seth snapped, "Don't look back!" So she stared instead at the wrinkled distant sails of the *Lizzie Ann*.

Then, from the corner of her eye, she saw another boat. Consider West was in the head, wildly grinning, his hair whipping across his right cheek. Together, the two boats bounced along the water.

Time passed ... passed. His tone urgent, Seth said, "Lower the sail." The canvas was shipped with harsh rattling noises. "Unstep the mast." She heard Gustavus and Dutchie heaving, and then the mast bumped as it was laid alongside her, several feet sticking out over the pointed stern of the boat. "Man the oars." Abby took a huge breath, and felt Seth's fist lodge by her hand again.

His strength was amazing. It was impossible to believe that just days ago she was terrified he was dying. "Pull ahead!" he barked in his husky voice. He helped her. Without his physical power, she would be floundering. Then she heard him snap, "Hold it." The men panted as they leaned on their oars.

Mr. West's boat sped past just as, with a sucking and surging of water, a whale rose and rose and then spouted so *close*. She turned. She couldn't help it. The whale lay in the trough of a wave and she could see the hump of its back and then she jerked as a hard hand gripped the front of her shirt and jerked her round. She collapsed on the thwart, her heart hammering, and heard Mr. West yell to his boatsteerer to stand.

"Give it to him, George!" he yelled, and then she heard a wild shriek of, "Fast!"

Seth cried out, "Stern all!" She grabbed her oar with frantic hands and shoved with the rest. The boat jumped back and the whale threshed gigantic flukes high into the air and then sounded. The larboard boat went hurtling by, hauled by unseen motive power, behind a rope that dug into the sea and ran so fast that it left an arrow of froth behind it.

She heard a distant shout. In a bare few seconds they had gone—*so far*. Then Seth said, "Take your oars." His voice was calm. "We'll have to bend on, I think." Bend on? What did he mean? Then she understood that Consider West's boat was in danger of running out of line. The whale was sounding and taking the line with him: Seth's boat would have to pull up so they could join their line to Mr. West's. Which meant that they would have to take over that unbelievably huge bull.

The pace Seth set to catch up was back-breaking. Abby's sight became as blurred as her hearing with the thump of her pulse and her sweat. Then she glimpsed the other boat, now sitting still in the water. They were pulling alongside as Seth said, "Hold it." Their oars were peaked. Her mouth felt parched. Then she saw the huge whale breach again.

"We'll fasten," Seth decided. "Gustavus, stand up."

Abigail heard the rattle as the Swede moved into the harpooner's stance, and a muttered word as Dutchie passed him the iron. Then: "Now!" Seth roared. The line sang out, and "Stern all, for your lives!"

Panic spurted through her, dissolving exhaustion. She shoved at the oar, great flukes rose up and up—and smacked down on the blade of the oar as she raised it. Jerked out of her seat, she went cartwheeling through the air.

The water closed over her head. Water! She was in the

same small patch of sea as a hurt and furious bull whale! Abigail surged to the top in a spurt of sheer horror, saw a boat, dived under it, avoided oars with her salt-washed eyes wide open, came up on the other side, and grabbed for the gunwale.

Of which boat? She didn't know—until she heard Consider West's frantic cry only four feet from her ears. He shouted, in wild horror, "Oh, my God, where is little Abby?"

She didn't answer. Instead, she tumbled over the side, and crashed into the bottom of his boat.

Dutchie pulled the starboard boat onto the whale and Seth wielded the lance with clinical efficiency. Within seconds the huge fish lay on the water, fin out, dead. From just two boat-lengths away, Mr. West's men watched their captain silently, and then one by one they turned to stare with blatant fascination at the captain's wife. Abigail scowled back at them from her sea-cleaned face.

As far as she could tell, Seth had no expression at all. Businesslike as ever, he ordered his boat pulled up to the dead bull. Dutchie leaned over with a boat knife, and cut a hole in one fluke, and a rope was drawn through the hole and made fast to the loggerhead. Then Mr. West's bow oarsman fastened a rope to Seth's boat, and together, without a word spoken, the two crews pulled hard, towing the whale to the *Lizzie Ann*, which was bearing down on them.

Abigail stayed in Mr. West's boat as it was hoisted up. Once it was secure in the davits she gathered the wet rags of her dignity about her and walked across the roof of the house to the ladder. When she turned from jumping down, Seth's boat had arrived, and Seth was climbing up the side of the ship. She watched him in an apprehensive paralysis— and his eyebrows were curled so grimly downwards and the crescents of his eyes glittered so coldly that her nerve broke, and before she knew it she was halfway up the mainmast and still climbing.

What was she doing? She couldn't stop up there forever! But she couldn't stop, either. Panic had taken over. Then, to her horror, she felt the shrouds vibrate. She looked down and shrieked. Seth had lost his head as well, and was pursuing her up the rigging.

It was like a game. She found herself gasping on the edge of wild laughter. She threw herself up the topmast shrouds in an undignified scurry. Then, in the topgallant crosstrees, he caught up with her.

She looked at him, contemplated whistling down a topgallant stay, and abandoned the notion. He held onto a lanyard and studied her. Abigail, his cabin boy, Abigail. She had shipped as his cabin boy. He felt drunken with delight and relief ... the crazy young minx was alive and here.

He knew he should be furious. The gossips of New Bedford would feed on the tale for years. Below, on deck, every man of his crew was staring. Seth could feel their slack-jawed amazement. He said, "Oh Abigail."

"Seth," she said. She smiled tentatively, tilting her head to one side the way she did when she was trying to coax something out of him. "Are you very angry with me?"

"There's every reason to be very angry. You could have been killed by that whale; you could have fallen from aloft. Why? Why did you do it?"

Abigail's expression became more cautious than ever. Then she dimpled and said, "I've come to collect."

"I beg your pardon?"

"You promised me a box of cigars a long time ago, and you never delivered. So I've come to collect."

"Dear God," he said. He couldn't believe that she had the nerve to be coquettish at a moment like this.

"Please?"

Seth paused. When he looked down he could see the decks and the upturned faces of the men and the half-submerged carcass of the whale.

The sea glittered all the way to the horizon. It was all ... so peaceful, and yet he had fizzing champagne in his veins instead of blood. "Abigail, get down to deck and go below," he said gruffly. "And get dressed in something decent. We'll talk later — after the whale is cut in."

"The men will be saucy and independent now," Peabody pronounced. He was saucy and independent himself — after all, he was the man who had raised the whale and won the bounty.

The cutting falls hung ready, and he and Pease and Hunter leaned on the starboard rail, watching the two boats' crews who were trying to secure the whale to the ship. "Cap'n Morgan is a fine man, one who will have order," he declared. "But how may he expect his instructions obeyed when his lady indulges in scandalous behavior?"

"Cabin boy, eh?" said Pease. He sniggered. "The kind of cabin boy every captain dreams of, huh? Tucker didn't know what his cripple eyes was missing."

"I knew alla time," Hunter said smugly.

"Balls you did."

"I reckon it's romantic."

"I beg your pardon?" Peabody cried. "Romantic? When the captain's lady provides fodder for scandal and slander? How can Captain Morgan expect loyalty and obedience, when the tabernacle is so greatly flawed?"

The two boats' crews were rowing on either side of the half-submerged carcass with a drooping rope slung between them. They were trying to snag the small of the whale's tail. One man dropped his end of the rope, and a curse sizzled up off the water."I think she's good grit, like a woman in a novel," said Hunter.

"Exactly. Like a vulgar interlude in a low kind of literature. Why those men who have the privilege of reading vitiate their tastes with pernicious —"

"He's right, yer know," said Pease.

427

"I beg your pardon?" said Peabody. He seemed astounded at this unexpected support.

"The men will never take kindly to discipline when they know that the captain's wife can get away wiv behavior like that."

"Balls," said Hunter, and spat. There was a shout from below as the rope was set, and the men shifted, ready for the order to haul the fluke chain. The whale bumped solidly against the hull. It was enormous, quite as long as the ship herself.

"A buster," said Peabody complacently. Then all three were distracted by the odd sight of Willie Cotton going by with his mattress over his shoulder.

"Wotcher taking yer donkey's breakfast for?" cried Pease.

Willie blushed. "It ain't—it's Mrs. Morgan's duds."

"What?" said Hunter. He shouted with loud laughter. "You been a-sleepin' on her wardrobe? He knew more than you did, that boy," said Hunter, and shoved Pease in the ribs.

"Wouldn't wanter **be in his shoes, when the cap'n finds out he aided and abetted,**" Pease said. "Curses instead of rations fer his supper."

"Balls," said Hunter, and then they all shut up as Mr. West arrived and barked at them to bear a hand and help.

"There's a treat in store, if you move smart and lively," he added.

"Wot yer mean, sir?"

"Cap'n's ordered dinner for when the fish is secured, and splice the mainbrace for a hundred-barrel whale."

A glass of grog? "Gawd almighty," said Pease, and the men moved with alacrity to the windlass. "D'yer think the old man's pleased that his cabin boy turned out to be his missus?"

"Dunno," said Hunter. "But he's shrewd enough ter keep us all a-guessing."

The officers had a celebratory glass as well. The warmth of the rum joined the warmth of relief in Consider West's belly. Gemini, but he'd lost nine lives in his fright when he thought Abby had been killed by that whale. Seth, in his armchair at the head of the table, was uncommunicative in the extreme, but Mr. West was certain that if Mrs. Morgan had been hurt, Captain Morgan would have had his intestines for a bandanna.

Now, he comfortably mused, everything was perfect. Mrs. Morgan was walking around the table filling coffee mugs as if she'd never been away. Then she took her accustomed seat on the bench opposite, at Captain Morgan's right hand. She was wearing a blue dress and her hair sprung in a bright and damp disorder of curls. Her expression was careful, and Captain Morgan watched her every second of the time. Consider thought he would not like to be in her shoes. But he wasn't worried for himself, no sir—for, let's face it, it had been a bet between two men.

He grinned and said, "My men think it romantic."

As soon as he saw Captain Morgan's face, he wished he hadn't spoken. He added awkwardly, 'They admire Mrs. Morgan's spunk."

"Is that so?"

"Ah ... yes, sir."

To Consider West's vast relief, Ichabod Jones broke the heavy silence by observing, "A sentimental species, sailors."

Captain Morgan's frown shifted to the third mate's weather-seamed face. "Yes?"

"I remember how the men used to grumble about the captain's daughter, when I sailed on the brig *Pandora*, and Mrs. Morgan was just nine years old."

"They did?"

"Aye, on account of they reckoned she got in the way. Then one day the crew sent a deputation to the captain, refusing duty—and you know why, sir?"

"Tell me."

"They were all upset, every single one of them — because Captain Sherman had lost patience with little Abby's mischief, and spanked her."

Dead silence. Consider West could have sworn he heard Captain Morgan murmur, "I know exactly how he felt" — but it must have been his imagination, because after clearing his throat, Captain Morgan pushed back his chair and said in a perfectly businesslike fashion, "It's time we attended to our whale."

Then he headed up the stairs to the deck. Consider West followed him with a breath of relief.

The sun was at the meridian. It was very hot. The hard light bounced off the curve of the ocean and the slowly bobbing carcass. Tom Kanaka had supervised the lowering and lashing of the cutting platform. Now it hung on the far side of the whale, parallel with the side of the ship.

Seth gave Tom a nod of approval and then edged out onto the plank. The rail dug into his belly as he leaned over and inspected the carcass. The water boiled every now and then as a shark slithered up to snatch a mouthful. Mr. West took a boarding knife, leaned far over, and hacked a hole in the corner by the long jaw of the whale, where the blubber started. The cutting falls, dangling from the main yard, were poised overhead.

Seth took a long-handled cutting spade, and he and the mates began to slice systematically into the fat, scarfing it into a spiral strip two or three feet wide. The blubber on this great bull was more than a half-yard thick. The sun beat down on Seth's back as he worked. When a shark slid right up the whale's side, he jabbed at it, but missed. It fell back with a jawful of blubber.

Someone would have to be lowered onto the whale on a rope — the monkey rope — to insert the blubber hook into the hole that Consider West had hacked.

It was a heavy, cumbersome hook, dangling from the cutting falls, and it jerked up and down as the men tried to steady the windlass. Getting it into place was the most dangerous job involved in cutting in, and it was always given to the smallest and lightest man on board. Willie Cotton had been assigned the task. He now stood shivering on the waist deck with the monkey rope tied round him. Two muscular boatsteerers held the line. Seth could hear their muttered encouragement. Then Willie visibly braced himself, and dropped over the rail and onto the carcass.

A shark darted at once. Seth stabbed. The shark fell off, and the water briefly boiled. No one said a word; the tension was palpable. It was only the line about his waist that held Willie upright: the whale was slippery and bobbed in the water. He reached up for the hook — and another shark lunged.

Seth jabbed, Willie jumped back — one foot slipped, and he fell in a tumble. Seth jerked his spade back, afraid that he had cut the boy, but Willie was fine. He reached up again for the blubber hook, snagged it in his hand, and used it to heave himself back onto his feet. Then he jabbed it at the hole , but slipped repeatedly, kept out of the water only by the boatsteerers' hold on the monkey rope.

Then abruptly, all at once, the nervewracking business was over. The hook was firmly in place. Willie was swiftly hoisted back on deck.

"Man the windlass!" The men heaved at the handles, stamping their feet. The cutting falls straightened, and the heavy blubber hook took the strain.

"Heave!" sang Gustavus.

We'll heave him up from the sea below
Way ho, Susy-anna!
We'll heave him up, and away we'll go
We're all bound o'er the mountain, ho!

The maintop creaked like a tree in a storm, and the massive pendant groaned. Seth leaned over the rail and sliced powerfully at the junction of blubber and fiber to start the strip of scarfed fat moving up and away from the carcass. "Heave!" cried Mr. Jones, and the mainmast shuddered. The *Lizzie Ann* quivered, and every timber throbbed. The blubber held onto the carcass, and held... and held, while Seth and Tom and Consider West jabbed with their spades.

"Heave!"—and slowly the old ship leaned over the whale. How far before the blubber wrenched away from the carcass?

Groaning in every timber, the *Lizzie Ann* leaned a full fifteen degrees with the massive weight of the blubber, the hull leaning like doom over the whale and the cutting stage. Everyone stared at the hook in primitive terror—and then with a huge tearing noise the fibers parted, and the strip of blubber began to unwind from the rolling whale.

The *Lizzie Ann* tipped back to an even keel, and water washed back and forth beneath the cutting stage. "Heave!" cried Mr. Jones.

We 'll heave him up from down below
Way ho, Susy-anna!
Up from where the sharks do grow
We 're all bound o 'er the mountain, ho!

The blanket strip of blubber rose jerkily into the air, suspended from the maintop, as the hook was hauled higher and higher; the men chanted as they worked at the windlass. Then, abruptly, it jammed. The hook had reached the top; it could go no higher. The great ribbon of thick fat alternately stretched and wrinkled as the *Lizzie Ann* rolled. Ichabod Jones took a boarding knife and hacked a hole in the strip near the level of the deck.

A second set of cutting falls was lowered, with a toggle

at the end. Mr. Jones threaded the toggle through the hole, then slashed right through the strip just above the hole. The strip hanging from the first set of falls immediately shrank, bouncing, casting great drops of grease all over the deck and the laboring men.

Seth straightened, his back aching already. Ichabod Jones cried, "Lower away!" The freed strip of blubber was slowly lowered into the blubber room in the forehold, where a gang of men waited to cut it up into small pieces, ready for boiling into oil. The second set of cutting falls was now attached to the windlass. Seth returned to the backbreaking job of cutting blubber loose.

At supper time there was soft bread for all hands, freshly baked. Seth and the others ate hastily, and returned to work. By two in the morning, the blubber was almost all in. The great head was baled of its store of clear spermaceti oil, more valuable than gold, and then the carcass was cast away, to drift off, bobbing as massed sharks tugged and tore at cartilage and flesh. Still, the work continued, pieces of blubber being constantly forked into the pots in the tryworks, and hot oil constantly taken out, to be stored in holding barrels until it was cool enough to be pumped into the great oil casks in the hold.

At four in the morning, change of watch, men tumbled below and slept in the clothes they stood up in. Seth threw a canvas on the sofa in the transom cabin, and lay there for four brief hours, grasping some sleep in the cool of the early morning.

When he opened his smarting eyes, Abigail was sitting at the chart desk writing, her back to him. The low early sun shone in the stern lights and made a bright halo of her head. Seth lay watching her, drawing out the moment.

She turned, sensing his eyes upon her, and he sat up and said, "What are you doing?"

She smiled. "The log."

"What!" He jumped up, grabbed the book from her, and scowled at the rounded writing. It was the same hand that had kept the log while he was ill.

He said, "You did not do that!"

She held up her pen in ink-splotched fingers, her eyes glinting in a wicked smile. The awful jealousy twisted inside Seth again ... she was so pretty, this mischievous young minx. How could he have sailed without her ... and how could she have run off with that English peacock, Nicholas?

Infuriated by her insouciance, he snapped, "I prefer to keep my log myself."

"I can do it, you know," she pointed out. "I was taught by experts—my father, my mother, and a procession of first mates. My mother kept the log of the *Pandora*. And," she added broodingly, "my father appreciated her help."

"Help?" His echo was sardonic.

"Yes! I could be so useful, if you would only let me. I could do so much—if you would only listen."

"*Listen?* What the devil are you talking about?"

"If you had listened to me the night Broddy murdered Tamati, you'd have the brig for your own. We just needed to board her—it would have been so easy to claim her, because I had the ownership papers with me. But you wouldn't listen, and now God knows if we will ever find her again. She could be anywhere!"

"You told me the papers were stolen in Aspinwall."

She nodded. "But Obed was carrying notaries' copies, and I'd made him give them to me, because I was so angry when he lost the run of the *Lizzie Ann*."

"Copies—of the ownership papers?"

"Yes! They were made in New Bedford, before Obed sailed. I had asked him to take me to New Zealand on the *Curtsey* so I could reclaim the brig, and when he flatly refused to carry me, I flatly refused to give him the papers, and so he took notaries' copies, instead."

Seth's eyebrows were high.

434

She'd defied Obed. His smug cousin had met his match in this young spitfire. His anger was melted by warm amusement.

"And while I was waiting for you in Valparaiso, I went to the customs house to ask about the *Lizzie Ann*—I was so worried, Seth, that you might be wrecked, and even though I nagged, Obed did *not* take enough trouble to find you—and after the customs house men had reassured me on that score, I asked about the letter and they told me about the brig. They were nice," she said resentfully. "And attentive. And they told me that the *Pandora* sailed up and down the coast. So I set to and made another set of papers. I did not want to give up the only set I had, the others being stolen. And I badgered Mr. Melvin into signing and sealing them, though he didn't want to do it at all."

"He didn't?"

"At times, Seth, it is not easy, being a married woman. Mr. Melvin said, I am scandalized, ma'am, I do not like it, it is more proper, ma'am, to deal with a woman's husband."

Seth bit back the twitch of his lips and said severely, "He was absolutely right."

"But why? I wanted to file the claim as soon as possible, before the man who stole the originals in Aspinwall put in a claim of his own. It would have all worked out, if you had only listened!"

"But I thought the burglary was opportunistic."

"That's what I thought, too—but then I became convinced that the thief deliberately carried Emily out of the room to clear the coast so he could search for the papers and steal them. And, Seth, I think I know who it was. When we first arrived in the House of the Ewer, Emily and I were walking down the stairs, and Victoria and Obed were in the courtyard having drinks with Mr. and Mrs. Perry—and Emily was terrified, Seth; she said she saw the man who carried her out into the Aspinwall street. It must have been Mr. Perry!"

"There was no one else in the courtyard?"

"Just the servant with the tray of drinks. And when you think about it, it makes sense. Mr. Perry is a shipping agent, so he would have known that the *Pandora* was commanded by a native with no papers; that all he needed was to get hold of the documents, and then he could claim the brig for himself."

Seth was abruptly intrigued; like his Aunt Fanny, he was always fascinated by a mystery. He said, "But how did he know you were carrying the papers? How did he know you were the rightful owner?"

"Victoria told him, perhaps — or Broddy. He and Broddy seem to be very close, so... But because I was so sure of it I searched his office whenever I could."

"You ... *what?*"

"Searched his office."

"Oh, my God." Seth had thought things were bad enough when he'd arrived in Valparaiso, but now it seemed that it was only by the grace of heaven that he hadn't found his wife under arrest in the fort.

"But my search was a failure. So I made my own copy, as I told you, and gave them to Lieutenant Nicholas so he could file a claim of piracy."

Nicholas. Seth snapped, "How dare you."

"But I did it for us, Seth. I so very much wanted to give you the brig."

For a moment Seth trembled with the conflicting emotions inside him. He wanted desperately to haul her into his arms and kiss some sense into her scatterbrained head ... but he was embroiled in the hellish business of cutting in and trying out. He had slept all standing, in his clothes, and the clothes he wore were filthy.

He turned on his heel and went back to work. The door slammed as he went.

Nineteen

The whale made one hundred and thirty barrels of oil, which took thirty hours to boil out.

The last oil was rendered just before dinner, and while they ate the fires went out in the furnace. In the afternoon the watch began to scrub ship, with sand and lye from the ashes and endless salt water, and at dogwatch all hands got on their knees and holystoned until the chipped yellow pine planks were clean again.

There goes one!
Hurrah for us, got one!
Now one whale is done!
And there's a-plenty more to come!

One hundred and thirty barrels, a tally that fully warranted the round of grog that Seth issued to all hands. It would be written up in the papers, and talked about for years—and would fetch the handsome sum of four thousand dollars, at the current market price. Seth, a warm glow inside him, ordered the yards braced and sail shortened for the night. Then he went down to his stateroom, where, by arrangement with Tucker, a canvas bath of hot water was waiting.

The door opened while he was luxuriating. He glanced up through steam and the smoke of his cigar and saw Abigail. The long late-afternoon light came in the sidelights and glinted on the bright hair and the plain brown dress she wore. She had a towel slung over one shoulder and she was carrying a bucket that steamed and smelled of an infusion of old tea.

He bit down the hunger at the sight of her, and said, "What the devil are you up to?"

She smiled beautifully. "I've come to give you a scrub." Then she set the bucket down. Abigail liked to add odd and imaginative potions to her rinsing water, Seth remembered. She added vinegar to the final rinse when she scrubbed down cabin walls. Tea, he gathered, was for rinsing people.

She had a small bottle in her other hand, and she set that down, too, as she knelt down beside him. Seth, very conscious of what was going to happen when she put her hands on his skin, said quickly, "I've been in the habit of washing myself for quite some years, now."

"But when you have a wife, you should take advantage of it! Anyway," she meditated, "I don't know how old you are."

"Twenty-six last Christmas."

"Oh dear! At twenty-six last Christmas you need all the comfort you can get. You don't mind, really, admit it."

He scowled, feeling like Methuselah, and she put her head a little on one side, and smiled a coaxing smile. How could he resist her?

He nodded and she set to, looking pleased. Her hand dipped in the water and felt about for the square of flannel, while his body responded with unseemly excitement. "Christmas," she said, lathering his back, and clicked her tongue. "I missed your birthday." Her head came round from behind his shoulder. "If you give me those cigars, I'll give them to you for your birthday."

"Very generous," he grunted, and she moved behind him again. The square of flannel moved over his neck and back and shoulders, and goose flesh rose with the delicious sensation. Then she poured water over his hair, and he hurriedly snatched the cigar from his mouth.

She rubbed a cold lotion from the bottle into his hair, and he listened with his eyes shut to the foaming sounds. There was a strong smell of ammonia and rosewater. Her fingers probed and scrubbed, massaging his scalp, her thumbs low in the places where the knots of tension throbbed. His head bobbed with her movements, and he could feel her breasts pressing against his back. He was a vessel of pure sensation.

She wet his head again with a mug of water from the bucket, and the scent of the tea mingled with the sting of the shampoo. She massaged soap again, and murmured wickedly close to his ear, "You like this, I can tell."

He blinked his eyes open, and her face came round from behind his shoulder again, and she smiled. She was bewitching him with her smiles. He said, "Yes, damn it, I do."

"Did you miss me when you lost the run of the *Curtsey?*"

Miss her? He had thought he would go crazy. He snapped, "You shouldn't have been there."

"I know, and I'm sorry—but you should admit that it was Obed's fault, not mine. He took advantage of me. I was most terribly angry with him."

"So you said." It occurred to Seth with some amusement that Obed might have been very glad to get rid of Abigail in Valparaiso.

"And that oil! I may be doing Obed a severe injustice, Seth, but I truly think that if he had beaten you to that whale, he would never have allowed that our ships were mated. However," she sighed, "that's the way Obed is, and we just have to accept it. He's too old to change, and after

439

all, he *is* family."

She gave him a dimpled smile, and disappeared behind his shoulder again. Her soapy fingers landed on his neck and rubbed, and his entire being responded. He felt as if his bones were dissolving into liquid sensation. She kneaded the hollows of his spine, moving down, down, and then she massaged the broad kite-shaped muscles of his back. Waves of warm languor rocked him, and his mind seemed detached from his body.

He mumbled, "It's amazing Obed did not claim the brig."

"What?" She laughed. "I hadn't thought of that! But I didn't go to the customs house until after the *Curtsey* sailed, and I had never told him about Ichabod Jones and his story of sailing from Rarotonga on the brig. Mind you," she ruminated, "it could have been a close run thing. The customs house men said a captain had asked after that New Zealand letter, and it must have been Obed. It's lucky he didn't think of checking up on the *Pandora*."

"Letter?"

"Yes, the one that Obed carried for a little while, that was addressed to me in New Bedford. The customs house sent it back to New Zealand; they said it belonged there. Isn't that strange? I suppose they returned it to sender, such a waste after all those miles."

The letter; Seth had forgotten about it. He said, "It might not have been Obed who asked."

"But who else could it be?"

"Some other man who knows your affairs."

Her fingers stilled, and then left his back. "Seth, what do you mean?"

"I was the last to hear about your flight from Panama, for instance, and it took McGhie to tell me that you had run away with a man, that you and that man gambled on the steamer—that you married me because Nicholas wouldn't have you."

She was in front of him, her face stricken.

"Broddy told you that? For God's sake, Seth, when did he tell you that lie?"

"A lie?" he shouted. "You deny it? When McGhie spent four days recounting the details, and you confessed to poker-playing yourself!"

"Four days—on the *Lizzie Ann*? Did he come with you from Talcahuano on the *Lizzie Ann*? And spin those—those fabrications, those lies? He twisted the truth, Seth—it was nothing like that!"

"You're denying you were in love with Nicholas?"

"*What?*" She laughed in amazement. "No, of course I wasn't. The very idea is ridiculous."

Ridiculous. The word touched a chord in him, and suddenly, abruptly, with a shaft of relief so acute it was like a pain, he believed her. McGhie had indeed twisted the facts—but why?

Abigail said angrily, "And it's unfair, too, to insinuate that other men know all about my affairs."

"Yes? And what about the riddle? Obed knew of it; Jireh knew of it. Can you say without a word of a lie that no other men knew about it before you bothered to tell me?"

Abigail took a breath, ready to shout at him. Then she stopped, her eyes widening. Seth said, "Well?"

"There was someone ... on the mule ride to Panama ... but it was just idle conversation."

"Who?"

She bit her lip. "Mr. Nicholas."

After the intense relief it hurt, bitterly and utterly without logic. He snapped, "Get out."

"But—"

"Pray leave me. I didn't ask to be scrubbed, and I don't want it."

"Seth Morgan, you are absolutely impossible!" she exclaimed, and stood up, and tipped the bucket of water over his head. Then she slammed out of the stateroom.

When the door opened again Seth was furiously mopping his body with a towel. The cigar was floating in the tub. Abigail was flushed, her expression contrite. "Seth," she said, "I'm sorry."

"For which of your sins?" he tartly inquired. Water had slopped all over the floor.

"For tipping the water over your head; it was childish and silly, but you made me very angry. Why Broddy told you that nasty nonsense, I have not a single notion, but it's absolutely untrue. Mr. Nicholas simply helped me carry my bags, and when we boarded the steamer, Mrs. Perry took me under her wing. They coaxed me into trying to play poker, but Mrs. Perry was there all the time."

"What?" He stilled, staring at her. "The *Perrys* were there?"

"Of course! It must have been Mrs. Perry who told Broddy about the poker playing—but only to entertain him, I'm sure. She wouldn't have meant any harm—after all, she's the person who knows best how much I love you, Seth."

"*Love?*" Water dripped off him. "You *love* me?"

"Of course. Didn't you know?" She blushed deeply, and said, "As Mrs. Perry deduced, I love you an awful lot. I think I've loved you since the day I first met you, though I was too young and stupid to know it—and most immodestly, too, I'm afraid."

There was a story there, he knew it, but he didn't care. He was brimming with primitive lust and joy and he said, "Oh God, how wonderful—why didn't you tell me before?" Then, without waiting for an answer, he grabbed her up and tumbled her onto the bed. The bed swung and Abigail shrieked, and he covered her with his body, damp and naked as he was.

She wriggled, intensely alive beneath him on the bed, and he said, "Oh God, how I love you, Abby," and dipped his head and kissed her passionately.

To his delight and amazement, she was as hungry for him as he was for her. She writhed with eagerness, caressing his cool back with feverish hands, her mouth sweet and hot and intimate as she responded to his kisses, and she squirmed to help him as he undressed her. He dropped the chemise on the floor. She was naked, and when he kissed her pretty breasts she gasped and arched and hollowed to receive him, caressing him with her seeking hands. When he slid into her the sensation was exquisite, like tightly enclosing, pulsing silk.

Abigail whispered, "Seth." He stilled, and she shifted under him in a series of little easing jumps, making herself comfortable, bending her knees to twine her legs about him. He grunted with surprise and shifted a little himself, and suddenly he was within her more deeply than he had ever been before.

He lanced her slowly, trembling as he reached for her heart. The pleasure was shocking in its intensity. The ship creaked around them, and the evening air was blurred with their panting and the hammer of his pulse. He thought his ears would burst with the mounting tension, and that his blood would boil. He gasped, and thrust hard. Then, in his shuddering crisis, he heard her exclaim, and felt her clench and throb about him, and it was like nothing ... ever ... that he had felt before in his life.

When he opened his eyes the stateroom was dark. They were inextricably entangled: it was very hard to decide where Abigail, his wife, ended, and he himself, Seth, began.

Her voice was wondering. "Seth?"

"M'm?"

"Does that ... sensation ... have a name?"

"What?"

"That ... feeling, like falling over a waterfall, into forever."

He smiled, his mouth in the curve of her throat. "They call it *spending*."

She was silent a moment, then said tentatively, "Seth, do you think I'm a shameless hussy, behaving like that?"

"No, of course not." He kissed her. "You were wonderful."

"So Mrs. Perry was right," she said, sounding enlightened. "A husband really does want a harlot in his bed."

There was no answer. Seth was fast asleep, still holding her cradled close to his chest.

Some hours later Seth wakened, to find Abigail shaking him. It was very dark and hot and quiet. The decks above were silent, and the sea was calm. Seth said dazedly, "What...?"

"You were having a nightmare, crying out my name."

A nightmare. Abigail had been standing frozen in the Valparaiso alley, while Tamati pushed her and pushed her to try to get her out of the way, and all the time McGhie had the pistol in his fist, aiming, ready to fire.

Seth pulled Abigail into his arms and held her tight, and said, "Oh Abby, I dreamed you were dead."

It was the same dream that had haunted him during his fever, when he had believed that they were sailing away from Abigail. He had dreamed then that she was in some horrifying danger and that he would never see her again.

She kissed his damp forehead. "Well, I'm here and as alive as ever." Then she said curiously, "How did I die?"

Seth was silent, struggling to separate nightmare from memory. In his dreams Tamati shoved at Abigail but she didn't fall. Instead she stood frozen, staring at McGhie and Seth, and then the pistol shot rang out. In the dream she had taken the bullet that had killed Tamati.

The reality: striding up the street, torn with jealousy and rage, hurrying to get to Abigail and face her with the truth of what McGhie had been saying, McGhie at his side ... and McGhie really did have the pistol in his hand, raised and aimed.

444

Seth could remember the silhouette of the thick finger on the trigger. Why? How had he anticipated the attack? The Maori wasn't even in sight then ... or had he recognized the brig *Pandora* as they had come into the harbor?

Then Seth saw what McGhie had seen — Abigail, standing at the mouth of the alley. Seth had stopped short in surprise, McGhie had started running ... Tamati had come bursting out, and with a savage screech he had hauled Abigail into the alley — and shoved her until she fell, out of the field of fire.

McGhie's pistol had been one of Colt's revolvers; Tamati had an old musket. The same instant that Abigail tumbled inside the building McGhie's pistol fired, and the sound of the musket shot had come like an echo.

The pistol and *then* the musket.

Seth lurched up in bed, and exclaimed, "Oh, my God!"

Tamati had been killed by the bullet that had been intended for Abigail.

At dawn, the *Lizzie Ann* anchored in the shallow dark-green waters of Lord Chatham Island, in the Galápagos group.

Seth gave the whole crew the day's liberty — and why not, for no one could desert at the island, there being nowhere to run away to? He and Abigail stood at the rail, watching the boats pull away from the ship. Everyone went, except for the cook and the steward — and Ichabod Jones, because Seth had particularly asked the third mate to stay behind.

The early morning sparkled. There was a mist on the upper peaks of the island. The shallows were thick with tossing kelp, and reptiles lumbered and flopped from the rocks. They watched the men land, and could hear them hollering to each other.

They would spend the day roasting crabs, and hunting the huge, slow tortoises that the New Englanders called *terrapin,* though they knew quite well that they were

445

tortoises, just as they called whales *fish,* even though they were perfectly aware that whales were warm-blooded sea-going hippopotamuses.

Abigail said, very subdued, "But why would Broddy want me dead?"

Dead. Seth put his arm around her, and she leaned against him a little, in the confiding way that she had. McGhie had been determined to get Abigail away from her husband's protecting presence, Seth brooded; that was why he had put her escape from Panama in the worst possible light, why he had worked so hard to fuel Seth's jealousy.

What would McGhie have done if Abigail hadn't shipped as Seth's cabin boy? It would have been easy enough to knock her over the head on the steamer passage, and drop her overboard. Then McGhie could have left the steamer at Paita; he would not have been forced to quit this coast.

He said, "The brig."

"The *Pandora?"*

"I don't believe Perry stole those papers. I know him well; he's my agent on this coast, and he's too lazy to be dishonest. You said you rushed to file a claim in case the thief beat you to it—but how do you know that he hadn't beaten you to it already?"

Abigail stared at him, her eyes widening. She remembered how Mr. Nicholas's face had gone blank when he saw the name of the brig on the papers she gave him, and how slowly and thoughtfully he had read them.

And then, after Tamati was dead, Broddy had run after Mr. Nicholas, calling out his name.

Seth nodded. "God knows where the brig is now, but I'd bet anything you like that Nicholas and McGhie are on board of her."

He turned and called down the skylight to where Ichabod Jones was sitting at the table, and the third mate came up at once. When he saw Abigail he took his pipe out of his mouth, and ducked his head in the dignified way he had.

Seth said, "The brig you sailed on from Rarotonga to California—you're certain she was the *Pandora?*"

"Positive, sir. I served on her for over a year."

"But you didn't recognize the captain?"

Ichabod Jones paused, frowning. "He was Maori—a New Zealand kanaka—but I couldn't tell much more than that, as he was so terribly scarred. It was a wonder he didn't die of those wounds. And he raved something dreadful, too. No, as far as I could tell, I had never seen him before."

Abby asked, "Would you be surprised if I told you he was Tamati?"

"Tamati?" Mr. Jones had to think, but then he said, "You mean the young Maori who worked for your father, and helped him on the brig as well?"

She nodded, and he said, "I would indeed have trouble believing you, ma'am."

"Believing me? Why?"

"Well, the captain of the brig raved of revenge—and it was revenge for the murder of his father. And I was under the impression, Miz Abby, that Tamati didn't have one."

Abby made a big batch of gingerbread, and at dinnertime she and Seth went with Tucker and Ichabod Jones to the beach, where she gave the treat to the men. They looked so happy, wading in the surf and loafing in the shade of the scrubby trees.

Seth took Abigail off to explore the ruins of the convict huts. She climbed a broken wall and declaimed at the empty sky:

With sugar and rice and apples I'm nice
Although I am wood, I taste very good.
When I am high, all sails fly
When I am low, watch for a blow!

"What am I?" she cried, and launched herself at her husband. Seth fell over when he caught her, and they rolled together on the grass, laughing. Seth had never known it was possible to feel such concentrated happiness. He had so nearly killed her with the blindness of his jealousy. If she hadn't shipped as his cabin boy... Cabin boy! He hoped the gossips of New Bedford would find the yarn too incredible to repeat.

He gently bit her earlobe and shoved a caressing hand through her hair, and said, "A barometer." She was like a barometer, too, he thought: even after the worst of storms she bounced back to being sunny.

"And cinnamon," she said.

She was like that, too—sweet and spicy. He kissed her and she kissed him back and they lay together a long time.

Then she sighed, rolled over, and sat up, and said, "I should have known all along that Tamati couldn't kill my father. And I should have known he would want revenge for his death."

"Your father? I thought he raved about the death of his own father."

"His father was my father. Tamati considered himself Sherman. He was totally ours. My father was his."

Seth sat up too, and said, "My God."

So, he realized, McGhie had killed Nathaniel Sherman. Tamati had done his utmost to protect his adoptive father, and had been horribly wounded in the fight. Then he had escaped on the brig *Pandora* ... and had pursued McGhie as far as California.

"That was why Broddy wanted to kill me. As long as I was alive, there was a chance I would find out that he had murdered my father, and would report it to the authorities. And there was always the chance, too, that Tamati would find me, and tell me the truth, and so Tamati had to be killed, too. It was nothing to do with the brig."

"Why not?"

"While it's possible that it was Broddy was the thief who ransacked our room and stole the papers while Victoria and I were searching for Emily, he could not have been the man who carried Emily out of the room. He was talking to me at the time. And she was so sure she saw that man in the courtyard of the House of the Ewer—and Mr. Perry was the only man there."

"No, he wasn't."

"Well, there was Obed, of course, but—"

"The servant. The man with the tray of drinks. To a little girl, Spanish servants would look all the same. McGhie bribed a servant to carry Emily outside. Who knows what reason he gave, if any?—but it was to make sure the coast was clear for the theft. It had to be him—the only people there who knew you had the papers for the brig were Victoria and McGhie. Then, the next time he was in Valparaiso, he used the papers to register his claim for the brig."

Abby thought about it, nodded, and sighed. "Yes, that makes sense. And he either stole our clothing to muddy the trail, or other people saw their chance and grabbed it when they saw the state of the luggage in the empty room. But why would Broddy do such horrible things, Seth? He and my father were great friends ... they laughed and drank and played billiards together."

"And no doubt McGhie was your father's proxy. Only he wanted to keep the money from the sale of your father's property all to himself."

"But Broddy's so poor! He can't have the money—he's dirt-poor, and he hates it. You should have seen his face when he talked about his bad fortune—it mortifies him. That's why he stole the papers, and then the brig."

Seth lay back on the grass, his arm under his head, frowning as he stared at the sky and wondered what had happened to the money from the sale of Sherman's lands. The proceeds must be somewhere ... money that belonged rightfully to Abigail. Like that fortune Nathaniel Sherman had been so secretive about, sending riddles instead of letters...

Seth sat up with a jerk. "The letter! The letter that went back to New Zealand — that letter must have been from your father!"

"My father?" Abigail's eyes widened.

"With the name of the proxy!"

"Surely not!"

"Maybe not — but McGhie would fear so, and I'll bet you anything you like that it was McGhie, not Obed, who asked after that letter in Valparaiso. And the officer would have told him exactly what he told you — that it had been returned to New Zealand."

At that moment Seth became utterly certain that he knew where the brig *Pandora* was headed. Next day at dawn the *Lizzie Ann* weighed anchor, set all sail, and steered sou'west, to catch the trades on the way to New Zealand.

Twenty

At daylight Hunter, in the topmast, called out that he had raised land, and by breakfast New Zealand was in sight from the deck. It was dead calm, with the islands called Three Kings about fifteen miles off their beam. It was a day of bracing yards for every breath.

Next dawn, the mauve-and-blue hills became green and brown. Abigail stood at the rail and watched the landscape of home rise from the sea. The winds were light and baffling, and for a long time the shadowy shapes became no clearer, but then the wind picked up, and an hour later she could see kauri forests and gullies.

By mid-afternoon the green arms of Doubtless Bay were closing about them, with the fortifications of the two extensive Maori villages to each side. Then Mangonui was in sight. She could see the river where Consider West and his crew had picked her up on that fateful fishing day. The three European houses were there, just as before, and she remembered exactly where she would find Captain Butler's house, at the end of a creek, on the point. She could see the ruins of her father's burned-out house on the crest of the hill where she had ridden so often. Greenery was sprouting in the ashes. On the beach where Tamati had waited with her old mare, Rosie, there was now a straggle of thatched huts, and a store with a rusted iron roof.

It was winter, well outside the whaler-recruiting season, so instead of a flock of whaleships in the harbor, there was just one. The *Erasmus!* What was Jireh doing here? Then Abigail forgot it, for she spied another vessel, one with just two masts—a brig, almost hidden behind a little headland. And the brig was the *Pandora.*

"Seth!" she cried, but he was too busy to hear her. With sails clewed up and main topsail backed, the *Lizzie Ann* was heading sedately for a mooring by the *Erasmus*, and Abigail could see men in the rigging of the other vessel turning their heads to watch. Then everyone started yelling at once.

"Hard down on the helm!" Seth roared—but too late. Instead of obediently dropping her anchor, the *Lizzie Ann* kept on going, steering as if by deliberate intent straight for the bow of Jireh Mitchell's ship.

It was not Consider West's fault: it was the fault of the anchor chain. It had kinked on the windlass drum. Mr. West ran about the foredeck and Seth cursed picturesquely, but there was nothing they could do about it. *Lizzie Ann* larboard davits grappled the *Erasmus* fly-jibboom in a long splintering collision, and both ships spun with the impact, and crashed together again.

When the banging sounds finally stopped, the two ships lay just a few fathoms from the beach, almost in reach of the scruffy little town. There was a long appalled silence, then Jireh Mitchell came bursting out onto his deck."It's that pirate Morgan again!" he shouted.

"Jireh, it's no joking matter!" Abigail exclaimed, still very shaken. "How long has that brig has been in port?"

"What brig?" said Jireh. "Oh, that one. I can't say I took much notice."

He had come in three days earlier, after leaving Martha at Russell in the Bay of Islands, and since then had been busy.

Now, as he bitterly complained, he was going to be busier still, while Seth was silently grim. The *Erasmus* and the *Lizzie Ann* were united by a tangle of spars, but that was not the worst of it. The *Erasmus* jib rigging was a tangle, and her fore topsail hamper was not much better, while on the *Lizzie Ann* the three boats on the larboard side were smashed to kindling.

Jireh and Seth spent the last hours of daylight surveying the wreckage and making lists of work to be done. When dusk descended, Jireh and his men jumped from the *Lizzie Ann* onto their own ship, and disappeared below, intent on supper. As soon as they were gone, Seth lowered the surviving starboard boat, and he and Mr. Jones and Tom Kanaka, with three oarsmen, headed quietly out to the brig.

Abigail stood at the rail and watched them go. Her shawl was hugged tightly about her, and she shivered every now and then. Lights flickered in the string of huts along the waterfront, and she could see the distant glow of fires in the native villages, but otherwise the water was perfectly black. Just as remembered, packs of dogs barked and howled in the distance. Cobwebby mists touched her hair and her face.

The splash of oars was startlingly close when she first heard it. Then there was a stealthy rattle as the starboard boat hooked onto the falls. Seth was the first to clamber on deck. She ran to him. His sleeve was heavy with dampness. He gave her hand a reassuring squeeze and then they went below to the transom cabin.

As soon as the door was shut she said, "Is she the *Pandora*?"

"Yes."

"And?"

"She's abandoned—but only just recently, I think. There's even food in the pantry."

"So she's still seaworthy?"

"Aye—with work and money. And," he added, "a new suit of sails."

"Her canvas is that bad?"

"It's not there at all. All her sails have been taken away — there's not a stitch left upon her."

Abigail stared. It was incredible. Why would anyone take away her sails? A ship was useless without them; the most ignorant of thieves would know that a brig with her canvas was a great deal more valuable than a few sheets of canvas.

Before she could speak, there was a thud as someone jumped from the *Erasmus* onto the *Lizzie Ann,* and then Jireh's hearty voice as he called out from the companionway door. He was carrying a full bottle of brandy, and was obviously in great need of company. Seth sighed, and invited him in.

Abigail fixed a tray in the pantry with fresh bread, ham and pickles, and plum cake from a recent baking. She put hot coffee on the tray, too. Seth took his mug gratefully, and ate with single-minded appetite, but Jireh's whole attention was taken up with drinking brandy and talking: it was obvious he had been drinking already.

He was lonely, too, having lacked good company over the past three days. "You won't find an American in this far-famed city of Mangonui, let alone a consul," he said. "All the trading is done through an Englishman by the name of Butler, who lives up the creek. If I remember a-right, his advertisements in the New Bedford shipping papers claim that there are no grogsellers in the place, but that's a lie, because there is a grogshop on the beach that sells that most pernicious kind of liquor, well adulterated with tobacco juice to keep carousers awake and buying more his poison. Butler is a decent, businesslike fellow, otherwise, with ambitions to be the customs house officer here. He will pilot your ship too — for a price."

This came with a meaningful look at Seth, who grimaced, being fully aware that the collision was his fault — though what difference the presence of a pilot would have made to a kinked chain was debatable. And the damage to his ship was far greater than to the lucky *Erasmus*. Despite the spare boat, and having boards in his hold to build more boats, if necessary, the loss of all three larboard whaleboats was a severe blow.

"I can sell you three boats," Jireh said, with his usual facility for reading minds.

"But surely you can't spare them?"

"I don't need 'em. My ship is full."

"What!" Seth tried to remember how many months had passed since he had left Mitchell at Capricorn Island. Back then, Jireh had reported something over one thousand barrels, all taken while mated with other ships.

"Four thousand barrels," said Jireh, and grinned as if he had cracked a joke.

Seth was not amused. Even with the famous luck of the *Erasmus,* completing the tally in such a short time was astounding. How the devil had Mitchell done it?

Jireh said, "I did it the easy way—traded for two thousand, five hundred barrels of shore-caught oil in Port Nicholson."

Seth wondered what Jireh had paid for that oil, but knew he wouldn't get an answer. "So you're homeward bound?"

"Nope. I'm off to Manila to sell my oil. Then I'll head for Canton, to speculate in China goods."

"You're giving up the whaling business?" Seth was astonished—almost shocked. Then he remembered Jireh's meanderings when he had first met him at Capricorn Island, and thought that he should not be so surprised.

"They all say that it's the smell of cutting in and trying out that keeps Martha so sick. She tells me that whalemen's work is a vile business, anyway. And who am I to disagree?"

Seth was silent. Young bloods like Consider West enjoyed the thrill of the dangerous chase, but everyone loathed the ghastliness of cutting in and trying out: it was only the fact that everyone had a share in the oil that kept the men at work. But Mitchell's oil was worth well over one hundred thousand dollars in the Manila market. There were few ways, if any, for a seafaring man to make that kind of money. He wondered what profit there was in trading Chinese goods.

"But I dropped Martha at Russell anyway—it might be the whaling that makes her sick, but I didn't want to risk watching her vomit her heart out all the way to Canton and back. Russell is a popular place for captains' wives to stop, to await—"

"Await?" said Abigail alertly.

"A happy event," said Jireh, but his expression wasn't happy. Then he said, "I got letters from home when I was at Russell. Charity is married."

Abigail exclaimed, "*Married?*"

Then Seth saw her quickly look at him: she was wondering how the news affected him, he realized. All he felt was astonishment, as he couldn't picture Jezekiel Mitchell without a cowed female in the house. As for Charity, he could scarcely remember what she looked like.

"To a cleric by the name o' Smith," said Jireh.

"That's nice!" said Abigail, and actually did look pleased.

"And," Jireh added wryly, "my father is also wed."

So that was why Jezekiel Mitchell had allowed his daughter's nuptials to take place—and why Jireh had come seeking company, Seth realized. A letter like that, so full of the changes back home, would unsettle the most placid of men.

He said, "So you have a stepmother now. Who is she?"

"That's the problem. My father mentioned a widow named Mary—but which Mary is beyond me to guess. I can think o' three that fit the description."

"Only three?" said Seth, his expression perfectly bland. "I can think of four."

"Oh God," said Jireh, and winced. "I'd forgotten the one in Dartmouth."

When Seth looked at Abigail she was red in the face from holding in her laughter. Then both abruptly sobered, as Jireh said, "Have you figured out the riddle yet?"

Seth said tersely, "No."

"But Mangonui is the place, is it not, where the fortune is to be found—once its nature is puzzled out? Isn't that why you came here?"

"There's no gold in that valley, if that's what you mean."

"Did I mention gold?" Jireh's smile was apologetic.

Seth paused, and then observed meaningfully, "You said you came in for potatoes."

"Aye, I did."

"And you expected to have any luck, at this time of the year?"

"Well, it didn't look hopeful," Jireh admitted. "Butler told me the natives are all a-planting their potato plantations, and that there were none of last season's left to trade, but when I steered for the nearest village I found the folks very obliging with a few barrels o' their native sweet potatoes, which are just as good. Tobacco is the only currency, but I have lots of that. I can sell you some, if you're short."

Seth flicked an eyebrow and said, "Thank you kindly, but no." Then he added, "It's a relief they're not demanding guns and ammunition."

"The chiefs are very much in control here. They're a friendly set, very generous with their hand-shaking and their hospitality, but determined on keeping the peace. Some can speak good English, too, and weren't hesitant about telling me the rules. There's a curfew, and if any men are found on shore after dark, the ship is fined. Any drunken misbehavior, and you can be certain that it won't go unpunished." Then Jireh said more slowly, "I wonder if I could ask a favor?"

"Of course."

"You'll have to go to Russell if you want letters, as they're all deposited there, Butler not having been appointed customs house officer yet. And I'd be greatly obliged if you'd leave Abby there for a few months. Perhaps while you whale on the Line."

Seth arched his brows, very aware of Abigail's stiffening. "Why?" he asked.

"Martha is being a trifle unhandy. She swears she won't be in Russell when I get back from the Orient — but if you left Abigail to live with her, I know she'd be a lot more agreeable."

When Seth looked at Abigail, she was staring at him, her eyes wide, and her expression an eloquent mixture of horror, appeal, and challenge. He thought of the weeks she had been stranded on the *Curtsey*, tending to Victoria and her fractious baby while he searched the ground for her.

"Seth?" Jireh prompted. His smile was coaxing.

Seth shrugged. "I'll give it some thought."

Seth saw Jireh to the rail with a distinct sense of relief, but Jireh refused to go until they had settled the sale of the three whaleboats. Seth bargained him down to a fair price easily — Jireh was definitely giving up the whaling business, he concluded, and wondered again what profit there was in trading.

Even after the bargain was made, Jireh lingered on, obviously waiting for an answer to his proposition that Abigail be left in Russell. At long last he gave up, vaulted the rail and disappeared. Seth turned on his heel and ran down the companionway.

Abigail was tidying up in the transom cabin. As soon as she heard him she stilled and exclaimed, "Seth, you wouldn't — "

He interrupted her, saying, "Look at these." He took two wads of papers out of an inner pocket, and handed them to her. Then he picked up his untouched glass of brandy and sat on the sofa, watching her as she spread the papers on the desk.

The documents, stained at the edges with seawater, were all signed and sealed, and both were sets of papers for the brig. One was the original set, the one that had been stolen in Aspinwall, and the other was the set of copies Abigail had made in Valparaiso, and had given to Lieutenant Nicholas.

She said, "You found them on the *Pandora*?"

"I broke open every locker. They were in the corner cuddy."

"So Broddy really was the thief," she sighed. "You were right—he must have bribed a servant to carry Emily outside. Oh dear God, Emily could have died, just so he could have the leisure to hunt for these papers, and steal them."

"Yes. And there is this, too."

It was a clipping from the San Francisco paper *Alta California,* reporting a letter received from Captain Mara of HMS *Nympha,* which announced the piratical seizure of brig *Pandora* by persons unknown, and testified that papers certifying the ownership of said brig *Pandora* had been entrusted to him by Captain McGhie, who could depose to their authenticity, and requested that the Governor of California should take steps for the apprehension of the offenders, and the recovery of the vessel. It had been published many months ago, not long after Abigail had absconded to Paita.

"It seems strange that he went off without the papers, seeing they served him so well," she said.

"What would be the point of keeping them? The brig's abandoned."

"But that's another mystery—why abandon her, and take her sails away?"

"I don't know. There's still cargo in her holds." Seth shivered. In the dark, cluttered hold, for just a second, he had been transported back to that nightmare forehold on the *Pierrot*, when Edmund had been lurking in a crevice, gripping that boarding knife. There had been the same smell of fear and rats. Something had rustled, and the hairs had stood up on the nape of his neck. Then he had moved more quickly than intended, springing up the ladder to rejoin Tom Kanaka and the others on deck.

Abigail said ruefully, "And you were right about Lieutenant Nicholas, too. I was a fool to trust him with those copies I made. Now that I know about it, it's obvious he knew that Broddy had already laid a claim to the brig. His face went blank when he saw the brig's name, and then he took a long time to read them. Undoubtedly, he was working out a way to blackmail Broddy into giving him a share."

Seth paused to drain his glass, then reached into another pocket. "There's more—another set of papers," he said. These documents were ship's papers, too, signed and sealed and travel-worn, with a Bill of Sale on the top. He handed them to her, saying grimly, "They tell us what McGhie did with your father's money, Abby—and the reason he murdered your father."

The papers were for the clipper ship *Rainbow*. The Bill of Sale transferred ownership of the ship from a merchant in Port Nicholson to Captain Broderick McGhie, of the same port. And the time of the sale pre-dated Nathaniel Sherman's murder by a week.

In the morning, Seth dressed in his shore-going clothes, and put the original papers for the *Pandora* in his pocket, along with the copy of the Bill of Sale that Abigail had made. She had written an affidavit for the English authorities in Russell, giving Seth authority to claim the brig on her behalf, as her husband, and also to claim any letters held for Miss Sherman. Then at the rail she clung to him.

"You'll take great care?"

"Of course." Tom Kanaka, looking amazingly different in a black broadcloth suit with a white stock tied under his tattooed chin, strode self-consciously up to them. He was going with Seth, along with four men to help sail the boat.

"And you have to be gone for two whole days?"

"Not two whole days. I'll be back midmorning tomorrow, with luck," he said, and dropped over the side.

Abigail held the rail, watching the boat as the lugsail took the wind. Within minutes it was lost to sight, tacking around a headland on the way south to the Bay of Islands. The deck was busy, with carpentering gangs working on the broken davits, and others clearing up broken spars. The larboard watch was assembling in the waist, talking animatedly as they waited to go on shore for four hours' liberty. Abigail turned and trudged down the stairs.

After the cleaning was done, and the dough left to prove, time hung heavy on her hands. She couldn't settle; the papers and their implications were gnawing at her mind. At length she took out the brig's documentation that Seth had left behind, and studied it again. It was very fortunate, she thought, that she had insisted on making copies of the *Pandora*'s papers—not once, but twice. After folding the pages and putting them away again, she spread out the papers for the *Rainbow.* For quite five minutes, she sat very still, thinking.

Abruptly, she rummaged in the desk for pen and ink and paper. Then she slowly and carefully began to make a copy. It was like old times. She worked the rest of the day and far into the night, copying by the light of a lamp. Even then, sleep proved elusive: the bed was too empty, her mind too full. She was pleased to get up at the first light of dawn, to find the bay shrouded with fog.

At the rail, she tried to peer into the mist, but could see nothing. She heard paddles before she knew that there was a canoe nearby. The narrow prow nudged through the gray curtain. It was a small canoe, with two Maori boys in it. She summoned half-forgotten words and called out to them in their language.

They hesitated, and then paddled up to the side. She signed to them to wait, dashed below, and came up again. Consider West was too busy and bad-tempered to pay attention—one of the men, Jim Pease, had not come back from liberty the day before, which meant a search party had to be assembled and the local chiefs placated. He would not even notice if she went.

She jumped down into the canoe. The copy of the Bill of Sale for the *Rainbow* was in her apron pocket. She gave the boys some tobacco, and they took her out to the brig.

The *Lizzie Ann* was lost to sight before they were halfway there. Abigail had forgotten the quick surging motion of a Maori canoe, and how the boys chanted as they dug their paddles. Then the canoe bumped against the *Pandora*'s side. She climbed up lithely, just as she had done as a child, straightened and turned. To her horror, the boys were paddling away.

She shouted, but they paid no attention, but bobbed off into the mist. She should not have paid them until she was safely back on the *Lizzie Ann*, she ruefully realized. She stood some moments at the rail, deeply regretting her impulse. The whole world was gloomy and hidden, and her skin crept with a sense of danger. Then she braced herself and went below.

She was immediately transported back to her childhood—though everything looked so much smaller than remembered. Because she had grown—or because the *Lizzie Ann* was bigger? And Seth was right; the brig felt utterly abandoned. Why? Why had she been left here without her sails?

There was the dent in the cabin table where her father had once dropped a knife. Now the table was ingrained with dirt, and the panes in the skylight were green with mold. The mattress in the captain's stateroom was soiled, too, and the blankets thrown upon it were dirty. Thank God, she thought, her mother was not here to see her seagoing home reduced to this state. The cover on the sofa was the one her mother had crocheted, but it was as torn and stained as the blankets on the bed. The lockers had all been broken — by Seth, of course, Abby thought … and then heard the stealthy step.

Her entire body went rigid with shock. She heard another step … and then the whisper of a chantey. "*Was ye e'er in Doubtless Bay... Oh, me lassie, bonnie lassie...*" The sound was so faint she did not know if it was real or merely in her head, but her hair was trying to stand on end. Then, all at once, a clatter on the deck overhead, and a click as the companionway door was opened. Someone came running down the stairs.

She was too frozen with panic to try to hide in the captain's stateroom. When the door to the cabin opened, she thought she would scream — and Jireh came in.

He stopped short. "God, Abby, but you gave me a fright. What the hell are you doing here?"

She could ask him the same question, she thought, but said, "Did you hear someone singing?"

"What?" Then, without answering, he said, "Where's Seth?"

"He took the starboard boat to Russell. He should be on the way back."

"The *boat*? Why didn't he wait until the *Lizzie Ann* is fixed? And why didn't you go with him?"

"He was in a hurry for our letters."

"But Martha would want to see you — just as she would love you to stay…"

Abby cut him short. "There's a letter from my father waiting there for me — one that was returned to New Zealand by mistake." Then she was saved by another thunder of bootsteps above. "What's that?"

"My boat's crew. Two of my Brand bomb-lance guns

have been stolen, and I thought the thief might have hidden them on this brig. After all, an abandoned hulk is the last place anyone would look. Abby, you didn't tell me what you are a-doing here."

"This brig was my father's. I asked some Maori boys to bring me in their canoe, as I thought..." She swallowed, and went on, "Stupidly, I paid them before they delivered me back, and they left me stranded. It was a stupid idea, altogether. All I achieved was to scare myself. I'm most thankful you arrived."

H grinned affectionately. "I imagine you want a ride back home."

"I'd be much obliged," she said with great relief.

As they approached the *Lizzie Ann* the sun came out, and the mist instantly dissolved. Abby, with a surge of joy, saw that Seth was back. He was standing on the roof of the hurricane house with Consider West, conferring about something.

When she saw his dark, preoccupied expression, though, she wondered with a tremor if he was angry because she was in Jireh Mitchell's boat. He was too preoccupied, however, to pay attention to how she returned, or even notice that she had been away.

There was a stand-off on shore between a war party and the men Mr. Jones had taken on shore to find the missing Jim Pease, and the liberty men from the *Erasmus* had got involved, too. Something had upset the natives greatly, but no one knew what it was.

Seth and Jireh hurried ashore in Jireh's boat. As Seth jumped out and waded to the beach with his rifle in his hand, the scene on the rise of the nearest hill was like a picture of a battle scene, tense and static.

Maori warriors in motley native and European clothing were ranged in ranks, confronting twenty or thirty whalemen, who stood in a restless group on the lower slope.

There had been no fighting so far, Seth saw to his relief, most probably because the Maori men greatly outnumbered the thirty-odd whalemen. During the recruiting season, when a dozen or more whaleships were in port, there would have been bloodshed by now, but luck was on his side—along with Ichabod Jones, who had been keeping the men under control.

Above, coming from beyond the ashes of Captain Sherman's house, a Maori on horseback was circling down the hill. As Seth ran up, with Mitchell close behind, the horseman weaved through the Maori ranks to the bare patch of ground that separated the two groups. An ominous bundle lay across the horse's neck.

He arrived just as Seth reached Ichabod Jones. Without stopping, the horseman tipped his burden onto the dirt in front of Seth. Before it even hit the ground, he had wheeled swiftly away.

It was a body—Jim Pease. Pease had been clubbed with something sharp-edged; his skull was deeply gashed, and his head was a mask of dried blood. Behind Seth, Hunter snarled a curse, an incoherent sound that was followed by wild yelling from the other whalemen, and an intent shuffling of massed movement.

Whirling to face the seamen, Seth fired his rifle into the air. They all stopped short, rebellion in their faces. He could hear rapid talk from the Maori ranks, and the beginning of a warlike chant. His neck crept, but he stayed stock-still, staring the sailors down.

Then, like an echo of normality, he heard a man clear his throat as if he was getting ready for conversation. Seth turned very warily, to see that three middle-aged Maori men had emerged from the crowd, and had ranged in a formal row in front of the ranks of warriors.

The one in the center was holding an elaborately carved stick, and all three had intricate facial tattoos. They wore European shirts buttoned tightly at the neck and cuff, and dungaree pants, and one had a bowler on his head. They could have looked comical, but instead, they emanated immense dignity. Seth realized to his surprise that he was glad he was wearing his formal broadcloth suit.

They introduced themselves with decorum, and when he reciprocated by saying his name and shaking hands with each one, he found to his relief that they all spoke English. They told him a great deal about themselves and the surrounding territory, evidently because it was their tribal area and this pinning down of their location was part of the formality. Then they got down to business.

The dead man, their spokesman communicated gravely, had molested one of the young girls of their village. Though the sailor had been drunk, he had been given hospitality, and in return he had raped and then murdered a child. As Captain Morgan could see for himself, vengeance had been exacted by one of the girl's male relatives. The killer had been restrained, and was now under guard in the village, to be judged according to their own standards. However, there was still the matter of recompense from the ship; as an honorable man, Captain Morgan should take responsibility for the horrible crime committed by one of his men.

Seth bit down anger. He couldn't believe that even the crude and dirty Pease would do anything so foul. The story, he was immediately convinced, was an elaborate cover-up for his murder—if it had been murder, and not just the outcome of some brutal fight. Then, just as he was set to express his belief that the three chiefs were playing free with the facts in the politest way possible, Ichabod Jones spoke up.

"Sir," he said. Seth turned to look at the grim expression on the seaman's weathered face.

Ichabod Jones said, "They are telling the truth, sir."

"What?"

"Pease had a venereal disease—and reckoned he could get rid of it by forcing himself on a young virgin."

466

"*What?*"

"I heard him boasting about it, but didn't take much notice at the time, as the men told him he was being filthy. Now Hunter informs me that he was raving on about it again in the boat on the way to shore, yesterday. Hunter says he told him again that it was just a nasty invention, but evidently Pease took no notice."

Seth muttered, "The ignorant, foul..." He broke off and looked down at the body. Pease's end had been brutal, but he had had a swifter death than he deserved.

And the Maori chiefs were right—he himself had been at fault. As captain, he was in charge of the medical chest, and should have known about Pease's condition. His only excuse was that Pease had never come to him for clap medicine— probably because he had known that he would be banned from going on shore if his venereal disease was logged. He sighed, and braced himself to negotiate.

It took a long time. The chiefs kept on veering off the subject of recompense to make polite conversation, evidently to keep the conference civilized. Once, they broke off to give him permission to take the body away. Seth nodded to Ichabod Jones, who signed to two men to drag it away for burial somewhere.

Even with the evidence of the murder gone, the conference had an intent audience. The *Lizzie Ann* men had disliked Pease, but followed the details of the bargaining as if they wanted to make certain of the worth of a whaleman, while the motionless Maori warriors, most of whom could not have understood a word, listened in disciplined silence. As it turned out, Pease was worth two casks of tobacco. Seth rose to his feet, and shook hands on the deal—and Abigail shrieked a warning from the *Lizzie Ann*.

The words were lost with distance, but the urgency was plain. Seth turned with a lurch of alarm ... and smoke was billowing from the quarterdeck of the *Erasmus*. As he watched, aghast, the after rigging caught alight.

A single gust, and the *Lizzie Ann* would catch fire too; when the blaze got hold of the oil in the holds of the *Erasmus*, the linked ships would go up like a torch. Seth ran for his boat, surrounded by loud splashing and cursing as all his men followed. Every boat and canoe on the beach was shoved out into the water, as everyone, Maori included, rushed to bear a hand.

Frantically, they swarmed on board the *Erasmus* – and the *Lizzie Ann*, too, as sparks whirled into her rigging. Hand pumps were rigged, buckets lowered, and wet sailcloth and blankets flogged the flames. The blaze was fought as far as the hatchways of the *Erasmus*, but at last ... at last ... with a hiss the final flame went out.

Seth felt a million years old. Every bone and muscle was stiff. His face and hands were scorched and he was black with soot, and so were all the men who had fought the fire. The grim day wasn't over yet, for the ceremonial presentation of that tobacco still lay ahead – but the fire was out and both whaleships were safe.

Then, for the first time since he had heard her shriek of warning, he thought about Abigail.

She was not below in the cabins. He searched for Consider West, found him, and said urgently, "Where's Abigail?"

Consider West said, "What?" He seemed dazed by the near-calamity. Someone had thrown a lighted truss of straw over the rail of the *Erasmus* while he was on the deck of the *Lizzie Ann*; he hadn't seen who it was, but somehow he felt responsible.

"Where is my *wife?*"

Consider West shook his head, as if he had to clear it. "When it looked as if the *Lizzie Ann* might go, I sent her off to safety."

"On shore?"

"The brig." Consider West even smiled, though exhaustedly. "She's safe – I left Dutchie to look after her."

As Seth's boat pulled round the headland, he heard the sharp crack of a shot. From the brig? Oh God, he thought, and urged the men to pull faster.

But everything was silent when the boat pulled up to the brig, and there was no movement on the deck. The *Pandora* looked as deserted as the night he had searched her. Seth opened his mouth to call out, but a nagging sense of calamity persisted, and he changed his mind. Instead, he waved his oarsmen to slow their stroke as he stood at the steering sweep and listened.

The brig bobbed and water chuckled faintly. Dutchie should have been on watch, but there was no sign of the German. The boat pulled slowly in under the jibboom, and Seth reached up to hold onto the martingale chains, every fiber of his body taut as he listened.

Not a sound from the deck. His nape crept with a warning of ambush. With slow, stealthy movements, he climbed the chains and crept along the bowsprit and onto the bow. Mr. Jones and the oarsmen were watching him. When Seth reached down, Ichabod Jones handed up his Henry rifle.

The stock felt reassuring. Holding the rifle ready, Seth sidled into the space behind the windlass. Then he peered around the starboard end, keeping his profile low.

Dutchie's body was lying sprawled on the amidships deck. The German sailor's head was cracked where a pistol shot had got him from behind. Seth cried out with panicked horror, "*Abigail!*" — and Abigail walked out from the shadow of the deckhouse.

She was perfectly white and did not speak. Seth moved to get about the windlass — and stopped. Broddy McGhie had followed her. McGhie was holding a squat, heavy gun to his shoulder, and had two pistols in his belt. The shoulder gun was aimed at Abigail.

He said in quite natural tones, "Come on out, Captain Morgan, with your hands up."

For a moment Seth was too frozen to move. Then he leaned the rifle against the back of the windlass, and went out onto the deck, holding up his empty hands.

Sweat was gleaming in bubbles on McGhie's high red forehead, and his gun — the gun aimed at Abigail — was a bomb-lance gun. Seth remembered Jireh showing it to him, back at Capricorn Island. It was a new device, designed by a Connecticut gun-maker named Oliver Allen, and sold as the Brand harpoon gun; Seth did not like it, because he somehow did not feel it was honorable to shoot whales ... and it was utterly unthinkable that it should be used on the fragile form of his wife.

Seth slowly, slowly, walked towards them. Abigail said, "He was... was waiting, Seth, and boasted how he set the *Erasmus* on fire, and then ... then he shot Dutchie. For no reason at all, he made him turn round and shot him in the back of the head."

McGhie said, "Tell your men to move off, Captain."

Without hesitation, Seth waved the boat away. The men obeyed at once. He wondered how much they could see. The bulwarks of the brig were high; she was built to take a deck cargo. Then he turned back and studied McGhie and the weapon he held.

He remembered what Jireh had told him. The lance was designed to kill a whale by exploding in its belly. A slow match led from the breech to the end of the bomb lance that went into the barrel of the gun. When the lance was fired into the whale, the slow match ignited, and after a few seconds the fire reached the powder packed in the head of the bomb. Then it exploded.

Oh God. And McGhie had two of the guns. The other, also loaded, was propped up by the Scotsman's leg.

Seth said with outwardly icy calm, "What do you want?"

"Ah," said McGhie, and actually smiled, a taut, vicious grimace. "Captain Morgan, there is a great deal ye can do for me, by replacing the seamen who ran away from me—and the sails they took off with them. But first of all, Captain, ye can hand me that letter."

The letter. The letter he had collected at Russell was in his pocket. How did McGhie know he had it? *How?* Seth could feel sweat trickling in a cold line between his shoulder blades.

He said, "Why do you want the letter? What do you think is in it?"

McGhie jerked the gun. Seth's abdomen clenched. McGhie hissed, "Gi'e it tae me—if ye cherish your wife."

Seth paused. As Abigail numbly watched, he moved his hand, and slowly, very cautiously, felt in his pocket. Then he slowly drew it out. The letter was open; he had read it.

She watched him tensely, listening to Broddy's harsh breathing, smelling his awful stench of foul breath and sweat and desperation—and to her horror Seth stepped forward and put it in her hand, instead of into McGhie's.

Broddy swore, close to her ear. She sucked in a breath of sheer terror. Then she looked down at the page on the top. Her eyes were too blurred to read the writing at first. Then she recognized the script—and her mind went blank.

"... for I love a man who owns a ship and that ship is none other than the Erasmus! Yes, Captain Cambridge has sold her and your own cousin's son Jireh will take her on her next voyage to the Pacific. Jireh is kind and handsome and greatly attentive, he dances attention all the time, and I shall marry him, and we shall sail to New Zealand together, and then I shall give him my brig, for my dowry."

She cried out involuntarily, *"No — oh no, Seth, no!"* Then, in a hot rush, anger saved her. She jerked her face up to stare at Broddy with utter loathing. "Did you think that this was

471

my father's letter, in which he named his proxy? Did you think it might send you to the gallows? All this was unnecessary, you ... you *creature*, for the letter was written by me—by me!—when I was a silly, deluded child! I wrote it in New Bedford, and it was returned to sender because my father was dead, and then it was returned again by the customs house at Valparaiso! You bastard!" she screamed—and threw the letter at his blank, uncomprehending face.

Broddy went white, and jerked back. The bomb gun fired. Stinging smoke shrouded the deck, and she was more terrified than she would have thought possible. She cried out, "Seth!" in an agony of grief, and then, like a miracle, Seth's hand gripped her. There was another explosion and another billow of smoke as the bomb exploded over the water, and Seth's voice shouted in her ringing ears, "Climb!"

He shoved her at the mainmast. Broddy was rolling, diving for the other bomb lance gun. Then Seth's strong arms and hard hands shoved her upwards and he was shouting in her ear but her head rang too much for her to understand what he yelled. She had dungaree pants on instead of a petticoat, and she gathered her skirts under one arm, and scooted up the shrouds. Her panting breath scorched her throat, and she was sweating with terror. Seth was right behind her, sheltering her with his big body. She could hear his hurried gasping, too.

Then his strong hands grabbed her, and threw her outwards and up over the sill of the maintop; his strength was incredible. She scrabbled onto the platform, sliding to safety on her belly. Terrified, she heard Seth slip on the futtock shrouds. A pistol shot ripped through the air. Seth's legs flailed, and then he was wriggling onto the maintop, lying on his stomach beside her.

With shaking hands she felt him all over. He was unhurt. The air stung and stank of powder. There was a boat pulling round the headland towards the brig with ... Jireh in the stern.

Broddy was … where? At the foot of the mast, with the bomb gun — the second gun — at his shoulder. She could see the hole in the end of the barrel like a baleful eye as he aimed it upwards. Seth shoved her flat on her face. Then, to her horror, she sensed Seth leave her, heard his feet thumping as he darted up the rest of the mast.

Jireh's boat was pulling up to the brig. She lifted her face and shrieked, "Jireh, go away!"

Seth was in the topgallant crosstrees. Then he skidded along the main topgallant stay, shouting as he went. The rigging trembled and sang, and with a crash he was in the foremast hamper.

Jireh, staring upwards at him, was scrambling up the side of the brig. Abby cried despairingly, "Jireh, get back!" — and Seth, with another primitive yell, slid down a stay and arrived with a crash on the jibboom.

Abigail cried, "No, oh, no!" but Jireh came over the gangway. Broddy roared with savage fury — and focused his rage. The bomb lance gun was aimed, no longer trembling, at Jireh's chest. Abby thought with despair, "Oh, dear God." She couldn't bear to look.

Seth launched himself over the bow to the back of the windlass. His out flung hand gripped the rifle. He stood, brought it up, swung the barrel round, aimed, and fired — all in one savage movement. The bang was followed by a ringing echo, and then silence, dead silence.

And then the bomb exploded, with a curiously muffled thump.

When Seth edged around the end of the windlass, he had to brace himself with a trembling hand on the greasy metal. Then he slowly and stiffly walked up to Jireh and the bundle that lay at Jireh's feet.

The rifle shot had caught McGhie with his finger around the trigger. He had fallen on the gun at the same instant that his finger jerked. The bomb had exploded underneath him. Now he lay in a heap of bloodstained rags on the deck.

Abigail climbed down from the mast. Broddy McGhie moved just as she arrived. He was lying face down, with one arm out flung, reaching for a pistol that had slid away on the planks.

Seth kicked it out of reach, and Abby crouched down.

Broddy's clothes seemed empty; it was incredible that he was still alive. He turned his head and glared up at her with a single hating eye. There was a little pool of blood in the other socket. Broddy blinked slowly, like a mortally wounded lizard. He did not seem to be in any pain.

Abigail felt no pity, just bitter contempt, so why were there tears on her cheeks? This ... creature ... would have slaughtered Seth; he had betrayed, cheated, and killed her father and horribly wounded Tamati; he would have murdered her on the way to New Bedford—and all for a ship, a mere construction of wood and rope and canvas. She felt with trembling fingers for the Bill of Sale and the pencil in her apron pocket, and put them by the outstretched hand.

She said very coldly, "Sign this paper, Broddy."

The shattered mouth worked before McGhie whispered. Then the thready voice was sarcastic. "What be it? Me last will and testament?"

"You can call it that." When she had copied out the Bill of Sale for the *Rainbow*, she had altered the names of both the buyer and the seller. "... Whereas Captain Broderick McGhie has this day sold to Captain Seth Morgan ship *Rainbow* and outfits as she now lies in the port of San Francisco..."

She said harshly, "Sign it."

She shoved the paper closer, listening to the laboring rasp of Broddy's breath. The single eye blinked slowly at the paper. With a sudden movement, McGhie seized the pencil and scrawled his name. Then, without another sound, he died.

Abigail was still shaking uncontrollably when she fell asleep in Seth's arms. She had recounted the events of her day over and over, as if to exorcise them from her mind, ending with a terrible confession: "When Broddy came out of the *Pandora* deckhouse to meet me and Dutchie I ran to him, Seth—I *ran* to him! My childhood memories all rushed back, and he looked so familiar ... and *dear* to me. And he *laughed* at me. He always knew I was a fool, he said. Yet all those years, I thought he loved us, me and my father—he was jolly, and kind, and all the time there was that cold, greedy heart underneath. He must have been so jealous of my father's success."

"Hush," said Seth, stroking her hair, and she had eventually fallen asleep. Now he held her as she breathed softly into his throat, feeling her relax in slumber. She became heavy, and he shifted, making himself comfortable, but despite his bone-deep exhaustion he could not go to sleep himself. His mind was too busy, too full of what he had gained this day.

Three ships, he thought. The *Lizzie Ann*, the brig *Pandora*—and the clipper ship *Rainbow*. He'd had the presence of mind to get Jireh Mitchell to witness McGhie's signature—right there on the spot. Jireh had been staring at McGhie's corpse in numb shock, but he'd had enough sense to understand what he had heard. Now the Bill of Sale was with all the other papers in Seth's chart desk. Everything was legal—the ownership of all three vessels. The customs officer at Russell had had no trouble at all in confirming Seth's claim to the *Pandora*.

Making the brig fit for sea was the first job—after repairing the scorched rigging of the *Lizzie Ann*. The *Pandora* might have to be hove down to inspect the planking of her hull, but he thought she would prove sound, once her bottom was scrubbed. The cabins and holds had to be cleaned up, of course. He didn't even know the nature of the cargo in her holds—something McGhie had picked up in the islands on the way to New Zealand, perhaps. Pearl-shell? Bêche-de-mer?

Nathaniel Sherman had traded in bêche-de-mer before he had met McGhie and started his New Zealand speculative career, Seth remembered, and he wondered what profit there was in sea slugs—and how they were cured. Perhaps a casual conversation with Jireh Mitchell would yield a few hints... Sherman had done well, though, with that and his trading between Sydney and New Zealand, and his holdings in this country—he would have been a wealthy man still, if the English had not taken control.

But the *Pandora* was going nowhere with no sails. Seth tried to remember how many bolts of canvas he had in his holds. The *Lizzie Ann* had some spare sails, and maybe he could manage without one or two of those ... Gustavus had served some time as a sailmaker.

And there was the matter of crewing her. Jireh, he thought, was certainly giving up the whaling trade, which meant that he would not need so many men. A merchantman needed far fewer crew than a whaler— McGhie had sailed the *Pandora* from Valparaiso with just Nicholas and three hands. If he could get four or five *Erasmus* hands to ship with him, the *Lizzie Ann* and the *Pandora* could sail in tandem to San Francisco, to see what he would find there.

It was not much more than a year since McGhie's crew had abandoned him and his ship, but anything could have happened. The *Rainbow* could be a coal hulk, or a floating brothel. Even if she was in a reasonable state, it would take money to get her to sea again ... but still Seth was filled with optimism. The future might be indistinct, but there was a brightness that beckoned.

He fell asleep, but his mind was still active, and he dreamed vividly of Nathaniel Sherman. He and Abigail's father were riding in the pumice valley again: the scent of sulfur and warm mud filled the air, with the rustle of leaves, and again he saw the old chief, Te Wharenui, being given a therapeutic mud bath by bare-breasted girls.

Sherman talked on and on about the mysterious fortune that lurked here ... and then, from a distance, unable to do anything about it, Seth watched Nathaniel Sherman ride off with Broddy McGhie; he saw them laugh over a joke McGhie told, and then, still laughing, McGhie fell behind, drew out a Colt's revolver, and cold-bloodedly shot Sherman in the back of the head. Sherman's body fell; his horse bolted with fright—and another horse came galloping out of the bush. Tamati, his face contorted with rage and grief, threw himself at McGhie with a club in his hand. The pistol fired ... and fired ... hitting Tamati every time, always in the head, but still the Maori kept on coming, and when the club cracked down on McGhie's shoulder, the Scot let out a piercing scream—

Seth woke up with a jolt. God, he thought with a wince, had it really happened like that? It seemed eerily possible that being in this place had opened a window into the past. Whatever the details, however, the truth was that McGhie had both robbed and killed the man who was supposed to be his closest friend, leaving the daughter of that friend with no legacy except for a silly riddle.

The riddle. *When I am low, watch for a blow*: a barometer. *With sugar and rice and apples I'm nice*: cinnamon. Barometer. Cinnamon.

No. The other way around. *Although I am wood, I taste very good—When I am high, all sails fly.* Cinnamon, then barometer.

But the barometer rhyme was unfinished, he abruptly thought. Four lines were missing—*Long foretold, long last; short notice, soon past; first rise after very low, indicates a stronger blow.* Only one-third of it was there in the riddle, so should he take two-thirds of the word away? Bar, not barometer. Cinnamon, then bar ... *cinna ... bar...*

"My God," Seth whispered.

He had solved the puzzle.

"It's cinnabar," he said to Abigail at breakfast.

"What is?"

"The answer to the *What am I?* part of your riddle. You take the first two syllables of *cinnamon* and the first syllable of *barometer*, and you get *cinnabar*."

She blinked. 'And what, pray, is cinnabar?"

"Cinnabar is the ore of mercury."

"Good heavens," she marveled. "How do you know that?"

"I don't know. I read it somewhere."

"And that's my father's mysterious fortune?"

"Well, mercury — quicksilver — is very valuable. It's used in the extraction of gold — and is worth over a hundred dollars per flask."

"How much is there in a flask?"

"That I do not know."

"Well, I'm glad you're not all-knowing." But despite her teasing smile she shook her head in wonder. "So we're going to stay here, and mine for that ... *cinnabar?*"

"Good lord, no," he said, and spread baked beans on a slice of bread.

"You've made up your mind already, when we haven't even looked for it yet?"

"I have no intention of looking for it. That valley is considered sacred by the local natives, and they would send me packing if I even tried. Just as they sent off your English friend, Nicholas, and the three sailors with him, when they turned up with their tools and the sails they had turned into tents, with every intention of digging for gold."

"You know all that?"

"The chiefs told me about it yesterday, while we were conferring about tobacco — which I still have to send over to the village. McGhie," he observed, "was unlucky twice. He lost his crew to the lure of gold in Mangonui, just as he did in San Francisco."

"So where did Mr. Nicholas and the seamen go, after the chiefs sent them off?"

He shrugged. "To dig elsewhere."

"For gold?"

"No. They were scared enough of McGhie not to come back—and in Russell they told me that there's a new craze, for digging for a valuable kind of gum that's found in the ground where kauri trees grow. So they have turned to that. Do you care?"

She said hotly, "Of course I don't—and Mr. Nicholas isn't my *friend*, as you know perfectly well!" Then, much more quietly, she said, "Seth, are you very angry with me?"

He studied her over the rim of his coffee mug. "What makes you think I am angry?"

"That stupid, childish letter, for a start. Broddy was right, I *was* a fool—a fool to fall for Jireh Mitchell's smile. To tell the truth, I don't even particularly *like* Jireh now. I may be doing him a grave injustice, Seth, but I don't think he wants this child that he and Martha have made. And this hardhearted decision to leave her in Russell—"

"Sons who have been the favorites of their mothers sometimes are not over-keen on being fathers."

"Maybe so," she conceded. "But I actively *hated* him when he ignored my shouts and came on board the *Pandora*. He could have killed us all—he could have killed you, Seth—just because he refused to listen!"

"But I have to thank him for your life."

"What?"

"Yesterday morning, you went alone to the brig— because you thought you'd find McGhie there, and you had the romantic notion that if you talked to him, and appealed to his conscience, he would sign that bloody Bill of Sale you had ready—right?"

Her voice was very subdued. "It wasn't really as bad as that..."

"Yes, Abigail, it was! If Jireh hadn't turned up, he would have killed you—he would have smacked you down the way a cat kills a mouse. Then he would have tipped your body overboard with a weight at your feet, and I would never have known what had happened."

"But Broddy wasn't there."

"But indeed he was. That's how he knew I was coming back with the letter—because you told Jireh about it, right? McGhie overheard you."

"Oh," said Abigail in a very small voice. She looked down at her hands, her lashes dark on her flushed cheeks. "So that's why you're angry with me," she muttered. "And that's why you're going to leave me in Russell."

Seth paused. A sly glint entered his eye. "Would you care to place a bet on it?"

Seth watched his wife as she lined up her cue. He was going to win—he was determined on it—but he would never have expected in his wildest dreams that Abigail would give him such a good game. Who had taught her? McGhie? Her father? Experts, obviously. She needed just three points to win, while he was short of five. The slightly uneven bed of the table had foxed him for a while, so she had got further ahead then he intended.

Abigail, in fact, Seth meditated, played billiards better than most men of his acquaintance—for he knew very few men who could score a break of more than thirty. He was enjoying himself immensely. They were in the house that Captain Butler had built for the accommodation of captains, and the billiard table, it seemed, had been bought from Abigail's father, sometime after she had left Mangonui, and sometime before McGhie had burned the Sherman house to the ground. Though a grim indication of Sherman's dire financial straits, it was also a blessing that the table had been saved.

The billiard room was very pleasant, too.

A large glassed-in verandah had been made of materials imported from Sydney. The windows overlooked the bank of the creek that wound from the river to Butler's property, edged with tree-ferns and trees with filmy foliage. As Seth turned back to the table, a movement outside caught his eye—a whaleboat, coming up the creek. He recognized Victoria—and Obed. Oh lord, he thought, Obed had come for his share of that whale. He watched the boat come to a landing, and then returned his attention to Abigail.

He watched her drape herself along the edge of the table, balancing herself with the toe-tip of one slipper on the floor. Her head was tilted, marigold curls falling down the side of her neck as she sighted along the tapering rod of the maple-wood cue, and he wondered if she had the slightest notion of how seductive she looked. Obviously not: her concentration was remarkable. But then, the bet he had made with her was the one most likely to make sure she played her very best.

At stake was the answer to Jireh Mitchell's plea to Seth for Abigail to stay in Russell with Martha. If Abigail won, the decision was hers; if Seth won, the decision was his. Abigail slowly drew back her arm. Seth was fascinated by the difference that a girl's shape made to her handling of the cue. He saw her breast swell and tighten as she took in a breath and held it. Then she began the slow stroke.

The garden door opened. Victoria said in her clear, precise voice, "Abigail, what *is* this talk I've been hearing?"

The cue hit the cue ball hard, with too much spin. The white ball clicked against the red, and the object ball spun as it fled to the far corner pocket.

Seth watched the red ball run, then saw Abigail shut her eyes and her shoulders slump. The red ball spun into the pocket. He heard its busy rattle. It bounced out again, and ran six inches. Then it stopped, lined up as precisely as a ruler with Seth's spot ball and the pocket.

"My decision, I think," said Seth.

He stepped forward and tapped smoothly, using plenty of top. The double click as the red fell in and his cue ball followed was clean and poetic. He put down his cue, and said, "Hello, Obed."

Abigail ignored this, protesting, "That wasn't fair! You won by accident—and now you're going to make me stay in Russell!"

"Did I say that?" he demanded.

"No ... but ... that bet..."

"I wanted a good game—and that I had. In fact, my pretty scatterbrained minx, you would greatly favor me with another game tomorrow. And I never, not for an instant, entertained the idea of leaving you in Russell. The suspense of wondering what adventures you'd got up to while I was away would kill me."

"Oh Seth, you are such a beast," Abigail exclaimed, and threw her arms about his neck.

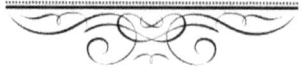

www.oldsaltpress.com

Old Salt Press is an independent press catering to those who love books about ships and the sea. We are an association of writers working together to produce the very best of nautical and maritime fiction and non-fiction. We invite you to join us as we go down to the sea in books.

Joan Druett is a maritime historian who is an expert on whaling history and women at sea, and is also the author of the bestseller *Island of the Lost*. She lives in New Zealand with her husband, the internationally acclaimed maritime artist, Ron Druett. Her website is *www.joan.druett.gen.nz*

www.ingramcontent.com/pod-product-compliance
Lightning Source LLC
Chambersburg PA
CBHW051937020726
47501CB00001B/160